Discovering THE NIGHTINGALE

—◆— A CHILTON CROSSE NOVEL —◆—

TRACI BORUM

Discovering the Nightingale

Chilton Crosse™: Book 5

Red Adept Publishing, LLC

104 Bugenfield Court

Garner, NC 27529

https://RedAdeptPublishing.com/

---

1.   http://StreetlightGraphics.com

For Teri, my aunt and my friend

Chapter One

Love is a smoke made with the fume of sighs.
~Shakespeare

Chelsea Barrett pushed the last pin into the corkboard then stepped down from the chair to view the final results. The *Romeo & Juliet* poster hung prominently in the center of her classroom's largest wall, along with an assortment of photos and quotes from Da Vinci, Marlowe, Donne, and Petrarch. The major theme for the upcoming term would be the Renaissance era, and Chelsea couldn't wait to dive in. She knew what she was up against—competing with her teenage pupils' obsessive interests in gaming and social media. Still, she hoped their excitement about events that happened hundreds of years in the past—the incredible surge of philosophy, art, science, and literature—might eventually match her own.

Most teachers her age looked ahead to a new school term through tired and jaded eyes, but Chelsea was still new to this, and the shine hadn't worn off. In fact, it hadn't even begun to fade. There was nothing typical about Chelsea's journey to the teaching profession—she'd grown up in Chilton Crosse, attended university in Bath to study writing and literature, then substituted in local schools and hated it. After that, she spent her twenties floundering in various clerical positions, none of them offering even a molecule of true satisfaction. So when given the chance last year to return to her home village and teach at the secondary school, she'd snatched it up, wanting to give the teaching profession one more try. At the ripe age of thir-

1

ty-three, Chelsea had only recently experienced the rough patches and frustrations and endless grading nights of a brand-new teacher. But with that first year fully behind her, mistakes made and lessons learned, she was facing the new term with a little more confidence and a fresh sense of enthusiasm.

Tucking a lock of chestnut hair behind her ear, Chelsea threaded between the desks to reach the center of the classroom and survey the entire space from the pupils' perspective. Almost three years before, this centuries-old school had been part of an enormous restoration project headed up by Adam Spencer, a London architect who now lived in the village. Chelsea had heard many prerenovation horror stories of crumbling infrastructure, damp ceilings, and poor lighting. But viewing this clean, crisp space with its freshly painted walls, enormous bank of windows opened to the stunning Cotswold countryside, and updated technology—new computers at the back wall, a fancy projection system up front, and smooth-running Wi-Fi—it was hard to picture the space any other way.

Only one blank wall remained, but Chelsea had already formulated some strong ideas for it. At least she had several more days before pupils would once again be filing into her classroom...

"Progress!" a voice said from behind.

Chelsea whirled around to see Rachel, her teaching colleague and best friend since childhood.

"It's getting there." Chelsea inched toward Rachel through the narrow aisle of desks. "How's your room coming along?"

Rachel taught at the primary school in the opposite building. "Well enough. I'm cutting out paper stars in my sleep these days. You'd think it would get easier with each new term, but this part of the process always leaves me knackered. There's so much to *do* before classes begin. It never feels like enough time."

"Especially for you." Chelsea winced.

Her friend, though naturally beautiful with her shoulder-length blond hair, creamy skin, and sparkling blue eyes, always looked tired—because she *was* tired. Rachel held, essentially, two full-time jobs. Her husband, Michael, was the vicar of the village, and as the vicar's wife, Rachel was on practically every village committee in addition to leading the church choir and singing the occasional solo during services. Very few people witnessed all the quiet work Rachel did behind the scenes—comforting grieving parishioners in their homes, preparing soup for elderly villagers, organizing fundraisers or church-hall celebrations. The list was endless. At the end of each term, Rachel would contemplate letting go of her teaching position and making more room for her vicar's-wife duties, but each year, she knew she couldn't bear to leave teaching. Not yet.

"Well, what about you?" Rachel lobbed the topic back at Chelsea. "Taking on this Renaissance festival single-handedly?"

Chelsea blew out a puff of air and pulled her jumper sleeves down over her knuckles. "I'm absolutely barmy," she admitted. "That's the only explanation. I can't believe I let myself be talked into this."

"Mrs. Pickering can talk people into *any*thing."

"True." Chelsea tilted her head. "How exactly does she do it? Subliminal persuasion? Mind tricks? Hypnosis?"

Rachel chuckled. "All of the above, I presume."

"Well, it works every time."

Rachel surveyed the room again with a definitive nod. "I think we've both earned a break. How about a coffee and a scone? You haven't seen the new bakery yet."

"Perfect idea. I'm in."

A scone would be delectable, especially on a damp, chilly, nearly September afternoon.

THE HIGH STREET OF Chilton Crosse always looked in top form, but it became especially postcard worthy on rainy days, Chelsea noticed. It was something about the shimmer of wet cobblestones, the reflection of glossy-tiled roofs atop honey-colored buildings, and the crystalline translucence of raindrops dripping from leaves.

Chelsea had moved a handful of times in her twenties, always restless, always searching for that place to call home. But it took her more than a decade to realize that home was right here, in the village where she'd been born and raised, where she'd made friends, learned about life, and fallen in love. Her roots were strong in Chilton Crosse, and she could feel them with each step as she walked with Rachel past all the familiar shops—the market, a flower shop, a novelty shop, an Indian takeaway, and across the street, Holly's bookshop, a boutique, a clock shop, and Joy Valentine's famous art gallery.

With such character and charm, it was no wonder that this Cotswold village had become a popular tourist attraction over the past few decades. Fortunately, in late August, the crowds had thinned as tourists returned to their jobs and homes in the States or various European countries, filled to the brim with memories.

"Hello, Mr. Bentley!" Rachel called out as they approached the bakery.

The elderly man sitting outside the building waved a withered hand. "Hello there, young ladies. Would you care for a scone today?"

Alton Bentley was the bakery's original owner, but recently, his daughter, Julia, had taken over. After enduring a kitchen fire several weeks earlier, the bakery's interior had been completely renovated. Chelsea was eager to view the results.

She closed her umbrella then leaned in for a toothpick-speared bite of scone. "Are you chilly, sitting out here?" she asked, seeing Mr. Bentley's thick coat in addition to a blanket draped over his legs.

The generous striped awning above offered plenty of shelter from the gentle pattering of rain.

"No, no. I feel marvelous. Fine English weather, good for the soul." He nodded his tweed-capped head.

Chelsea thanked him for the scone as Rachel held open the bakery's door.

The aromas of freshly baked goods and strong coffee hit Chelsea's senses as she entered. The place was packed with villagers, probably curious to see the renovations. Chelsea noticed the new changes immediately—fresh-painted buttery-colored walls, dark wood tables and chairs, and a larger display case up front. But the interior still somehow managed to retain its familiar comforting atmosphere.

"Your usual?" Rachel asked, heading toward the counter.

"Sure. I'll fetch a table." Chelsea found one in the corner and wriggled out of her coat as she sat. The days were becoming only marginally cool, but since Chelsea was cold natured, she took a light coat with her everywhere, even when it might not be necessary.

She caught sight of another new addition on the wall beside her table—a framed recipe, faded and worn, holding stains of various ingredients. Presumably, it came from Julia's mother, Rose, for whom the bakery was named. Chelsea's eyes drifted toward the counter, where Julia Bentley had made a rare emergence from her kitchen, the place she spent most of her time. Chelsea didn't know Julia well but had noticed a significant transformation in her over the past few months. Julia had fallen in love, and it showed.

Will that ever happen for me again?

Chelsea usually avoided comparing her life with other people's—what a juvenile thing to do, really—but she couldn't help herself. She didn't even have time for a relationship at the moment, so it was pointless to desire one.

"So, back to this festival..." Rachel had appeared during Chelsea's daydreaming and set down two coffees and scones. "Any regrets about saying yes?"

Chelsea slid the plate closer. "Not really. I may be the committee's head—regrettably— but there's a whole team of people helping out."

"Including me!"

"True. Plus, most of the teachers are on board. I'm getting calls from new volunteers almost every day. They're already requesting specific tasks, which means that many elements of the festival are already underway... before we've even had our first official meeting!"

"That's a relief. I pictured the burden of the whole project on your extremely petite shoulders."

Chelsea grinned as she pinched off her first bite of scone. "Well, if I'm truthful, this really isn't Mrs. Pickering's fault. All she did was present the idea, and then I ran with it. I have no one to blame but myself."

Weeks before, Chelsea had brainstormed an idea—her pupils could put on a production of *Romeo and Juliet*, an abbreviated performance for parents only, nothing elaborate. But when several pupils began showing enthusiastic interest, Chelsea presented the idea of a mini-Renaissance festival to Mrs. Clementine, the school's headmistress, who greatly approved. Soon, other teachers contacted Chelsea, so she decided to move the whole affair to the garden area near the school buildings.

When the news reached Mrs. Pickering's ears—as news inevitably did, in Chilton Crosse—she appeared at Chelsea's cottage door, unannounced, with the notion of turning the little school event into a full-blown village-wide festival.

"Oh, but there's no time," Chelsea gently protested, handing over a cup of tea to Mrs. Pickering, who was seated in her living room.

"We only have a few weeks, as it is, to throw together a small school festival."

"Then let's push it to the October half-term holiday. That would afford us another fortnight, at least."

"Even so, I don't see how we could accomplish it for the entire village in a handful of weeks. The last time Chilton Crosse held a proper Renaissance festival was..." Chelsea pondered, but she was ill-equipped to answer. She'd been absent for most of the past sixteen years of village life.

"Eight years ago. And it's high time we have another." Before Chelsea could protest yet again, Mrs. Pickering held up her hand. "My committees have been known to throw together a produc-tion—or in this case, a festival—swiftly and capably. It *can* be done."

There was no use arguing with her, so as Mrs. Pickering exited the cottage, Chelsea promised to "strongly consider it." When Mrs. Pickering had gone, Chelsea did more than consider it. She hopped online to research other village festivals, but the more she scrolled and read, the more discouraged she became. There was so much to consider. Everything had to be authentic—costumes, food offerings, jewelry, and music. Also, period-specific activities, such as jousting and flame throwing, seemed to be popular for many of the local festi-vals. The enormous scope of the entire undertaking was overwhelm-ing. Chelsea *had* been right. There was no way a few weeks of plan-ning would do a festival like this any justice. In fact, most villages usually spent at least a year putting together these elaborate produc-tions.

But as she closed her laptop, a thought occurred to Chelsea. *Why does it have to be a copycat replica of every other Renaissance festival in every other Cotswold village? Chilton Crosse is unique, so why can't this festival reflect that?* If they condensed and managed their expec-tations thoughtfully, then Mrs. Pickering was correct—it could be done.

Chelsea scrolled back in her mind to the studying and research she'd been doing for most of the year, on her own, in preparation for the Renaissance unit she would present to her pupils this upcoming term. The term *Renaissance* covered a broad time period and was spread out over multiple nations, involving unique and varied subjects—art, literature, science, math, philosophy. Perhaps a Chilton Crosse festival could be broad as well. *Why box ourselves in?* The village was filled with creative people—painters, musicians, craftspeople, and teachers. They could use their talents and blend them with echoes of Renaissance examples, putting on a festival that incorporated and celebrated *all types* of creativity and ingenuity, whether from hundreds of years in the past or today.

When Chelsea finally relieved herself of the pressure of a rigid festival with specific expectations and strict authenticity, and of meeting other people's standards of what a festival should be, the whole idea came alive. She stayed up half the night brainstorming, and by the time she met with Mrs. Pickering the next day, she'd mapped out the bare bones of a realistic plan, which Mrs. Pickering had adopted instantly, promptly naming Chelsea the head of the Renaissance Festival Committee.

"I'm sure it will be amazing." Rachel reached for her coffee mug. "You know you can count on me. Anything you need."

"Thanks. I'll take you up on it." Chelsea dusted the scone's fine crumbs between her fingertips and changed the subject. "Is Michael in Bath today, seeing his father?"

Rachel lowered her voice. "Yes. And he's not doing well."

Michael's father, Emmett, had come to Chilton Crosse almost eighteen years before to take the position as vicar of the village church. But almost as soon as his younger son took over as vicar, six years ago, Emmett's faculties began to decline noticeably. When his dementia became too great for Michael and Rachel to deal with on their own—he nearly burned their vicarage down one afternoon while trying his hand at a cottage pie—Michael scouted surrounding areas for the best possible care-home facility available, which happened to be located in the nearby city of Bath. Since then, Michael had been making regular visits to see him.

"I'm sorry," Chelsea said, matching Rachel's reverent tone. "I know he and Michael have a special bond."

"Like you and your dad did."

Chelsea nodded wistfully at the mention of her father, who'd had a sudden heart attack three years before—so sudden, in fact, that she hadn't been at his bedside when he died. His loss hadn't quite reached the depths of her heart yet. And she didn't want it to.

"I was such a daddy's girl," she admitted.

"I remember." Rachel took a sip of coffee, clinking her wedding ring against the mug. "Listen to us. We're supposed to be taking a *break* from real life. Sorry I turned the conversation maudlin."

"You didn't—I'm the one who asked about Michael's dad."

Rachel's mobile buzzed on the table with a text. "Mrs. Hannigan," she muttered, glancing at the screen. "I'm supposed to meet her in... five minutes. Goodness, is that the time? Sorry. I'll have to grab a takeaway cup for my coffee."

"No worries. We'll try this again soon."

Chelsea was accustomed to cut-short chats and briefer-than-intended calls. Her friend was in high demand in the village, especially today with her husband being absent. Rachel scurried off with an apology and a goodbye wave, leaving Chelsea to finish her scone and coffee alone. She let her gaze wander over toward the counter in time to see Tristan, Julia's new love, plant a quick kiss on her cheek before he left the bakery. Chelsea returned to her last bite of scone, pushing her envy down with a quiet sigh.

CHELSEA DIDN'T NEED an umbrella on her brief walk back to the school. The raindrops had ceased, and the gray skies had parted, if only momentarily, to reveal a rare glimpse of a bright English sun. She ticked through her mental list of items to finish in the classroom before heading back to her cottage for an early dinner. As she neared the end of High Street, Chelsea recognized a familiar figure, hunched and leaning against the edge of Mrs. Pickering's market shopfront.

"Sienna?" Chelsea called softly as she approached, seeing the teen's thick dark hair covering her face as she stared down at her mobile.

Sienna snapped her head toward Chelsea, lips parted in surprise, cheeks wet with tears. "Oh. Miss Barrett. Hey."

Chelsea inched closer, squinting. "Is everything all right?"

Sienna offered her teacher a tiny reassuring smile as she wiped a cheek with the back of her hand. "Sure. Fine."

Sienna Brighton was Chelsea's favorite pupil. She wasn't supposed to *have* favorites, but Chelsea couldn't help it. Sienna reminded her of her fifteen-year-old self—awkward, overly sensitive, curious about the world, a rule follower, a people pleaser, and her own worst critic. Sienna never gave Chelsea any trouble, which by itself made her a dream pupil. She always submitted assignments on time, was the first to answer a question Chelsea might pose in class, and sought Chelsea's tutoring occasionally after school. Sienna wanted to be the best at everything—which meant she was too often hard on herself.

Chelsea faced Sienna squarely and made eye contact. "You can tell me."

Tears came again, and Sienna nodded, unable to speak.

"Here, let's move out of the way," Chelsea suggested, noticing the occasional passerby eyeing Sienna with a concerned gaze. Chelsea didn't want this becoming a spectacle. Her small village was lovely but gossipy, and a crying teenager could quickly become the source of speculation among the villagers.

Chelsea remembered a private area nearby. "I have an idea. Follow me."

"Okay," Sienna managed to say between sniffles.

During the swift walk to the church, Sienna's tears dried, and by the time they entered the sheltered porch leading to the grand double doors—away from prying eyes and listening ears—she seemed ready to talk.

"Boys are so daft, aren't they?" Sienna plonked down on the stone bench then plucked a tissue from the packet Chelsea had fished from her bag. "I don't understand them."

As Sienna blew her nose, Chelsea tried to craft a concerned-but-casual facial expression. Over the past year, she'd learned that teenagers tended to shy away from adults who reached out to them too earnestly. They wanted to handle most things on their own, and Chelsea didn't want to scare Sienna away.

"What happened?" Chelsea asked.

"Matthew broke up with me today. Just now, actually. By text." She lifted up her mobile and pursed her lips, likely trying to force away more tears. Her eyelashes were already clumped together with moisture.

Matthew Donovan was an average pupil but a gregarious young man, popular with everyone in the class—always pleasant and joking. Although Chelsea could sometimes observe new flirtations and friendships forming between her pupils throughout the terms, Chelsea had never seen Matthew and Sienna even communicate with each other, apart from the occasional assigned group work. She'd had no idea the two were dating.

"I'm so sorry," she told Sienna.

Sienna squeezed the tissue into a tight ball then set her mobile in her lap, screen side down. "I've had a crush on Matthew for two whole years, but he barely knew I was alive. He has loads of friends and never even talked to me. But then, at the start of summer holiday, I ran into him at the bridge. I stopped in my tracks and nearly went the other way, but he called out my name." Sienna looked with watery blue eyes toward Chelsea. "He knew my name."

The corners of Chelsea's lips lifted in a grin. She hadn't expected this much vivid detail.

Sienna blinked and continued. "And so I went over to him at the bridge. I always see him joking around in class. But that day"—her focus drifted down again to her lap—"he wasn't smiling. We ended up talking for two hours. He told me about his uncle and this rift that was tearing the family apart. He opened up to me right there. And I just listened. After that, we talked every day—texts, calls, walks in the village. He kissed me at the bridge two weeks later." She smiled. "I couldn't believe it was happening. It's like I saw everything differently after that kiss. The whole world turned... brighter somehow. Like I'd put on special glasses or something." She gave a soft chuckle. "That sounds completely daft."

"No, it doesn't. It sounds extremely accurate." Chelsea vividly remembered that same sensation from when she fell in love the first time—her world coming into clearer view, all the dull edges sharpened and crisped up, with her heart permanently lifted inside her chest.

"I've never been so happy. But now..." Sienna frowned at the mobile, her expression sour, as though all her pain were the fault of the phone. "I don't know what I did wrong. Matthew started ignoring all my texts. I thought maybe he was just busy. But then he messaged me this morning, that he 'needs some space' and wants to back off for a while. I don't understand..."

"First," Chelsea said, "you didn't do anything wrong. It's an issue Matthew is probably having on his own." She thought back to her own painful teenage days. The image of Luka McKane floated up to the fringes of her mind—the anxiety, the drama, the hundreds of tears she'd wasted on him. "I think young men his age are... struggling. They've got all this boundless energy, all these expectations for the future. Plus, their maturity level doesn't quite match that of girls their age."

Sienna's eyes widened. "*So* true."

"And sometimes, they view a serious girlfriend as an extra pressure, holding them back. They might not be mature enough to handle a real relationship. I think Matthew got scared. He's not ready now, but it doesn't mean he won't ever be." Chelsea hated to give Sienna false hope—first loves rarely lasted a lifetime, she knew from experience—but she also didn't want Sienna to close the door on something that could, given some patience and nurturing, become a precious and lasting relationship. "My best advice is to give it time. Give Matthew the space he wants. If it's meant to be, as clichéd as that sounds, it will happen. But if it's not, you will still be fine all on your own."

Sienna sniffed then uncrossed her arms to reach for the phone again before it slid off her lap. "Thank you, Miss Barrett. I knew you would have the right words."

Flattered, Chelsea placed a hand on top of Sienna's and gave it a squeeze. "These teenage years can be brutal, but you will survive. I'm glad our chat seemed to help."

"It did." Sienna pushed off from the bench and stood. "I can't believe school is almost back in session. But I'm glad you'll be my teacher again."

"So am I." Chelsea had been thrilled, months back, when the headmistress handed her the next-level literature course for this new term—it meant she would have many of her former pupils in this particular class.

Chelsea stood to walk into the warm sunshine with Sienna. "How are your lines coming along?" The pupils interested in auditioning for *Romeo and Juliet* roles had the entire holiday break to memorize lines. Sienna was trying for the part of Juliet, but after her painful breakup, that might change.

"Good, actually. I'll be ready for next week. I'm nervous, but I really want this. See you next week at school?" Sienna gave a shy wave as she backed away.

"Next week," Chelsea confirmed, watching her go.

NIGHTINGALE COTTAGE came into view, with its newly restored Tudor exterior looking particularly crisp and clean after the recent showers. Turning the key to her front door, Chelsea heard the familiar clanging and banging coming from upstairs. She tipped her damp umbrella onto the stone floor, set down her bag and keys, then shrugged out of her coat and shut the door.

"Mac?" she called out, with no response. He likely hadn't heard her over the clanging.

If polled, most villagers would probably say that Mac MacDonald was the village's most beloved resident. He was known to all as gardener, handyman, jack-of-all-trades, and faithful friend. He worked quietly on the fringes of the villagers' lives, repairing their taps, trimming their shrubs, or retiling their rooftops. And—keeping their secrets. Throughout his years of work, Mac had probably heard enough gossip to last him a lifetime but had never revealed even a sliver of it to others. People trusted him, including Chelsea, especially since he had been one of her father's best mates in the village. In fact, months before, she'd given Mac the key to Nightingale Cottage so he could come and go as he pleased while doing the renovations, which were almost completed.

As she moved into the living room, Chelsea heard Mac tromping down the stairs. She waited for him to appear.

"Oh. Hello, lass." He carried his toolbox, which had become an appendage over the years, and wore his usual dusty dungarees.

"You've been busy," she noted. "How's the wall coming along?" The replastering of the master bedroom's walls and ceilings was the final stage of the renovations.

"One more section to go. I can probably complete it over the weekend." He scratched at his silver hair with his free hand.

"That's perfect timing. School starts next week. Maybe I can move some of my things in before the first day." The thought of doing that, in addition to prepping for classes, was actually overwhelming. But it would be worth it to finally be settled and make this a home again. "I'm about to put the kettle on. Will you have some tea?"

"Can't, thanks. I need to be off on another call. Mrs. Cartwright's Aga is on the fritz again." He trilled the *r* in *fritz* as only a Scotsman could. Over the years, Chelsea had become accustomed to Mac's thick accent, and only now and then did her ears have trouble translating a word or two.

"Okay, next time, then."

Mac nodded then moved past her. "Have a good evening, lass."

As Mac opened and shut the door to leave, Chelsea heard the patter of rain again. A cup of tea *did* sound good, paired with a fire burning in the fireplace and a Westie on her lap.

Chelsea cracked open the study door, and out came her mum's eleven-year-old West Highland terrier, Socrates. These days, the dog plodded more than sprinted, but his bright eyes and eager panting showed the youthfulness that still existed inside.

"Hey, boy." She bent to scoop him into her arms and pet his silky bright-white fur and received a wet lick on the cheek in return.

Her mum had to leave Socrates behind when she'd left the village, and it took a few months for Chelsea and the dog to bond. She stayed patient, letting him warm to her in his own time. It had paid off, and before long, he was at her heels wherever she went, hoping for a head scratch or some belly rubs.

"Did all that clatter upstairs scare you?" She carried Socrates into the kitchen then placed him gently onto the flagstone floor so she could free her hands and make a cup of tea. The dog found his bowl and lapped up the water while Chelsea milled around the kitchen, one of her favorite things to do.

Within minutes, Chelsea had snuggled into the plush oversized chair near the fire in the living room, cup of tea in hand, quilt wrapped firmly around her legs, and Socrates at her side. She listened to the gentle *rat-a-tat* of raindrops plonking on her recently tiled roof, glad that it was the first repair Mac had insisted on making. Looking around at the familiar wood beams overhead, the white plastered walls, and the oak table nearby, she knew that this cottage had finally become her true home.

When her mother had first offered the cottage to Chelsea, she'd said yes out of obligation. Her mother wanted to relocate to Bristol to help out her ailing sister. The move was an unexpected blessing, as Chelsea's mother pushed her grief aside to care for someone else. Puttering around the cottage alone after Chelsea's father had died had been a challenge for her mother most days. Plus, she couldn't face the paperwork and tedious details of trying to renovate and sell the cottage on her own.

So for the time being, Chelsea had agreed to move in—which included keeping Socrates, since her aunt was allergic to dogs. Chelsea took the teaching position to sustain some sort of income until she could get things in order and sell the cottage.

But as time inched forward, Chelsea had developed an unexpected affection for teaching, and she'd slowly integrated back into village life—and, most importantly, renewed her friendship with Rachel. Chelsea was reminded of how lovely and comforting village life could be, especially in Chilton Crosse. It was different living here on her own as a grownup. When she was a child, people had known her mostly as "the police constable's daughter," and she'd felt their prying eyes on her constantly. This time around, she could be reintroduced as just Chelsea—teacher, cottage owner, village contributor. As the cottage renovations came to a close over the past few weeks, the answer had been clear. She wouldn't sell after all. She would purchase the cottage for herself. The act of moving into her parents' bedroom, refurbished and redecorated with her own touches, would be her final stamp on creating a real home.

As Chelsea sipped her tea, her thoughts moved back to Sienna. The anguished look on her face and the pain in her eyes were familiar. At that exact age, Chelsea had been wildly in love with the vicar's oldest son, Luka. Even sixteen years after he left the village, she could picture him vividly. She stared toward the fire and saw his dark eyes always deep in thought, his perfect lips that sometimes surprised her with a smile, and that thick, wavy, near-shoulder-length hair. Her thoughts shifted to other, stronger images, a slideshow clicking through specific moments they'd shared together. Luka cradling his hands around hers to demonstrate snapping the perfect photo. The glistening of his chest as he bailed hay at Mr. Elton's farm on a hot summer day. The tender strength in his arms as he pulled her in close for a kiss. The quiet stutter as he told her "I love you" for the first time. The way he looked at her like she was the only person in the room, or on the planet.

She remembered the first time she ever laid eyes on him, standing at the front of the church with his father and his brother, Michael. Staring at Luka from four rows away, Chelsea had sensed a physical tug inside, as strongly as she'd ever felt anything in her life. It was the moment her heart left her chest and never truly returned.

Chelsea closed her eyes tight and shook her head, banishing these unwelcome images, willing them to disappear. Opening her eyes, she realized she'd spilled her tea onto the blanket. "Blast," she whispered, startling Socrates as she dabbed at the wet spot with a nearby napkin.

Over the years, thoughts of Luka had drifted in and out of her mind. A song, an image—almost anything held the potential to trigger a memory. But by staying busy with other things, she'd always been capable of tucking the memory snugly back where it belonged, firmly in the past.

After she'd finally managed to heal parts of herself—which took years after the breakup—Chelsea had made a choice never to lose perspective that way. She would never again flash completely out of time, walk back in her mind, and revisit him in living color. But Rachel's earlier mention of Luka's father being ill, combined with the angst of Sienna's teenage love on full display, had apparently been a lethal combination, and the Luka memories managed to rush to the surface, pushing through Chelsea's carefully constructed barrier.

Resentful, she set down her tea then lifted Socrates with one hand and threw off the blanket with the other. There were things to do around the cottage—dinner to make, old items in boxes to sort, colors to choose for her new bedroom. Plenty to keep her thoughts focused safely elsewhere.

THE NEXT MORNING, GROGGY from lack of sleep, Chelsea rolled over in bed to view a new text alert. Propping herself up and blinking hard to clear the sleep from her eyes, she spied a message from Rachel.

Call me? I have some news...

That couldn't be good. Chelsea rose to a sitting position and rang Rachel's number while Socrates yawned audibly from his bed in the corner of the room. Chelsea noticed the haze of morning light filtering through the guest-bedroom window.

"Hey, Chels," Rachel answered. "I didn't want to tell you in a text. It's about Michael's father. He's gone. It happened in the middle of the night—"

"Oh, no. I'm sorry to hear it."

"Michael had decided to stay there late, since the nurse told him things were looking grim. Emmett had stopped eating, and his breathing was shallow. Michael was with him when he died."

"Well, I'm glad of that. He wasn't alone. I know this will be hard on Michael."

"It will," Rachel said. "I'm not sure how to help him, what to say..."

"Just be natural. It will come, and you'll know the right words at the right time."

"Thanks. So... I actually need to start planning the funeral and reception straight away."

"Can I help with anything?"

Rachel sighed through the phone. "Not yet. I'm only in the planning-and-calling stages. A lot of tedious details to sort through."

"Well, I'm here when you need me. I mean that. Use me."

They said their goodbyes, and Chelsea clicked off and stared again at the diamond-paned window. She hadn't known Luka's father terribly well. She'd attended church regularly as a teenager, but other than hearing the vicar's sometimes-stern sermons, she knew little of the man himself except the small tidbits she'd been able to glean through Luka. They'd had a tumultuous relationship. Chelsea wondered when Luka had last spoken to his father. *Months? Years?*

Chelsea was aware that Luka had been trotting around the globe since he left the village as an eighteen-year-old. He was an award-winning photographer for journals and newspapers and rarely visited the UK. He'd surely been told of his father's death—if Michael had been able to reach him.

Chelsea tried to imagine Luka's reaction to the news. *Immediate sadness? Painful regret? Or only numbness?* But a more pertinent question barged its way through all the others: *Will Luka come home for the funeral?*

Chelsea chucked her mobile onto the bed then curled up in her sheets again and shut her eyes, craving the oblivion of sleep.

Chapter Two

*Perhaps out there, somewhere, someone is sighing for your absence;
and with this thought, my soul begins to breathe.* ~Petrarch

Chelsea jangled the set of keys at her side and strolled buoyantly along the path toward the vicarage, hoping Rachel would be pleased with her surprise. Her friend needed a definite pick-me-up after having spent the better part of three days making somber decisions—the color and size of a casket, the number of lilies to purchase, the selections of songs and Bible verses that would best suit the upcoming funeral service. Chelsea knew, from helping her mother make funeral arrangements for her father, how surreal and daunting the entire process could be. Especially the part where you pushed the searing grief away to force a small, comforting I'm-all-right smile until the service was over and you'd convinced everyone—including yourself—that it was true.

Michael and Rachel's vicarage was a quaint stone cottage that stood beyond the church, hidden from view of the village. Chelsea raised her hand to the door, but before she could knock, it opened wide. Michael appeared, wearing his vicar's collar and looking flustered.

"Oh. Hi, Chelsea."

"Michael." She leaned up on her tiptoes for a brotherly kiss of his clean-shaven cheek, which he reciprocated. "I'm so sorry about your father." She hadn't seen Michael since the news broke.

"Thanks." He offered a reverent pause then added, "It was his time."

Chelsea wondered if this was the standard line he would be handing to people attempting to comfort him this week.

"But it doesn't make the grieving process much easier, does it? It still hurts."

"Yes. Yes, it does." He nodded, momentarily dropping his vicar mask—as Rachel called it—then stepped outside the cottage to let her pass through.

Chelsea shut the door, remembering her mission. She stepped inside the living room, which was cozy and humble with dark beams overhead, a stone floor beneath, and a fire burning brightly in the fireplace. Rachel stood near the sofa, folding a navy-blue towel. When she saw Chelsea, her tight expression relaxed into a wistful smile.

Chelsea rounded the sofa to join her. On the way, she set down Rachel's keys on a corner table, atop a notepad that contained a long list of funeral arrangements with some items marked off and some still remaining. The sofa was lined with neat stacks of folded laundry—jumpers, towels, trousers, and socks.

Chelsea gave her friend a gentle side hug then reached inside the basket perched on the sofa. She picked out a bath towel and began to fold. Rachel was forever tidying up around the cottage—clearing tables, dusting bookcases, washing dishes—more out of duty than a personal compulsion or pleasure. She'd once told Chelsea, "The vicarage has to be spotless always. You never know who could be dropping by, even on weekends."

Chelsea nudged Rachel's arm. "How are things today?"

Rachel offered the same shrug her husband had given. "Fine. Busy. But fine. Head above water at least." She set down the folded towel and made eye contact. "You know what the hardest thing is?"

Chelsea paused her folding to listen.

"I can sense this... pressure. Right here." Rachel tapped her own shoulders then clasped her hands at her waist. "Pressure to make this funeral perfect. Nothing less will do. For Michael, for the villagers, and for Emmett's memory. He was beloved when he was vicar, and the turnout will be large—we're even having the reception at the church hall. Our vicarage is too small. But if anything goes wrong or isn't perfect... I'll feel like I mucked things up." She selected another towel then paused. "That sounds selfish, making it all about me."

"Rach, you're the least selfish person I know. It will all be perfect and appropriate. You'll see." She balanced her folded towel on a ready-made stack then pulled her mobile from her jeans pocket. "I have something to show you. Here, let's sit. Take a break."

Chelsea had proposed, over and over again, making calls or seeing to some of the funeral details to relieve her friend's burden. But Rachel had insisted on doing it all on her own. Seeking another way to aid her friend, Chelsea had whisked by the vicarage earlier that morning to pick up Rachel's classroom keys, saying that she needed to check the Wi-Fi connection, by order of the school's headmistress. But it was all a ruse.

They settled into the two cozy chairs that flanked the fireplace. "I've done something," Chelsea confessed, "and hope you'll be pleased." She scrolled through some photos she'd taken of Rachel's classroom minutes before then handed the phone across to Rachel. "You haven't had a single moment to concentrate on your room, so now you won't have to."

Once inside Rachel's classroom, Chelsea had gotten straight to work. There were only two major projects to complete. First, she filled a blank board on the wall with the materials Rachel had already bought or cut out. Second, she did a general tidying up—dusting, straightening curtains and desks, and even decluttering the wardrobe filled with supplies for the new year. Then, just as she was ready to leave, Chelsea remembered that Rachel always bought, with her own money, treats for the pupils each new term—something to lay out on their desks when they first arrived in her class. Chelsea poked around, and finally, underneath Rachel's immense oak desk, she noticed two canvas bags, each filled with brand-new pencil boxes, laminated times tables, crayons, pens, pencils, and protractors. Chelsea had sorted and arranged them on each pupil's desk as meticulously as she imagined Rachel would have done.

Rachel scrolled through the photos, and her crinkled expression dissolved into a gasp of surprise as she understood what the pictures meant.

Chelsea explained, "You would've told me another no if I'd offered to help. So I didn't even ask this time. You're all set for the first day of school."

Rachel shook her head. "This must have taken you hours."

"Only two. And I'll change anything you want me to." Chelsea pointed toward the mobile's screen. "I put the pens and pencils *inside* the boxes on the pupils' desks, but I can take them out and display them. Or that jungle-themed board. If you want me to swap the rhino with the giraffe, for instance? I can—"

Rachel grasped Chelsea's hand in midair. "No. Nothing needs to be swapped or changed. Nothing at all. It's absolutely perfect."

Chelsea watched tears form in Rachel's weary eyes then squeezed her hand. "I wanted to take something off your plate."

"You have." Rachel removed her hand to dab her eyes with the towel she still held. "I can't thank you enough." She handed back Chelsea's phone.

"How's Michael doing? He looked so tired just now." Chelsea pointed toward the front door.

Rachel shifted in her seat. "He wrestles with sleep, can't seem to get comfortable. He doesn't want to talk about it yet, the grief. Keeps telling me he's 'fine.'"

"He'll let you in," Chelsea reassured her. "When all this has passed—the service, the formalities, the social obligations. He needs to be strong, and he's probably afraid he'll crumble if he leans on someone right now."

"You're right. But sometimes I miss him. I miss *us*."

Michael and Rachel had always been the sort of couple people envied—in tune, in sync, best friends enduring the ups and downs of life together with a cheery outlook. But over the past several months, Chelsea had noticed a specific distance growing between them, due partly to the busyness of life but mostly to the struggle to have a family. Rachel had tried for nearly eight years to get pregnant and had suffered three devastating miscarriages. Two years before, she and Michael decided to try adoption and even made it through home visits and training classes but were told the process could be agonizingly slow. Not having the funds for another logical route—expensive in vitro and hormone treatments—Rachel and Michael chose to put the family planning on indefinite pause. She didn't let on how much this decision affected her, but Chelsea could still see the disappointment lingering in her eyes.

"About the funeral..." Rachel steadied her gaze. "There's something you need to know."

Chelsea tilted her head.

"Luka might come. He said he's trying to make it."

Neither Chelsea nor Rachel had uttered *that name* to each other in years. It was jarring to hear it spoken aloud, almost as shocking as a profanity or blasphemy would have been. At any time in the past, Chelsea could have inquired about Luka's exact location. It would have been a simple enough question to ask and an easy one to answer, since Michael often received Luka's postcards from Switzerland, Russia, or Brazil—Chelsea had seen them over the past year and a half, on occasion, lying on the entry table of the vicarage during her visits. But when Luka broke Chelsea's heart all those years ago, Rachel had flown into best-friend protective mode, and Luka's name became in-stantly taboo between the two friends. Rachel had wanted Chelsea to forget all about Luka and move on with her life.

Chelsea's pulse raced as she pictured Luka back in the village again, within proximity. She ached to hear Rachel's details but tried not to show it. "I admit, I was curious about him..."

"I wasn't sure when to bring it up, or how. Or even *whether* to."

"I'm glad you did." Chelsea waited as patiently as she could, preparing to devour every word.

"Luka told Michael he'll try his best to come, but I think it's... iffy. He's in South America on some photo shoot. The weather looks dodgy, but he's getting a plane out tomorrow. Mac has agreed to take his place as pallbearer, in case..."

"In case Luka doesn't show."

Surely Rachel, too, was wondering if Luka might develop some sudden excuse to miss his own father's funeral. Luka had created an excuse of "a terrible bout of dysentery" to skip his brother's wed-ding twelve years before, and Chelsea had been relieved. She'd been able to perform all her duties as chief bridesmaid to Rachel without having to worry about Luka's presence casting dark clouds over the whole thing.

"Well, you know how I feel about my brother-in-law, so I hate admitting this, but Luka's actually surprised me lately. Since Emmett was moved to Bath, to that facility, Luka has been visiting him. It was quiet at first—he didn't want anyone to know he was seeing his father. But one day last year, Michael happened to catch him at his father's bedside. And since then, every time Luka's come to Bath, Michael has dropped everything to join him. Brothers in solidarity." She added in a quieter tone, "Luka never came to the village, though. Just slipped off again to who knows where on his next project."

Luka, in the vicinity of Chilton Crosse all this time. Chelsea imagined him at his father's bedside, offering comfort and companionship, even perhaps making some much-needed amends.

"I always assumed Luka left England and never glanced back," Chelsea mused.

"He's kept in touch with Michael, and in the early days, when you were at university, he even reached out to Emmett, came into the village for a couple of brief and awkward Christmas dinners—arranged by yours truly. I couldn't stand having a fractured family and wanted to mend things."

"I had no idea."

"The tension was strong on both sides of the table for those Christmases. I could see Emmett make a small effort, but he was never warm toward Luka. I can understand why he quit coming for holidays after that. It wasn't doing much good." Rachel winced. "Was I right to tell you about Luka maybe attending the funeral?"

"Of course. I needed to know. And I'm glad we can talk about it. I think it broke through some sort of unspoken wall. I mean, we never, ever talk about him."

"That's my fault. I drew a hard line when I watched you crumble after he left. But maybe acting like he never existed wasn't the best approach. I regret it now. I didn't let you talk when you probably needed to. I thought I was helping, but maybe the opposite was true. I didn't want him hurting you again."

"I know."

Suddenly, the fire's heat became strangely unbearable, and Chelsea found herself squirming, needing to get out and take a walk in the crisp nearly autumn air. "I'd better get going."

They stood together, then Rachel leaned in for a tight hug. "Thank you for finishing my classroom. What a lovely surprise."

As Chelsea exited the cottage, one word floated in her consciousness above the others Rachel had spoken. *Iffy*. It was possible Luka might not show up after all.

WHEN CHELSEA ENTERED the bookshop, she hoped to find a journal—nothing fancy, just something functional to hold all her ideas and meeting times for the upcoming Renaissance festival. As she browsed the shelf, her gaze came to a dead stop at a leather-bound journal, its cover embossed with a colorful peacock, which happened to be one of the many symbols of the Renaissance. *Perfect*.

While paying at the till, Chelsea received a text from Noelle Spencer, asking her to drop by. So instead of her original plan of pivoting homeward, Chelsea went in the other direction toward the art gallery.

Noelle was the American who'd made Chilton Crosse her home four years earlier, whose architect-husband, Adam, had helmed the school's restoration project. When Chelsea contacted various villagers for their participation in the festival over the past weeks, Noelle had been one of the first to volunteer her talents. She was the great-niece of Joy Valentine, a famous Cotswold artist who'd lived in the village for decades. Joy had passed away a few years back, bequeathing both her cottage and her art gallery to Noelle.

As Chelsea entered the gallery, she immediately smelled the strong scent of turpentine and paint. The space was cool and inviting. As a teenager, she would wander around the gallery, losing herself in the paintings. Sometimes, Joy would set up an easel in the back room, and villagers and tourists could quietly mill about, watching her create a new masterpiece before their eyes. Noelle, a talented artist in her own right—she'd been taught as a teenager by Joy—occasionally painted inside the gallery to keep that tradition going.

Chelsea rounded the corner and tapped on the wall, catching Noelle's eye from behind the canvas. She gave a friendly smile as she waved Chelsea closer.

They seemed to be the only two in the gallery. Sometimes, Noelle's eight-month-old son was with her, but Adam must have been sitting with him that day instead. Frank, the curator, was probably on a lunch break.

"Thanks for coming by." Noelle swiveled on her stool and gestured toward a chair in the corner.

"I was out and about today anyway, running errands." Chelsea sat down and crossed her legs, perching the new journal on her knees.

Noelle was close to Chelsea's age, with the same petite stature and a similar haircut—a shoulder-length bob with long side-swept fringe. But Noelle had blond hair instead of Chelsea's brown and clear blue eyes instead of Chelsea's hazel.

Noelle set down her paintbrush then wiped her hands on a cloth covered in smudges of various paint colors. "I didn't want to show you this until it was nearly completed."

She craned her neck toward the canvas, and Chelsea's eyes followed, settling on the painting. She recognized the scene immediately—the high street of Chilton Crosse, with its honey-colored limestone buildings, towering trees, and colorful flower boxes. The sturdy stone gazebo, familiar shops, restaurants, and pub all led toward the church's noble spire. As Chelsea stood to see the painting up close, she noticed it was dusk, with faint wisps of orange-and-pink clouds dotting the sky. It all looked utterly quintessential, but then Chelsea realized what was so special about it. Noelle had captured the festival. Down along the cobblestone street, tourists and residents roamed about—some even dressed in costume. Chelsea spotted a colorful string of medieval banners hanging between the shops.

"This is absolutely beautiful."

Noelle's face relaxed. "I'm so glad you like it. I had an impulse and went with it. I'm not sure I got all the details right. I can make changes if I need to."

"No, I think it's perfect. In fact, I'll text Tristan today, see if he can get this onto the website when you're ready. And on the brochures he's having printed up. This painting can be the face of the festival."

"You really think so?"

"If that's okay with you."

"Of course. I'm flattered." Noelle's mobile pinged beside her, and she glanced at the screen. "Sorry, I should respond to this. It's Adam with a question about little Adam."

"It's fine. I need to be on my way. Thank you for... this." Chelsea pointed at the painting, knowing that any sentiment she expressed would be wholly inadequate. "It's more than I could've imagined."

Outside the gallery, Chelsea paused and clicked her pen, filling her first entry in the journal: *Noelle painting. Centerpiece for advertising—website and brochures and flyers. Tell Tristan.*

CHELSEA SQUINTED INTO the mirror, holding the mascara wand steady then brushing it against her upper lashes while trying not to blink. She only hoped the *waterproof* claim on the bottle was accurate. This would be a day for shedding tears.

She placed the mascara in her makeup bag then searched for her lipstick tube, which seemed to be missing. She broadened the search, gingerly shifting the hair products on the tiled countertop, lifting up a towel, sorting through her toothpaste and floss and powder. *Did it fall out during the move?*

The night before, after Mac had finished all his projects, Chelsea gained an unexpected spurt of energy and moved all her essentials—bedding, toiletries, makeup, and hair products— into the cottage's master bedroom. She could move the rest later. Her first night spent in her new room felt strange. This had been her parents' bedroom for so many years, but soon, she would put her own stamp on it with wall hangings and furniture and all her clothes inside the wardrobe.

"There you are," she told the lipstick tube peeking meekly from behind her hair spray bottle. "Little bugger."

Thunder rumbled low in the distance as Chelsea uncapped the tube and peered at her reflection again. For the service, she'd chosen a modest black dress with tiny colored jewels at the neckline and a burgundy shawl. Earlier, as she'd selected her funeral attire, her fingers had grazed the black coat she'd worn to her father's service years before. She couldn't bear either to chuck it out or wear it again, so there it hung in the wardrobe, a lingering reminder of that somber day.

She pressed the tube to her upper lip and dabbed on the mauve shade, careful that it matched her muted makeup—nothing too bright or noticeable. Rain began to patter on the window, and part of her wished she could stay indoors. Trekking outside in low heels and risking the splatter of mud wouldn't be pleasant, but there was no other option. She was attending the funeral in support of Rachel more than anyone else. Chelsea had already insisted on helping out with the refreshments after the burial service. Rachel would need all the aid she could get.

Finishing her lipstick, Chelsea thought of the *vicar veil* that Rachel and Michael hid behind. She understood, more than anyone, the behind-the-scenes work that went into a day like this one—the brave but weary smiles they would have to plaster on, the small demands parishioners would place on the couple, and the many ways Michael and Rachel would do their very best to accommodate everyone.

Peeking behind the veil had actually started back in Chelsea's teen years, when the vicar had first arrived at the church with his two sons. Chelsea and Rachel were already heavily involved in the music program and because of this, they spent more time at the church than most villagers, preparing for performances, rehearsing, and sometimes just hanging out. It wasn't uncommon for Chelsea to be there after hours or on days without services or activities. The church was almost her second home.

One evening, a year after the vicar had arrived, sixteen-year-old Chelsea came out of choir rehearsal alone. Rachel had stayed behind to spend extra time with Michael—the two had become smitten with each other months before. The evening was dusky with a strong chill in the air, and Chelsea was on her way home to study for an exam. But as she moved in the direction of Nightingale Cottage, she heard raised voices. She paused to listen and realized they were coming from the vicarage.

She should have continued on her path, back to the warmth and safety of her cottage. But curiosity got the better of her, so Chelsea changed course and walked slowly in the direction of the vicarage as the shouting intensified. The words were muffled, but the tone was clear. Luka and his father were having an argument. Twenty feet from the cottage's entrance, Chelsea froze as the front door flew open wide with Luka's frame in the doorway.

"I will *never* be good enough for you!" he yelled into the cottage then slammed the door shut.

Chelsea held her breath, wishing she could be invisible, praying Luka wouldn't see her. But the first step he took away from the cottage was in her direction. He froze, too, and stared her down, his expression sullen.

"What are *you* doing here?"

"Nothing. I... I just..." Chelsea tucked a lock of hair behind her ear and shifted where she stood. "I was coming out of rehearsal. Choir rehearsal. And I heard shouting, and so—"

"So you thought you'd come over and eavesdrop? Listen to something that was none of your business?"

His dark eyes glared. She should have been rattled, even slightly afraid. But all Chelsea felt was compassion. He was angry, yes. But the source of the darkness in his eyes was actually pain.

For months, Luka had been her private obsession. Since the moment she first saw him at the church, being introduced to the parishioners, her heart had been stolen away. She couldn't explain the intensity of these feelings for someone she didn't even know. They'd had minimal contact at school, since he was a year ahead of her, and also at church, since he rarely attended. And any efforts she'd made to draw closer to him had been rebuffed. Conversations she might initiate ended abruptly as he found excuses to leave. At first, she took it as rejection, deciding she wasn't pretty or interesting enough. But as she observed him with other people, she understood that he treated everyone that way—coldly, at arm's length, with disregard. Which only strengthened her curiosity.

Chelsea took a deliberate step toward Luka, but it backfired. He moved from his spot, walking swiftly in the other direction.

"Wait. Luka, please!" Chelsea tried to match his pace, her new heels scuffing against the rocky unpaved road toward the countryside.

When they were well past the high street, at a fork in the road, he stopped in his tracks. "Why are you following me?"

"I wanted to make sure you're okay." She heard the sheepish tone in her own voice and cringed. "That's all."

Luka blew out an audible sigh and looked around him at the early evening—the trees, the darkening skies, the stone walls separating property from property. She wondered what he was thinking.

"C'mon." He took a backward step toward Chelsea, wrapped his warm hand around her own, then led her up the path.

He didn't say a single word during that swift journey, but Chelsea didn't care. All she could focus on was her hand inside his. She had held her ground, stayed tenacious, and chipped away at that thick wall of his. And it had paid off. His veneer was cracking.

When he arrived at Mac MacDonald's property, Luka opened the gate for Chelsea then closed it behind them. He didn't reach for her hand again but led her toward the barn at the south end of the property. Inside, he flipped a switch, and a couple of lights overhead cast a weak glow. Chelsea had never been on Mac's property before and hadn't even known he had a barn. It didn't seem very functional—one stall held an old mare who snorted now and again, but the other stalls were empty.

Luka unraveled a nearby horse blanket and laid it down on a long hay bale for Chelsea, who sat to watch him pace. He rubbed at his face with both palms then ran his hands over the top of his wavy hair and crossed his arms. "Sorry you had to hear all that." He paused and made eye contact for the first time since they'd left the vicarage. "What *did* you hear?"

"Nothing. Not really. Some shouting." Chelsea shifted on the uncomfortable hay. "And something about not being good enough."

Luka continued his pacing. "It's only the truth. Always has been."

"You don't really believe that, do you—that you're not good enough for your father?"

"He thinks so." Luka stopped and faced her squarely, his hands still folded across his chest. "I guess you've heard the rumors by now—rebellious son stirs up trouble for the perfect vicar and his favorite son. A constant thorn in their side, an embarrassment to the family. Am I close?"

Chelsea *had* heard those rumors almost verbatim, in fact. The moment the congregation laid eyes upon the two young men for the first time, judgments had been formed and solidified, rightly or wrongly. The brothers couldn't have been more starkly different in appearance. Michael had a light-brown flop of hair and a joyful smile as he gazed eagerly at the parishioners, and Luka had jet-black wavy hair down to his collar and tucked behind his ears—*How shocking!*—and dark eyes that stared intently at the floor in front of him, hands clamped at his waist as though he'd rather be anywhere else. Chelsea remembered that day in vivid, colorful detail.

"People like to talk. Is it important, what they think?"

Luka smirked, his tone softening. "Not to me. It's my father. He cares. Too much." He untangled his arms and scratched at his neck. "If I'm honest, I guess I don't help things. I had agreed to A levels, but now I want to quit. And I'm refusing to go to university—a cardinal sin in my father's eyes. That's what started tonight's row. And I've been known to get smug and stomp around the cottage in foul moods. And to miss curfew and skip church."

"Self-fulfilling prophecy." Chelsea remembered that section in her textbook from the year before. She saw Luka's confusion and explained. "It's when you already know what people will expect from you, so you sort of... maneuver into that role. Without even meaning to."

"You're the cerebral type, aren't you? I see you studying under trees in the village. Or at the bridge."

Chelsea was almost more gobsmacked by the knowledge that Luka had watched her around the village than by the fact that she'd been having a real conversation with him after several months of trying. "You do?"

"I pay attention." The old mare snorted again from her stall, and Luka shifted his focus. "It's late. I'd better get you back home."

Chelsea had barely noticed the dusk outside fading to dark or the chill seeping into her bones from the cooler temperatures. Luka held out his hand, and she grasped it to stand up. She dusted loose hay from her backside as he removed his coat and draped it around her shoulders.

"Thanks," he muttered. "For listening."

That night had changed everything. A wall between them had crumbled. From that moment, Luka seemed to trust her more than anyone else in his life. He let down his guard and told her things he never let other people know. And for the next whole year of her life, Chelsea was the happiest she'd ever been—or ever would be.

Gazing down at the lipstick tube, Chelsea realized the time. If she didn't leave for the funeral service immediately, she would be late. Ignoring the ominous clap of thunder, she slipped into her heels, fetched her bag and shawl, then headed downstairs and out the door.

NINETY MINUTES LATER, Chelsea stood in the drizzling rain underneath an umbrella at Emmett McKane's graveside while Michael recited comforting portions from Ecclesiastes 3:

> To every thing there is a season, and a time to every purpose under the heaven: a time to be born and a time to die... a time to weep and a time to laugh, a time to mourn and a time to dance.

Standing in the cemetery, she had her answer. Luka hadn't come after all. Though she'd trained her eyes not to look and her brain not to care, she couldn't help sneaking an occasional glance around the packed service earlier inside the church. And even as she'd walked the short distance to the graveyard on the outskirts of Chilton Crosse, she'd let her eyes wander to look for any sign of him.

But minutes later, as she stood beside Rachel, watching Michael take a clod of soil and cast it into the open grave, Chelsea's gaze drifted behind him, past the other gravesites. And there he stood on a hill—a dark figure leaning against a tree, watching the mourners from afar. *Luka.*

Once her eyes had found him, Chelsea couldn't stop staring. He was so far away that all she could see was a suit that matched the black hair nearly down to his shoulders. She couldn't make out the details of his face. But it was unmistakably him.

"Chelsea?" Rachel whispered then craned her own neck to follow her friend's gaze.

"He came."

When Michael dismissed the crowd, Rachel left Chelsea's side long enough to approach her husband and point toward the figure still standing beside the tree. Michael nodded then turned to walk the distance to his brother. It was clear that Luka had no intention of moving any closer. He stayed where he was, letting Michael come to him. Chelsea wondered if he'd seen her—if he had recognized her among all the other females dressed in black, huddled under umbrellas to escape the drizzle.

"Do you want to wait and talk to him?" Rachel asked.

Chelsea tore her focus away from Luka and turned to her friend. She had promised to help Rachel with the reception at the church hall, and that was precisely what she would do.

"No. It's fine. We can go now."

"Okay. If you're sure."

"Completely sure."

It might be the last time she ever saw Luka. Chelsea stole a final glimpse of the tree and saw the brothers embrace. Then she turned her back on them and walked with Rachel toward the church hall.

Chapter Three

Absence from those we love is self from self – a deadly banishment.
~Shakespeare

He'd missed it. After thirteen and a half hours spent in a stuffy plane's cabin, sandwiched between an obese businessman and a nervous teenager, he had missed his own father's funeral. Luka McKane had thought the flight he'd booked would give him ample time. But hours' worth of technical problems and weather delays had him leaving Heathrow Airport too late to make the service. As a seasoned traveler, Luka should have known better.

By the time the cab pulled into Chilton Crosse and parked outside the familiar church, they were gone. Everyone, including his father in the casket, had already moved to the gravesite. Luka hoisted his backpack over his shoulder, gripped his duffle bag, and walked the distance toward the cemetery in the drizzling rain. Seeing the graveside service in progress, he set his bags onto the spongy ground then stood beneath a leafy oak tree to watch from afar. He could only see the back of his brother. Luka imagined him choking back tears as he read some scripture over his father's body.

Luka wished he could have offered his brother some comfort or even stood by his side. But walking up to the scene this late, disrupting and interrupting, would have been anything but a comfort. So he waited respectfully until the graveside service was finished to make his presence known, catching his brother's eye.

During the quick minute Michael walked briskly toward him, Luka had spotted someone else among the mourners. She was a black dress in a sea of other black dresses, but her walk and demeanor were unmistakable. *Chelsea.* He scanned the area around her, looking for signs of a husband or children, but found none.

Michael reached him, blocking Luka's sight of the mourners somberly drifting away from the grave. "You came." He wrapped his arms around his brother and squeezed tight, and Luka reciprocated.

"Too late," Luka muttered as they backed out of the hug. He made eye contact with his brother. "I'm sorry."

Michael waved a forgiving hand between them and tsked, his eyes glassy from tears. Luka placed a hand on his arm and gave it a squeeze. "How did it go?"

"As well as expected, I guess. I put myself aside, pretended it was someone else in the coffin. I've performed this service dozens of times, so the pretending was easier than I thought. It was the only way to get through it. I can mourn later in private."

Luka understood. He hadn't fully dealt with the news either. He had always known he probably wouldn't be there for his father's last breath, not with his sporadic and unpredictable traveling schedule. But the reality that he'd missed those last moments—and now the funeral—was almost too much to bear. He wondered when it would all stop feeling like some dream he was plodding through.

Before the tears could even begin to form, Luka sniffed them away and changed the subject. "I don't want to hold you up. You've got people looking for you. There's a reception now?"

"At the church hall. Come!"

Luka shook his head. The very last thing he could endure was empty chitchat from villagers or lengthy anecdotes about his father or worse, the inevitable twittering gossip whispered behind his back. "Is that Luka, the prodigal son finally returned? He missed his father's funeral. Shame! What else did we expect? Typical behavior, so disrespectful..."

"I can't. Mac's expecting me. But maybe I can drop by tomorrow to catch up."

"Aren't you staying with us at the vicarage? Rachel's set up the spare room."

Luka winced. "I already told Mac I'd stay with him."

Michael couldn't cover his disappointment. He'd been like that as a little boy too—his emotions usually showed up on his face, inside the crevices of his crinkled brow or in the subtle shift deep inside his eyes. "Well, okay, then. How long are you staying?"

Luka slipped his hands into his pockets. His dark suit was crumpled from the plane ride. "Not sure. One night, two at the most. I've got a small break between jobs."

"Well, if you're not staying with us, I insist you come for dinner tomorrow night. I'm not taking no for an answer." Michael's eyes shifted to the ground between them. "I've missed my brother. And especially now, with it being just the two of us..." He lifted his eyes toward Luka. "Stay longer."

Luka gave both a nod and a shrug, unable to commit. "There are some other factors involved."

"Chelsea?"

His candor surprised Luka. Michael had only ever mentioned her name to inform him casually of the major life events over the years—her engagement and subsequent breakup with some bloke from Bath as well as her father's untimely death. But nothing since then. Luka had assumed Michael and Rachel had lost touch with her entirely.

"I wasn't expecting her here," Luka admitted.

"She lives in Chilton Crosse."

"Since when?"

"Last year."

"You never mentioned it."

"Would it have changed things? Brought you back home?"

Luka knew the answer before the question was asked. *No.* He looked down to kick a pebble in the dirt. His life was far away from Chilton Crosse, far from the UK. He could never have made Chelsea any promises he could keep—even if she'd considered them in the first place. The way he'd abandoned her all those years ago, with barely an explanation, was unforgiveable.

"In any case, she's living in her family's cottage," Michael added. "Rachel said she was planning to sell it, but I think she's changed her mind. She's gotten a job at the school. Looks like she might be here to stay." He peered down at his watch—their father's old watch, Luka noticed. "I'd better get back to my duties. I don't want Rachel handling things alone." He paused and extended an open hand. "I'm glad you're here."

The brothers exchanged a hearty handshake, then Michael stepped away and moved toward the church hall with the others while Luka remained. He stood beside the tree, waiting until every last person had disappeared and the cemetery was empty. Then he left his bags beneath the tree trunk and stepped down from the hill toward his father's grave.

He came to a stop at the edge of the sunken hole to peer down at the glossy coffin lid tarnished with a spattering of Michael's dirt. Luka squatted down to scoop up his own handful then stood again. He'd already made amends—as much as had been possible with his father's state of mind the past few years.

"I didn't know my last time with you would be the final one," he whispered to the coffin, picturing his father in his hospital bed, withered hand reaching out to hold Luka's. "I waited too long to try to make my peace with you. I'm stubborn that way. But I cherish the time we had these past few years. I know that you loved me. And I hope you know I loved you too." Luka broke up the clod of dirt in

his palm, muddy from the rain, and tossed it into the ground to join
with Michael's. "Be at peace."

With one last glance at the open hole, Luka brushed the dirt
from his hands then went to retrieve his bags from underneath the
tree, his heart heavy and light at the same time.

WHEN LUKA ARRIVED AT Mac's property a few minutes later—he'd taken the long way round, reacquainting himself with the
village's outskirts—the rain had ceased, and a glint of sunlight
emerged through a distant cloud. One thing about England that Luka could never get out of his system was the rain. He remembered
complaining about it while he was growing up, but as he traveled
abroad, he missed it—the damp soil, the glistening cobblestones, the
sleek sheen of persistent rainy days. There was nothing like it.

After setting down his bags on Mac's front porch, Luka stretched
out his tired back, still sore from the lengthy plane ride, then rapped
his knuckles on the door and waited. It only took a few seconds for
Mac to respond. When he opened the door, Luka grinned.

"Look at you." Mac paused in the doorway, matching Luka's
grin, taking him in. "What has it been... ten years? Twelve? Haven't
changed a bit, 'ave you?" His Scottish accent seemed to have only
grown stronger in the passing years.

Mac had always had prematurely gray hair, even when Luka was
a teenager, so the same could be said about him. "Neither have you."

They stepped into a strong embrace, squeezing tight before letting go. Luka stooped for his bags then entered the cottage he remembered so well. It was humble and sparse, with the same rustic
charm that Luka recalled—hunting and tartan pictures gracing one
wall, beams overhead, and worn leather furniture in the living room.

Luka followed Mac through to the compact kitchen and set
down his bags.

"Still milk, no sugar?" Mac said, pouring a cup of tea.

"Good memory." Luka sat at the table and accepted the tea from Mac, whose own steaming cup was already set in front of his chair.

Mac joined Luka with a quiet grunt. "I didn't see you at the service." He sipped his tea.

Luka knew Mac well enough to know it wasn't an accusation, only a passing observation.

"I missed it completely," Luka confessed. "My flight didn't cooperate. But I've just come from the gravesite. Saw Michael."

"'Twas a good service. Your brother did a fine job." Mac's gray-blue eyes held a strong reverence.

"Thanks for taking my place. As pallbearer," Luka clarified.

"My pleasure, son."

Luka took a long sip of hot tea, comforted by the restorative warmth sliding down his throat. *Strong English tea. Something else I've fondly missed.*

This would usually be the part of a conversation where they caught up on each other's lives, filled in the gaps of the past several years. But the gaps were already filled—in monthly phone calls back and forth, in postcards sent from Luka from every place he'd visited, in occasional handwritten letters from Mac that told Luka some bits of recent Chilton Crosse news. *With the exception of Chelsea, apparently.* Luka had stayed in touch more regularly with Mac than with his own brother or father, probably because he felt more at ease with him than anyone else. As a teenager, Luka had been forced by his father to work for Mac. "It'll be good for you, getting your hands dirty. Time to earn your keep. Take on some responsibility." His father had probably had no idea that working alongside Mac would provide Luka with a paternal figure—someone who never judged or second-guessed him. Someone who trusted Luka and respected him and would never make demands on him. With Mac, Luka could be himself. He had nothing to prove.

"Did you say your goodbye?" Mac asked. "At the gravesite?"

With his finger, Luka traced the groove of wood in the table near his mug. "I did. I stayed behind, had my moment with my father."

"Good."

"Why is it easier to say things after someone's gone? To stare into a grave and have a one-sided conversation? Things I couldn't say to him when we were face-to-face."

"'Tis a mystery," Mac admitted, his graveled voice softening. "We keep our guards up around people, even those we love, for our own protection. Human nature."

"True. But it also costs us in the end. Leaving things unsaid." His mind drifted back to Chelsea, slim and petite in her black dress.

"What are your plans?" Mac asked.

"I'll stay a night or two. I have another job soon."

Mac reached backward to retrieve a key from the kitchen counter then placed it in front of Luka. "The stone cottage isn't much—'tis old and crusty and falling apart in places, much like yours truly. But it has running water and a working cooker. 'Tis yours as long as you want it."

"Thank you, Mac. For everything."

And he meant it. *Thanks for your kindness, loyalty, and willingness to take me in—for being a mate for all these years.* But rather than say all that, Luka smiled in Mac's direction and accepted the key, hoping Mac sensed every word.

LUKA PUNCHED THE SAGGY pillow and rolled over again, trying to get comfortable. He'd hoped that the long journey, the jet lag, and the weight of his father's death would be enough to lure him into a deep and comforting sleep. But Luka couldn't shut down his mind. He'd lain in bed for the past hour, squirming and wrestling with covers—too hot, too cold—until finally he gave up.

He swaddled his body in the top sheet then tromped down the hallway in bare feet toward the back door. If he remembered correctly, the cottage's back garden contained a handmade bench that Mac had crafted years before. And as he shut the door to walk outside, Luka spotted it instantly, in need of a good tidying but otherwise in fine condition.

Not even bothering to clear the dust and grime away, he sat down and let the cool air sift through his hair, brush his cheeks. The moon was exceptionally bright, probably because he was deep in the countryside with few city lights. It shone down onto the garden with a glow, illuminating the stone walkway, the nonworking fountain, the overgrown hedges. Luka twisted his head back toward the cottage and noticed the shadow of Virginia creeper crawling up the stone's surface. Soon, the leaves would be transformed into autumn colors—rich, vibrant shades of red.

Luka returned his stare to the moon beaming high in the sky. He closed his eyes and could still see its shape in his mind's eye, glowing strong. And without even trying to conjure it, Chelsea's image came into view once again. Rather than nudge her away, he gave in.

Unmarried. Moved to Chilton Crosse. Here to stay.

For so many years, Luka had tried to extract Chelsea from his thoughts, as though she'd never existed. It was easier that way. He dulled the pain with other relationships—which never lasted, mostly because of his globe-trotting—and even with alcohol for a period of time when he first left Chilton Crosse. But his saving grace had been work—never sitting still, catching the next plane, tackling the newest adventure, accepting a new assignment. He was passionate about his photography, and he was lucky that it legitimately allowed him to escape. He never stayed in one place for long, and that lifestyle suited him. Being back in Chilton Crosse was like putting on a pair of old, comfortable jeans. He never thought of the village as home—he hadn't lived there long enough to call it that. But wandering through woodlands with Chelsea, sneaking away to Mac's barn, snapping photos of her beautiful face, hearing her read her poetry aloud, opening up to her without hesitation—those tender moments had felt like home to him more than any other time in his life. He was safe with her. And since he'd left Chilton Crosse, he hadn't been able to duplicate that sensation, hard as he'd tried.

His thoughts drifted toward the first time he'd ever laid eyes on Chelsea, when he was seventeen. He had only been in the village for three days when his father had asked him to stop by the church and pick up the Bible he'd forgotten on the back pew after speaking with a parishioner that morning. Luka arrived at the solid door and paused, hearing a song drifting from inside. It was a weekday afternoon, and he hadn't expected the church to be occupied. He cracked the door open and let it close behind him as he entered, his eyes directed toward the front of the church. A beautiful girl in a yellow dress stood near the organ with her eyes closed, singing "Abide with Me" a cappella. Her delicate hands moved in rhythm with the music, and her soprano vocals soared inside the acoustics of the room.

Before she had a chance to open her eyes and catch him gawking, Luka fetched the Bible for his father and slipped discreetly out the door. But he lingered there, leaning his back against the door, to hear her finish the song.

Something had stirred in him that day, something he didn't expect and couldn't explain. But he knew one thing—a girl like that was too good for him. That notion was only confirmed as later in school, he heard about her getting good marks, being hand-picked for leadership positions, and receiving praise from all the adults in the village. She was beloved by everyone. So he'd done his best for the following year to avoid her, to spare her from the cloud of negativity that had seemed to follow him from village to village as he'd moved with his father.

Eventually, though, Luka's resistance wore down, and in a moment of weakness one night, he'd let Chelsea in. He never regretted it, but looking back, he thought that she probably did. If she'd simply walked away that night after his row with his father, she would never have suffered the pain of their separation a year later.

Opening his eyes, Luka watched a cloud pass over the moon, darkening the garden, and decided it was time to go inside and wrestle with sleep once again.

Chapter Four

Is love a tender thing? It is too rough, too rude, too boist'rous;
and it pricks like thorn. ~Shakespeare

Chelsea tipped the bedroom curtain back to see the moon in full view. It was so bright that she swore it had awakened her, shining through the diamond-paned window, urging her to take a peek. But something else was responsible for her restlessness. She wanted to believe that the upcoming first day back to school was to blame, and it was, partly. But Luka McKane's presence in the village was the true culprit. She'd spent years having no clue where he might be at any given moment. But for the first time in a very long time, she knew precisely where he was.

Chelsea had stayed purposely busy at the funeral's reception hours earlier, helping Rachel fill teacups, restock sandwich trays, and replace paper napkins, forcing herself to concentrate only on the tasks at hand. When it was clear that Luka was staying hidden and would likely leave the next day without a word, Chelsea chose to push from her mind that haunting image of him standing at the tree and move on with her life. She had things to do—final touches on her classroom, a load of laundry at home, a call to Mrs. Pickering to return, an early meal to make. Whatever Luka decided to do with his time would not factor into Chelsea's life. She had a choice, too, and that was to leave Luka behind. She'd managed to hold that emboldened attitude for the entire day, up until the moment she'd slid her bare feet underneath the covers and clicked off the nightstand light.

Inside a foggy haze from lack of sleep, with her resistance down, Chelsea suppressed a yawn, stared back at the lovely round moon, and let herself wonder what Luka was doing underneath it.

"OKAY, EVERYONE, TAKE your seats. It's time to begin!" Chelsea shouted over the pupils' raucous chattering.

She knew that on the first day back, especially during the first lesson, they would all be eager to catch up and socialize. When the pupils were finally silent, she clasped her hands at her waist. Earlier in the morning, she'd selected her favorite rose-colored dress, the one that gave her confidence even when she didn't have much to spare.

"Welcome back to the new term. I hope you had a restful holiday break. As you can see"—she moved a hand to gesture around the classroom—"this term's theme is the Renaissance. We will be studying artists, philosophers, writers, and great thinkers. And as you already know, we'll have a Renaissance festival in conjunction with our *Romeo and Juliet* production. What you might not know is that the festival has expanded to village wide, and yours truly is the committee chair." She saw some raised eyebrows. The word hadn't quite gotten around yet. "Auditions for *Romeo and Juliet* are scheduled for Friday, and rehearsals will begin next week. There's no time to waste if we're going to be ready for the big day."

Her eyes wandered over to Hugo, who was clearly texting underneath the desk. Chelsea cleared her throat and waited for him to make eye contact. When he finally did, he gave a sheepish smile. "Sorry."

"You've reminded me..." Chelsea stepped backward to retrieve the ample wicker basket she'd purchased from the novelty gift shop. "I have a new rule about mobile phones. Each morning before class, all pupils will place their mobiles—turned off—into this basket. You can retrieve them when our time is over. This classroom is officially a text-free zone. When you're here, I want you to be fully *here*."

She ignored the anticipated moans and groans as she passed the basket to Hugo first. He stared longingly at his mobile, as though he were losing his best friend, before depositing it hesitantly into the basket.

"Really, miss?" he asked with pleading eyes.

"Really." She suppressed a powerful urge to grin then handed the basket over to Sienna, who dutifully placed her mobile into the basket then passed it to the next pupil. Chelsea returned to the center of the room and drew the pupils' attention to her once more. "If you fail to put your mobile into the basket, you will have extra homework that evening. So don't think you can get away with it. I'll count them if I have to..."

Chelsea had learned, from certain incidents the previous year, that she needed to be stricter with her pupils, especially at the start, so they wouldn't take advantage of her kind, sometimes naive nature.

She retrieved her textbook. "Let's dive right in. Open your books to page 137, 'A Biography of William Shakespeare.'"

ALTHOUGH CHELSEA HAD spent nearly every day of her holiday break prepping and planning for the new term, she'd still found time to relax, sleep later than usual, browse the village shops and gallery, take leisurely coffee breaks with Rachel, or go for long walks around the village's outskirts at sunset. During those weeks, she'd somehow forgotten the frantic and unrelenting pace that a school day could hold, especially the first day. By the time her final group of pupils had filtered out of her classroom, Chelsea realized how drained she was. Holding young people's attention, filling their brains with knowledge, keeping the material relevant and interesting—it all amounted to a pouring out of herself that left her empty.

Earlier, during her lunch break, she'd scurried back to the cottage to feed Socrates and let him stretch his arthritic legs in the garden while she closed her eyes in the warm sunshine and mused whether Luka was still in the village. She'd pictured him packing up and boarding a plane to whatever exotic destination was next on his agenda—Africa, Peru, Brazil, or maybe India.

As the last pupil closed the door behind him, signaling the school day's end, Chelsea rounded her desk and plonked down in the chair, reaching for her mobile, which had been switched off all day. As it came to life in her hand, she saw text after text, call after call, and became suddenly overwhelmed. She skimmed through the messages then played the voicemails, all related in some way to the festival. Tristan had texted an answer to an advertising question, Noelle had emailed a photo of the finished painting, Mary Cartwright had texted a question regarding costumes, and Mrs. Pickering had left two voicemails about the time of the committee's first meeting this week.

Chelsea set down the phone and rubbed her temples, wishing she'd waited until later to check her messages. In her mind's eye, she foresaw nothing but packed, busy days ahead—no time to breathe or rest, at least until the festival was over and done with. Weeknights, weekends, and lunch breaks would all be spent scrambling to catch up.

What have I gotten myself into?

Like it or not, though, she was committed. She would see this festival through, and it would be the best one this village had ever seen, if she had any say in the matter. At least, that was what she told herself as she pushed her mobile aside and focused on the most crucial task at hand—tomorrow's lesson plans, plus a bit of grading. Everything else would have to wait.

TWO HOURS LATER, CHELSEA'S mind refused to look at another page of text or glance at another paper. Her brain had reached its absolute capacity. She grabbed her bag and mobile, pushed up from the chair, and stretched her aching back. Then she paused at the mirror that hung beside the door. Peering into it, she saw tired eyes reflected back, smudged with a bit of mascara, which she rubbed away with her fingertips. She scanned the classroom to make sure everything was in order for the next day—no crooked desks or left-behind umbrellas—then clicked off the lights and shut the door.

Emerging from the school building, Chelsea felt like a hermit exiting a dank cave into the fresh air. She hadn't seen or talked to Rachel all day, which wasn't surprising. They taught in separate buildings and had different schedules, and they both kept busy from the moment they entered to the moment they left, which didn't leave much room for socializing.

Wanting to see how her friend's first day had gone and knowing a text or call wouldn't suffice, Chelsea headed toward the vicarage. She also had a bit of gossip to share. During her grading session, someone had stopped by to convey that Tara Ridley, a popular maths teacher, had been sacked over the break—the direct result of a scandalous dalliance she'd had with one of the married administrators.

At the vicarage's front door, Chelsea knocked and waited. The door opened, and Michael emerged, beaming. "Chelsea! Come in." He stepped aside to let her in.

Chelsea smelled something delicious—lamb, perhaps—as she entered the cottage. "I'm interrupting your dinner," she said with a wince.

"Not at all." Michael waved away her concerns.

Rachel came in from the kitchen and stopped short. Chelsea had trouble reading her friend's expression—an odd mixture of cheerfulness and distress, like a smile wrapped inside a frown. Perhaps her first day had been as daunting as Chelsea's, and she was having trouble hiding it.

"Hey," Rachel whispered, coming in closer.

"I hope it's okay I stopped by," Chelsea said. "I wanted to see how your day went."

Rachel clasped Chelsea's hands tightly as her eyes widened and darted around. "It was okay, I guess. Fine. Busy but fine."

Chelsea had never seen Rachel this jittery before. "Are you all right? I came at a bad time, I think..." Just as she'd decided to politely exit the cottage and leave them to their dinner, Chelsea's eyes drifted past Rachel's shoulder toward the kitchen, where Luka stood in the doorway, a dish towel slung casually over his shoulder.

Chelsea's heart jolted inside her chest. She should have seen this coming.

Rachel bowed her head slightly and released Chelsea's hands then stepped aside, allowing them to face each other.

"Chelsea," he whispered.

This time, unlike at the gravesite, she could see all the details of him up close—plaid shirt, faded jeans, light beard, and jet-black hair. His coloring came from his Italian-born mother, she recalled. And those eyes. Dark brown and still able to sear through her with one unblinking gaze.

She willed her heartbeat to slow down, but she was powerless. Luka stepped toward her, and everything else faded away. He gave a shadow of a smile and stopped in front of her.

"You're still here," she heard herself say. "I mean, in Chilton Crosse."

Luka gripped the towel and slid it off his shoulder but kept his eyes on her. "Yes. Staying at Mac's."

Social decorum finally got the better of her, and she recalled Luka's reason for being in the village. "I'm sorry. About your father."

"Thanks. I'm sorry about yours too. Michael told me..."

Chelsea gave a little shrug. She hadn't expected to talk about her father today. *Especially with Luka.* Her breathing relaxed, but her shoulders remained rigid. She studied Luka's face, noticing new creases at the edges of his eyes. The last sixteen years had been exceptionally good to him. He was merely an older version of himself, without the weight changes or balding tendencies that seemed to render some people unrecognizable in their thirties. This was still Luka standing in front of her.

She wondered how he was seeing her—older, too, with new wrinkles and tired eyes from a lengthy workday. The rosy glow of youth he'd last remembered on her was likely gone.

"Stay for dinner," Michael said from behind her, clearly unable to contain his eagerness.

Chelsea forced her gaze away from Luka. "No, thanks. I can't. Too much to do..."

A timer buzzed in the kitchen, and Michael moved swiftly to quiet it.

"It's lovely to see you again," Luka said, drawing her focus back to him.

"You too," she lied.

The truth was too impossible to utter—*It's shocking to see you again. It's harrowing, distressing, even slightly traumatic to see you again.* She could think of a hundred descriptors other than *lovely.*

"I'd better go," she said. Past these polite niceties, she couldn't imagine having a real conversation with Luka, especially in front of Michael and Rachel. It would be pointless anyway. Luka would soon be gone.

"I'll walk you out," Rachel offered, placing a gentle hand on Chelsea's arm.

Chelsea turned without a goodbye, or even a backward glance at Luka, and followed Rachel out the door. Closing it behind them,

Rachel stood on the porch to face her. Even in the shadow of a dusky evening, Chelsea could see the stark concern in her friend's eyes.

"I am *so* sorry. I had no idea you would drop by tonight," Rachel said in an urgent whisper, even though the cottage's door was thick enough to prevent Luka from overhearing.

"Why didn't you tell me he was coming over? I would have avoided the cottage."

"I know. I'm sorry," Rachel repeated. "I meant to. But it's been an insane day. The pupils were bouncing off the walls, and I didn't have a moment to breathe. Michael didn't even tell me Luka was coming until a couple of hours ago, so I had to race home and put the dinner on. I actually texted you but got interrupted. Here, I can show you..."

She started to produce her mobile, but Chelsea put her hand on Rachel's wrist. "I believe you. It's okay. Well, not okay, but it's over now."

Rachel peered into Chelsea's eyes. "How did it feel to see him again?"

That was a loaded question Chelsea couldn't possibly answer only seconds after seeing him, while he still stood mere feet away inside the cottage.

"I'll be fine," Chelsea said, knowing that eventually it would become the truth. Maybe it was better this way, being surprised by Luka, with no time to prepare for the encounter. "When is he leaving?"

"Michael says maybe tomorrow. Luka didn't commit one way or another."

"Naturally," Chelsea muttered, peering out toward the fading sunset that cast a beautiful glow on the countryside. Suddenly, she ached to physically remove herself from where Luka was. She couldn't stay another minute. She leaned toward Rachel for a quick kiss on the cheek. "I'll call you tomorrow. No worries. This wasn't your fault."

Chelsea took the first few steps toward her own cottage, knowing that Rachel hadn't moved a muscle from the porch as she watched her friend and fretted over her. Chelsea wondered why it was *her* job to make everyone else comfortable—why she felt the need to set them all at ease, to reassure them that she was okay and that all was well. As she moved away from prying eyes and toward home—a place of refuge where Socrates and hot tea and a warm bed awaited her, a safe place where she could shed her social mask—the frustration and anger began to seethe and curdle inside.

The last thing she wanted to be in front of Luka was polite and distant. Unaffected. The still-raw parts of her heart wanted to beat against his chest with her fists, look him straight in the eye, and ask "Why?" After sixteen years, she still had no answer to this pertinent question, only futile speculation. "Why did you leave without warning? Why did you profess your love to me, make plans with me, build a future with me, then in one fell swoop smash everything to bits and change the entire course of my life? Why did you leave me to pick up the broken parts and move on as though nothing had happened? And the biggest *why* of all—why did you look so casual tonight, so utterly calm and composed as though you were simply saying hello to any old person rather than to someone who had, at one time, meant everything to you? Why?"

By the time she reached the front porch of her cottage, Chelsea's mask had crumbled away, her social wall dissolving into sobs. She leaned against the cottage's stone wall, supporting her weight with her hand, and let the tears splash down onto the porch. Soft wails came from deep inside her throat. She couldn't stop them if she tried and didn't care if anyone heard. Not that they would—she was too far from the village center out here. Even closing her eyes tight against his vivid image couldn't stop her from seeing Luka staring back at her. She couldn't escape him this time. The ghost had come back to haunt her.

Finally, after the heaving had made her ribs sore and her head pound, Chelsea opened her eyes, took slow, purposeful breaths, and regained control. She cringed, removing her hand from the stone—she'd cut her palm against the rough surface during her breakdown. With her other hand, she wiped her cheeks and straightened her spine.

She couldn't remember the last time she'd cried over Luka. Perhaps she was due. As she scrambled to find the cottage keys inside her bag, Chelsea realized that her primal outburst had been cathartic. She felt strangely better.

When she entered the cottage and watched Socrates ambling toward her, metronome tail wagging, she reconsidered her reaction to Luka. She was glad she hadn't shown him her true feelings and had maintained her dignity. She hadn't let him see how much his presence disturbed her. She hadn't let him know how he'd broken her. For all he knew, she'd viewed him, too, as "any old person." And that gave her enough of a mild satisfaction to see her through the rest of the night.

Chapter Five

Begin doing what you want to do now. We are not living in eternity.
We have only this moment, sparkling like a star
in our hand—and melting like a snowflake. ~Francis Bacon

It didn't matter that his sister-in-law had gone to incredible lengths to cook one of his favorite meals. Luka had no desire to eat it. Half an hour into the lamb dinner, he still hadn't finished even a quarter of his portion. Since Chelsea had left the cottage and he'd sat down with Michael and Rachel, Luka had let his dinner hosts fill in the conversation gaps as he stared at his plate and picked at his food.

Earlier, when he had rounded the corner of the kitchen to see Chelsea standing there, a shot of adrenaline had burst inside his chest. His senses took in every detail as he approached her—the sleek chestnut hair, the delicate color of her dress, and those deep-set hazel eyes that showed weariness, making her gaze seem all the more intense. Being near her again was like breathing oxygen he'd been deprived of for too long.

Even being back in Chilton Crosse, knowing that coming face-to-face with his first love would be a strong possibility, Luka hadn't prepared for it. He hadn't planned out the conversation in his head or thought ahead to what he would ask her after all these years. He was tongue-tied at first, completely stilted. His knew his words came out as overly formal and distant. Inside, though, he was anything but. It was clear she hadn't expected to see him either. As he stepped closer to her, he noticed a tiny glint of emotion in her eyes those first few seconds, but past that, Chelsea seemed entirely poised and composed, even disengaged.

What did I expect—for her to fling her arms around me with a happy-to-see-you smile? Hardly.

But he'd hoped to be able to read her at least—and to find, beneath that polite shell, any evidence that she had an iota of feeling left for him. Gazing into her face as they exchanged empty chitchat, Luka knew that whatever fire Chelsea once had for him had been extinguished. And he alone had been responsible for that. It was clear that Luka was only a wisp of a memory from her past. She had moved on from him, in her life and in her heart.

"Luka?"

He blinked, realizing that Rachel was bending her neck forward, peering at him.

"Is your lamb tough?" Her eyes darted toward his full plate.

Luka shook his head and took a quick sip of wine. "No, no. It's delicious. I guess I shouldn't have eaten the sandwich Mac offered before I came. My fault. Sorry." He picked up his fork once more.

ON HIS TREK BACK TO Mac's cottage, with only the beaming moonlight above to light his way, Luka received a text, a confirmation of his flight the following day, which he'd booked that afternoon. His next assignment was in Bali, to take some travel shots for a brochure, part of a slick, expensive advertising campaign. Luka enjoyed the variety of his job—nature photography for magazines, human-interest stories for news outlets, travel photos for various companies. Over the last decade, he'd even published two coffee-table books with compilations of his photography. His work was steady and satisfying.

He stared at the screen and clicked off the text then shoved the phone back into his pocket, his mind still on Chelsea. Bali seemed far away, and not just physically.

As he made his way up the dirt road toward the outskirts of the village, Luka thought about the breakup. It had been painful enough for him to wrench himself away from her, to leave her behind and not look back. But he wondered how Chelsea had taken it. He'd never dared to ask Michael how she was doing in that respect. He didn't know if he could handle the answer.

Up until the night he left Chilton Crosse, Luka and Chelsea had been blissfully in love, spending every free moment together, talking softly on long walks, falling asleep arm in arm in Mac's barn, stealing glances in church when no one was looking. There was no hint that their relationship was doomed. They'd made specific plans to stay together, and Luka had committed without an ounce of hesitation. But everything changed that week, and Luka was left without a choice. Palms damp, head spinning, he prepared to talk to Chelsea—who was oblivious to what was coming—and searched desperately for the words that would make her understand. He'd bumbled and stumbled, trying to explain—he couldn't even remember the exact words he'd used. Something pat and meaningless along the lines of "It's not you. It's me." He hadn't given her even one substantive answer.

No wonder she hates me. Luka stuffed his hands deep into his jeans pockets and trudged up the hill, wishing he hadn't laid eyes on her again. He'd been hoping to board the next day's flight to Bali and simply whitewash this whole Chilton Crosse visit, gaining distance from it as the plane lifted higher and higher and England grew smaller and smaller. But after seeing her, it was impossible to shake the image—like closing his eyes against the sun but still seeing its powerful glow behind his lids.

When he reached Mac's property, Luka wasn't in the mood to have a conversation, but he needed to say goodbye and thank Mac for his hospitality. He tapped on the cottage door then entered the living room to find his friend relaxing in the shadows of a crackling fire, a fluffy sheepdog asleep at his feet.

Mac closed the book in his lap. "You look knackered. Sit." He gestured toward the chair opposite the fireplace.

Luka didn't want to sit. He wanted to keep moving, go to the cottage, pack his bag, stay busy. But it was his last chance to see Mac for a while, so he sat.

"You came from dinner at your brother's?"

Luka nodded, staring into the fire.

"Did it not go well?" Mac laid the book down on a table, jarring his dog from sleep. "I thought you and your brother were getting along."

"We are." Luka moved a hand through his hair and sat back in the chair. "Things are good with us. But there was an unexpected visitor tonight."

"Chelsea?"

"She came to see Rachel. She didn't know I'd be there. I guess Rachel forgot to warn her off."

"How was it?" Mac folded his fingers across his chest, and Luka found the gesture oddly comforting. He could let down his guard with Mac.

"It was bound to happen in a small village—running into her. But when I saw her standing there, time stopped. She was seventeen, I was eighteen, and the time in between melted to nothing. I felt things stronger than I have in years, like I woke up from this deep sleep. But then her eyes shifted. A wall came up. I could practically see it rising. We only said a few polite words—'Hello, sorry to hear about your dad'—and that was it. She took off." Luka stared at the fire again and muttered, "Who could blame her?"

Mac shifted forward, elbows on knees, one half of his face glowing from the fire, still prepared to listen.

Luka moved his focus from the fire and set his gaze on Mac, unblinking. "I love her. I still love her." The words felt foreign, tart on his tongue.

"Then do something, son. Stick around, play things out. Give it a chance."

Luka scoffed. "It's over. Chelsea made it obvious tonight. She probably even hates me. There's no way I have a chance with her now. I can never earn back her trust. Not after all this time, with the way I ended things. Plus, I have another job ahead. It's already booked..."

"So you're running away again." Mac nodded, raising an eyebrow.

Luka flashed a glare at Mac. "You know it's not that simple. I didn't have much of a choice back then."

"But you have a choice now. Isn't sixteen years enough time wasted? Son, what are you waiting for? What are you afraid of?"

Luka softened, knowing Mac *never* got involved in people's personal lives or offered casual advice. This had to be important enough for him to break his own rules.

"Mac, if you could've seen her tonight. There was no connection, no recognition. We were strangers. She's forgotten what we used to have."

Mac shook his head and sat back in his chair. "She hasn't forgotten. She was being brave, proving to you that she's okay. Part of her wall."

"Maybe. But what if she was telling me it's over for good? She'll never forgive me."

"How do you know? You haven't even tried." Mac reached for his book and opened it again.

Their talk was over, Luka knew. Mac wasn't the type to strong-arm anyone. He would leave his words dangling in the air for Luka to ponder. It was Luka's choice to accept or reject them. He stood and walked to Mac, gave his shoulder a friendly pat, then headed out the cottage door.

THE NEXT MORNING, LUKA still had a couple of hours to throw his stuff into his bag, organize his passport and flight information, then order a taxi for the drive to the airport. But he couldn't motivate himself. Instead, he procrastinated by clearing leaves in the cottage's overgrown garden, dusting off Mac's bench, and sweeping the living room floors.

Even these small distractions couldn't stop the words from echoing in his mind, loud and clear: *Sixteen years wasted. She hasn't forgotten. What are you afraid of?* Mac had handed him truth more filling than any lamb dinner.

Luka had admitted it to Mac, said it out loud without even hesitating. He loved Chelsea. But what Luka hadn't recognized until that moment, as he took a break and sat at the edge of his bed, was that he loved not only the teenage version of Chelsea, but he loved this current older version too—the one he admittedly barely even knew. For Luka, whatever connection they'd established as teenagers in the village had been cemented in time, still available to draw from. This wasn't nostalgia or reminiscence. This love was here and now, living and present. Fully alive.

Heart pumping, Luka stood to find his mobile, which was buried underneath a pile of shirts on his bed, and rang up the magazine editor. "James!" Luka hoped his cheery tone would make up for the big, fat mess he was about to create. "Listen, I've had a change of plans..." He explained that he couldn't make the Bali shoot—something had come up in his personal life, and he had to cancel.

James did not take this well. "We have no one else to cover it. The crew is already headed there. How can you leave me in the lurch this way?" After some prodding questions, then some swear words, then more guilt tripping, the inevitable other shoe dropped. "Our association is finished." *Click.*

"That went well," Luka muttered, making his second call, knowing it would probably go just as well as the first.

His agent, an American he'd only met twice in person, answered with his usual friendly tone. "Luka, what's up?"

"Listen, Todd, I need to talk to you." Luka sat down on the bed.

"Uh-oh. This doesn't sound good."

"Well, it's good for me. Not so much for the magazine." He explained the Bali situation, being vague again on the personal details. "I thought James needed to hear it from me directly rather than from my agent. I saved you from an angry, profanity-laced conversation, if that helps."

After a lengthy pause, Todd replied, "Look, I get it. You just lost your father—I lost mine last year, so I understand. It's devastating. But maybe after you take a week off, you can get back to it, make amends with the magazine. I can smooth the way."

"You don't understand. This is a long-term break. I want you to cancel my next three shoots for me. Tell them whatever you need to. I have to stay here in Chilton Crosse, and I'm not sure when I'm leaving."

"You're serious about this."

"I am."

Todd took another pause then said, "Well, I can tell by your voice that I can't change your mind. I'll cancel your shoots. But I can't guarantee they'll want to pick you back up. You're well respected, but if word gets out that you're undependable—"

"I understand the risk. But this is something I have to do."

"Fair enough. Have you thought about what else you'll do for work?"

Actually, no. Luka hadn't thought that far in advance. "I've got some savings. And I had this idea on the taxi ride from the airport. You've been needling me for ages to consider another book. Well, how about the Cotswolds?" He pitched the idea off the cuff, having no idea where it would go. "You know, the charm, the beauty, the villagers, the quirky customs, the festivals. Americans would eat that stuff up."

"No kiddin'. And didn't you tell me that your hometown has that famous artist? Valentine?"

"Joy Valentine."

"You could highlight a few villages or maybe even just yours. And she could be a focal point."

"Yeah, maybe." Luka didn't want to tell Todd that he was only trying to appease him with the new book idea and that he really had no intention of seeing it through. It was only a bone to offer his agent, to keep him happy.

They wrapped up the call with Luka promising to keep Todd informed about the book's progress. Then he made one final call to cancel his Bali flight. Luka clicked off and stared at the bedroom wall. *It's done.* He'd made swift decisions without any real thought of the long-term consequences, stepping onto a high wire with no safety net below. But deep inside, Luka knew this was his only real choice. Net or no net.

Chapter Six

Everyone sees what you seem to be, few know what
you really are, and those few do not dare
take a stand against the general opinion. ~Niccolò Machiavelli

Chelsea had finally learned her lesson. If she waited to check her messages until the school day's end, they would pile up and overwhelm her. So between classes, she glanced at her mobile's screen, hoping the messages might be more manageable in small doses, and saw three texts—one from Noelle, one from her mum, and one from Rachel.

She tapped Rachel's first: *Luka is staying in CC. Michael just told me. "Extended visit" is all the detail he gave. Sorry.*

Chelsea read it again to be sure, heart dipping at the possibility of running into him at any moment, anywhere.

The timing seemed ironic. After breaking down outside her cottage two nights before, Chelsea had eaten some dinner and gone upstairs for the best sleep she'd had in ages. The next day, she'd awakened refreshed, relaxed, and ready to face the day with a vibrant spring in her step. She'd had some sort of breakthrough regarding Luka. She had pushed through the storm of facing him and had come out the other side even stronger. But—that was when she'd assumed he would soon be hopping a plane for a far-away-from-Chilton-Crosse destination.

"*Why* is he staying?" she asked her phone, wishing it could answer her.

JOURNAL, CHECK. TABLET, check. Tote full of handouts, check. Mobile and bag—check, check.

Chelsea finished her mental list before clicking the door shut to Nightingale Cottage and making her way to her first festival meeting. Being overprepared helped to ward off the nerves flittering in her stomach at the thought of being the committee chair. She'd never been the chair of anything before. It had all seemed doable on paper for the past few weeks. But the idea of facing a small crowd of villagers, even friendly ones whose only mission was to help her, filled her with a bit of dread. The responsibility was thick and weighty on her shoulders—especially knowing Mrs. Pickering would be there, judging her every word and attempting to meddle in all the decision-making.

As she neared the church hall, Chelsea noticed a cluster of tourists milling about the edge of the church, pointing and aiming their mobiles for a photo. The centuries-old structure was always an attention grabber. When the group cleared off, someone else remained. She hadn't seen him at first, blocked by the tourists. Chelsea squinted for a clearer view of the man, who was crouched down, his camera pointed upward toward a leafy oak tree.

Luka.

Rachel's text had succinctly warned her that this would happen. But the sight of him thirty feet away, casually snapping photos in the village, was still jarring. Accepting the fresh September air into her lungs with renewed purpose, Chelsea set her shoulders back and continued on her one and only mission: walking briskly to the church hall with her eyes on the entrance, hoping to avoid Luka's attention.

But she heard him calling her name. "Chelsea!"

She might be able to get away with gripping the door handle and walking through, pretending she hadn't heard. But there was no point in avoiding the inevitable. *Extended visit*, Rachel's text had said. This sort of encounter might not be a rarity, so Chelsea might as well face it head-on.

She swiveled around to see Luka jogging up the path toward her, gripping his fancy camera. It was strange to see a "real" camera these days. They'd almost been rendered extinct, with everyone using their mobiles for taking photos.

"Hey." He stopped in front of her with a half smile, a loose lock of hair dangling at his neck. She remembered preferring his hair that way, long and wavy, whenever he would grow it out during school holidays. It always reminded her of some roguish character in a Brontë novel.

"Hi." She forced a polite smile.

"Stellar day. Nice weather. Thought I'd capture a few shots."

"Yeah, the blue sky is a novelty these days..." At the risk of being put under his spell, she only let herself look at him for a few seconds at a time. Then her eyes wandered away, scanning the sky.

"I'm staying for a bit. In the village."

"Rachel mentioned it." She tried to include a shrug in her voice. "Michael will be glad." She looked down at her bag, pretending to search for something inside it.

"Yeah, we've needed to catch up. And it's great to see Mac again."

"He's the best."

"He said he's been renovating your mum's cottage. Well, your cottage now."

"Yeah, he finished up over the weekend. Did a beautiful job."

"And I've heard about this Renaissance festival coming up. You're on the committee?"

Tired of fake searching, she closed her bag and looked at him squarely, wondering what else Luka knew about her life. *Has he been conducting research, asking people questions, taking notes?*

"In charge, actually. Mrs. Pickering sort of talked me into it..."

Luka gave a husky chuckle. "She's got a knack for that." He looked down toward his camera with a knowing nod.

Chelsea let her eyes linger on his perfect lips, the shadow of a dark beard. He returned his gaze to her, and she cleared her throat. "Tonight's our first meeting, actually." She pointed behind her toward the hall. "I'd better get inside."

"If you need a photographer—you know, some photos during the festival... I should be available."

This information stunned Chelsea. The festival was still weeks away. *Is he planning to stay* that *long?* She remembered, as a teenager, how much he despised any type of festival or community activity in the village. He shunned them, even mocked them privately. And here he was, asking to be at the center of it all, taking photos.

"Oh. Well, we couldn't pay you for it." Chelsea prayed this might deter him.

"I wouldn't ask for anything. Strictly voluntary."

Before she could form an answer, she saw someone approaching from behind Luka—Mrs. Pickering on her way to the meeting, early. Chelsea's heart sank at the thought of having to endure her for an extra hour. She'd hoped to be alone in the hall before the meeting to spread out her notes and sign-up sheets, perhaps even to rehearse her opening speech to the newly formed committee.

Mrs. Pickering noticed Chelsea first and nodded as she stopped to join them. Then her eyes rested on Luka. She couldn't hide her surprise and disdain. "It's you." The wrinkles on her brow gathered into a V-shaped point above her eyes. "I'd heard you were back in the village."

Luka flashed a warm smile in her direction. "I am. How are you, Mrs. Pickering?"

Clearly not expecting polite chatter, Mrs. Pickering narrowed her eyes. "I'm perfectly fine. How long will you be in the village?"

Luka paused, searching the air for his answer, then whispered, "Indefinitely."

Chelsea suppressed a giggle while watching Mrs. Pickering blink hard at the answer.

"Hmph," Mrs. Pickering replied then turned on her heel toward the church hall.

Luka took a broad step toward the door, brushing Chelsea's sleeve in the process, and opened it wide before Mrs. Pickering could reach the handle. She paused, frowned again, then passed reluctantly through.

Luka let the door close on its own then stepped back to his earlier spot opposite Chelsea. "Well, that wasn't *quite* as brutal as I expected. At least she didn't berate me in front of a whole group of parishioners, like that one time."

Chelsea remembered. She'd been standing with her father outside the church, talking to the elder vicar, when Mrs. Pickering's agitated voice rose high above all the others. Chelsea, along with everyone else in the vicinity, paused to watch Mrs. Pickering wagging a finger in Luka's direction as he bowed his head, hands in pockets, enduring her verbal abuse—something about being a bad influence, not knowing his "place." When she'd finished her rant, she turned and left Luka standing there, all eyes still on him. After a beat, he'd disappeared quietly in the other direction, leaving Chelsea aching to follow him.

This unexpected memory had brought a shadow with it. The strangeness of talking to adult Luka while having a flashback of teenage Luka was too surreal—they couldn't occupy the same space.

Chelsea blinked away the memory. "I'd better go."

Luka reached for the handle to let her through. "Think about my offer. Photographing the festival."

"I will," she promised, entering the hall. She heard the door close behind her.

Mrs. Pickering was already near the table's head, unwrapping her scarf then digging through her own notes. Chelsea walked to the table and set down her bags and devices.

"Can you believe that man?" Mrs. Pickering still hadn't lost her scowl. "The nerve of him, coming back to this village."

"His father just died," Chelsea reminded her, keeping a calm tone. "He was here for the funeral."

"Well, he missed it, didn't he?" she spat out. "So disrespectful."

Something inside Chelsea burned. It all came flooding back—the way Mrs. Pickering and others in the village, even her own father, had judged Luka from the start all those years ago. He never even had a chance to change their minds, to challenge their prejudices. Whatever had happened between Chelsea and Luka at the end, whatever ill feelings or wounds she still silently bore, he didn't deserve such treatment. Not then, not ever.

Chelsea abandoned her tote bag and stared hard at Mrs. Pickering. "I don't think it's disrespectful. Luka tried his best to make the funeral on time. Flew all the way from South America, in fact." She wanted to add that Luka had made great efforts to see his father in the care home, quietly, for years—never making a spectacle of it, never seeking glory or gratitude. But that was private information that even she wasn't supposed to know. Besides, it would be lost on Mrs. Pickering anyway.

"Well." Mrs. Pickering scoffed. "It's time for him to leave. His kind doesn't belong here, never did."

"His 'kind'?" An angry flush rose to her cheeks. All her life, Chelsea and others in the village had kept quiet, not stirred trouble, not pushed back whenever Mrs. Pickering gossiped or judged or name called. But Chelsea wasn't certain she could stay quiet this time. "What exactly do you mean?"

"You know. Troublemakers. Rabble-rousers, whatever you want to call them. Poor Vicar McKane. To have such a heathen for a son. Remember the graffiti incident? The church headstones?"

Of course Chelsea remembered. Everyone did. The village had had a rash of vandalism the year after Luka and his family arrived, and Chelsea's father had been in charge of the investigation. And even though no suspects were arrested, no charges were ever brought forward, the suspicions still lay heavily upon Luka's shoulders, and Mrs. Pickering was likely the reason.

Suddenly, oddly, Chelsea's frustration began to dissipate into pity as she watched Mrs. Pickering—hunched, shuffling through papers, utterly unaware that her judgmental words had the power to hurt people, change their lives, and permanently alter the way others saw them. This woman would never change, and she seemed to be getting more bitter year by year. She was set in her ways, determined to believe fallacies and think the worst of people. Chelsea pitied her for living in a world where everyone was impossibly flawed or, even worse, irredeemable. How tragic to see people through only one warped and biased lens instead of seeing them for all that they were and all they could be. *Who's the real heathen?*

In the end, nothing Chelsea could possibly say would sway this woman's opinions, so she only said, "Mrs. Pickering, not everything is as it seems. People aren't always what they appear to be on the outside."

Mrs. Pickering grumbled her reply, still shuffling papers. Chelsea heard the door open, grateful for a distraction as Mary Cartwright walked through. This was not the way Chelsea had wanted the meeting to begin—a shaky impromptu encounter with her ex, followed by a showdown with the village gossip. She only hoped the rest of the evening would be less eventful.

HALFWAY THROUGH THE meeting, with ideas being tossed around, added to, and sorted through, Chelsea felt a specific adrenaline rush, the same type that occasionally hit her when a school lesson was going fluidly—pupils being engaged and asking questions, Chelsea having all the right answers, everyone in sync. Joe, the pub owner, had brought sandwiches for the committee, and Julia had brought along some freshly baked biscuits. All sixteen members attended, each brimming with excitement over the possibility of making the festival the best yet.

All Chelsea had to do was facilitate, listen, jot down ideas and notes in her peacock journal, and make occasional suggestions. Even the financial aspects had been completely accounted for. The village kept an ongoing yearly fund for community events—fetes, festivals, parades—and whatever funds were lacking, Duncan Newbury, the wealthiest man in town, always took care of.

Early on in the meeting, someone had overridden an idea of Mrs. Pickering's, so she'd decided to slouch in her seat and mope about it for the rest of the time, which kept her silent, fortunately. But toward the end, Chelsea was aware of her own hypocrisy. She was guilty of viewing Mrs. Pickering through only one warped lens, seeing her as nothing but uncooperative, unbending, and sour. She was the one who'd first presented Chelsea with the idea of a village festival and made her the committee chair. Mrs. Pickering *did* add value to the village and was often the brains behind their celebrations and gatherings. As insistent and difficult as the woman could be to work with, Chelsea had to admit that she always got the job done. Perhaps she'd had a bad day at her market or was having health issues Chelsea was unaware of.

People aren't always what they appear to be. Chelsea needed to heed her own adage, or else it would mean nothing.

Before ending the meeting, Chelsea gathered the group's attention. "I wanted to thank Mrs. Pickering for organizing this committee and for having the initial vision and foresight that I didn't have." She noticed that Mrs. Pickering's expression had lightened. "It's very much appreciated."

Someone at the table applauded hesitantly, causing others to follow. Mrs. Pickering accepted the accolades as Chelsea assumed she would—with an odd mix of humility and pride, a bowed head, and a growing smile. She was eating this up, and Chelsea was fine with that. Maybe Luka's earlier example—taking the high road, opening the door for Mrs. Pickering—had rubbed off on her.

Just because the meeting was over didn't mean the brainstorming ideas had ceased. In fact, Chelsea was held up for almost an hour, fielding questions and ideas from various villagers. She jotted swiftly in her journal, hoping she could translate her messy handwriting later on, as people came to her one by one. Holly mentioned her younger sister, Rosalee, who had become a rather famous actress in the past couple of years, recently starring in a BBC remake of *Great Expectations*.

"I was thinking she could play some sort of role in the festival. But I don't want to interfere with your plans or draw too much attention to Rosalee," Holly insisted. "I know that your pupils are putting on a production of *Romeo and Juliet*. She wouldn't want to overshadow it."

"Including Rosalee is a brilliant idea. In fact, we'll have various people reciting monologues from Shakespeare and Marlowe plays while the festival is going on. Maybe your sister would be interested in something like that?"

"I'll ask her. I think she's been looking for an excuse to come home to the village. Her recent texts tell me she's homesick."

Tristan, Mrs. Pickering's nephew—and Julia Bentley's new boyfriend—was the last to approach Chelsea.

"I saw your latest mockup of the festival webpage," Chelsea told him. "The colors and photos and fonts are perfect. It looks really professional."

"Thanks. Those were only stock photos, but they fit well enough for the moment. By the way, have you seen Noelle's painting?"

"Yes, but not the end result."

"It's finished." Tristan clicked his phone and swiped photos until he found the right one. Then he swiveled the screen to show Chelsea. "I took this yesterday."

She leaned in and noticed some detail in Noelle's painting that she hadn't seen in the previous version. "It's beautiful. Can we add it to the website?"

Tristan lowered his mobile. "Well, that's the problem. I fancy myself a pretty okay photographer... with a phone. But that oil painting deserves something better. I was thinking we could get it photographed—high quality, high resolution—so that it would look even better on the site. Do you know a professional photographer around here?" Tristan had only been in the village a few months and was still getting to know the villagers.

It would be easy for Chelsea to say she didn't know of anyone. But that wouldn't be the truth. Luka had offered, and she needed to try to remove her own emotions from this equation. This was all for the good of the village.

So she caved. "Actually, I do. Luka McKane."

"The vicar's brother?"

"That's the one. He's a professional, and he might be willing to help out."

"Cool. Do you have his number?"

"I'm afraid I don't."

"Could you pass along my contact info to him, then? I want to jump on this."

"Um, sure. I can try."

She watched Tristan walk away, wondering what she'd just committed herself to and pondering how she could pull this off with the least amount of contact. Enduring the occasional spur-of-the-moment run-in with Luka was one thing, but tracking him down and courting trouble on purpose was entirely another.

IT WAS A RARE LUXURY for Chelsea to have an actual homemade meal in her own cottage in the middle of a school day and a friend over to share it with her. The pupils were having a special gathering in the assembly hall after their lunch, which gave the teachers an extended free period. So Chelsea had texted Rachel that morning: *Shepherd's pie at my cottage?*

Rachel had sent a swift *Yes!*

Chelsea had barely had enough time to race home, feed Socrates, and heat up the pie she'd created for the previous night's meal before she heard a knock at the front door followed by Socrates's series of yips. She raised the bubbling concoction carefully out of the Aga.

"Coming!" she called, moving the heavy dish to the top of the stove with a small clunk.

At the front door, Rachel held out a pan of a sugary-smelling concoction.

"What's this?" Chelsea asked, letting her inside.

"You know I can never go to someone's home empty-handed. It's a habit."

"Bread pudding?"

"Your favorite. I made it this morning before school. It's Michael's favorite, too, and he needed a pick-me-up."

"How's he doing?"

"I think it's really hitting him now, about his dad. He's had time to process the funeral. He still won't talk about it, and I can see this vacant expression on his face sometimes when he thinks I'm not looking. But then he presses on, keeps busy with his work."

"Easier that way?"

"I think so."

Chelsea led her back to the kitchen, where a bank of windows surrounded a circular kitchen table, the one where Chelsea ate most of her meals.

"Here, I'll take it." She unburdened Rachel of her scrumptious bread pudding and set it aside on the counter.

As Chelsea prepped the plates with steaming shepherd's pie and Rachel poured the drinks, they chatted about how school was progressing. Rachel had a particularly trying pupil in her class, a little boy who didn't realize that talking out of turn, especially while the teacher was speaking, was rude and inconsiderate. Chelsea's main problem was being buried alive under paperwork—stacks of grading that never seemed to shrink, no matter how much she accomplished.

"It's the well that won't run dry," she quipped. "Although I want it to." They settled at the table, forks in hand, with Socrates snoozing nearby. "Let's tuck in!"

And they did, silver clinking against plates, bites savored. "You've outdone yourself," Rachel told her after a couple of tastes.

"Oh, you always say that. You know this is the only thing in the world I can cook. But thanks anyway. It's really a matter of assembly."

Rachel scooped up another bite. "The meeting last night went well. High attendance with strong participation."

"I couldn't believe it! I guess I had low expectations. But it's really inspired me, the enthusiasm everyone has for the festival. Well, except one person amongst them."

"A certain Pickering?"

"We actually had an encounter before the meeting began. And Luka was involved."

Rachel nearly choked on the sip she'd taken. "Luka? You didn't mention seeing him last night."

"I didn't have a chance. I haven't really seen you until now."

"Well, here I am. Begging for details."

"I was walking up to the church hall yesterday, and there he was, taking photos of a tree or the church or a headstone—who knows. I thought I could manage to slip by him unnoticed, but he approached me for a chat." When she saw Rachel's eyebrows rise at this, she added, "Not that kind of chat. Nothing significant. You know, polite, shallow conversation that strangers make. But we did talk about the festival. He said something sort of telling—that he wanted to take photos during it. Rach, that's weeks away. Sounds like he won't leave anytime soon."

Rachel shook her head and waved a hand. "Michael hasn't said anything more to me, I promise. This is the first I'm hearing of it. So you mentioned Mrs. Pickering too—an 'encounter.' Were there any casualties?"

Chelsea snickered. "Thankfully, no. But the tension was thick. Mrs. Pickering had wandered up and scowled when she recognized Luka. She said, 'It's *you*' with this tangible hatred in her eyes. I felt kind of sorry for Luka—I expected him to be sarcastic or unkind, but he was the opposite. The perfect gentleman, in fact. Even opened the door for her."

"Nice one."

Chelsea paused and broadened her thoughts. "You know, this village is hard to label. I mean, on one hand, we have Mary Cartwright or Mac or you—people who would drop anything and everything to come to someone's aid. We even have a mystery Claus, a secret do-gooder who spends hundreds of pounds on one villager to meet their needs each Christmas."

"Like your mum."

"Exactly." The month after her father had died, Chelsea's mum had been the recipient of a brand-new washing machine, though Chelsea wasn't sure how anyone knew the old one was broken. Her mum had also received a six-month cleaning service to take that particular chore off her shoulders.

"And then we have Mrs. Pickering," Rachel added. "I suppose *every* village has its own Pickering."

"Right. Well, after her rudeness, Luka left, and I went into the hall. But that's when Mrs. Pickering really let loose. She said all these nasty things about Luka, calling him a rabble-rouser and a heathen." Chelsea set down her fork. "And something in me got stirred up. He wasn't in the room to defend himself, and there she was, saying the vilest things. She even brought up the graffiti incident."

"That was years and years ago! And they never proved he did it."

"Exactly. Rumors only."

"So how did you handle her?"

"Well, I wanted to tell her off, accuse her of being wicked and judgmental. But I kept cool and told her that Luka was here for his father's funeral and that he took great lengths to come. And then I told her that people aren't always who we think they are."

"Sounds like you put her in her place... but gently." Rachel squinted across the table at Chelsea and gestured with her fork. "Wait a minute. You *defended* Luka to Mrs. Pickering. Without hesitation. Does this mean... are you softening toward him?"

The same question had been nagging at Chelsea in the hours since their encounter. She wondered why it had been so easy to defend him—and whether she would have done the same for anyone else.

"I don't think so," she said truthfully. "I still bristle when I see him. It's this weird physiological reaction, almost the start of a panic attack. That doesn't sound like softening. It sounds like... fear. Which tells me that keeping up this wall is my only defense against him.

Honestly, I'm hoping he changes his mind soon and leaves the village. It'll save me the trouble of searching my feelings. I can get back to my life again, move forward."

"Meaning...?" Rachel prompted.

"Everything was going well for me. The last year or so, I've felt centered and mature, taking on this new career, finally having a cottage of my own—and friends, a community, a church. And just when I feel balanced for the first time in years..."

"Here comes Luka to muck it all up again."

"Precisely."

"I'm sorry, Chels. I don't know what to make of it myself. It's a mystery, why he's staying around. I guess he's between jobs and wants to spend time with Michael. That's the easy answer. And quite honestly, Michael's glad to have Luka around for a bit. It still amazes me, how Luka never resented Michael for being the favorite child. Michael really looks up to him—always has."

Chelsea thought ahead to the next couple of weeks. "I wonder how the rest of the villagers will treat him while he's around."

"Well, one thing's for sure. There will be a *lot* of Poldark comparisons." Rachel smirked.

Chelsea faked a gasp. "You are so cheeky!"

"What? I'm only stating the obvious. Seriously, though. That hair! I'm completely jealous of it."

"Me too!" Chelsea snickered. "But he can totally get away with it."

"Totally."

As the girls giggled into their napkins, Chelsea felt sixteen all over again.

CHELSEA HAD ASSUMED that sitting through several auditions for a Shakespeare play would be thrilling and energizing. But after two solid hours of audition after audition—some marvelous and some not so marvelous, with most of the pupils using the same three monologues—Chelsea was unable to suppress a yawn or stop her thoughts from drifting away.

At least she'd had some help with the process. Four other teachers, including the school's drama teacher, had volunteered to be on the panel to help choose the roles. They'd scheduled the auditions a couple of hours after school, so at least Chelsea had enough time to pop home, change clothes, and feed Socrates before riding her bicycle up the hill. The new assembly hall—built as part of the renovations—was the perfect place for the school's concerts, plays, and awards ceremonies as well as these auditions. It held three hundred seats, all crimson velvet covered, and the space was equipped with the latest digital technology for lighting and sound.

Finally, the last pupil took the stage, but this one snatched Chelsea's full attention. Sienna crossed to the center and took a noticeable breath then fidgeted with her long hair. She was nervous.

"Whenever you're ready," said Mr. Harper, sitting near Chelsea.

Sienna clasped her hands at her waist then cleared her throat. Before she began, Chelsea noticed some movement nearer the stage—most of the pupils and parents had exited the building, but one person remained. A man leaned forward, elbows on knees, his gaze on Sienna. Likely her father, there for support.

Sienna's monologue was an unexpected one. Every other Juliet hopeful had chosen lines from the famous balcony scene. But Sienna had chosen something from a later, lesser-appreciated scene in which Juliet impatiently awaited Romeo's response from her nurse:

Now is the sun upon the highmost hill
Of this day's journey, and from nine till twelve
Is three long hours, yet she is not come.
Had she affections and warm youthful blood,
She would be as swift in motion as a ball;

My words would bandy her to my sweet love,
And his to me...

It was one of Chelsea's favorite moments in the play, even though it was a quiet one, often overlooked. Juliet's panicked, frustrated tone revealed the passion and impatience of youthful love, as though Juliet suspected her time with Romeo would be all too brief, foreshadowing the play's tragic end. And as Sienna uttered the words—timid at first, but growing in courage—Chelsea realized her student was likely thinking of her own love, Matthew, as she impatiently waited and pondered, "Does he love me too? Will he ever be mine?"

By the time Sienna had finished the piece, the selection panel had broken into applause—something they'd refrained from doing with all the other auditions so as not to give their opinions away. The man down front stood and put his fingers to his lips to whistle, which made Sienna's surprised grin widen even more.

The panel thanked her for the audition then dispersed, eager to get home. They would be making their final decisions by Monday morning. Chelsea stood, waiting to congratulate Sienna on a strong audition.

"Miss Barrett! How did I do?" Sienna, along with the man, came to a pause in the aisle.

"You were perfect. The monologue was natural and organic. I have a good feeling about this." Chelsea couldn't tell her she'd gotten the part, but based on the panelists' reactions, she had no doubt about it.

The man stood tall and lanky, with ginger hair and fair skin, and placed his hands on the girl's shoulders. "Thank you, Miss Barrett, for being such a wonderful teacher to my daughter. She speaks of you highly. You've been inspiring."

"Oh, well, that's lovely to say. She's been inspiring to me as well."

The man chuckled. "Forgive me, I've forgotten to give you my name. It's Dan."

"Lovely to meet you. And please, call me Chelsea."

"So, I'll know the results on Monday?" Sienna asked, her eyes filled with hope.

"Monday," Chelsea confirmed.

"Fingers crossed." Sienna made the sign with fingers on both hands.

Dan asked Chelsea, "Will you... I mean, do you want to walk out with us? Back to the village?" He pointed toward the exit.

"Oh, thanks. But I brought my bicycle."

As they parted, and as Chelsea slipped on her coat and gathered up her bag, she tried to recall Sienna's home situation. Her parents had been divorced the previous year, but Chelsea hadn't met either one until that night.

The ride home was refreshing but chilly, and by the time she arrived at her cottage, Chelsea was ready to fill her system with a cup of hot tea then fall into bed. It had been a particularly grueling couple of days, and she eagerly looked ahead to the weekend. Maybe, just maybe she could get some real rest for a change.

Chapter Seven

It is not in the stars to hold our destiny,
but in ourselves. ~Shakespeare

Luka lifted the camera to his eye and adjusted the exposure until he was satisfied, then clicked to capture the length of Chilton Crosse's high street before the last traces of dusk faded away. He lowered the camera to gaze at the scene through naked eyes: the empty cobblestone slick with earlier rain, the dark shops closed up moments before, the streetlamps issuing a comforting glow.

As a teenager, he hadn't fully appreciated the beauty of this village or noticed its charm. He only viewed it as an oppressive, boring place he couldn't wait to escape. But returning as a man who had seen much of the world—the poverty in Zimbabwe, the civil war in Somalia, the jam-packed streets of New Delhi, the rainforests of Africa—he saw the place differently. To him, Chilton Crosse was straight out of a fairytale.

Luka snapped the cap onto the lens, tucked the camera into his bag, then walked the short distance to the pub. It had been Michael's idea to share a pint. The brothers had been trying all week to meet up ever since the lamb dinner at the vicarage, and finally, Michael had sent an urgent text that afternoon: *7pm pub. Be there.*

Luka clasped the edges of his leather coat, trying to shut out the autumn chill as he watched a laughing couple exit the pub. His father used to call his church "the beating heart of the village," but Luka had always believed otherwise, and his travels had only confirmed it. The local pub was always the heart and soul of any small town or village. Friendships were formed and maintained, satisfying meals were devoured, and the world's problems were often solved over a few pints.

As a teenager, Luka hadn't spent much time in the pub. Still, he knew this structure well—its honey-colored limestone exterior, its low-beamed ceilings and dark mahogany bar inside—because he would accompany Mac on occasional visits to repair a lager dispenser or see to a plumbing issue in one of the upstairs bedrooms.

Luka reached the pub's entrance and opened the door to a blast of warm air. A blazing fire popped softly in the opposite corner, where a pair of old men played chess. Scanning the room, he didn't see Michael anywhere. The pub was barely half-full, likely because this was a weekday evening. Luka approached the bar, a U-shaped behemoth that took up the center of the room.

A heavyset man wiped down the bar's glossy surface while humming a tune. Luka recognized the man as Joe Jr., whose father had run the pub when Luka was a teenager.

Joe looked up when he saw Luka then tilted his head. "I know you…"

Luka set down his camera bag on a barstool. "Luka McKane."

He waited for the dots to be connected as Joe's smile grew wider. "Right! It's been years. How are things?"

"Good. Hectic."

"You're a photographer," Joe noted, resuming his bar-wiping duties. "Traveling the world. Lucky sod." He paused again as another lightbulb clicked on. "Your father's funeral was a few days back. I was sorry to hear it. A good man, that one."

"Yes, thanks. He was." Luka drummed his fingertips lightly on the wood. It still hadn't quite hit him—the weight of grief, the sting of certain regrets that would follow him for a lifetime. Talking about him in casual conversation seemed surreal. His father, gone for good.

"So..." Luka felt the sharp urge for a change of topic. "You've taken over the pub, then?"

"Years ago." Though Joe's eyes and smile were completely familiar, his stocky frame appeared nothing like the scrawny twentysomething Luka recalled. "And got married a while back—to Lizzie Gallagher. In fact, she's due to have our twins in these next few weeks."

"Twins! Congratulations, mate."

"Thanks. So, what can I get you?"

"A lager."

"Comin' up." Joe flung his towel over his burly shoulder and reached for a glass just as the pub's front door opened.

Michael, whose eternally boyish features had him looking deceptively younger than his age, brightened when he saw Luka. He shut the door then came to stand beside his brother.

"Vicar, haven't seen you for a bit." Joe deftly placed a brimming pint in front of Luka without spilling a single drop. "Things well with you?"

Michael seemed to conjure up a cheerful response. "Very well. How about yourself? How's Lizzie?"

"Miserable. Keen to deliver. But she's healthy, which is all we can ask. So, what'll you have tonight?"

"Same." Michael nodded toward the pint as Luka found his wallet.

"But tonight was my idea," Michael protested.

"You can pay next time." Luka placed the notes on the bar then sipped from his lager to prevent a spill. He clutched his camera bag and maneuvered toward an empty corner table beneath a diamond-paned window. Michael joined him with his own lager then wriggled out of his beige coat, revealing his usual vicar's collar.

"Hectic day?" Luka noticed the deep circles under Michael's eyes.

"Every day seems a hectic day." He set his mobile beside his glass. "I don't even have the luxury of turning this thing off. Someone might need me."

Luka removed his own coat with an understanding nod. Michael's job was one of total service, as Luka knew very well, having observed his father for all those years, growing up. Michael and Luka had been obliged to share their father with the entire village. The parishioners' needs sometimes felt as time sensitive and pressing as those of the vicar's two sons. Michael's job didn't have him only preaching on a Sunday or conducting some church meetings. Luka knew, without having to ask or be told, that Michael also attended to multiple needs throughout the village, day or night—visiting ailing parishioners, conducting marital counseling, spearheading committees, pacifying disputes and disagreements, performing weddings and funerals, and the list went on.

Luka weighed his own profession against his brother's and came up short. *What do I contribute to people—to the world—with only my camera?* He hid safely behind its lens, taking photos of hummingbirds or castles or Porsches for advertisements and calendars. Sure, sometimes he would fly to a war-torn or poverty-stricken country, assigned to document lives and shed light on people's plight for a serious journalistic article in a well-respected publication. But he was never sure if his efforts did any good or whether anything had changed as a result of them.

"Sorry. Didn't mean to start off having a moan." Michael shrugged. "Things are good. I can't complain. Good health, gorgeous wife, lovely life." He raised his lager. "Cheers."

"I'll drink to that."

They clinked glasses then took careful sips of the brimming nectar. Luka was content to be in a cozy pub, sharing a pint with his brother. The past few years, the only venue he'd seen Michael in was a dreary, sterile care home with colorless walls, where they'd spent time exchanging sad, knowing glances about their father's withering condition as they watched him sleep—or worse, attempting to calm him down when he had one of his spells of not recognizing his surroundings or even his own sons. Since the elder vicar was always the sole focus of their visits, the brothers rarely had time for relaxed chats or updates on each other's lives beyond a few whispers in the hall before they parted ways. A pint in a pub was a refreshing change.

"So, catch me up," Michael said with a wave of a hand. "You've had a good week in the village, staying with Mac? What else have you been up to?"

Luka shifted in the chair. "Not much. Helping Mac with the odd job or two, taking some photos around the village, contemplating my next move."

"If I'm honest, I expected you to leave after the funeral. I know how busy your life is."

"It's as busy as I want it to be. I've cancelled the next couple of jobs. It's time for a break."

"And time for something else?" Michael raised an eyebrow.

"What else?"

"Admit it. You're not staying for Mac or for me and certainly not for the people in this village. You're staying for Chelsea. When you heard she was in Chilton Crosse, you couldn't resist."

Luka could have fudged the truth and pretended to be in the village because of the new book. But why lie? He had nothing to be ashamed of.

"I hadn't planned on staying at first. I'd even booked a flight out for my next project. But yes. Seeing Chelsea again..." Luka shook his head as he pinched the corner of the paper napkin under his glass.

"It was written all over your face when Chelsea came to the vicarage. You could have cut the air with a butter knife. There's still something between you."

Luka wasn't sure if Michael was only seeing what he wanted to see or whether his assessment of that surprise meeting was accurate. Michael had always been a Chelsea advocate. Ages before, in another lifetime, he'd told Luka how perfect she was for him. He'd always hoped they would end up together.

"Well, I'm not sure she sees it that way," Luka said. "She's been distant whenever we meet."

"You've seen her again?"

"I ran into her near the church hall last night. We had a quick chat, nothing significant."

It had been a stroke of good luck, with Luka snapping photos of the church and seeing Chelsea round the corner toward the church hall. He swallowed his insecurities and spoke to her, and for a moment, he thought he sensed her relaxing into the conversation. He even made her smile, revealing those familiar dimples dotting her cheeks. A hopeful sign. And as she'd disappeared behind the door to leave, Luka wanted more. Their chat had been *too* quick. He wanted to follow her inside, create an excuse to speak with her, and be in her presence a little longer. But in the end, he'd respected her boundaries and walked the other way.

"Progress," Michael noted, reaching for his glass.

"Not sure about that. The thing is..." Luka folded his hands on top of the table and stared across at his brother. "I don't want to scare her off. Chelsea didn't expect me to stay. She was probably hoping I'd leave by now. She's not ready for this, ready for me. I can tell."

Trying to ease back into Chelsea's life would take some delicacy. Their meetings needed to happen organically somehow. He didn't want to stalk her or pester her. He didn't want to pop up too often, unannounced, in places he knew she might be. Mostly, he didn't want to force his way in. He'd already forced his way *out* of her life years before.

"Well, here's what I think, for what it's worth." Michael wiped his mouth with the back of his hand and peered back at Luka. "Maybe if you're in her orbit enough and she gets used to seeing you around the village, the shock of your presence will wear off. Right now, she keeps seeing the teenage you. That's all she's ever known. But maybe she needs to get acquainted with the adult you."

Michael had put into words what Luka, until that moment, hadn't quite been able to. Every time Luka was around her recently, he had trouble aligning the Chelsea he was seeing with the Chelsea he'd known before. And if Luka was struggling with it, he could only imagine how hard this was for her. Michael was right. Chelsea needed to be reacquainted with him—*this* Luka, with all his life experiences, maturity, and depth—and to start viewing him as the man he was now, not the immature eighteen-year-old who'd abandoned her so abruptly.

"Thanks, brother. What do I owe you for the counseling session?"

"Nothing. It comes with the job." Michael grinned.

They spent the next hour drinking their pints and shifting the conversation to memories of their father, which included the good times, because, Luka had to admit, there *were* good times. When Luka was a little boy, the vicar's high expectations of him hadn't seemed out of reach. Those early days had been filled with distinct moments of laughter, family bonding, and meals shared with their mother. Even as he viewed his father through the filter of adulthood, Luka respected him for the burdens he'd silently carried after his wife died, privately grieving while trying to raise two young boys on his own and still fulfilling all his vicar duties. It couldn't have been easy.

As expected, Michael's mobile began to vibrate on the table while he was in midsentence, recounting a trip the family had made one summer to Scotland. "Sorry," he muttered, checking the screen. He tapped to see the full message. "Duty calls." He typed out a quick response then put on his coat. "It's Mrs. Bates. Her health has taken a turn for the worse, and I promised I'd be available. Could be a long night."

"I'm glad you had time for a pint at least." Luka slipped on his coat, too, grabbed his camera bag, then followed Michael.

At the bar, they shook hands and held steady eye contact—a warm, unspoken exchange between brothers glad to be reunited—before Michael turned to leave. With time on his hands, Luka was contemplating a solo darts game when he heard someone else enter the pub.

"Your order is ready in the back," Joe told the man over Luka's shoulder. "I need to fetch it."

"No hurry." The man came to lean against the bar.

"Have you met Luka?" Joe nodded in his direction. "Our vicar's brother."

"Nice meeting you. I'm Tristan." His eyes wandered down toward Luka's camera bag, then he wagged his index finger. "I know who you are..."

Luka cringed inside, waiting to hear what the villagers had told him about the elder vicar's wayward son.

"Chelsea mentioned you after the festival meeting. You're a photographer, right?"

Luka brightened at the unexpected mention of her name. "I am."

"I run the festival's website, and I need a high-quality photo of a canvas. It's this painting that Noelle has done of the village's high street. I asked Chelsea who could take the photo, and she told me your name. I don't know if you'd even be willing. We might be able to pay you—"

"No need. I'd do it free of charge."

"Excellent!" Tristan pulled his mobile from his pocket and began tapping out a text. "I'll let Noelle know you can do it. What day is good for you?"

"Tomorrow's fine."

"Tomorrow," Tristan muttered, still tapping. He sent the text then looked up. "The painting is at the gallery across the way. That's where Noelle will be." His mobile pinged, and Tristan gazed down again. "She says tomorrow is great. Anytime."

"So Noelle runs the gallery now?" He vaguely recalled her name from Mac, who'd mentioned the change of ownership a few years before.

"Yeah, she inherited it. She's Joy Valentine's niece from the States. And an artist too. Taught by her aunt."

Luka was glad to hear the gallery was still thriving and that Joy's legacy lived on. The gallery had been his sanctuary during his teen years in Chilton Crosse. The art hanging on the walls, the cool, dark interior... and Joy. She was a hard one to read, a woman of few words, but he and Joy had connected on an artistic level when he'd first wandered into the gallery, yearning for an escape from his father. Joy seemed to know why he was there and had let him explore and peruse the paintings in silence. When he finished, she paused her paintbrush to mention the camera hanging around his neck then made a comment about photography being an important art form too. She asked to see some of his work, and she later used a couple of his photos as the basis for paintings in her Cotswold landscape series. Shortly after he left the village, Luka heard from Mac about Joy's descent into reclusiveness. Mac had also been the one to tell him about her death years later.

Joe appeared again, placing Tristan's order onto the bar. Based on the scent, it had to be fish and chips.

Tristan had been tapping another text into his mobile. "I'm letting Chelsea know you've said yes."

For a moment, Luka imagined Chelsea receiving a text with Luka's name attached to it. Although she'd been the one to mention him to Tristan in the first place, he worried she might wrongly assume that Luka had instigated this. Perhaps his volunteer work would have the opposite effect of what he was hoping for. He watched Tristan send the text, helpless. It was already done.

"Can I get your contact info, mate?" he asked Luka.

"Sure. I guess I need yours too." Luka produced his mobile as they swapped information. "So, once I take the photos, I'll send the proofs to you, then?"

"Send them directly to Chelsea. She'll approve them first, since she's the committee chair, then she'll send them to me."

Before Luka knew it, he'd received another *ping* on his mobile from Tristan, with Chelsea's number.

Tristan slid his mobile back into his jeans pocket then paid Joe for the food. He took hold of the bag and turned to Luka. "I've had a new idea, to drum up more interest in the festival in these next few weeks. Like, some behind-the-scenes stuff—costumes, rehearsals, food, that sort of thing. We could put photos on the website as a way of advertising it. Would you be willing to take some shots I can add to the site? Chelsea didn't mention how long you were planning on staying at the village, but—"

"Done. I'd love to."

"Well, that was easy." Tristan's smile broadened. "Great to meet you. Thanks for helping out. Cheers."

As Tristan exited the pub, Luka put away his mobile, even more grateful he'd come to the pub that night.

"Lucky timing," Joe said, reading Luka's thoughts.

Luka looped his camera bag over his shoulder. "You have no idea."

CLICKING THROUGH THE slideshow of recent proofs, Luka blew out a sigh. Though he hadn't really intended to create a coffee-table book of the Cotswolds, he'd been unable to suppress the urge to capture certain images as he walked around the village the past few days. Suddenly, he'd compiled a vast collection of photos that he could easily visualize as colorful, glossy pages in a published book—a closeup of a squirrel munching on an acorn, a set of crooked headstones gracing the churchyard, the bridge that crossed over a bubbling stream, the stone gazebo that had become the centerpiece of High Street, a flock of tourists pointing toward one of the charming shops, and just this morning, a perfect shot of Joy's gallery before he walked inside to meet Noelle.

He clicked the laptop shut and rubbed his eyelids.

"Troubles?" Mac asked, entering the room with his toolbox.

Luka set the laptop aside on Mac's sofa. "I'm realizing I've got more work in front of me than I counted on."

Mac squatted down beside the coffee table and flipped it over with a quiet grunt.

"Need some help?" Luka asked.

"Nay, this only needs an adjustment. Wobbly leg," he explained, sifting through his toolbox.

Minutes before, Luka had knocked on Mac's door after biding his time at the too-quiet guest cottage, waiting to see whether Chelsea would respond to his text about the canvas proofs he'd taken at the gallery that morning. Over the years, Luka had taken thousands of photos of people, nature, and architecture, but never of an oil painting. He was afraid he wouldn't do justice to this masterpiece painted by Noelle that had captured the charm of Chilton Crosse almost as well as her aunt had done. When Luka arrived at the gallery, Noelle had politely introduced herself then was pulled away by a lengthy call, which left Luka alone to concentrate on his photography. He'd spent time setting up his portable strobe flashes, dispersing the light evenly across the canvas, then finding a suitable highlight-to-shadow ratio. In the end, he'd taken what he'd hoped were some viable shots of her canvas then texted them to Chelsea.

"What plans have ye for tomorrow?" Mac asked, searching for the right-sized screw.

"I need to visit my flat in Bristol—check my post, pay some bills. Plus, I'm running out of clean pants!" He laughed and saw Mac return a grin.

For the past decade, Luka had kept a home base in the UK—a tiny, cheap flat in Bristol where his post could be delivered and where he could store furniture or seasonal clothing or extra equipment. He barely spent a handful of nights there each year, but at least it gave him the illusion of having stability in the world.

Luka flinched as his mobile buzzed near his thigh. He turned the screen toward him and saw Chelsea's response. He opened the text wider to see that she'd also added Tristan to the conversation.

I prefer 4 and 6. Tristan, what do you think?

Simple, to the point. Even businesslike. And ignoring Luka entirely. *Does she hate the photos but is too polite to say?*

Tristan texted back immediately: *I think 4 is the one. Thanks, Luka!*

After that, the texts stopped cold.

"Bad news?" Mac observed.

"No, just... the text I was waiting on from Chelsea. She's unreadable."

"Give her time, son." Mac twisted the screwdriver.

The phone pinged again in Luka's hand, another text from Tristan in the same conversation thread: *An idea. Aren't rehearsals for the play on Mon? Luka could take some behind-the-scenes shots for the website.*

Rehearsals. Luka had heard Mac mention a Shakespeare school production earlier in the week—he'd agreed to construct the sets. Before Luka typed a too-eager response, something told him to wait. So he did.

And finally, Chelsea responded: *Okay. 5:00 after school. Assembly hall.*

Luka made a small fist-in-the-air gesture as he smiled toward the screen. He waited a handful of seconds then slowly tapped out his response: *I'll be there.*

Chapter Eight

All the world's a stage, and all the men and women merely players:
they have their exits and their entrances; and one man in his time
plays many parts... ~Shakespeare

C helsea crunched on the corner of her buttered toast, eyes still
focused on the essay in front of her, then scribbled *Add more
detail* in the margin with her red pen. In the past year, she'd become
quite adept at the "eat with one hand, grade with the other" technique, careful to avoid leaving crumbs or jam stains on the papers.
She'd learned that marking up compositions wasn't simply a task she
could carve out of her day in a regimented manner—rather, it was
something that required her constant attention as she squeezed a few
papers inside her lunch breaks or between classes or late at night or
in the few moments she could spare before hauling herself off to
school for the day.

After marking the grade atop the paper, Chelsea set down the
pen, swallowed her last sip of tea, then grimaced in the direction of
the dirty dishes peeking up from the sink, still waiting for her to tidy
them. She'd been too lethargic to do the job the previous night.

The dishes were the result of refreshments offered at her meeting
over the weekend. The selection panel had met at her cottage to
determine which pupils had won parts for *Romeo and Juliet*. The
production would be an abbreviated version of the play, but still,
there were a lot of roles to fill. The panel—made up of teachers with
various subject specialties including history, arts, and theater—was

unanimous in its selections, especially when it came to Juliet. Sienna had won the role in a landslide vote.

Chelsea pushed off from the kitchen table and stacked the essays to create a neater pile then slid them into her tote bag, hoping the mild headache she'd awakened with would evaporate. She didn't have time for it. She had lectures to give, group work to facilitate, an exam to hand out, and then rehearsal to attend after school. Fortunately, the drama teacher would take charge of the entire play, though he wanted Chelsea to be present at some of the key rehearsals. The play *was* her idea, after all.

Adding to the day's burdens was the new invitee who would be attending the first rehearsal. She could barely believe her eyes when she'd received Tristan's text a few days before. Chelsea had been stooped over, filling Socrates's food bowl, when the message came through: *I'm at the pub, met Luka, that photographer. He's agreed to snap a photo of Noelle's canvas.*

That was jarring enough, but Tristan followed his text with the contact info for Luka. She stared at the screen as though it contained toxic properties. She assumed Tristan had given Luka her contact information, too, right there at the pub. Luka McKane now had her mobile number.

Then, the very next afternoon, she'd received a text from Luka containing the expected proofs of Noelle's canvas. Rather than answer him immediately, she clicked off the phone and moved along with her day, finally responding to his text after dinner. The proofs Luka had sent were so good that she'd had trouble choosing. He'd captured all the vivid colors and details, and Chelsea could swear she even saw a brush stroke or two. *Art meets art.*

She sent her response—adding Tristan to the text conversation so it wouldn't just be her chatting with Luka—then flipped through pages of her book to prep for classes, thinking her text had settled the matter. But Tristan responded, pushing further, asking whether Luka could attend the upcoming rehearsal for some behind-the-scenes shots of the play.

At that, Chelsea abandoned her book and stared at the screen in her hand. With a *yes* from her, Luka would essentially become the festival's official photographer. And it wouldn't be long before he would be attending weekly committee meetings. *What can I say? What possible out can I dream up that won't look suspicious?*

She pictured Tristan and Luka, their mobiles poised, awaiting her answer. If she said no, even with a legitimate reason, Luka would see right through it. He would know that it bothered her too much to be anywhere near him. And then he would know the truth—that a part of her, however small and however deeply buried, still wasn't over him. She couldn't have that. So she begrudgingly typed *Okay* then shut off her phone and placed it, screen down, on the table.

BY THE TIME CHELSEA had left school for the day, changed into jeans and a jumper at the cottage, eaten a bite of reheated dinner, and graded a few more papers, she'd unexpectedly softened on the idea of Luka becoming heavily involved in the festival. She recalled Mrs. Pickering's scowl the previous week, her unabashedly poor treatment of Luka, and his cordial attitude toward her. If he could willingly endure Mrs. Pickering at committee meetings, perhaps he'd earned a right to be there.

Besides, when Chelsea tilted the situation, studied it from the outside in and not from her own deeply biased perspective, she realized that Luka was actually doing the village a great favor when they had done him none. He was a world-renowned, award-winning photographer, and he'd decided to reject future work in order to remain in this humble village and snap photos—for free—to help their wee festival garner more attention. In fact, his name alone might produce some significant interest online.

In the end, the most comforting thought was that Chelsea was the chair. She still held enough power to do some delegating—to pair Luka with Tristan and let the two of them work out the particular photos and behind-the-scenes situations. Perhaps she wouldn't be seeing Luka that often. And at least with the upcoming rehearsal, it was a planned situation rather than their usual surprise run-in. She could be somewhat prepared, bracing herself for the sight of him this time.

CHELSEA ENTERED THE assembly hall early, but she wasn't the first one there. Fred Rutherford, the school's drama teacher, sat in the middle row, flipping through what Chelsea presumed to be the script. He wore his usual tweed cap and thick-rimmed glasses. He was probably only in his early forties, but he dressed at least two decades older.

"Hi, Fred," she said, hoping not to spook him.

He craned his neck to see her entering the row. "Oh, hi, Chelsea. Good timing. This one's for you."

He held out the script, and she took it then wriggled awkwardly out of her coat, one-handed, keeping her scarf looped around her neck for added warmth. She set down her bag then sat beside him while he explained that this first rehearsal would only last about ninety minutes and would consist of a quick read-through. He wanted the pupils to be comfortable with each other, relax, and have some fun with it. The blocking and stringent rehearsals without scripts would come later.

While Fred was in midsentence, Chelsea heard the back door of the building open and close. It could have been anyone, but she wondered if it was Luka. Her mind tuned Fred out completely as her ears pricked up, paying attention to the steps approaching their row.

When Fred paused to look up, Chelsea followed his gaze to Luka. He stood at the edge of their row, dressed in a black leather coat and jeans, a backpack slung over his shoulder. He carried a white paper bag at his side.

"I'm interrupting."

"No, it's fine," Chelsea said. "Fred, this is Luka. He's a photographer. *The* photographer, I mean. For the festival."

Fred stood, gave a friendly nod, and crossed his arms. "Tristan told me you were coming. I was just telling Chelsea what today's rehearsal would look like. Casual vibe, relaxed mood. I want to establish trust with the pupils."

"My plan is to stay invisible," Luka said. "Out of the way. I'll snap some candid shots around the rim."

"Perfect."

Chelsea could hear the door opening again, coupled with the sharp, distinct laughter of two female voices entering the assembly hall.

Fred checked his watch. "I'd better get some things in order before the chaos begins. Wish me luck!"

He snatched up his script and coat then exited the other end of the row, leaving Chelsea and Luka to themselves. Before she could scramble to find a new topic—it was clear Luka wasn't ready to follow Fred's lead and move toward the stage—one of the female voices came closer. Sienna bounded up to her teacher, so Luka stepped aside in the aisle to offer more space.

"Miss Barrett!" Sienna gripped a rolled-up script between her hands. "I can't *believe* I got the part! I wanted to thank you in class today, but I knew Jenny Newman was crushed at not getting it." Her voice had hushed to a whisper, even though Jenny Newman was nowhere in sight. "I didn't want to rub it in."

"I understand. And you don't have to thank me. You earned the part. All of us on the panel agreed. You *were* Juliet."

Dipping her head, Sienna grinned then looked toward Luka and seemed to notice him for the first time.

"This is Luka," Chelsea explained. "He'll be taking some photos tonight for the festival."

"Congratulations on getting the part," Luka told Sienna.

"Thanks. I was so nervous last week at auditions. But I knew Miss Barrett was in the audience, cheering me on. She's the best! Well, anyways, I'd better hop on stage. Did you hear that? I'm going 'on stage'!"

"Yes, you are." Chelsea snickered, watching Sienna bound away and join her friend.

Chelsea recalled that Sienna's ex, Matthew, had been cast as Romeo. It was a split decision by the panel—Matthew's audition had been a bit clunky and unsure, but his nervousness made him rather endearing. Chelsea was curious about how Sienna would handle being "his" Juliet but assumed she was thrilled to have an excuse to see him on a weekly basis, not to mention being forced to play romantic scenes with him multiple times...

The energy in the building had heightened considerably as more teenagers entered in clusters then gathered at the stage, their excitement palpable even from the middle row.

"Were we ever that young?" Chelsea wondered aloud.

"A lifetime ago," Luka said.

Fred was clapping his hands, trying to reroute the teenagers' attention toward him. "It's about time to begin, folks. Power off the mobiles, get out your scripts..."

"That's my cue," Luka said. "Oh, here." He stepped closer and plopped down the white bag in the empty seat beside Chelsea. "I figured you didn't have much time to eat today." Then off he went, headed toward the stage, focused on his mission.

Curious, Chelsea opened the bag and peered inside. The familiar scent rose up before she even saw what was inside—two Chelsea buns, a yeasty treat dotted with fruits and spices. It was their little inside joke from years before, when Luka had brought her a bag of them from the same village bakery. "Named after you, eh?" he'd said with a wide grin. "Sweet and spicy with surprises lurking inside." It was one of the rare moments Luka ever showed his corny side, but Chelsea loved it best. It meant he was being vulnerable, showing her every layer of himself. She'd had to boycott the delicious Chelsea buns altogether when Luka left the village. The association with him was just too strong.

Watching the rehearsal begin, Chelsea pinched off a corner of the bun and drew it to her lips to take a bite. It was as delicious as she remembered—buttery and spicy, pure heaven. She scrunched the bag closed then retrieved her peacock journal and opened it to the next fresh page, intending to jot down some notes.

A man ducked into the assembly hall from a side door—she recognized him, from his ginger hair, as Sienna's father. He caught Chelsea's eye and gave a small wave then took a seat up front with a couple of other parents. Chelsea assumed the pride would eventually wear off a bit and the parental attendance would become scarcer as the weeks wore on. But it was refreshing to see their early enthusiasm.

Chelsea crossed her legs and moved her attention to the stage. Fred had the pupils sitting cross-legged in a circle for a relaxed read-through of the script. At first, they were shy, stumbling and giggling and elbowing each other through their lines. Shakespeare's formal *thou shalt* and *whither* and *forsooth* probably felt strange on their tongues. But as the rehearsal moved on, their confidence increased, and even from her seat several rows back, Chelsea noticed the deep concentration on the pupils' faces. Some even used hand gestures and inflections as they delivered lines with growing self-assurance.

Luka skulked around the outskirts of the circle, silently crouching and aiming his camera then taking a few more steps and clicking again. Occasionally, he would pause and stand upright, examining the camera's screen and making adjustments. He was in his own world, utterly oblivious to anything but that circle of pupils and their teacher. Chelsea could see the intensity of his gaze from where she sat, his dark eyebrows furrowed, his lips pursed in concentration.

It was a familiar sight—Luka with a camera in hand. She'd first seen him with it as a teenager, shortly after he'd arrived in the village, back when they barely knew each other. She would notice him at various spots around the fringes of the village, snapping photos. It seemed like such an intimate connection he was having with whatever subject he happened to be shooting—a puddle in the road, a bird in a tree branch, an unsuspecting villager walking past—so she always watched him from afar then continued on, respecting his privacy.

But after they'd gotten to know each other—starting with the night she'd caught him in that awful row with his father—Luka's boundaries had quickly dissolved, and he began to let her in. And that included his love for photography.

Chelsea recalled one particular lazy summer afternoon, strolling with Luka along the manicured Italian gardens behind Chatsworth Manor—the hidden gem on the outskirts of Chilton Crosse, where fancy parties were held or films were shot. She could still remember feeling the warmth of his hand holding hers. In the two weeks since their talk at the barn, she and Luka had seen each other every day, stealing moments together in private places, talking about life or school or nothing at all. So far, their physical contact had been limited to innocent hand-holding or a stroke of a cheek.

On that day, Luka had released her hand to take photos of a robin perched on a nearby branch. Chelsea had waited for him to take the photo then crossed her arms in faux frustration. "I'm always in competition with that thing," she teased. "What's the appeal, anyway? It's just a bird." She pointed to it as it flew away, leaving behind a quivering branch. "They're commonplace."

Luka faced her and chewed at his lip. "It's hard to explain. It's not just a bird. It's something else." He balanced the camera in his palms. "This forces me to see the world in a different way."

"Show me."

Luka searched around for a new subject. "There, on that flower." He pointed. "A butterfly you might've passed by. But I would've been looking for it, seeking it out." He waved her toward him, careful not to disturb the insect as Chelsea joined him.

Luka placed a hand on her hip to shift her in front of him until they both faced the butterfly squarely. He extended his arms around her shoulders then lifted his camera in front of her eyes. "Hold onto it," he whispered, guiding her hands as she gripped the camera. "Tell me what you see."

Chelsea could feel his breath on her neck, making it difficult to concentrate. She closed one eye and peered through the viewfinder to focus in on the butterfly. Luka showed her how to make adjustments to the lens, and suddenly, she could see the colors, vivid in the sunlight.

"Beautiful," she whispered, her smile wide behind the camera.

The details of the wings came into stunning view as they clapped together, hypnotic. Chelsea could even see the tiny black legs, the antenna, a beady eye.

"Push this when you're ready," he told her. His finger navigated hers toward a button as she tried to keep the camera steady.

Breathless, praying the butterfly wouldn't disappear before she could capture it, she pressed the button and heard the shutter close and open in a microsecond. As they lowered the camera together, the butterfly drifted away.

"Let's see it." Luka remained in place, his chest still pressed against Chelsea's back, and clicked a button on the digital camera—a birthday present from Mac, she later learned. The small screen revealed Chelsea's butterfly, perfectly centered, wings spread apart at a slight angle. It looked like a professional photo.

"I did that?" she asked.

"You did," he whispered. "I'll have it printed for you."

As Luka lowered the camera to his side, Chelsea swiveled in his arms, realizing that his free hand had grasped her waist. She stared at his mouth and wondered, not for the first time, what it would be like to press her lips against his. He must have been reading her mind, because the next thing Chelsea knew, Luka had broken eye contact with her and started to lean in.

Heart thumping, she closed her eyes tight and let him kiss her, let him sweep her away. She felt the bliss of his soft lips, the tenderness in the kiss. He grasped her waist and drew her even closer. Chelsea felt a jolt from the pit of her stomach to the top of her head. The electricity that passed between them was otherworldly. As he backed away, her thoughts remained fuzzy and scattered. When she opened her eyes, she saw his lips form a smile.

A series of thumps broke Chelsea's thoughts as she watched pupils eagerly bounding down the stage's steps. Rehearsal was over, and she wondered how much of it she'd missed. She glanced down at her journal and saw a blank page. In her mind's eye, staring at the page, she could still see the butterfly's colors, feel Luka's hand pressing her waist, taste his lips...

Chelsea closed her eyes tight then rubbed the lids with her fingertips, sensing her earlier headache returning. This was what she'd been most afraid of—that Luka's constant presence in the village would trigger vivid memories beyond her control. She would have to be more diligent in the future, prepare for them and halt them before they had a chance to run wild.

"Chelsea? Are you okay?"

She lowered her hand and opened her eyes to see Luka standing once again at the edge of her row. He held his camera at his side as he had on that summer day. *Does he remember that day like I do? Or remember it at all?*

She took in a sharp breath. "Staving off a headache. It's been a really long day."

"Anything I can help with?"

"It's nothing that a strong cup of tea and some sleep won't cure."

Luka pointed toward her journal. "You're still writing?"

"Oh. No. This is all for the festival." She ticked through the other pages, each filled to the brim with brainstorming. "Notes, scheduling, and so forth..."

"I remember your poetry. And you were attempting a novel, weren't you?" He busied himself with his camera, placing it gingerly into his backpack.

Chelsea hadn't thought about her novel in ages. She'd been inspired after reading Jane Austen one summer and had attempted her own hand at a love story. She didn't remember telling Luka about it. She tsked. "I don't have time for that anymore."

She shut the journal and moved to gather her things, hoping Luka would finish packing up and politely be on his way. He'd gotten what he needed—candid shots of pupils in midgesture, quoting Shakespeare on a stage. His job was done. But after Luka hoisted his backpack onto his shoulders, he remained in the aisle, waiting for her even as she pushed her arms through her coat sleeves, biding her time, hoping he would take the hint.

"Good rehearsal!" Fred called suddenly from center stage. He gave a thumbs-up that turned into a goodbye wave.

Chelsea waved back, watching him turn to exit stage right. The teenagers and parents had all bounded out by that point, leaving

Chelsea and Luka as the only stragglers. She slid the journal into her bag then looped the strap over her shoulder.

"Don't forget your buns." Luka pointed to the white bag.

"Oh. Right. Thanks for these." She grabbed up the bag, weirdly irritated at having to thank Luka—she didn't want to owe him anything—then moved toward the aisle, brushing his sleeve as she slipped out past him.

As they gravitated together toward the exit, she intended to make it completely obvious that they were parting ways. Luka stepped in front of Chelsea to open the door wide for her, and she passed through. Before she could issue a casual goodbye, Luka spoke.

"I need to ask you a question."

She paused, the evening air brushing her cheeks, and frowned. "Okay?" It came out more as a question than an answer.

Luka took slow steps forward, apparently wanting to talk *and* walk. She followed his lead, uneasy about where this conversation was headed. Anything was possible.

He shoved his hands into his coat pockets, his focus on the paved road as they moved in the direction of the village. "So, my agent has been pushing for me to do another of those books. You know, a coffee-table book with classic Cotswold photos—cottages and churches and shop fronts and the like. We're even thinking of adding a whole chapter about Joy Valentine and her gallery."

Relieved that Luka was talking business, Chelsea relaxed. The photos she'd watched him take last week made more sense—he was staying in Chilton Crosse for a specific purpose. And it wasn't her.

"Anyway, I'm confident about the photos but not about the writing. So I just wondered... if you..." His eyes drifted toward her as she walked by his side, then he shrugged. "I think you'd be really great at it. Helping with the photo descriptions. You know, writing paragraphs for each page with some details or history, that sort of thing. You'd get paid for it, of course."

Chelsea knew the answer immediately and shook her head, her eyes returning to the road. "No. I'm sorry, I can't." It sounded harsher than she'd intended, so she clarified. "I'm overwhelmed already. With grading and school, the committee, the festival. And now these rehearsals. It's too much already. I can't commit to anything else."

A lonely bird called out from a faraway tree, the only other sound besides their footsteps and an occasional breeze rustling leaves.

Luka nodded. "Right. Of course. Say no more."

She could sense his disappointment but couldn't do anything to lessen it. She'd told him the absolute truth—she literally couldn't commit to another thing at that point. She was stretched too thin. Plus, it would have been yet another project that would put her in close, possibly daily proximity to Luka.

"I'll send you the proofs of tonight's rehearsal, after I've had a chance to sort through them," he said.

"No rush."

They'd reached the turning point in the road—one path would take her to her cottage, and the other would take Luka toward the village. He paused, his dark eyes resting on her.

A faraway yipping broke the silence, and Chelsea realized it was Socrates, inside her cottage down the path. She sometimes opened the front curtains so he could peer out and bark at squirrels or birds.

"Your dog?" Luka asked, staring toward the cottage.

"Mum's dog. Eleven-year-old Westie. Socrates."

"Great name."

"Dad's idea, actually." Chelsea's mind drifted back to the Christmas Eve she'd spent with her parents at the cottage. "It was his gift to my mum. This tiny white ball of fur. And when it was his turn to hold the dog, Dad lifted it up, eye level, and stared into its face. Then out of the blue, he told us, 'He looks like a Socrates to me. He has wise eyes.' And the name stuck." Chelsea paused. "The dog sort of be-came Dad's dog—followed him around everywhere, begging for food and attention. Dad pretended not to notice the favoritism, but we all knew better."

"You miss him. Your dad." Luka peered down at her in the shadows.

"I miss him every single day." She shifted the bag on her shoulder and realized that Socrates had finally quieted his barking. Picturing her father's face always brought him closer, but it also emphasized the sharp ache of loss. "It never quite goes away. Some days—like today—I get too busy with things, and he doesn't seem to enter my thoughts at all. But then when he does, it's so... fresh again. Like he's still right here."

Luka blinked hard as he moved his gaze to the path. His own grief was still raw, Chelsea knew, and was probably magnified because his father's passing meant that *both* his parents were gone. Luka wasn't a stranger to this kind of pain. He'd been ten when his mother died, and he'd had to grapple with that enormous weight of grief at a tender age. *How can a child possibly process what that loss means—the permanent hole it will leave behind?*

"Rachel told me that you'd been visiting your father. In the care home." Even as the words came out, Chelsea realized it was probably a secret Luka wouldn't appreciate her knowing.

But he didn't seem irritated or surprised. He likely assumed that Chelsea and Rachel shared everything. His tone was matter-of-fact. "I visited when I could. It never seemed enough." He shook his head and kicked the dirt. "Hideous way to die—struggling with your memories, losing all sense of place and time. My whole life, I'd never seen my father look afraid, not ever. But in those final months, not knowing who I was, not knowing who *he* was... this panic settled into his eyes. And there was nothing I could do. Trying to prod his memory only made it worse."

"Heartbreaking," Chelsea whispered.

"Yes." Luka rubbed at his eyes then cleared his throat. "Well, I won't keep you longer. I'm sure you've got papers to grade."

"I'm convinced they reproduce when my back is turned."

Luka chuckled. "Sounds about right. Thanks for letting me tag along tonight. The rehearsal, I mean. I got some good shots."

"Tristan will be pleased. And I meant to tell you earlier, the festival meetings have been set for every Thursday until the big day and maybe even a couple of emergency meetings squeezed in on other days if we need them. You're welcome to attend. Or not. Whatever you want."

"Okay." Luka's eyes lingered on her an extra half second before he pivoted to walk down the other path, toward the village.

Hearing Socrates yipping again, Chelsea moved in the cottage's direction. "I'm coming, I'm coming," she whispered, knowing Socrates probably needed an urgent walk in the back garden. As she made her way up the stone path, she realized that her conversation with Luka had left her feeling oddly satisfied. She rarely had the chance to talk about her father, and she guessed that Luka could say the same. That loss, at least, gave them something in common that wasn't rooted in their teenage past. Something mutual, something safe.

She entered the cottage, dropped her bags to the floor, and picked up Socrates, receiving a series of frantic licks in return. "Did you miss me? Were you lonesome?"

She kicked the door closed with her foot and cradled him as the licks continued. Her father would have been pleased at the sight of her living in this cottage, taking care of Socrates, finding her career path, and becoming involved in village life. She only wished he'd been able to see it for himself.

Chapter Nine

*The aged love what is practical while impetuous youth
longs only for what is dazzling.* ~Petrarch

"And when I got to the chemist's, it was six pounds more than I expected. Six pounds! I'm not made of money. But still, what's a soul to do? So I paid them and moved along..."

Chelsea had already heard this same story from her mother earlier in the week, but she let her tell it in full and glorious detail again, only half listening this time. She shifted Socrates in one arm while trying not to drop the mobile in her other hand. Reaching the cottage's narrow staircase, she suppressed a yawn as her mother finally wrapped up the story.

"Are you still there?"

"I'm here, Mum. Taking Socrates up the stairs."

"How's he doing?"

"You need to come and see for yourself. He misses you!"

"I miss him too. When did you say this festival is?"

"Only a few weeks away. Mid-October."

"Oh my. Will everything be ready by then?"

"It'll have to be. The panic will probably set in as we get closer, but having a big committee helps. Everyone's working hard, and I'm getting daily updates. Right now, I'm weirdly Zen about it—just taking things day by day." Chelsea had reached the top of the stairs, slightly winded. She set down Socrates and watched him waddle off to her bedroom at the end of the hall. "Anyway, you've got a lovely guest room here if you fancy a visit sometime."

"Thanks, love. I'll certainly try. It depends on how your aunt is doing."

"Of course."

They exchanged goodbyes, promising to touch base again in the next few days, then Chelsea clicked off. She still hadn't told her mother that Luka was in town. She wasn't even sure her mum would recall who Luka was, especially in terms of what he'd meant to Chelsea. She and her mother hadn't had a close relationship back then. While other girls might have asked for romantic advice or openly told their mums about their first loves, Chelsea kept Luka to herself in those days. Her parents had known vague details about their relationship, and she remembered the concern in their eyes whenever his name came up. But so many years had passed since then that Chelsea doubted her mother would remember him at all.

Chelsea sensed another yawn coming on and didn't suppress it this time. The weight of another school day sat on her shoulders, and she stretched her arms above her head to release it. The previous night's rehearsal, followed by another lengthy workday, had taken its toll. The basic necessities of life, such as sleep and food, were almost luxuries these days. Chelsea brought her hand to her waist to verify it—she'd lost some weight these past couple of weeks. Sometimes her only solid meal of the day was squeezed in after school, when she was too hungry to *feel* hungry anymore.

She imagined what her mother would say. "Your stomach has shrunk. You need to eat—you're too thin." Maybe before her mother arrived for a visit, Chelsea could regain the weight and avoid that conversation altogether.

Eager to slip into her flannel pajamas—the September nights were getting chillier and chillier—Chelsea started to follow Socrates down the hall but paused at the guest room, originally her childhood bedroom. A thought came. She flipped on the light then moved to open the wardrobe doors and spotted what she was looking for—a cardboard box on the top shelf. She'd intended to sort through it during the past weeks' renovations but had always put the task off till later.

She set down her mobile then pulled down the box and placed it on the bed. She hadn't peeked inside this particular box in at least fifteen years. It had been tucked away since the day she'd moved out of the cottage and gone off to university. She'd practically forgotten about its existence until recently.

Chelsea lifted the lid and peered inside, smiling at the tokens and treasures of those youthful days—awards ribbons for school attendance, badges from her Girl Guides accomplishments, a paper-mache project she'd completed at school, a palm-sized stuffed bear her father had given her for a birthday. She removed the items one by one until she struck gold. A candid shot of her carefree teenage self stared back at her—squinty eyed, laughing, dimples showing. Luka had taken it. She flipped it over, hoping to see a date, but the backside was blank. She took another glance at teenage Chelsea—the easy smile, the joyful expression—and tried to recall how close to their breakup the snapshot had been taken. She felt a powerful urge to enter the photo and clutch her teenage self by the shoulders to warn her of the impending heartache—to plead with her to walk away from Luka before he could walk away from her.

But life didn't work that way. Things had to take their own course. And even if she *had* been warned, she probably wouldn't have changed a thing. She would have kept on loving Luka, no matter the dire predictions—either not believing them or loving him in spite of them. Chelsea occasionally missed that naive part of herself that used to hold inordinately high expectations of people and thought the world should function a certain way, living up to all her desires.

Chelsea set the photo aside and moved along in her excavation. Farther into the box, she discovered a thick brown notebook and drew it out carefully. "I remember this..."

She cracked it open to find pages and pages of notes compiled from three lengthy interviews she'd done with Joy Valentine. It had been a school project. "Select a respected member of the village's community and write a profile piece on them." Chelsea remembered approaching Joy with trepidation the day she'd selected her for the project. Joy rarely smiled, and she was known to be crotchety. Chelsea hadn't ever spoken directly to her, but that day, she'd gathered up her courage, entered the gallery, and stuttered her way through an explanation of her school project as Joy sat behind her canvas, paintbrush poised, eyebrow raised.

"Certainly, I'll do it," Joy said, lowering the eyebrow and returning to her painting.

After that, Chelsea relaxed and spent three separate afternoons with Joy, asking detailed questions about her art, her family, and her accomplishments. At times, Joy would issue a slightly gruff "Off-limits. Next question." But for the most part, she seemed candid about her life, especially when it came to her art. Joy's eyes would sparkle, and she would grow animated, her words spilling out faster and faster so that Chelsea could hardly jot down the answers quickly enough.

Peeking out from the notebook's final page was a photo of Joy at her easel that Chelsea didn't remember taking. She tucked it securely inside the notebook then set both aside in order to remove the final item in the box, a black leather journal. Cringing, she opened it to the first page, entitled, "Untitled: A Novel," and read the clunky prose she'd penned as an eager teenager: *Lindsay Baker didn't realize it then, but this day would end up changing the rest of her entire life!*

"So melodramatic." Chelsea shook her head as she skimmed through page after page of too-lengthy, too-flowery descriptions and overhyped, unnatural dialogue. From what she could gather, Lindsay Baker, a wealthy aristocrat's daughter, had fallen madly in love with a farmer's son, Timothy. Their love was doomed from the beginning, it seemed. But Chelsea would never find out for sure. She had completed only forty pages of the novel. In fact, the work had ended abruptly—midchapter, midsentence.

She closed the journal then fished inside the box for anything else she might have missed. In the back of her mind, she remembered a personal diary with Luka-centered entries, all about meeting him, falling for him, then recuperating after he abandoned her. If that diary still existed—a pink book with a unicorn on the cover—it should certainly be in the box.

But then she recalled that she'd always kept the diary tucked underneath her mattress. No one knew the diary even existed, so it wouldn't be out of the realm of possibility that it had remained there, unmoved and untouched, for all those years. She could hear Socrates clicking down the hall, probably wondering why she wasn't coming to bed.

"Soon," she said, seeing his small frame halt then sit inside the doorframe.

She abandoned the box and stooped to lift the mattress with one hand then patted around underneath with the other, hoping to touch the corner of a book. Nothing. She bent down on her knees, eye level with the mattress, and hoisted it upward with both hands to take a legitimate look. Still nothing. She moved to the end of the bed, then to the other side, to do the same, but all she found for her efforts was some dust. Just when she was about to abandon the idea, her index finger touched the edge of something. Pushing farther, she felt the shape take form beneath her hand. Definitely a book. Breathless and hopeful, Chelsea coerced it closer, sliding it toward her until she drew the book all the way out. Cupping it in her hands, she saw the unicorn on a pink cover with bald corners, worn from use.

She couldn't pretend that her curiosity didn't push well beyond a nostalgic walk down Memory Lane. She wanted to know, with fresh urgency, if her teenage accounts of Luka, frozen on the page, would match her aging memories, dulled by time.

Chelsea lowered herself onto the bed, flipping gingerly to the diary's beginning, and saw Luka's name on page one. She'd started the diary the first day she laid eyes on him. She groaned at the wording, straight from a cheesy romance novel: *mysterious eyes that hold a secret... flowing hair that moves when he moves...*

The first few pages were written months apart, scattered and brief, and were all about how she *thought* Luka *might* have looked at her on purpose, or how she *desperately* wanted to talk to him but was too afraid. But something changed a fourth of the way through the diary, detailing the night of Luka's argument with his father. Even Chelsea's handwriting had become clearer in this passage, her prose less flowery and more intense. She used the word *love* several pages later and detailed their various dates and excursions around the village.

Chelsea flipped pages, skimming, remembering, and realizing that, yes, her adult memories did match the strength of the emotions she'd experienced during that year. Near the end, she noticed references to her *big plans* with Luka—postpone university for at least a year while they backpacked around Europe, staying in hostels, using their savings for meals, and seeing the world together. After that, maybe attend university, then get married and have a family. These things *had* been discussed between them, and the proof was in her hands. And the wording indicated that Luka had been equally committed to it—in fact, the European trip had been his idea from the start. Teenage Chelsea understood how important university was to her parents, and she'd already begun her A levels. But Luka wanted to be with her, and that was all that mattered to her then. Everything else—even university—could wait, as far as she'd been concerned.

As she came to the final pages, Chelsea wondered whether she had documented the night of the breakup. But the last page only contained a brief list of items Chelsea had planned to pack for her Europe trip with Luka. The only content in her hands was pre-breakup. Flipping through the rest of the pages, making sure she didn't miss a single sentence or word, Chelsea realized the end of the diary was blank—no clues, no hints, no revelations concerning the fateful conclusion to their story.

Disappointed, wishing she hadn't even sought the silly diary in the first place, Chelsea closed the book, outlined the unicorn with her fingertip, then placed the diary where it had always truly belonged—deep inside the box of dusty old memories, which she shoved into the top corner of the wardrobe, to be forgotten once more.

Socrates whined from the doorway, watching with tender eyes as though he could read her frustration. She closed the wardrobe doors, grabbed her mobile, then went to scoop Socrates up and nuzzle his soft coat.

"There's nothing in there for us, after all," she whispered into his fur.

CHELSEA HAD GRAPPLED with it all morning—while brushing her teeth, while picking out her favorite crimson skirt, while unlocking her classroom door, then while watching pupils filter in and out of her class throughout the day. But in the end, texting Luka had been the right thing to do. Chelsea had something that he needed, and she couldn't deprive him of it.

She could have waited another twenty-four hours to see him at the meeting the next night, but he might not attend. And even if he did, their chatting together, even for a brief minute, might cause villagers' heads to turn and tongues to wag. Texting was a better option.

Chelsea peeked at the wall clock again—still twenty minutes left of her free period. She'd asked Luka to stop by sometime during the hour, at his leisure. She decided to organize the essays on her desk to stay looking busy. But before she could put her hands around the stack of papers, she saw Luka standing in the doorway.

"Sorry I'm late." He threaded through the student desks. "Mac had me 'on assignment' at the pub. Leaky tap." As though to prove it, he raised the toolbox in his hand.

"It's fine. I was just grading."

Luka peered around the room. "You did all this?" He pointed with his free hand at the boards covered in Renaissance quotes and posters that Chelsea had painstakingly filled up weeks before.

"All me. Hoping to get the pupils into Renaissance mode." She relaxed a bit as Luka's attention turned elsewhere. But when he set down his toolbox and took a seat across from her desk, she felt that familiar nervousness rise. She shifted swiftly into business mode. "So, I found something last night at the cottage. I thought it might be helpful." She drew out the brown notebook and set it between them. "It's a project I did in school, ages ago. We were asked to choose someone in the village and write a profile piece on them. I chose Joy Valentine."

"Really?" Tilting his head, Luka moved forward and leaned across the desk for a closer look. "This is quite a find."

"I'd forgotten about it, honestly. It was so long ago. But as I was rummaging through this box last night, there it was." She opened the first page to show him her teenage scribblings, then he drew the notebook closer and flipped gingerly through its pages. "I interviewed her three separate times, asked her all sorts of questions. She probably thought some of the questions were daft, and they were. 'What's your favorite pudding?'"

"Favorite bird." Luka nodded with a half grin, reading from a page.

"Right. Those were warm-up questions, I guess. But then my dad coached me, offered me deeper questions to ask. And by the time we finished the final interview, I got some substantive answers from her."

Luka's lips parted as he skimmed a page. She stayed quiet to let him peruse the notebook but couldn't help letting her eyes roam over his masculine hands, thick eyelashes, jet-black hair...

"This is fantastic." Luka glanced up suddenly. "How did I never know about these interviews?"

Chelsea shrugged. "I guess the assignment happened the first year you were in the village, before I knew you. Before we... knew each other. Anyway, I thought this might help with your coffee-table book. Use anything you want from it—I've already texted Noelle for her permission. She loves the idea of her aunt being highlighted this way. She even said you could photograph some of Joy's paintings for the book."

"Brilliant!" Luka said, louder than he'd probably intended. "Thank you. I mean, you didn't have to do this."

"I wanted to. The book sounds like a lovely idea for the village."

"Does this mean...?" Luka closed the notebook but kept his hand flat on top of it. "Have you changed your mind about contributing?"

Chelsea's firm no had tempered a bit since he'd first asked—and since flipping through her first attempt at a novel. She remembered the elation she felt when she'd brainstormed those original ideas, put pen to paper, and crafted sentences, no matter how clunky. *Why did I ever stop?* A part of her, long buried, wanted to rediscover that creative side of herself and try her hand at writing again. And maybe this village book could at least nudge her slowly in that direction.

"I don't know... time is still a *huge* factor, realistically." She shifted in her seat.

"There's no rush," Luka assured her. "I don't even have a deadline for the book yet. Maybe I could send you some proofs and see if they inspire you. Then you can make your decision from there. Dip your toes in rather than plunging headfirst."

No pressure, no time crunch. Receiving beautiful photos on her mobile and putting words to them whenever she felt inspired. It was almost too perfect to resist.

"Well, okay. But *no* promises," she told him firmly. "This isn't any sort of yes."

"Understood. It's only a maybe."

"Right. Barely a maybe." Chelsea grinned as she realized what had happened. Luka McKane had just talked her into a maybe. She wasn't immune to his charm, even as an adult.

Luka craned his neck slightly, searching her face across the desk.

"What?" she asked.

"Your dimples are showing."

"Are they?" She covered her mouth and smiled even wider behind her palm.

"What's making you smile?"

She lowered her hand. "You... have this way of persuading people, that's all."

"Do I?"

"Don't be too pleased with yourself. That wasn't necessarily a compliment."

"Well then, I'd better leave before your maybe changes back to a no." Luka stood and grinned as he raised the notebook. "This is in good hands."

Chelsea stood, too, and crossed her arms. "I think Joy would appreciate being included in your book. She's the heart of the village, really. Even being gone."

"Agreed. I'm already getting inspired with some ideas for that chapter." He pushed the chair back in place. "I'm glad we met here in your classroom. I'm getting to know a whole other side of you."

That hadn't been Chelsea's intent—having Luka find out more about her life. She'd only invited him to her classroom for convenience's sake, squeezing him into a crowded sliver of her busy day. She started to say a politer version of this, but he continued.

"You're a good teacher." He said it definitively, as though he had it on strong authority.

"You've never seen me teach. How do you know?"

"I watch people. It's part of my job. I saw you the other night at rehearsal, the way you interacted with your pupils. They're at ease, probably because they know you won't judge them. That's one of your best qualities—always has been. You let people be exactly who they are."

A peal of laughter broke Chelsea's thoughts, and a cluster of teenagers entered the room, chattering away.

"Guess that's my cue." Luka found his toolbox and pivoted to walk out of the room, dodging a boisterous teenager along the way.

"Miss Barrett?"

Chelsea blinked, shifting her gaze from the door to Sienna standing beside her. "How can I help you?"

Sienna lowered her tone to a whisper. "That's the same man as before, at the rehearsal? Luka?"

"Yes, it is."

"Your... boyfriend?"

Chelsea's lips parted in surprise. Sienna wasn't usually this bold. "You know that's an inappropriate question for your teacher," she chided gently. "And no." Chelsea kept her voice low too. "He's not my boyfriend. He's just an... old friend. A ghost from long ago."

Sienna turned, murmuring, "He doesn't look like a ghost to me..."

Chapter Ten

Truth bears the same relation to falsehood as light to darkness.
~Leonardo da Vinci

If someone were ever to quiz Chelsea about her favorite season in Chilton Crosse, she would have been stumped to answer. Each season held its own beauty—crystal wonderland whites in the winter, bursting floral colors in the spring, rich deep-green leaves in the summer. But if pressed, she would probably choose autumn.

As she stepped out of Nightingale Cottage on the way to her festival meeting, she saw that the edges of autumn had begun to appear on a handful of trees, unseasonably early. The change was subtle—if you weren't looking for it, you might miss it. Most leaves were still fully green, but the tips of certain other leaves were already turning crimson or gold. She could only imagine the spectacular colors that would be offered in the coming weeks.

As she approached the church-hall doors, Chelsea half wondered if the meeting was even necessary. She'd already heard from everyone on the festival committee over the past two days, texting or ringing her up to tell about their individual progress. Mary had completed nearly a third of the costumes, Mac was hard at work on the sets and outdoor stage, Julia and Joe were experimenting with Renaissance foods, the school's madrigal singers had chosen their music selections, Tristan had finalized the village's website, and Mrs. Bennett had ordered special Renaissance jewelry to sell. Every single person was on task, and as far as Chelsea could tell, they were ahead of schedule. This committee practically ran itself.

Chelsea settled in at the table, thankful Mrs. Pickering hadn't arrived early this time, then moved her attention to her notes and jotted down more ideas. Julia and Rachel came in to set up the treats—biscuits and scones and a kettle for tea. Then, one by one, the rest of the committee members filtered in, all chattering away while setting down scarves, coats, and bags.

Rachel briefly left her duties to set down a plate of food in front of Chelsea, who gave her a smile in return. The elongated table filled quickly, with Mrs. Pickering taking her usual spot at Chelsea's right hand. Frank O'Neill took a seat at Chelsea's left. He wore a navy suit tailored to his exceptionally thin frame, complete with a handkerchief peeking out from his lapel pocket.

Leaning in, he said, "Noelle won't be here tonight. Sick child. I'm taking her place."

"Oh, sorry to hear about little Adam." Chelsea tsked. "I'll text her later to see how he's doing."

Frank nodded then pinched the end of a scone for a taste. He'd become the gallery's curator during the years Chelsea was absent from the village, so she didn't know him terribly well. But he struck her as a rather odd man—somewhere in his thirties, or maybe forties, but dressed as though he'd stepped from the pages of a 1950's men's catalogue. At times, he could be peculiar and temperamental, but at other moments, he became warm and animated. She supposed he had an artist's temperament. *Fitting*...

As Chelsea stood to begin the meeting, she noticed a vacant chair—the one she'd set out purposely for Luka. Perhaps he'd changed his mind about attending.

When Chelsea's polite waving and timid "May I have everyone's attention" did little to hush the group, Mrs. Pickering brought out the dreaded gavel. Chelsea cringed as she watched the wooden hammer crack down on the table—but it seemed to do the trick. After only two quick raps, the entire committee had halted their jabbering and eating and was staring with wide eyes in Chelsea's direction.

She cleared her throat to address the group. "Welcome. Let's first thank Julia for once again supplying us with delicious refreshments."

As a smattering of applause broke out, Chelsea consulted her list again. She would have to skip the first order of business—introducing Luka—so she seamlessly moved on to the next. "The first item on our agenda comes from Holly. She's on a deadline to order the banners that will hang above the street, between the shops, during the festival. I believe she has some samples."

Holly shuffled through a folder of papers. "I'll pass them around the table."

As she explained the size and cost differences between the banners, a noise at the back of the room caught Chelsea's attention. Most of the committee members were too absorbed in poring over samples to notice Luka entering the hall. He flashed a smile toward Chelsea as he made his way to the table's opposite end.

"What's he doing here?" Mrs. Pickering had leaned in to ask the question, but Chelsea's attention remained on Luka as he found his seat.

"He was invited," she whispered back. "I'll explain in a moment."

Someone thrust a banner into Mrs. Pickering's hands, forcing her to pay attention to the current task. Chelsea took a couple of peeks down the length of the table to see that Mary and Tristan had befriended Luka, handing him banners and discussing them.

Soon, Holly spoke up again. "Has everyone had a chance to look them over? Which do you prefer?"

Several piped in with their opinions. "This one is too colorful." "This one is too small." "This one is too busy." But it was clear that one pattern had emerged as the group's favorite, and after a swift vote conducted by Chelsea, it became the chosen winner.

As the samples were returned to Holly, Chelsea took in a breath, praying this would go well. "The next item on the agenda involves our new photographer." She gestured toward Luka, and the group's attention followed. "This is Luka McKane," Chelsea explained. "Many of you know him already—our elder vicar's son and a world-renowned photographer. He has agreed to photograph our little festival, including some behind-the-scenes shots in the coming weeks."

"Oh, I saw some photos on our village website this morning." Mary turned to Luka and tapped his arm. "Were those yours, then? All the young people rehearsing a play?"

"That's right," Luka said.

"We're hoping these behind-the-scenes shots will drum up interest in the festival, get people talking," Tristan said. "We're using them as a bit of advertising."

"So," Chelsea continued, "you might see Luka now and again snapping photos of your preparations for the festival."

"I promise to be discreet. I won't invade your privacy," Luka assured the group.

Mrs. Bennett piped in. "Well, I'm not sure *my* participation is all that exciting. I'll be pulling some jewelry pieces from my boutique's collection and ordering more for the festival."

"But those are the shots we need," Luka said. "I can make your jewelry look dazzling. And you might even get some early sales."

"Oh!" Mrs. Bennett brightened. "Well, in that case..."

Chelsea's senses had been half-attuned to Mrs. Pickering the entire time, trying to gauge her expression. It had started with indifference, but as the discussion continued, the scowl on Mrs. Pickering's face deepened.

"I think we need a vote!" Mrs. Pickering insisted in a gruff tone, which shushed the entire table.

"A vote on what?" Chelsea asked.

"To make him"—she waved her hand dismissively in Luka's direction—"part of *this* committee. He's an outsider. Not one of us."

"That's not true, Mrs. Pickering. As I just explained, Luka is the elder vicar's son—"

"I know precisely who he is. We don't *need* a festival photographer. Every one of you has a mobile at the ready and can take photos at any moment of every day. Plus, we haven't even discussed how much he'll cost us."

Chelsea somehow, miraculously, managed to keep her tone calm and even. "Nothing at all. He's volunteering his services."

"Even so, I'm calling for a vote," Mrs. Pickering insisted. "You can't deny me that. It's in our committee's standing rules—which I helped to write."

Chelsea had hoped that her words to Mrs. Pickering the previous week had shamed her even a bit. But apparently, this woman knew no shame. Chelsea took in a sharp breath to dampen her frustration. She couldn't let Mrs. Pickering's negativity win. Plus, Chelsea was the chair. She was obligated to set the tone for the meeting. The members would be looking to her for guidance.

She removed her gaze from Mrs. Pickering and addressed the committee. "Well, I still believe I'm within my rights, as chair, to choose all the members of this committee. But Mrs. Pickering wants a vote. So let's give her a vote."

Chelsea hadn't thought this all the way through—it could go horribly wrong. She only hoped that her faith in this community would be proven. She skimmed their faces, praying they would come to the right conclusion.

"All in favor of Luka McKane, award-winning and world-renowned photographer, becoming a member of this committee and our official festival photographer, please raise a hand and state 'Aye.'"

She expected at least a split-second pause between her statement and the vote as some waited to see what others would do or even considered the lifelong repercussions of going against Mrs. Pickering. But she saw no hesitation. All hands around the table rose high instantly, with a sure and collective "Aye." All except one.

Chelsea beamed then confidently finished the process. "And those opposed?"

In her peripheral vision, Chelsea saw Mrs. Pickering's hand shoot upward.

"The motion carries. Overwhelmingly," Chelsea added, grasping Mrs. Pickering's gavel and cracking it on the table. "Moving on to our next order of business..."

NEARLY TWO HOURS LATER, Chelsea declared the meeting adjourned. They'd accomplished more that night than she'd imagined they would, and the members' eager participation made it clear that the excitement over the festival hadn't waned a single bit. If anything, it had increased, which only helped to bolster her own enthusiasm. She still had enough energy, she hoped, to push through to the end.

Gathering her belongings, she noticed that Mrs. Pickering had been the first to abandon the table, but everyone else lingered leisurely behind, clearing away cups and plates, chatting about each other's weeks, and moving chairs back where they belonged.

Luka walked toward Chelsea, one hand grasping the shoulder strap of his smaller camera bag. "Sorry I was late." He stood next to her at the head of the table. "I lost track of time, helping Mac with those sets. Did you get those photos I sent? I wasn't sure if they came through."

The same evening that Chelsea had handed him the notebook with Joy's interview notes, Luka had texted her two photos, a closeup shot of a barn owl and a spectacular sunset. Then he'd sent another photo the next morning of the stone bridge. When she received his texts, Chelsea had gotten an unexpected case of cold feet. They were too good—crisp, gorgeous, and vivid. She had fretted over finding the right language to describe or enhance them. *He's a professional. I'm not.*

"They came through." Her fingertips grazed the peacock journal's cover. "And I actually jotted down some ideas on a break today. But—"

"What?" He inched closer, staring down at the journal as she flipped toward the back pages.

"They're not that good," she warned. "I mean, they're just some brainstorming. Some scattered ideas. Nothing polished." She waved her hand across the pages dismissively.

"Here, let me see."

He shifted the journal toward him as they stood side by side, then he lifted it higher.

"I wasn't sure what you were looking for," she explained. "Or what you needed. This is probably way off track."

"No, it's not." He lowered the journal and peered down sideways at her, waiting until she made eye contact. "It's poetry, just like I'd hoped. Expected."

"You're sure?" She searched his face to be certain he wasn't only being nice, telling her what she'd wanted to hear.

"A hundred percent. It's exactly what I was looking for." Luka handed back the journal between them, his stare lingering.

"Chelsea?" Mary had walked over without either of them noticing. Luka politely stepped backward to make room. "Oh, I'm sorry, dear. I'm interrupting." Mary winced.

"No, it's fine," he said. "We were finishing up."

"I'm awfully glad you're on this committee," Mary told him. "Tune out the naysayers in this village. You have many supporters—trust me. I have my ear to the ground."

"Thanks for that." Luka turned back toward Chelsea. "I'll send you more photos tomorrow, Chels. Goodbye, Mrs. Cartwright."

"Good night, dear."

Chels. He hadn't called her that in years...

Mary clasped her hands together and offered a wistful smile. "Isn't it good to have Luka back in the village? Well, most of us feel that way. You certainly did a fine job with Mrs. Pickering, letting her know—with grace and kindness—that she was in the vast minority."

"I'm not sure how graceful I was or how kind. I just did what was right."

"Indeed. That young man has been through enough in his life. He should be welcomed back into the village—don't you agree? It's the Christian thing to accept people for who they are..." She frowned and searched the air. "You know, I don't even recall what suddenly drove him away, all those years ago, or what's kept him gone since then." Her eyes returned to Chelsea. "But it's nice to have him back in the fold. He seems... relaxed. Different than what I remember. Perhaps he's matured over the years. No longer that rebellious teenager..."

"Yes. Perhaps so."

"In any case, everyone deserves a second chance, don't they?"

LILTING PIANO MUSIC drifted out as Chelsea opened the heavy church door. She didn't recognize the melody. It had to be one of Rachel's original compositions.

Chelsea saw her friend at the front of the church, perched at the piano, with one hand in her lap and the other hovering above the keyboard as she thoughtfully tapped out notes, oblivious to everything but the music. Chelsea paused and gazed at the colorful stained-glass windows, savoring the notes echoing inside the walls—a moment of unexpected tranquility during another hectic weekday.

When the notes came to a sudden halt, Chelsea's eyes darted toward the piano. Rachel was staring straight at her, hand delicately poised.

"Sorry!" Chelsea walked down the aisle. "I was trying not to interrupt."

Rachel lowered both hands to her lap. "It's fine. You didn't. I was... dabbling."

"I love it when you dabble. That was beautiful. Is it new?" Chelsea approached the alcove that encased the piano and leaned against its wooden ledge.

Rachel moved back toward the keys to stroke them silently with her fingertips then lowered the piano's lid. "I guess. I wasn't really concentrating, just letting my fingers move." She swiveled on the bench, her long paisley skirt moving with her. "I shut off my phone for a bit. How did you know where to find me?"

"Michael told me. Well, he guessed this was where you'd be. He said you were... pensive tonight." Chelsea searched Rachel's face. "Is everything okay? You do look a bit lost in thought."

Rachel cupped both hands in her lap. "It's something I can't tell Michael. He wouldn't understand. It sort of... breaks our agreement."

"What agreement?"

"The one where we forget about adoption for now. But I can't forget. So every few weeks, I ring up the social worker to ask for any possible updates. She didn't have any this afternoon. She never does anymore."

"I'm sorry." Chelsea wished she could remove the pain in Rachel's eyes. "What can I do?"

"Nothing. Listening is enough. I guess we'll keep playing the waiting game. Maybe it's not meant to be."

"There's still time. It could happen."

Rachel made eye contact with Chelsea, tears forming, bottom lip quivering. "True, but if I raise my hopes even a little... well, that's more painful than anything. I have to keep telling myself it might never happen." She sucked in a breath and returned her gaze to her lap. "Maybe it's best that I rang her up today. I needed to hear it again. A reality check."

Chelsea inched forward, the ledge still between them, and set her open palm out toward Rachel. Without looking up, Rachel placed her hand inside her friend's with a gentle squeeze.

After a beat, Rachel lifted her hand to the corner of her eye to wipe a tear before it could fall. Then she forced a half smile and a brave face. "So, you came looking for me. Did you need something?"

"Nothing. I need nothing from you. I hadn't seen you in ages, hardly at all this week. And I missed you. I miss us."

"Me too."

Rachel rose from the piano bench and rounded the edge of the alcove to join Chelsea. They sat together on the first pew, settling onto the velvety tufted cushion.

"So." Rachel perked up. "How's school going?"

"Oh, fine. I'm buried under exam grading and lesson plans. How about you?"

"Busy too. But the pupils are good. A few of them are soaking things up like a sponge. Maybe I'm making *some* sort of impact."

"I know what you mean. It's hit-and-miss in my class. Teenagers are incredibly hard to gauge. And yanking them away from those mobiles and texting... the world's biggest challenge. They're so addicted to those devices."

"I'll bet. Well, at least the committee is going well. Great meeting last night—everyone in good spirits, participating."

"They've been so willing to help out."

"Including Luka?" Rachel gave a sideways glance. "I noticed the two of you afterward, shoulder to shoulder, peering down at something together."

Chelsea shifted in the pew. "I was showing him some ideas. He's putting together a coffee-table book of Chilton Crosse, and he's asked me to write up a few descriptions of his photos. He's also including a chapter on Joy Valentine."

"I didn't know any of this. And Michael never mentioned it. Hey, didn't you interview Joy once?"

"Good memory. Yes, and I gave my notes to Luka the other day."

"The other day? You've been seeing a lot of each other this week, then."

Chelsea flicked Rachel's arm. "Not like *that*."

"But you're not as stressed about him. I mean, the last time we spoke, you bristled at the mention of his name. Are you warming to him now?"

"I wouldn't go that far." Chelsea pictured Luka's face, realizing how easily the details of his features came to her. "I admit, I'm getting used to seeing him around the village. It doesn't startle me as much anymore. And Mary Cartwright said something last night that stuck with me. She was talking about Luka returning to the village and how he deserves a second chance. How we all do."

"A second chance? You still have feelings for him."

Instead of denying or confirming it outright, Chelsea decided to tell the messy truth. "It's complicated. I think it's mostly remnants of older feelings bubbling up. Sometimes, I get these sharp memories of those days, the two of us. But that's from years ago. I barely know him now, as an adult. I don't know where he's lived the last decade, who he's dated, what he's seen and done. I don't know very much about his life, like he doesn't know much about mine. We're still strangers, really." She took in a slow, deliberate breath and tried to pinpoint the truth. "Luka and I knew each other intensely for this concentrated amount of time back when we were teenagers. So these feelings—if we're calling them that—are in the past, and I need them to stay there. I can't go down that road again."

Rachel's expression softened. "I get it. I do. But... be careful not to dismiss your history so quickly. Don't underestimate the power of a first love. Michael was my first love, and I can't imagine being with anyone else. It doesn't matter how many years ago it happened for you and Luka—what you feel for him is still alive inside you, probably stronger than you think. And even though your feelings are from the past, you're experiencing them in the present, or else we wouldn't even be having this conversation. They're relevant right now. Aren't they?"

"What are you saying?" Chelsea tilted her head. "That I should actively explore this? Give him another chance? You *know* I can't—"

"But blocking out your feelings, pretending they don't have any power over you... that's probably not healthy either. They can come back to bite you. I guess I just want you to be real with yourself, even if it's uncomfortable. Or scary."

Chelsea sighed deeply. Rachel was only telling her what she already knew but hadn't come to grips with yet. "But there's no middle ground. It's either give in to my feelings or ignore them entirely. And the giving-in option is off the table. It's too dangerous. You know what he did when he left. He broke me."

"*Almost* broke you," Rachel corrected. "You pushed past it, made a good life for yourself."

"Okay, almost broke me. But I can't go through that again. I won't do it. His leaving changed the course of my life. We'd made plans... talked about getting married, starting a family. Not right away but in the distant future. I know we were only teenagers, but those dreams were real to us. Or at least, they were real to *me*. And in one night, Luka shattered all of them."

"I remember."

Chelsea's chest tightened as she remembered too. "He changed his mind and decided he didn't love me anymore. Or maybe he did but got cold feet at the end. Or maybe he never loved me in the first place. There's this enormous question mark that still hangs between us, tainting everything. And I can't seem to get past it." She shook her head. "So when you see us together these days, it's not what you think. On the surface, we might be cordial, but it doesn't mean I've forgotten how things ended or that I can ever trust him. Maybe he deserves a second chance with this village. But not with me, not with my heart. Rach, I can't ever be that vulnerable again—that daft."

"You weren't daft. You were in love, and it was real. I saw it with my own eyes. I wish I had answers for you, but even Michael doesn't know why Luka went away that night. Can you...?" Rachel peered at Chelsea. "Would you ever be comfortable asking Luka about it—now that so many years have passed?"

The very idea of actually talking to Luka about that final day brought a sharp, swift wave of panic. "No. I couldn't. Call it stubborn pride, but I would be completely humiliated if I let him know it still matters. Besides, what if I don't like his answer? He might confirm that it was all one-sided. Or that maybe I did something to make him stop loving me."

"You know that's not true."

"But that's what my teenage self was telling me. That I pushed him away or said something that made him leave. That it was my fault somehow."

Rachel leaned in for a tight hug and whispered, "I'm sorry I brought all this up. I didn't mean to open old wounds. You don't have to justify anything to me."

Chelsea nodded into Rachel's shoulder and closed her eyes. They pulled out of the hug, and Chelsea tucked a stray hair behind her ear. If Rachel had expected tears from Chelsea, she would be mistaken. Though it was hard admitting these painful truths, a part of

Chelsea was still far removed from it all, as though it were happening to someone else. Her emotions seemed to shift day to day, and sometimes she wasn't sure *what* she felt.

"I'll be fine. The reality is I still have to put up with Luka being in the village as long as he's here. I only hope that, when the book is finished, he'll go on his way, get back to his life, and I can get back to mine."

"Can I give you one piece of advice?"

"Of course."

"Yes, be careful. And yes, protect yourself. But I've watched you make progress with Luka lately—defending him to Mrs. Pickering, having friendly conversations with him. When I've read your body language the past couple of weeks, you've seemed happy. Buoyant. And part of it *might* be because of Luka. So make the best of things as they are, here and now, while he's around. Keep the door of your heart cracked open at least a smidge..."

"Okay. But only a smidge. I can't afford more than that."

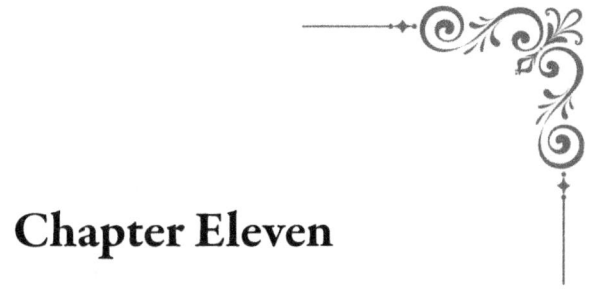

Chapter Eleven

My love, as it begins, shall so persevere. ~Shakespeare

"What's the most memorable location you've visited?" Mary Cartwright asked as she passed the new potatoes to Luka.

He accepted the bowl and pondered his answer. "Honduras was probably the most recent memorable one." He lifted four small potatoes onto his plate with the serving spoon. "But not in a positive way—it's incredibly unstable politically. Many people there are suffering. Those images will stay with me."

Luka hadn't planned on remaining for a meal at Mary and George's Mistletoe Cottage. He'd only meant to snap photos of Mary's handiwork with the festival's costumes—beaded and velvety and expertly made. But after he'd gotten what he needed with the photos, Mary had insisted on his staying, and he couldn't think of a single reason to refuse. A homecooked meal was too tempting.

"Honduras," Ben Granger said from across the table. He was another on-the-spot invitee of Mary's. "That's one of the countries listed on the Doctors Without Borders site."

Minutes before Luka sat down at the table, Ben had knocked at the cottage door, and Mary had let him inside with an embrace. She'd then introduced Ben proudly to Luka as "my nephew, the doctor," and the two men shared a firm handshake. Ben was near Luka's age, with dark-blue eyes, a clean-shaven look, and a tall, thin frame. Luka had noticed him around the village a couple of times, once at the pub and once near the church. Both times, Ben had seemed a bit lost in his own thoughts.

"Doctors Without Borders?" Mary repeated, staring hard across the table at Ben. "This is the first you've mentioned it. Isn't that a long-term commitment? And a dangerous one?"

Ben cut into his roast with his fork. "It can be. Depends on where you're sent. And the commitment time varies."

"Ben is a surgeon," Mary explained to Luka. "Our village is fortunate to have him as our doctor in residence." She returned to Ben. "But I was hoping it would be for longer than this. You've been here less than a year!"

For the first time since his arrival in the cottage, Ben grinned—just barely. He brought a forkful of roast to his lips. "Nothing's set in stone. I've only browsed online a bit."

"Well, that's a relief. More tea, dear?" Mary asked Luka, hand poised on the kettle.

"No, thank you." Luka's mobile buzzed inside his pocket. It would be rude to check it while at someone else's table, but he couldn't help himself. Besides, the meal was nearly finished. He reached down to tilt the screen, which revealed a text from Tristan: *Still stopping by?*

Because of Mary's unexpected invitation, Luka had lost track of time. He was nearly a half hour late to meet with Tristan about the website. Luka had wanted the text to be from Chelsea. They hadn't spoken in forty-eight hours, since the festival meeting, where they'd shared a quiet, intimate moment while poring over her descriptions of his photos. He'd left the church hall that evening filled with some measure of hope.

He pushed the mobile back into his pocket. "Sorry. I need to be going. I've got another appointment."

"Oh, gracious. I've made you late." Mary set her hand gently on Luka's wrist and patted it twice. "Let me package up a treat for you. I'll add in a portion for Mac. I've made some muffins..." She heaved herself out of the chair with some effort and moved toward the kitchen.

Luka assumed it was futile to protest, so he wiped his mouth with his napkin and peered across at George, Mary's husband, who chuckled through a bearded smile. "You realize this won't be your last invitation to a meal," he told Luka.

"That's all right by me. This was delicious."

"Thank you, dear." Mary had already reappeared with a firmly sealed Tupperware box. "You're welcome here anytime. And I'm glad you were able to meet Ben properly. Fortuitous timing."

After exchanging good nights, Luka made his way across the street toward the bakery, where Tristan was waiting after hours. Nearing the front door, Luka mused about how active he'd suddenly become in the village. Ever since Thursday's meeting, his mobile had lit up with texts and calls from shop owners and committee participants eager to have their photos taken behind the scenes.

It was all due to Chelsea. Had it not been for her enthusiasm and support, even in the face of Mrs. Pickering's dissent, Luka never would have been welcomed in the first place. Not this openly, at least. He thought back to the sullen circumstances, a mere fortnight ago, under which he'd first entered Chilton Crosse—the melancholy weather, the gathering of mourners, his father's open grave. That day, he'd intended to leave almost immediately, moving forward with his career and not looking back. The entire journey to Chilton Crosse was meant to be a momentary blip on the radar of his life. But he was becoming more ensconced in the villagers' lives and in their daily activities, even going as far as sharing meals in their homes. And the more they began to care about him, the more it became mutual.

Julia Bentley answered Luka's knock at the bakery door and opened it wide for him, inviting him in. If Tristan was miffed at Luka's tardy arrival, he wasn't showing it. He sat, laptop open, at a nearby table across from Mr. Bentley, who was reading a novel—some sort of Western, from the horse-centric cover.

Luka greeted them both, then took a seat as Julia walked up. "Anyone for brownies? They're warm."

"You have to ask?" Tristan winked. "I'll take two." Luka had heard that Tristan and Julia were newly dating, and it showed. Their affection for each other revealed itself in every sweet expression and subtle mannerism between them.

Mr. Bentley broke his attention from his paperback. "Brownies, did you say?"

"Yes, Dad. And a sugar-free batch just for you."

"She takes such good care of me," Mr. Bentley said.

"Luka?" Julia asked. "Brownie?"

"Sure, I'll take one." He didn't want to seem impolite by rejecting her offer—even though his stomach had already been filled to the brim.

As Julia went to retrieve the brownies, Mr. Bentley wagged his finger at Luka across the table. "Do you play poker, young man?"

Luka smiled at the random question being chucked his way. "I've been known to."

"Well, then, you should join our weekly poker nights here at the bakery." He tapped the table with his index finger. "*After* hours."

As Mr. Bentley returned contentedly to his novel, Tristan maneuvered his laptop to show Luka the festival's website. "I'm thinking of separate pages for each of these sections, but I'm not sure. Would a long page filled with random behind-the-scenes photos work better? Or should I organize them?"

Luka peered toward the screen. He knew nothing about advertising or websites, but Tristan seemed to value his opinion, which felt both refreshing and odd. Since Luka had been in a perpetual state of traveling for the past fifteen-ish years, he hadn't had time to form significant male friendships. His agent *sort of* counted—they would share the occasional chat about Todd's family life or Luka's background—but it was mostly business really.

"I think the random photos work well," Luka said as Tristan scrolled down.

Julia appeared again, this time with two plates of brownies—one for Tristan and Luka to share and the other for her father.

"Thanks, love," Tristan whispered, peering up at her.

Luka hadn't meant to, but he caught the tail end of Tristan finding Julia's free hand then bringing it up to his lips for a quick kiss. Looking away, Luka shook off a momentary prick of envy. So many times in Chelsea's presence, over the past couple of weeks, he'd wanted to do that very thing—to find her hand, kiss the tender surface of her skin, and express openly what he was feeling. He had worked hard to give her space and time to accept him again. But there were moments lately when he'd see a stray curl brush her jawline, and he would squelch the desire to reach up, stroke her cheek, and tuck the hair behind her delicate ear. Or he'd watch her fetch her coat and sense the urge to hold it steady for her so she could wriggle into it. And a few nights back, at the fork in the road, staring down at her face in the shadows and listening to her open up about her father, he had wanted to draw her in close, hold her tight, and feel her breath against his neck—to comfort her and let her comfort him too. And perhaps when they'd pulled out of the hug, she would have lingered and handed him the sign he'd been hoping for—that it was time to lean down and kiss her.

But these moments, all fantasy on his part, might never edge their way into actual reality. Luka knew there might come a day when he would conclude that Chelsea would never trust him again or let him in, no matter how long he stayed in the village.

Tristan handed the plate of brownies to Luka, breaking his thoughts.

"Thanks." Luka chose the square from the top then took a significant bite of the decadent chocolate.

ON HIS WAY TO MAC'S property, drowsy from a stomach full of roast beef, veg, a muffin, and *two* brownies, Luka heard something he hadn't expected—a screeching electric-saw noise that told him Mac was up late, working on the *Romeo and Juliet* sets. The light from the work shed confirmed it.

Luka had been pitching in with the sets whenever he was able, and it felt like the old days—Mac and Luka side by side, wordlessly toiling away on some project for the village. Back when Luka was a teenager, the act of working with his hands *and* with Mac had been completely therapeutic, an escape from his stifling home life at the vicarage or the frustration and boredom with school. Luka rounded the corner of the shed and laid his camera bag on a counter safely out of the way. Mac was bent over the electric saw and had finished trimming a long piece of lumber. He shut off the equipment and removed his safety goggles.

"Working late?" Luka asked.

"Aye. Feeling restless."

"Well, I've brought you something." Luka popped the lid off Mary's Tupperware, which held her muffins plus three brownies from Julia, and extended it toward Mac, who wiped his hands on a cloth, then selected a brownie off the top. "I had dinner at Mary and George's, then met with Tristan at the bakery."

"Busy days." Mac took a significant bite of the brownie.

"Ben Granger was at Mary's." Luka closed the Tupperware lid. "You've mentioned him before. He helped you last Christmas with the nativity set?"

"Aye." Mac finished off the brownie then took a long sip from a water bottle that sat nearby. Capping it, he added, "Ben's a good sort.

Smart. Making progress. It wasn't that way when he first came to the village. I think he still has a few demons from his past to rid himself of. But he'll make it—I've no doubt."

Luka wanted to know more. The lack of detail made Ben seem even more mysterious, if that were possible. But he didn't push further. Luka knew that was as much as he'd get from Mac.

"Can I help?" he asked, willing to push through his food-induced drowsiness to lend a hand.

"Nay, I'm finished for tonight." Mac perched on a nearby stool, crossing his arms. "Seems you're making some friends in the village. Quite the popular lad."

Luka chuckled. "I'm not sure 'popular' is quite the word for it, but yes. Something has definitely shifted. Aside from Mrs. Pickering, the villagers have been surprisingly welcoming. I think it's this project, the festival. It's sort of forced people to accept me, like it or not." He clicked his fingers. "Speaking of projects, I've been meaning to get your input about this..."

Luka retrieved his camera bag, which also contained Chelsea's notebook. He'd been carrying it with him everywhere, using the blank pages for his own scribbled notes as he asked individual villagers about Joy Valentine, hoping to fill in the information gaps and to prick people's memories. So far, the villagers had been quite forthcoming, eager to talk about Joy by spouting off tidbits of memories sprinkled with occasional gossip and speculation about her mysterious reclusive years. Luka wouldn't be including the gossip in his book, of course, but he'd jotted down the notes in front of the villagers all the same, out of politeness.

He found another stool in the shed's corner and brought it closer to sit across from Mac. "That coffee-table book I'm working on—my agent wants to include a chapter on Joy Valentine." Luka flipped through the notebook. "Chelsea gave me this a couple of days ago—a series of interviews she held with Joy back when Chelsea was a teenager. I did the math, and these interviews were Joy's last ones, right before she retreated into her cottage. Some of this stuff is really gripping." Luka found the page he was searching for and paused. "Here. Chelsea asks about her favorite childhood memories. Joy mentions her sister, starts to give this really vivid memory of a picnic at some place called Windermere, then stops short. Shuts down the interview." Unable to read Mac's stoic expression, Luka continued. "So now I'm carrying the notebook around with me, asking villagers about their own memories, trying to add more details for my book. A villagers' perspective. You were Joy's gardener for years, even when she was reclusive. Any memories you want to share?"

As he shifted the notebook on his knee, the photo of Joy came loose from the pages and drifted down to the concrete floor. Mac reached down to rescue it, and then he froze. Dusting the glossy side, he stared at the photo.

"She looks happy here." After a long, thoughtful moment, Mac handed the photo back then rubbed at his stubbly chin and stared down at the floor as Luka poised his pen. "Joy Valentine was a complex woman. Opinionated and temperamental one minute, compassionate and warm the next. But she was never anything but kind to me..." Mac paused. He recrossed his arms and squinted at Luka. "Off the record now, lad?"

Luka lifted an eyebrow, understood that Mac was serious, and closed the notebook. "Sure."

"It's time you knew."

Intrigued, Luka capped his pen and set his full attention on Mac.

"As you said, I was her gardener for many years." His Scottish r's trilled as he stepped backward in time, his gaze drifting beyond Luka through the open door, into the darkening night sky. "I was the only one who had contact with her when she... retreated. I would run errands for her, pick up her post, her groceries. She tried to pay me for it, but I wouldn't accept. I saw a woman in pain, and I was the only one she trusted. Over time, she let me in—into the cottage and into her life. We had coffee together nearly every day. She opened up, and I discovered the reason for her pain. I've never told a living soul and never will. But the event rocked her to the core. Once her admission came, a wall broke down between us and we... " Mac shifted on his stool. "We grew to love each other. Soul to soul."

Luka's lips parted. This was the last thing he'd ever expected to hear. *Mac was in love. With Joy Valentine.*

"I wanted to marry her, even knowing she would never leave that cottage. But she refused my proposal multiple times, saying she didn't want the villagers to see me only as the husband of the mysterious recluse. She was protecting me." The hint of a smile rounded the corner of Mac's lip. "You'd think our relationship would change or come to an end, since my proposals were rejected. But we went along our way, same as before, enjoying our time together until her passing. No one knew her the way I did."

"I had no idea," Luka whispered.

"Aye, no one does. Except the niece, Noelle."

"Why are you telling me this now?"

"You feel about Chelsea the way I did for Joy. 'Tis a timeless sort of love." Mac loosened his hand and pointed toward Luka's chest. "Sixteen years apart, and that fire is still there."

"True."

"The point is, son—this life, these years you have, they'll steamroll forward. Decades tumble into more decades. Looking backward, any day I spent with Joy was a good day. So whatever Chelsea is willing to give you now, accept it. Even if it's only a bit here and there. Even if it's not enough, it's something. It's everything. Better to live with her inside your life on her terms than to live without her at all."

The significant lump in Luka's throat wouldn't let him respond, so he nodded to make sure Mac knew he'd heard. Luka had experienced some form of this the past few days. He'd been gazing forward into his future to try to picture Chelsea absent from it. And he couldn't do it. The ache in his chest at the thought was too strong.

THE NEXT DAY, LUKA surprised Mac, and even himself, when he showed up on Mac's doorstep, dressed in trousers and a dark jacket, ready to attend Sunday-morning church. Luka hadn't been inside the building since he'd left Chilton Crosse. It had taken years for him to feel comfortable visiting *any* church after those tumultuous teenage years. Eventually, he began visiting both opulent cathedrals and rustic structures of worship during his photo shoots across the globe. As he observed worshipers in their element—mouthing earnest prayers with hands tightly clasped and rosaries kissed—Luka began to wonder how God fit into his own life.

Growing up, he'd only viewed this stern and faraway being through his father's eyes. Later, as an adult viewing human suffering across the globe, Luka's religious questions only expanded. But steadily over the years, through his lens, whenever Luka observed the smile of a child or the delicate feathers of a red-tailed hawk or the intricate design of a snowflake drifting from a vast gray sky, his belief in a Creator—an Almighty being—grew stronger and more certain than ever.

By the time he was ready to share his newfound faith with his father, he was unable to. He worried that his father might question his sincerity, make certain judgments, or even bring up past spiritual failures. But in the end, at his father's bedside, Luka was able to open up, hoping his father heard and understood. Luka often read him scripture from the Bible that lay permanently on the bedside table, the same familiar stories of faith his father had read to him as a child—David rising up to become Israel's king, Moses freeing his people from the slavery of Egypt, Daniel escaping the lion's den without a single scratch. In return, Luka would sometimes receive a nod from his father or a squeezing of his hand. Those had been comforting, poignant moments Luka would never forget.

"Don't you look dapper," Mac told Luka with a wry grin, stepping outside the cottage to join him.

"You don't look half-bad yourself. Thought I'd join you this morning."

"'Tis fine by me."

They walked toward the village together in silence, enjoying a crisp mid-September morning. The sun winked between branches as leaves dangled in the breeze. Luka wasn't sure what had made him wake up with a desire to visit the church. But he'd obeyed the desire and, after a refreshing shower, had put on the only suit that he'd brought back from his Bristol flat.

Mac and Luka were a couple of minutes late to the service, so they slipped into the back pew during Rachel's solo. As Luka settled in beside Mac, his attention moved to the organ, where Mary's nephew, Ben, sat at the keyboard, playing effortlessly. A man of many talents.

While the song continued, Luka scanned the building and took in all the familiar images from his teenage years—intricate stonework, stained glass portraying moments in Jesus's life, imposing decorative altar up front. None of it had changed in all those years. Well, his father was gone. That was a change.

Luka searched the backs of heads for a familiar brunette and found her almost immediately among the assorted hats and primped hair. Chelsea sat four rows from the front, eyes focused on her friend. Luka was glad she hadn't seen him enter the building. He wouldn't want to disturb her worshipful state of mind.

After a couple of communal hymns and prayers, Michael floated toward the podium in his full vicar's attire—distinguished neck collar, long black robe, thick Bible in hand. Luka had never heard his brother give a sermon and wondered whether Michael would emulate their father's gestures or mannerisms after all those years of watching him preach.

But Michael was his own man. His voice was gentler than their father's, meeker and kinder, yet the words in his sermon weren't sugarcoated. He spoke from Matthew 14, in which the disciple Peter walks on water to meet Jesus but then begins to sink as he loses his faith. Michael spoke of "keeping our eyes on the Savior" and "not being distracted by the world around us or by fear."

A fraction of Luka had always believed Michael had gone into the ministry, in part, to please their father—to preserve that favorite-son position. But watching his brother come into his own with a spiritual maturity and passion, Luka understood that Michael was always meant to be a vicar, and the choice had been all his own.

After the sermon and a parting hymn, Luka nudged Mac to see if he'd like to slip out before the rest of the crowd cleared, and Mac agreed. Luka would make a special point, sometime soon, to praise his brother and tell him how proud he was, but not when Michael was surrounded by villagers hungry for his attention. Luka was aware of how this part of the day went—the vicar would be swarmed by parishioners and lavished either with praise or with urgent requests for help and prayer. Luka would have his moment with Michael later. The same was true with Chelsea—church was a sacred time that Luka didn't need to disrupt. There would be other chances.

"A bite at the pub?" Mac suggested as they entered the sunshine again.

Luka agreed, and for the next hour, they enjoyed a leisurely meal at the coveted fireside table. Mac's quiet personality meant that he would only offer scant conversation during a meal, but Luka found that refreshing. After the past few days of heightened village activity, a silent meal after a reverent church service was what he needed most.

BACK AT THE COTTAGE, Luka reached inside his trouser pocket for his mobile—which he'd placed on silent mode during both the church service and the pub meal—and glanced at the screen to see a text from Chelsea, sent minutes before.

He sat on the edge of the bed and read the first line: *Tell me what you think about these.* Luka scrolled down and realized that the lengthy text contained two descriptions to go along with photos he'd sent a couple of days before—a picturesque stone cottage and a bright-yellow leaf on wet pavement.

He tried not to overanalyze her text and even decided not to send her an immediate response. He couldn't seem too eager. Every communication with Chelsea these days seemed delicate. He would tap out his reply—short and sweet—later in the day and hope it would be enough.

Chapter Twelve

I would not wish any companion in the world
but you. ~Shakespeare

With the crackling fire as a soothing backdrop to her task, Chelsea shifted her focus from textbook to notebook as she jotted down two more lines of a scene from *Romeo and Juliet*. Pleased with her progress, she grinned, eager to see what the pupils would do with this tomorrow.

During last week's lecture, seeing the pupils' boredom in their stifled yawns, Chelsea had come up with an idea on the spot. She paused her lecture midsentence, closed her book, and divided the pupils into groups. Then she assigned them four lines of Shakespearean text and had them translate the lines into modern English. She wasn't completely certain this would work. She expected them to mutter frustrations and give the exercise only their slimmest efforts. But five minutes in, she heard laughter bubbling up from one of the groups. Prepared to nudge them back on task, Chelsea glided over to the circle of desks and was gobsmacked to discover that the pupils were hard at work on the translation, bouncing words around until they came up with the right one.

A likely reason for the assignment's success was that Chelsea had encouraged modern-day slang as part of the translation. Shakespeare's "Go thither, and with unattainted eye, compare her face with some that I shall show, and I will make thee think thy swan a crow" had become "Go on, ya! Open your eyes so I can show you someone else. I'll make some fit girl look as ugly as a right munter."

Chelsea closed the textbook and reached for her lukewarm tea, nearly dropping it when a crack of thunder came out of nowhere. Socrates, who'd been snoring quietly beside her for the past two hours, jerked out of his dream and began barking at the air.

"It's okay, boy." Chelsea abandoned her tea to comfort him. "Only a bit of thunder."

As if to challenge her, the thunder cracked again, this time nearer by, and Chelsea suddenly recalled Mr. Bentley's weather forecast as he'd offered his plate of scone samples that morning before school. "Cold front coming tonight," he'd warned her.

She wondered why cold fronts always had to arrive with such nasty weather—warm air pockets hitting cold air pockets in a battle for ultimate dominance. Hearing the pelting of rain against the window, Chelsea remembered something else. Earlier, while eating at the kitchen table, she had raised a window to enjoy the lovely autumn breeze. But she had completely forgotten to close it.

Chelsea removed her thick blanket and wrapped it around Socrates's tiny white body to keep him warm and comforted. "Stay. I'll be right back."

She moved swiftly into the kitchen and saw raindrops already trickling through the open window, dripping down to the slate floor.

"Blast," Chelsea whispered through gritted teeth.

She rushed toward the window, placed her fingertips on the sash, and pushed down with all her might. Since her childhood days, this particular window was notorious for sticking. She had vivid memories of both her parents, at one time or another, struggling to close it. In fact, she had wanted Mac to fix it once and for all during the renovations but kept forgetting to ask him.

"Come *on*!" she pleaded as she gave it another try, risking more rain splashing against her face and jumper. But the tenacious window refused to budge.

Heart racing from her strenuous task, Chelsea noticed her mobile on the table. She grabbed it and retrieved Mac's number.

When the voicemail beeped, she tried to calm her tone and sound casual. "Hey, this is Chelsea." She ignored the rain, which was intensifying behind her, intruding into the cottage, and creating a fast-growing puddle on the floor. "I know this is a ridiculous reason to ring up, but I need your help. This window in the breakfast room is stuck, and it's raining... and water is pouring in. I can't close it. Could you please come by and give it a try for me?"

She clicked off, knowing Mac might not hear the voicemail for several minutes or even several hours, and decided on a Plan B. By that time, Socrates had shed his cozy blanket and joined her in the kitchen to see what all the ruckus was about.

"Stay back, boy," she warned him, gathering towels from a nearby hamper.

As she patted the wall and floor with towels, again getting sprayed with rain, Chelsea had an idea. She abandoned her task and went in search of the cling film in the kitchen drawer. It seemed like a barmy idea, but it was all she could think of—stretch the film tightly across the open window and secure it with... *tape?* But it would take time to go in search of packing tape strong enough to secure the window. It was somewhere in an upstairs craft drawer or maybe in the guest bedroom...

Holding the cling film's tube, Chelsea considered giving up. Though she tried never to use Michael as a stand-in husband during times like this, perhaps it was time to ring him up. This was quickly turning into a minor emergency.

A sharp rapping at the front door startled her.

"Mac!" She threw down the cling film and scooped up Socrates on her way to answer the door, wiping her dewy face with her sleeve.

She opened the door wide to see Luka running a hand through his damp hair. "Your window?"

"In the kitchen." She pointed backward.

Luka whisked past her in search of the problem. She slammed the door shut and followed him into the kitchen, where he'd already set down his toolbox and approached the window. Socrates trembled in her hands.

"It's okay, boy," she whispered, smoothing down his fur then kissing the top of his head.

Luka nudged the kitchen table aside with his hip and squared himself with the window as unrelenting rain sprayed his coat and jeans. Feet planted on top of the sopping-wet towels, he placed a hand firmly on each side of the sash, and with one decisive motion, pushed the window down. The rain was sealed out, the crisis over.

Chelsea had been holding her breath for the past few seconds, watching him work, hoping for success. When Luka turned to look at her, wiping his hands on his coat, he flashed her a smile—or maybe the smile was meant for Socrates. Thunder rumbled again, but this time it was farther in the distance.

"That should do it," he announced.

Chelsea marveled at how swift and easy the task had been for him. He probably could have done it one-handed but didn't want to show off. He wasn't even out of breath, the way Chelsea had been when she was struggling with that blasted window. She wondered why watching a man perform a simple task that she sometimes didn't have the physical strength to accomplish herself—close a stubborn window, open a tenacious jar lid, repair a flat tire—could be so incredibly appealing.

"I just... couldn't get it to budge," Chelsea explained, feeling suddenly foolish for having to ring up someone for a few seconds' worth of labor. *What else could I have done? Kept my pride intact while letting the kitchen flood?* And if Mr. Bentley's forecast was correct, the rain was expected to last throughout the night. She *had* needed help. There was no other option—and no shame in admitting it.

"Glad to help. Mac knew I was a couple of cottages down from here." Luka pointed behind him. "Electrical problem over at Mr. Carter's. I was finishing up when I got Mac's call."

Socrates squirmed in Chelsea's arms, and she set him down, expecting him to dart back into the warmth and safety of the living room. But he padded over to Luka instead and sniffed his wet work boots.

"Hey, boy." Luka bent down to let Socrates smell the back of his hand. "Adventurous night for you?"

While Luka was occupied, Chelsea returned to the window and added dry towels to the puddles. At least she could do something to contribute to the situation. Although she admired the specific help that a man could give, the other side of that coin was how uneasy she felt at being the helpless female in the room. Chelsea had lived alone much of her life and often took pride in doing things without a man—or anyone. And she didn't enjoy being obliged to Luka.

As she abandoned the towels to watch him straighten up from Socrates with a good-natured grin, though, she realized how overly sensitive she was being. *She* had been the one to ring for help, and she'd gotten it. Simple as that.

"In all the bluster, I forgot to thank you," she told Luka.

"Happy to help."

Attempting to shed the awkwardness of the moment, Chelsea shifted into manic-hostess mode. "You're soaked! Let me put the kettle on. Peel off your coat and go take a seat by the fire. I'll be there in a jiff." Cringing, she realized she sounded exactly like her mum—well, anybody's mum.

Luka didn't protest or say he had another job waiting, as she'd half expected. Instead, he headed toward the living room with Socrates at his heels. Performing menial tasks in the kitchen helped rid Chelsea of any lingering nerves. She moved about, swiftly filling the kettle, finding two cups, then adding a few top-quality biscuits to a plate. Luka's efforts had earned him a *proper* tea.

Her jumper was soaked, as well, she realized, so she removed it, thankful for the turtleneck underneath that wouldn't require a quick trip upstairs to change clothes. She gave her hair a gentle finger combing then entered the living room with her tray. She found Luka standing coatless by the fireside, open palms extended toward the flame. It was obvious he'd stoked it into a lovely blaze. Socrates nuzzled inside the blanket on the sofa while lightning flashed through a nearby window. As Chelsea set down the tray, Luka swiveled, his face covered in shadow. He took a seat near Socrates on the sofa, and Chelsea poured the tea, watching the nectar leave the spout in a lovely amber stream. She handed Luka the cup then poured herself one, added two sugars, then sat opposite him in the big cozy chair she'd purchased over the summer. It was originally meant to be her "reading" chair. The trouble was, she never had *time* to read, so the chair had instead become her grading-essays chair, her falling-asleep chair, and her catch-all-for-bits-and-bobs chair.

Curling her feet beneath her, she took a sip then pulled the quilt her mother had made firmly over her lap. "What a night," she said, breaking the silence. "It's still coming down out there." The raindrops splashed against the window, but instead of this being an alarming sound worthy of panicked calls and a scrambling for towels, it was welcoming and comforting.

"With more to come," Luka added.

Chelsea took a longer sip and tried to remember the last time Luka had been inside this cottage. He'd only visited once, the night her parents had invited him round to a meal. They'd spotted her with

Luka in the village the week before, hands locked together as they walked, and had questioned her later. She shrugged off the relationship as being casual—by that point, it was actually intense and all-consuming—but she didn't want her parents to know in case they disapproved. Her father's response was "Why don't you invite the lad to tea? I want to get to know him."

Grill him, more like...

At first Chelsea protested and made excuses, but then she figured, *Why not*? If Luka was willing to come, why not let her parents see in Luka what she had seen all those months—his quiet kindnesses, his dry sense of humor, his intelligence and thoughtfulness, the parts of him that few people knew existed. Perhaps some time spent together would alter her parents' misinformed view of him. And they might actually accept her and Luka as a couple.

But the tea did not go well, and it was the first and last one they all shared together. Chelsea struggled to keep the conversation flowing, but faced with Luka's unexpected shy streak—he seemed suddenly intimidated in the presence of a police constable—and her father's critical eye, she gave up trying and embraced the awkward silence and clank of silverware. She apologized to Luka afterward.

In response, he cupped her cheek gently and kissed her forehead. "It's okay," he told her. "We tried. They don't have to like me. We like each other, and that's what matters."

After that failed attempt at gaining her parents' approval, Chelsea had continued to downplay her relationship with Luka to them, seeing him mostly in secret to avoid village—and parental—speculation.

Luka cleared his throat, and Chelsea noticed that he was staring across at her.

"You seem lost in thought." He downed the last of his tea and set it aside.

"I'm thinking about this cottage. Old memories."

"That's been happening to me lately. Mostly with my dad."

Chelsea knew exactly what he meant. Shortly after her father had passed away, vivid memories would strike her at random times, lifting her out of the present moment and dropping her back into the past. She had little control over these memories, which had been a particularly cruel aspect of grief that she hadn't expected. Fortunately, they had lost some of their power over time, and that would eventually happen for Luka too.

When Luka didn't follow up on his comment about his father, Chelsea set down her tea, nestled into the quilt, and changed the subject entirely. "So, I'm ready for more of your book photos. If you want to send them." When Luka had responded so positively to her text descriptions from the day before, she'd gained confidence and found herself eager to try her hand at the next batch.

"I meant to text you several more last night, but things got busy. Mac had a couple of maintenance emergencies and left me working on the sets. I can text those proofs later tonight. And I should be able to go out for a shoot in the morning if weather permits. I'll visit Joy's old cottage, maybe the graveyard, and Mr. Elton's farm. My book needs some sheep in it."

"I'm jealous of you," Chelsea admitted.

"Why?"

"It's just... your lifestyle, your job. Making a career out of your art the way you've done. I mean, most people can't do that. And to travel the world, on top of it. You probably have loads of freedom in your schedule."

Luka shook his head and frowned. "It's not very glamorous—trust me. I spend more time in crowded airports and dank hotel rooms than anything else."

Chelsea played with a loose thread on the quilt. "Tell me about your life since leaving the village." Since the moment he'd stepped into the cemetery and leaned against that tree, she'd wanted to ask about his absent years. But she didn't want to hear the answers from Rachel or Mac or even Michael. She wanted to hear straight from Luka what had been important enough to pull him away from the village—and from her.

Shifting positions, and disturbing Socrates in the process, Luka stared at the fire. "Well, I went to work straightaway in Bristol, at a pub. Lived in a tiny flat with two other blokes and saved up enough money to take a photography class. The lecturer thought my work had promise, and I apprenticed for him. He set me up with my first job—a magazine advert for a toy company. Not what I was hoping for, but it was a start. I did a lot of adverts in those early days, then I got a break for a travel magazine, which got me my agent, Todd. After that, I did some work for news organizations, and things took off from there. It's been a good living. But it can also be really... isolating. Traveling alone, living alone. No roots, no home base. It's hard to maintain relationships."

Women, Chelsea translated, wondering about the string of them he'd likely left behind over the years.

"Almost sounds like you've soured on things."

Luka stretched his arms high then clasped his hands on top of his head. "Over time, I guess I have a bit. Maybe I just needed a break."

"Is that why you're staying here indefinitely?" She knew she was pushing but couldn't stop herself.

"Partly." Luka lowered his arms and crossed them over his chest. "It's surprised me, being here. I hadn't intended to stay."

His eyes rested on Chelsea, unblinking. The fire popped gently, having lost much of its earlier momentum, while rain continued to patter against the window. "Maybe I'm the one who's jealous of you."

"Me?" Chelsea said through a chuckle. "Living in this wee cottage, teaching distracted teenagers, and grading lengthy essays? Or managing a committee and dealing with Mrs. Pickering on a weekly basis? How could you possibly be jealous of that?"

"Well, the idea of it, at least. A place to call home."

"Maybe you're glamorizing *my* life now." She stared at him through the fire's glow. "Nobody's life is perfect."

"True enough. But you're happy here, aren't you?"

"I am. Finally." It was her turn to fill in the gaps of her time since they'd parted. "After university, in Bath, I took some pointless jobs where I felt useless and robotic. I wasn't making a real difference in anyone's life, my own included."

She almost said, "And then came George," but she held back. Chelsea was certain that Luka had received an earful from someone about her broken engagement—the humiliation of withdrawn invitations and returned wedding gifts while people buzzed and clamored for salacious details.

Those had been dark days. When Chelsea discovered the awful truth five days before the wedding—that she *knew* she could not marry George—she decided to meet with him face-to-face and answer all the hard questions. She couldn't send someone else to do her dirty work, and she couldn't take the cowardly way out with a quick note of vague explanation. She had to face the firing squad on her own.

So, scrounging up some final measure of courage, she knocked at George's front door with a trembling hand then sat on his sofa without looking him in the eye and told him the stark truth in quiet tones, hoping that, past that painful moment, her words might bring him closure someday: "I can't go through with the wedding. I love you, but not enough for marriage, for life. I'm so sorry." But even as she'd spoken the words and tried to answer his confusion with responses that might offer comfort or clarity, she'd realized nothing could soothe the jab of pain she had delivered. There was no good way to break someone's heart.

"Chelsea?" Luka had craned his neck to peer across at her.

She blinked away the painful memory. "What was I saying?"

"Pointless jobs."

"Right. Anyway, after floundering a bit, and then with my dad's passing, I felt lost. Like you're saying, no job that made me happy, no real place in the world. So I came back to the village, and the teaching position opened up. I took it, thinking I would hate it or be horrible at it, but I found out neither was true. When I look back, I guess it sort of fell into my lap—the cottage, the job. Funny, how your life takes shape over time. When I was younger, I didn't think my life would look anything like this. None of it was part of the plan."

Luka stared down at the table between them. "I think I'm responsible for part of that," he said softly. "There are things I regret. About how I left the village."

Chelsea's heart hammered faster. She might finally receive some answers.

"I know my leaving was really abrupt. And unexpected." He gave a lengthy pause. Then he added with a small shrug, "I was young and daft. And impetuous. I didn't know what I wanted from life, and I was itching to get out and explore the world. In any case, I'm... sorry about the way I took off. You never deserved that."

An apology. Well, that's something, at least.

But it was all he could seem to manage—the same broad, hollow clichés he'd handed her the night he went away, with no clarification. So nothing had really changed.

Chelsea could have prodded, putting Luka on the spot and making him explain further. He *had* opened the door for it, after all. But she couldn't find a way to ask the only question that mattered—"Did you ever really love me?"—without coming across as utterly pathetic. He had answered it by omission, though. By offering no clear-cut reason for leaving, he was telling her that he never truly loved her—at least, not enough to stay. He was sparing her feelings by being evasive.

Technology intruded rudely into Chelsea's thoughts, bringing her back to the here and now, as Luka's mobile jangled beside him. He retrieved the call too late—it had already gone to voicemail.

"Mac," he said, staring at the screen. "Probably putting me on another assignment. Busy night. I guess I'd better..."

He rose slowly as Chelsea tossed the quilt aside and stood to join him. "Your coat seems drier." She touched the material with her fingertips. Earlier, Luka had slung it over a chair near the fireplace.

Socrates gave an audible yawn from his spot on the sofa as Luka pushed his arms through the sleeves.

"And don't forget your tools," Chelsea said.

"Right."

As Luka went to retrieve them from the kitchen, Chelsea secured Socrates inside his blanket cocoon so that only his white head peeked through. When Luka reentered the room with his toolbox, she rounded the sofa to meet him at the front door. "Thanks for helping me out tonight. Can I pay you for it?"

"You already paid me in tea and biscuits. And good conversation."

Chelsea crossed her arms, not knowing how to respond. His hand was on the doorknob, ready to leave. But his body hadn't moved.

"I've enjoyed this, Chels." His voice was sonorous, lowered to a near whisper. "Spending time with you again."

She parted her lips to form an appropriate response, but before she could, Luka had already leaned in, brushing his scruffy cheek against her own. She closed her eyes as his lips pressed a slow kiss into the center of her cheek. He backed away without another glance, whispered a faint "Good night," then disappeared behind the door.

With the gentle weight of his kiss still fresh, Chelsea returned to her cozy chair and dwindling fire and replayed their conversation in her mind, specifically the part about the breakup. Then she thought about George again. She actually *had* been in Luka's shoes and knew what it felt to realize, from one moment to the next, that her love for someone wasn't as strong as she'd first believed. Chelsea had always assumed that Luka left Chilton Crosse that night without a single backward glance.

But what if his decision was just as excruciating as mine with George? Maybe breaking her heart hadn't been so easy after all.

Life was never as simple as *did* or *didn't*, *would* or *wouldn't*. Chelsea hadn't been inside Luka's head that fateful night, and she would apparently never receive a full or satisfying explanation for his exit. And she had to be okay with that. In the end, perhaps not knowing was actually more merciful.

Chapter Thirteen

Men at some time are masters of their fates. The fault... is not in our stars,

but in ourselves, that we are underlings. ~Shakespeare

Avoiding puddles on his way back to Mac's, Luka tried to ignore how cold he was. The rain had let up momentarily, but his clothes and hair were still damp from his recent outings—first to Mr. Carter's place, then to Chelsea's, then to the Indian restaurant for a refrigeration issue. It was a busy night.

But now, Luka had time to think about that kiss. He replayed it in his mind—the sudden impulse to lean in, the softness of Chelsea's cheek, the hint of floral perfume. In the moment it happened, he'd half expected her to stiffen or recoil or even nudge him away. But she hadn't. Instead of being buoyed by this reaction, Luka actually became deflated. That kiss represented sixteen years' worth of other kisses he and Chelsea should have been sharing.

Luka approached Mac's property and struggled to open the gate's latch, slick with rain, then trudged through the field toward the guest cottage. As the rain started up again, pelting his face, Luka pictured that life with Chelsea, the one they should have had together, in full, vivid detail—something he'd never let himself do before.

They would have traveled through Europe as planned, visiting the Louvre, the Tuscan countryside, and the Parthenon—two teenagers in love, experiencing the world together on a shoestring budget. After that, they would have returned to the UK to get married then lived in some tiny flat, with Chelsea starting university and Luka finding work. Would he still have taken those photography classes to become a professional? Doubtful, since it would have required heavy travel, and he wouldn't have wanted to be far from Chelsea. Maybe he could have worked for a studio, taking photos of weddings or graduation portraits. And maybe he and Chelsea would have had a family a few years later—a boy named Rupert and a girl named Emily. Rupert would have his father's dark eyes, and Emily would have her mother's dimples.

Luka reached the cottage and fiddled with the keys, dropping them in the process. He muttered a curse word, picked them up, and tried again. *This* was why he hadn't gone fully down that path of envisioning the road not taken—regret pulsed through every vein. The night he'd left Chilton Crosse, he had watched Chelsea's eyebrows crinkle in hurt and confusion and heard her ask questions he couldn't answer. That night had been a game changer of his own making. He had thought he knew the gravity of his decision then, but his eighteen-year-old self had no clue about the larger impact it would have—the permanent ache of anguish that would follow him for years into the future.

What if, what if, what if... Luka slammed the door behind him and dropped the toolbox to the floor, his hand cramped from carrying it all around the village, then walked through the pitch-dark living room, punctuated occasionally with flashes of lightning through the window.

He peeled off his sopping-wet coat then unbuttoned his flannel shirt, leaving them both crumpled on a chair in the corner of his bedroom. He plucked a clean towel from inside the wardrobe and buried his face inside it, breathing in the faint scent of lavender.

What good is regret now? It couldn't give him the do-over he craved with Chelsea. He couldn't step backward in time, face his teenage self squarely, and tell him, "Don't do this. There *is* a choice.

You don't see it now, but there is. Choose her. Choose Chelsea, no matter the cost."

Luka tousled his hair with the towel then moved down to dry his arms and torso. He didn't know how cold he'd been until he found himself shivering. He paused as he recalled the kiss again. Maybe it wasn't a do-over, but it was possibly a second chance to get it right. They'd wasted sixteen years, but Mac was spot on—what about the years still ahead? They hadn't been written in stone yet. There *was* hope. Luka had seen it in Chelsea's eyes, lit up by the fire's glow. He'd watched her relax, pick a loose thread on the quilt, and ask him questions about those years he'd spent without her. Something inside her still cared. Her efforts to offer him tea and biscuits had seemed more than just societal politeness—stronger than a thank-you for pushing down a window sash. She was offering him something else—a hopeful sign. A potential future. But maybe that was what Luka *wanted* to see and nothing more. Perhaps his mind was only tricking him into seeing a mirage.

The jangle of his mobile interrupted his musings. He pitched the towel onto the floor and walked to his coat, hoping to catch the call in time. His agent. Luka wasn't in the mood to talk shop, but maybe it would do him some good.

"Hey, Todd," he answered, trying to produce lightness in his tone.

"Luka! Glad you answered. I was gonna shoot you an email, but this deserves a call. I looked over those proofs you sent, of the village. The photos, the Joy Valentine stuff. It's incredible. I sent it off to the publisher this morning, and they loved it. Want to put a rush on it. They're pushing for an end-of-October submissions deadline, then it'll go straight into edits. I can send a contract your way this week."

That was not at all what Luka had expected—so much excitement about a project he'd half-heartedly pitched weeks earlier as an excuse to stay in the village. "Blimey. October." Luka rubbed his stubbled chin. "I suppose I could manage it." He thought of the festival and wondered whether Chelsea would be up to finishing her descriptions that quickly. He couldn't add any more pressure to her schedule. "I can't make promises, though. It has to be quality work."

"Of course. I'll let the publisher know you'll try. I think that's all he really wants. Go at your own pace. But make it fast."

"Thanks, mate. For everything."

Luka clicked off then chucked his mobile onto the bed. That was the second offer of interest he'd received that day. The other, earlier, had also been from Todd—a text that held a new opportunity for a photo shoot in Australia, one of the few places left on Luka's bucket list. He'd texted back a polite *Sorry, can't do it.* The shoot would fall too close to the festival, and he couldn't let Chelsea down. Not this time.

LUKA RAISED HIS FIST and tapped on the vicarage door then took a step backward to wait. After last night's storm, the Cotswold skies were pristine and clear, but the temperatures had plummeted significantly. He crossed his arms to stave off the cold.

The door opened, and Rachel emerged from the other side.

"Oh. I was expecting Michael."

"I live here, too, you know." Rachel smirked then backed away to let him pass through to the living room.

"I just... thought you'd be at school."

"Inset day," she explained, shutting the door. "Professional development. I've been in meetings all morning, but they let us go for the afternoon, to work on our classrooms. I'm getting some lunch before I head back."

Luka was surprised to receive this level of warmth and talkativeness from Rachel—it went well past their usual stilted formalities. From the beginning, many years back, theirs had always been a polite association built of nods and niceties and well-wishes. That was how in-laws often related, Luka assumed—reserved, slightly set apart, remaining on the fringes of each other's lives. Ever since he'd decided to stick around the village, Luka had feared his sister-in-law's reaction, knowing how close Rachel was to Chelsea and how protective they were of each other. But Luka was reading an unusual level of relaxation in Rachel's body language toward him. He wondered what had brought about the change.

"Michael texted me this morning," Luka said. "He mentioned Father's papers, getting them ready for the solicitor next week. I told him I'd help out. We were supposed to meet here. He's picking up some curry."

"Oh. Well, he didn't mention it to me. I guess he's running late." She rubbed her arms. "It's cold. Let's sit by the fire."

Luka followed her to the chairs near the fireplace and plopped down, holding his hands near the flame.

"How are you? I've barely seen you since you returned to the village." Rachel's eyes looked distant and tired.

Luka wondered how she was *really* doing, but he still wasn't comfortable enough with her to ask. "Yeah, I've kept busy. With the festival, the coffee-table book..."

"Chelsea mentioned it." Rachel crossed her legs and smoothed out her long skirt. "She said it's going to be really special. The book."

"I hope so. Her help has been inspiring. With the descriptions, I mean."

Rachel cast her gaze toward the fire. "It's bizarre, isn't it?" she asked the flame. "To have you both back here again, working together in Chilton Crosse." She made eye contact with Luka again. "Surreal, I guess, would be a better word for it."

"Surreal, definitely. At first, it was awkward. But lately, there's been a... shift in things between us. A slight one." He hoped he wasn't overstepping by inviting Rachel into this type of conversation. He wasn't asking her to switch loyalties, and he wasn't consciously fishing for confirmation of hope. But he wouldn't turn it away if she offered it.

Rachel recrossed her legs and settled back in the chair. "I know we never talk about this, about Chelsea. But maybe we should. She's my best friend in the whole world."

Luka imagined that Rachel was the one who had soothed Chelsea on the night he left, the one who had given her reassurance and comfort. He felt guilty and wanted to say so but couldn't form the words.

Rachel continued. "I only want the best for Chelsea. And for you. *Whatever* that ends up being between the two of you."

The open-mindedness of her response startled him. "I want the best for Chelsea too," Luka assured her. "Always."

The front door opened with a light thud, and Michael suddenly appeared. "Sorry I'm late." He juggled a briefcase and two bags of takeaway from the Indian restaurant. Seeing his wife with Luka, he paused. "Oh. I thought you were at school."

"I had an in-service day," she said with a tsk, pushing up from the chair. "I told you last night."

Luka joined her as they met Michael near the door, and Rachel relieved him of the bags. "I'll get some plates and silver for this. Soda to go with it?" she asked, looking back and forth between the brothers.

"Sure," Michael said.

Luka added, "Thanks," then Rachel headed for the kitchen.

Luka noticed a slight coldness pass between his brother and Rachel. They didn't seem as affectionate as they normally were. But then, he hadn't been around them enough in the last decade to determine what *normal* was for them as a couple. He'd missed a lot in the time he'd been gone.

"I've got the papers in a box somewhere," Michael muttered, setting down his briefcase on the sofa.

Luka could tell this would be an all-business lunch meeting on Michael's end of things. And if that was what Michael needed, that was what Luka would give him. Maybe someday, if the mood struck, Michael would open up and confide in him about how things were really going.

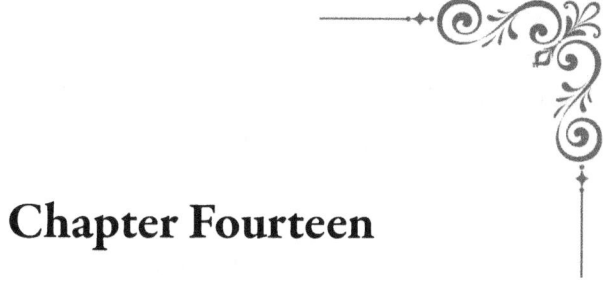

Chapter Fourteen

True happiness consists not in the multitude of friends,
but in the worth and choice. ~Ben Jonson

Chelsea knew from the start that it was a bad idea to keep her classroom blinds open to display the pristine sun-washed day outside while she tried to work. She'd managed to grade four essays before the lure of the outdoors became too powerful. She yearned for the sunshine and, against her better judgment, decided to pack up and take the papers home to grade later in the evening. She would spend the rest of the afternoon in her garden, jotting down notes for a new novel that had been swirling around in her head all week. Besides, the in-service day didn't *require* her to be at the school building that afternoon. It had only been a suggestion from the headmistress as she'd closed the final meeting.

Light and free, headed for the door, Chelsea heard her mobile ring. Wanting to ignore it, she instead set down her bag on the nearest desk and found the phone on its last ring. Chelsea answered Fred's call, hoping she wouldn't regret it.

"Chelsea. What a relief. Listen, I'm supposed to let Mac into the assembly hall—he's bringing the sets with him so my pupils can begin to assemble and paint them tonight. But I'm here in Bath, stuck at a doctor's appointment, and can't get there in time. I was hoping you'd use your key to let Mac in. He should be there soon."

"Sure, no trouble. I'm at the school right now, in fact, heading out. I'll make a detour in that direction."

"Wonderful. You've saved the day!"

Chelsea clicked off, gathered her bag again, and flipped off the lights, glad for this new distraction. She would technically be "working" but could still enjoy a lovely walk along the way.

CHELSEA TOOK HER TIME on the path toward the assembly hall, smiling up at the impossibly blue sky, squinting when her eyes drifted too near to the sun. Usually, with temperatures this brisk, she would be shivering and huddled into her coat, rushing toward her destination. But the beaming sun kept her warm, creating an odd hot-and-cold sensation on her cheeks. As her eyes skimmed the skyline, she noticed more leaves starting their autumn transformation. Deep burgundies, warm yellows, and dark browns had just begun to dot the landscape with some color and vibrancy.

Up ahead, she spotted Mac's flatbed lorry parked near the assembly hall's side entrance. Either Mac was early or she was late—she wasn't sure which. Chelsea sped up, feeling guilty about her leisurely walk, and returned to her original mission. Head down as she rushed, she flipped through her keys until she located the one Fred had handed her a couple of weeks before for such an occasion as this.

When she looked up again, she saw silver-haired Mac standing near the lorry beside Luka. She should have known he would be here too. He'd been aiding Mac with the sets for weeks. It made perfect sense that he would also help to deliver them.

Doing a swift mental checklist on her appearance—comfy jeans, burgundy coat, hair twisted up in a casual bun—Chelsea walked up to the lorry, making eye contact first with Mac. "Sorry. I just now got the call from Fred. He's been detained and asked me to come."

"No worries, lass." Mac dipped his cap toward her.

Chelsea offered a polite smile to Luka, which he reciprocated. She had wondered how it might feel, the first time seeing Luka after he'd leaned in to kiss her cheek at the cottage. But she didn't have much time to analyze it. Mac and Luka moved immediately into action, getting to work straightaway and unloading the sets.

Chelsea unlocked the building's side door—the quickest path for the sets to move from lorry to stage—and opened them wide. Next, she hunted for the panel to switch on the lights. She'd only seen Fred do this once, so she hoped she was doing it right. It took a few attempts to light the stage in time for Luka and Mac to bring in the first set—dozens of lumber pieces, expertly cut into various shapes and sizes.

"This is the balcony. Where do you need it?"

Chelsea stepped onto the stage and considered it. "Let's try over there." She pointed to the far end of the stage. "Fred didn't specify. And the set for the tomb scene could go over there, I guess." She pointed to the other end.

Weeks before, when Fred had suggested taking over the play's production, he'd told Chelsea about the new video projector designed to flash a photo or painting onto an enormous screen at center stage. Essentially, it would serve as the backdrop for individual scenes—the Italian countryside or the Capulets' fancy party or a starry night—which would save countless hours in manual labor, though he still wanted the two vital sets of balcony and tomb made the old-fashioned way. Fred was giddy about the new technology and had already trained his pupils to use the equipment. And though Chelsea was quietly skeptical about the play being Fred's guinea pig, she trusted his instincts. When she'd drummed up this idea of an abbreviated play weeks before, she'd had no idea that Fred—along with Mac and Luka—would treat it *this* seriously.

Mac and Luka set down the lumber then whisked past Chelsea to retrieve the rest of it, making several trips in the process. As the accumulated stacks grew larger and larger, Chelsea tried to envision the finished product. It was hard to do when all she could see were pieces of wood, unpainted and unassembled. Still, these sets made everything real for her—the play, the festival, and the group effort of the village. This was no longer only a collection of jotted-down ideas inside a peacock journal or a verbal brainstorming in a succession of meetings.

When all the lumber had been brought inside, Mac stretched his back and told Luka, "I'll take the lorry home. Need a lift?"

Luka shook his head. "I'll stick around to take some shots of the stage, pre-setup, for the website. I told Tristan I would." Luka moved toward his backpack perched at the edge of the stage. He must have brought it in during one of his trips from the lorry. It was never very far away.

Mac left the double doors open when he walked out, so the bright sunshine continued lighting up the side stage. Chelsea, in no particular hurry to leave, moved to center stage and peered out at all the vacant seats.

"This feels weird," she mused.

"What does?" Luka removed his camera from the backpack then came to stand near her.

"Being inside a huge space that's meant for a lot of people when it's only just us. Like we're trespassing. It's that way at school sometimes when the pupils aren't there, with all those empty desks. A sad ghost town... sort of soulless."

"That happened in church when I was in there with my dad on weekdays or with Michael. The space felt bigger without anyone else there. A little spooky."

"Exactly." Chelsea circled around toward the sets, imagining Sienna lavishly dressed in one of Mrs. Cartwright's gorgeous costume creations and delivering lines to Matthew. "This is still my favorite Shakespeare play, *Romeo and Juliet*."

"I actually prefer the history plays." Luka moved closer toward the future balcony set and snapped photos of the lumber. "*Richard III*, if I'm pressed."

Chelsea's eyes widened in Luka's direction.

He smirked. "What? Surprised I know my Shakespeare?"

"No. Well, maybe. I figure that nobody but us nerdy types read most of his plays. Beyond the preferred three they teach to everyone in school."

"There's a lot of downtime in my line of work. Long plane rides, layovers, sitting in the backs of cabs. A long time ago, I made a decision to use that time to do some reading—literature, history, science, even the Bible. Teach myself. Maybe it's old guilt over not going to university."

"Actually, you probably learned more that way because you *were* interested in it, without somebody forcing you to read it and be tested on it." She watched him take another few shots, this time of the empty seats. "I don't confess this often, but so many courses I took at university seem utterly pointless in hindsight. I'd love to go back and take some classes on my own—for me, not some degree."

"You should."

It was Chelsea's turn to smirk. "There's no time. Not now, anyway."

Luka lowered his camera. "There will be. Someday. Time seems to wax and wane, doesn't it? I mean, what you pictured as the next year of your life can become something entirely different." After a contemplative pause, he moved toward the side of the stage and squatted to return his camera to the backpack.

Chelsea moved to her own bag, close by, and pulled out the peacock journal. "I almost forgot..." She decided to get comfortable and joined him on the floor, sitting cross-legged. "I got sort of inspired last night."

They were near the open doors, and a cool breeze drifted inside. Chelsea inhaled deeply and smelled a hint of smoke from a fire burning somewhere far away. She flipped to the correct page then handed the journal to Luka as he sat down, one leg crossed, the other extended outward, with his knee almost touching hers.

"More descriptions?" he asked, browsing the entries.

"Yeah, several more. I was scrolling through the photos you sent last night and just started writing."

What she didn't tell him was the original source of her inspiration. A few minutes after Luka had left her cottage—after he'd kissed her cheek—she'd postponed her planned tasks of washing dishes, folding laundry, and checking on Socrates's water bowl in order to conduct some research. She used her phone to google *Luka McKane*, which she'd only done once or twice in the past several years. She discovered his official photography website and spent over an hour scrolling through photo after photo of Luka's work—colorful exotic birds, vibrant sunsets, slim women balancing jugs of water on their heads, sailboats poised on a vast ocean. They were remarkable, all of them. How amazing, for her to view so literally what someone else's vision of the world was in a particular moment. Every angle, every color, every image she saw—they were what Luka had been experiencing all those years, permanently recorded. She was seeing his world through his eyes.

Serendipitously, right when she had finished her "research," Luka texted the photos he'd promised to send. Seeing the first one—a horse standing stately in a field, practically posing for the camera—Chelsea grabbed her journal to write down ideas. She hadn't planned on penning more than a couple of entries, but once she'd started, she couldn't stop. By the time she had scrolled through Luka's last photo almost two hours later, there were twelve entries, finished.

Luka scanned the final journal entry then looked across at Chelsea. "You weren't kidding. These were inspired."

"But are they any good? Be honest. I finished them so fast, and I haven't had a chance to make any edits..."

"They're great." He closed the journal and squinted slightly. "It's almost like you're standing over my shoulder as I'm taking the photos. You're describing exactly what I experience in the moment."

"Well, your photos are easy to describe. They're beautiful."

A shadow of humility covered Luka's face as he handed over the journal. He grasped his raised knee with both hands, clearly in no hurry to get up and leave.

"I'll make some edits and type them up for you," she offered.

"It's ironic timing, actually. I talked to my agent last night. He says there's a publisher eager to put these into print. A contract is being sent."

"Seriously? That fast?"

"Apparently, they want the photos—and descriptions—as soon as I can send them. But I didn't want to pressure you or put a timetable on this, so I told Todd I'd do my best."

"Well, we're twelve ahead now. How many more does he need?"

"I don't think there's a set number. I actually took a few dozen more shots all around the village early this morning, which I need to sort through. Add in the festival photos, and we're getting pretty close. I need to reorganize all the proofs and put them into sections. And then there's the Joy chapter that still needs polishing. Lots of work ahead."

Chelsea shifted the journal in her hands. "Well, I'll do whatever I can to help. It's a worthy project. And you don't want the publisher to lose interest."

"Right. As long as I can keep Todd happy, we'll be good. But the festival comes first. And this." He pointed back toward the unassembled sets.

Instead of feeling the typical hefty weight on her shoulders at the thought of more work ahead, Chelsea felt oddly invigorated and excited about *all* the worthy projects coming into her life. They were offering a strong sense of purpose.

"Thanks for helping with the sets. I mean, that's not exactly part of your job description as festival photographer."

Luka shrugged. "I like using my hands. Reminds me of years ago, working with Mac. I missed those days but didn't realize how much until now."

"I know what you mean."

Chapter Fifteen

Time stays long enough for anyone who will use it.
~Leonardo da Vinci

Chelsea dusted sandwich crumbs into the bin then set her plate near the sink. It was the first time in two days that her stomach could tolerate anything besides soup and crackers. She'd spent the entire past weekend tucked inside her cottage, sleeping the days away and nursing some sort of stomach virus she'd likely picked up from one of her pupils. But her mum had a different theory.

"Your immune system is down," she'd told Chelsea on an earlier call. "You need more rest and good nutrition."

At least the virus had been merciful, leaving her weekdays alone. She couldn't afford to miss a single school day. She had managed to trudge to work this morning, still weak but gaining strength throughout the day, too busy to be ill.

Socrates whined at her from the kitchen corner. She found a soft toy then bent down to tempt him with it. He had clearly known something was wrong with her over the weekend, as he spent the majority of his time curled up on her bed or leaning against her on the sofa.

When her mobile buzzed from the kitchen table, she gave his head a regretful pat. "Sorry, boy."

She drew close to the phone to see a text from Luka: *Need your input. I'm at the bakery. Can you stop by?*

179

She hadn't seen Luka since last Thursday, at the committee meeting, and even then, they hadn't had a chance to speak. Frank immediately pulled her aside afterward to ask a question that required a lengthy response. In her peripheral vision, Chelsea noticed Luka slipping out the door to leave. He'd sent her a couple of photo texts over the weekend, but she'd been too ill to respond.

She stared up at the kitchen clock with a flower pattern that her mother had purchased during Chelsea's childhood, the one she still couldn't bear to part with. It was 7:10.

"Weird. The bakery's closed," she told Socrates.

Now? she texted to Luka.

Yes, he responded.

The only reason Luka might be at the bakery after hours was to see Tristan—who practically lived at the bakery these days because of Julia—in order to do some work on the festival's website. They obviously needed her input in person. Otherwise, they would be doing all this by a group text. It had to be important.

Chelsea hadn't intended to leave the cottage that evening and, in fact, had hoped for an early bedtime. But after having a satisfying meal and feeling significantly stronger, she thought, *Why not?*

She texted: *Be there soon.*

Luka's response was positively baffling: *Use secret knock. 2 raps, pause, 2 more raps. I'll explain when you get here.*

She read the text twice and shook her head, amused by all the mystery. Chelsea tossed the toy to Socrates. "Later, I promise," she told him, then fetched her keys and paused at the hallway mirror. She didn't have time to run upstairs and freshen her makeup after a long workday, so she pinched her cheeks lightly, pressed her lips together, then combed her side-swept fringe with her fingers. It would have to do. She pulled on a thickish coat—the autumn evenings had become chillier with each night—and headed toward the bakery.

The whole village took on a different hue in the darkness of evening. The sky was studded with stars, the breeze moved through trees with a soothing *shush*, and occasional streetlamps glowed yellow, guiding her steps along the cobblestones of the nearly abandoned high street.

By the time she reached the bakery, Chelsea had already forgotten the secret knock and had to double-check Luka's text. Feeling ridiculous, she rapped twice on the heavy door, waited, then rapped twice again, wondering if this was some sort of ruse. But within seconds, the door flew open, and there stood Luka, waving her inside with a bright smile. He shut the door then offered to take her coat.

As she wriggled out of it, Chelsea realized there was a party going on. Big band music drifted through speakers, the scent of cinnamon hung in the air, and a group of men—Mr. Bentley, Tristan, Michael, and Mac—were gathered at the center table.

"Chelsea! Welcome!" they said in unison. Julia waved, too, from behind the bakery's counter.

"What's all this?" Chelsea asked Luka, waving back hesitantly as he coaxed her farther into the room.

"Poker night!" He beamed like a little kid.

"I've heard of this... but I thought it was an urban legend."

Luka paused in front of her and peered down with an apologetic wince. "We need another player—we're used to having six. Are you up for it?"

So this had nothing at all to do with the festival or the committee or the website. It was merely a game night she'd been invited to, spur of the moment. No ruse at all.

Chelsea lowered her voice again, and Luka leaned in to hear her. "Um, I'm the only female here. It seems this is an all-boys event..."

Luka scoffed. "Not true. Women are always welcome. In fact, the wives have been invited, but they're not usually interested. Plus, it's only my second time here, so you're not the only newbie in the room."

"Okay, then. Count me in."

Luka smiled even wider and grasped her hand to lead her toward the men. Julia was approaching at the same time, with a plate of something delicious for the group.

"I usually sit in," she told Chelsea, "but I can't tonight. Busy prepping for tomorrow. You'll have fun." She set the treats on the table.

"She said yes," Luka announced, offering Chelsea the seat next to his.

Michael sat on her other side, still wearing his vicar's collar but seeming relaxed and content as he helped Chelsea drape her coat across the back of her chair.

"Go easy on me," Chelsea told them, watching Mac expertly shuffle the deck across from her.

"You can watch the first couple of hands," Luka said. "Five-card draw. I'll show you some tricks."

Chelsea suppressed a grin and scooted closer to the table as Mac began to deal. During the first game, Luka guided her through the process, explaining the basics, shuffling methodically through his own cards, and telling her why he was discarding the three of hearts and ten of diamonds.

"I'm hoping for a straight," he said as he accepted a card from Mac.

Each time he made a move, Luka would lean backward from the table and whisper his strategy straight into her ear. His breath tickled her neck, his low tone resonating softly. Luka actually won that round, much to the chagrin of the others, who chucked their cards onto the table with mock frustration.

Luka scooped up the chips he'd won and explained, "These are basically worthless. The night's winner gets a white-elephant gift brought by the last week's winner."

Mr. Bentley shuffled this time, his ninety-year-old hands surprisingly nimble, then dealt the cards. When he came round to Luka, Chelsea scooted her chair closer to the table and apart from Luka. "I'd like my own, please," she told Mr. Bentley. "I'm ready to give it a try."

Luka raised an eyebrow as he stacked some chips for Chelsea and placed them in front of her. On the first deal, she held two kings. She couldn't believe her luck. But she quietly sighed then frowned at the cards.

"Need some help?" Luka asked.

"No, I'll have a go on my own, thanks."

The round played out, additional cards were dealt, and chips were pitched into the table's center. Michael was the first to fold, then Mac, then Luka. In the end, Chelsea and Mr. Bentley squared off. Together, they showed their hands. Chelsea had a full house, while Mr. Bentley had a straight.

The men examined the cards, and a hearty shout went up as they congratulated Chelsea, who could finally relax her face into a broad smile. She stood up and scooped the chips gingerly toward her.

"Blimey." Luka watched her stack them up. "You're a quick study!"

By that point, the cheers had quieted, and Chelsea was handed the stack of cards to deal. She shuffled the deck, her fingers remembering how, and threw a side glance in Luka's direction. "Confession time. I played at university during study breaks. I became rather good."

Luka dipped his head and chuckled. "*Why* would I be daft enough to assume you didn't know how to play just because...?"

"I'm female?" Chelsea snickered. "It's fine. Poker's still considered a man's game, so it's an easy assumption. But there's a lot you still don't know about me." She bit the corner of her lip to hide a smile then ticked through the cards with her fingernails as she shuffled.

"Apparently so," Luka said with a lift in his voice.

Chelsea continued to win, losing only a couple of hands to Mac and Mr. Bentley. In the end, she'd won enough rounds to be called the winner of the night.

Mr. Bentley tipped his cap from across the table. "Well deserved."

"Here's your prize." Luka reached behind his chair to retrieve a shoddily wrapped parcel with gaping holes and half-taped corners.

"Um, thanks?" She poked her finger inside one of the corners and ripped open the gift to reveal a beautiful mantelpiece clock with gold trim and a decorative face. "This isn't a white elephant." She turned it over to look for the flaw, expecting a piece or two to fall off in her hands.

"Well, it's broken," Luka admitted. "It doesn't tell time."

"Ahh. You shouldn't have." She lowered the clock into her lap and crumpled up the paper.

"Chelsea, you are welcome at my poker table anytime," Mr. Bentley said, stacking the cards and gathering the chips, indicating that the night was coming to a close. "A worthy opponent."

"Thank you—that's really kind. But with rehearsals and this festival, I'm not sure I can make it very often. Maybe when things settle down..."

The men began to rise up from the table, clearing throats, yawning, and talking among themselves as they moved chairs back into place and exchanged goodbyes.

"Here." Luka held out Chelsea's coat as she stood.

"Thanks." She set down the clock then slipped her hands inside her coat sleeves.

Unlike some women, Chelsea had never been offended by traditional male gestures such as opening doors, helping with coats, or pulling out chairs. Her father had often performed these small, kind tasks for her mother, so for Chelsea, it was natural. She always took them as a sign of politeness on the part of the male, not an admission of weakness on the female's part. If that made her old-fashioned, so be it.

By then, everyone else had already filtered out—Michael had left after the prize was handed to Chelsea, and Mac had discreetly exited during the past couple of minutes without anyone noticing. Tristan, of course, stayed behind to spend more time with Julia. Chelsea and Luka waved good night then walked together into the chilled air.

"Beautiful evening," Luka noted, craning his neck for a look at the stars.

"It is." Chelsea held her broken clock close to her chest as they settled into an easy pace down the high street.

Luka nodded toward the clock. "I can repair that for you. Or maybe Mac could give it a go."

"This sounds weird, but I want it to stay the same as it is. I've *earned* this broken clock. Repairing it would be sacrilegious somehow."

Luka chuckled. "Well, if you feel that strongly about it..."

"I do."

The street ended at the church. When they reached the two paths—one heading toward Chelsea's cottage, and the other heading the opposite way, toward Mac's property—they paused to face each other.

"Thanks for including me tonight. I had fun," Chelsea said.

"I'll bet you did. Winning nearly every game *would* be fun."

She fidgeted with the clock then looked up at Luka. "Oh—but winning this means I'm providing the prize for next week?"

"If you can't make it, somebody else will take over. I think Julia keeps a stash of white-elephant gifts around in case someone forgets." Luka scratched at his beard. "Actually, I have a confession to make. I think I invited you tonight for selfish reasons."

"What do you mean?"

"I haven't talked to you much lately, not since Mac and I carried in the sets last week. And when Tristan said we needed another player tonight, you were my first choice. It was mostly an excuse to make sure you weren't avoiding me. Or that I hadn't said something daft to make you pull away. I thought we were... getting to a good place. Or a better one than when I first arrived."

Chelsea wondered how much of her face he could see in the shadows. There was only one streetlamp nearby, beaming behind her. "We were. We are. I wasn't avoiding you. I've been under the weather with some sort of stomach virus. I even had to bow out of the play rehearsal this afternoon. I still didn't feel up to it. But I'm improving—had some sleep and a real meal, finally."

Luka frowned. "You should've told me. I could've brought you some food over, helped out."

"I was trying to avoid everyone in case I was contagious. I managed. Socrates looked out for me. And I'm much improved, as you can see." She made a *ta-dah* motion with her free hand.

"That's good. I know you can't afford to be ill right now."

"True. Too many people depending on me." A pause lengthened between them as Chelsea stared down at the shadow pooled around her feet. "Well, I'd better go. Early day tomorrow." She started to pivot but paused. "One question for you first."

"What?"

She squinted up at him. "You didn't... *let* me win that final hand tonight, did you?"

"Chels. You know me better than that. I'm a huge competitor. Remember the darts games?"

She did. When they were teenagers, Luka had set up a dartboard inside Mac's barn, and she'd asked him to teach her how to play since she was too young to be inside the pub for a game. He would plant his feet near hers as she leaned back against his chest, then he'd grasp her right hand and poise the dart, offering gentle instructions. That was her favorite part. It took several weeks of practice, but she finally got better at it. "Don't ever let me win," she told him once after a losing game. "I'm serious. If I win, I want it to be genuine, all on my own. Not a fake win. Promise me." And he had promised. Soon after, they began to set wagers, and the stakes grew higher and higher. She would beat him occasionally, but he won most of the games—which told her he was keeping his promise. The rare wins had been sweeter anyway.

"I mean, I can be chivalrous," Luka said, "but I'm not *that* chivalrous. You won tonight fair and square."

"Good to know."

She caught his grin before he swiveled in the other direction. "'Night!" he called backward as he walked away.

INSIDE THE COTTAGE, Chelsea removed her coat, said hello to Socrates, then walked promptly to the fireplace mantel and placed the broken clock in the center. She adjusted it, stepped back, adjusted it once more, and was satisfied. She liked that it didn't tell time—that it was frozen *in* time. *Ironically perfect.*

Chapter Sixteen

He who possesses most must be most afraid of loss.
~Leonardo da Vinci

"Mrs. Pickering, I'm fully aware that the festival is less than two weeks away." Chelsea nudged her cottage door open with her hip, struggling to keep the mobile against her ear as she passed through.

"By now," Mrs. Pickering lectured through the phone, "you should have a detailed daily agenda that you send to all the members! Contacting them one-on-one, sporadically, is not good enough."

"I had planned to send out an agenda this very evening," Chelsea lied. "Be assured that everything *is* under control."

She refused to be a Mrs. Pickering, micromanaging the villagers and bothering them with daily agendas and updates—especially when they were the ones keeping *her* apprised most of the time. With the small exception of the advertising posters, which hadn't yet come in, Chelsea felt wholly confident that everyone was on task and on time. She wasn't going to let Mrs. Pickering fill her with unnecessary panic.

"What about the banners? Who's going to string those up between the shops? And when?"

Chelsea didn't have the energy or desire to sift through her peacock journal and locate that exact information, so she skimmed it from the top of her memory. "Mac and Adam have volunteered. The banners will be displayed at the end of this week." *I hope.* "Mrs. Pickering? I think I'm losing you... my phone is cutting out. I'll see you at this week's meeting—"

She clicked off before Mrs. Pickering had a chance to object. She knew it was evil to fake a dropped call, but sometimes, it was the only way to shut the woman up.

Chelsea tossed her mobile onto the sofa and set down her canvas bag—the one containing stacks of essays and literature quizzes—then kicked the door closed. She unclenched her fingers from around the plastic bag of takeaway she'd bought after school and moved toward the kitchen, grumbling, "Food. I need food."

Scrumptious scents rose from an open hole at the top of the bag—a hearty cottage pie and a side of chips. The protein bar she'd scarfed down during her too-short lunch break hadn't been enough to sustain her the rest of her workday. Her appetite had fully returned, and all she could focus on was the heady scent of beef and potatoes.

Socrates usually ambled along from somewhere in the cottage to greet her at the front door, but she realized he was noticeably absent.

"Socrates? Here, boy! Where are you?"

She rounded the kitchen corner and caught sight of his white paws underneath the table. A highly unusual place for him to nap.

"What are you doing under *there*, silly bugger?"

She set the takeaway on the table then knelt down in her skirt to pet Socrates. His watery eyes blinked up at her, but he didn't even try to move. He remained on his side, panting heavily. His tail gave two short wags.

"What's wrong?" She reached out, almost afraid to touch him.

She let her eyes roam the floor and noticed that his food bowl in the corner was completely untouched. He usually took his time eating throughout the day, but he always finished his portion and licked it clean by the time Chelsea got home.

Panicked, she knelt farther down and touched his fur. "Hey, boy. What's going on? What's happened?"

He remained lethargic, letting Chelsea's hand roam over his little body, checking for obvious signs of an injury. She found nothing. "Is it something you ate?" she asked, touching his abdomen, which contracted sharply as the pants continued.

Then she remembered. *The rawhide.* She'd given him a treat before leaving for work, purchased at the market a few days before. The bone had seemed harmless enough, and Socrates had leapt with pure excitement when she'd unwrapped it, waved it to let him sniff it, then dropped it before leaving the cottage. She couldn't recall the last time she'd given him a rawhide, but at Mrs. Pickering's shop, she'd seen the cute picture of a Westie on the package and bought it on impulse.

Keeping her hand on Socrates's panting chest, she checked the floor for other ominous signs and saw them—small circles where the dog had vomited and, in the corner of the room, a half-eaten rawhide.

Heart in her throat, she told Socrates in a calm, reassuring voice, "I'll be right back," then raced into the living room for her phone.

In the year and a half since she'd been in charge of her parents' dog, she'd taken him to the local vet a couple of times for vaccines and checkups. Dr. Renfro's contact info was on her mobile, easily accessible. After three rings, his secretary picked up.

"Cindy. This is Chelsea Barrett. Socrates is sick. Lethargic, vomiting, no appetite. It's short notice, but can I bring him in to see Dr. Renfro?"

"Yes, of course. We'll make time. I'll let Dr. Renfro know."

It only took minutes for Chelsea to retrieve the crate, pad it with a fresh towel, and carefully lift Socrates into her arms. "It's okay, boy. We'll get you all better. I promise." He blinked in response while she placed him gingerly into the crate.

Chelsea scrambled to get out the door in a rush without jarring him. She headed to her car, placed Socrates into the passenger side, and buckled him in, receiving a lick on the finger through the crate's door. When she tried to start the car, it wouldn't respond.

"Come *on*..." she begged the engine, realizing, even as she tried again and again, that the battery had died. Though she rarely used the car—she could walk everywhere in Chilton Crosse—she was usually diligent about driving it every few days to keep it running well. But with her busy schedule lately, she couldn't recall the last time she'd climbed inside it.

She found her phone again and rang Rachel. No answer. Then she tried Michael and got his voicemail. Finally, she rang Mac, her last resort. *Success.*

"Mac, I hate to ask you, but is there any way you could lend me your car or even your lorry? Just for an hour or so. My car won't start, and my dog is sick. I need to take him to Dr. Renfro." His office wasn't a simple walk away—it was located near a neighboring Cotswold village, centrally located to serve the farm animals and pets in the surrounding five villages.

"Sure, lass. Hold tight."

Minutes later, poised to remove the crate from the passenger seat, Chelsea heard the lorry. As it drew closer, she saw Luka in the driver's seat. It was becoming an obvious pattern lately. *Call Mac, and Luka arrives instead.*

Luka hopped out of the lorry after bringing it to a squealing halt. "I'll drive, if that helps. I know the way." He opened the passenger door.

Chelsea hadn't asked Mac for a driver, too, but Luka stood there, eager to offer help, and she would take it. *No time to waste.* Besides, she was much too shaky to drive—Socrates had begun to whimper inside the crate. She needed to get him immediate help.

She thanked Luka, handing him the crate as he whispered, "Hey, little man!" Then she hoisted herself up into the lorry's passenger seat. Luka passed the crate back to her, and she set it on her lap.

Luka entered the driver's side and shifted into gear without saying a word. He must have sensed that Chelsea wasn't in the mood to talk, which allowed her to focus on Socrates.

Soon, their destination came into view—an old farmhouse in the middle of the countryside at the end of a dusty lane. Dr. Renfro lived in one half of the house, while his vet office and exam rooms occupied the other half. Luka was already at Chelsea's side by the time she'd fiddled with the seatbelt and reached for the door handle. He took the crate from her with care.

When she'd stepped out of the lorry, Luka handed her back the crate then walked a few steps ahead to open the door to the farmhouse and let her enter.

Cindy rushed toward Chelsea. "I'll get the doctor." She disappeared into a nearby hallway and reappeared a moment later. "Come this way."

Chelsea followed through, leaving Luka behind in the waiting room. Dr. Renfro, a fiftysomething man with salt-and-pepper hair, took the crate from Chelsea and set it on a stainless-steel table. As he opened the door to coax the dog out, Chelsea described the awful details—Socrates's lethargy, lack of appetite, and vomiting, all probably from the rawhide bone she'd stupidly given him that morning.

The doctor eased Socrates onto the table while his assistant, Melanie, came to his side. Chelsea watched as Dr. Renfro pressed on Socrates's abdomen then listened for a heartbeat after examining his eyes, ears, and throat.

"The fact that he's vomited is a good sign," Dr. Renfro said, his voice calm and even. Chelsea assumed this was the professional don't-alarm-the-worried-pet-parent tone he used with all his patients. "But he's dehydrated." He looped the stethoscope around his neck. "Let's do some bloodwork, get more information. It'll only take about a half hour if you want to wait." He tickled Socrates's neck, but the dog barely blinked in response.

"I do," Chelsea said.

Luka stood when she entered the waiting room, and suddenly, she was very glad not to be alone. Half an hour of one's life could sometimes stretch into an eternity, especially when test results were at stake. She didn't want to trudge through those minutes all by herself.

She told Luka about the bloodwork as he returned to his seat and patted the one beside him. Again, he seemed to sense that she didn't want to talk. He patiently scrolled on his phone while she flipped through a magazine and let her eyes blur the words. She couldn't have cared less about how to give a puppy his first bath, but the article helped her pass the time well enough.

Finally, the doctor appeared again, smoothing out his white coat, wearing the same unreadable expression as before. Chelsea rose to her feet, and Luka followed suit.

"How is he?" she asked.

"The lab work shows a significant spike in his white blood cell count, so we'll put him on antibiotics. Because he's also dehydrated, as I suspected, we'll give him IV fluids too. We need to keep him one night at least, probably two. Based on what you told me, I suspect he was allergic to an ingredient in the rawhide. But we can never know for sure."

"Will he be all right?" Chelsea asked.

"Well, normally, dogs can rebound rapidly from this sort of thing. And you've brought him in a timely manner, which is good. But Socrates is... how old?"

"Eleven."

"Yes, eleven. So his immune system isn't as strong as a younger dog's would be." The doctor cleared his throat. "I can't pretend it's not serious. But stay hopeful. I'll ring you with updates. For now, he's in good hands, and we're doing all we can."

He ended his statement with a firm nod. Sometime during the doctor's prognosis, Luka had placed his hand around Chelsea's shoulder.

When Luka drove her back to the cottage, she didn't know what to do with her hands. She'd been too used to carrying the crate around like a carton of eggs. She clasped her palms together and peered out the window until her familiar cottage lane appeared.

When the lorry came to a halt, Chelsea opened the door to set her feet on the ground, the weight of the entire day meeting at the center of her soles. The sun had already begun to set, counting down the minutes until evening. She shivered, realizing the temperatures had already dropped significantly. She hadn't thought to wear a coat.

Luka shut off the engine and met her around the front of the lorry. "You okay?" He came closer, removing his own coat to swaddle her shoulders.

"I guess." But the tears splashing down both her cheeks told a different story as she clung to the lapels with both hands.

Luka leaned forward then brought her close to his chest. She didn't resist. The tears continued to fall as she buried her cheek into his neck. She squeezed her eyelids tight as Luka stroked the back of her head.

"He's so helpless." She didn't even know if Luka could hear her muffled voice. "I've never seen him that way. I didn't know what to do."

"You did everything right." Luka's voice reverberated deep in his chest.

She pushed gently away to look him in the eye. "But I'm the reason he's sick. I gave him that rawhide this morning."

Luka tilted his head then raised his hand to wipe her cheek. "It was an accident, Chels. How could you have known?"

"I've been distracted lately. I *should've* known. I should have read the label. Or watched Socrates more carefully. But I ran off to school this morning in a rush, like I always do, scrambling to move to the next thing on my blasted agenda. Always too busy..." Her eyes drifted past Luka's shoulder, toward her cottage. "I guess... I feel responsible because I'm the one taking care of him now. No one else. And because..." She gazed back up at Luka.

"What?"

"This sounds a little barmy, but that dog is the last thing I have left of my father. I didn't realize it until today." Her voice grew shaky, but she continued. "My dad named him, took care of him, led him on walks, fed him scraps under the table for all those years. And then it became *my* job."

"That's not as barmy as you think." Luka touched Chelsea's forehead and swept a strand of hair away from her eyes. "Let me show you something." He took a step backward and removed his wallet from his jeans pocket. He searched inside then produced a card, sandwiching it between two fingers. "Last week, Michael gave me one of Father's old Bibles. When I was thumbing through it, this yellow card fell out. It was a note from one of my teachers from when I was a boy, maybe eight or nine." He flipped the card to read it. "'Luka is a diligent young man with extremely high potential.' Maybe my dad was only using the card as a temporary bookmark, but finding it last week, I chose to assume it was significant, wedged inside his Bible for years, not just chucked out." Luka shook his head and looked out into the dusky sky. "It was probably the last time he was ever proud of me for anything." He placed the folded card back inside his wallet. "I'm keeping it here and will probably always carry it next to me—a reminder that, at least once in my life, my father was proud of me." Moving his wallet to his back pocket, he grinned. "So if you're barmy, then that makes me a little barmy too."

"You're trying to make me feel better."

"Did it work?"

He'd told Chelsea something he probably hadn't told anyone else, exposing himself to mockery, in order to comfort her. And for the first time since Luka had arrived in Chilton Crosse, she experienced an overwhelming desire to press her lips to his in a kiss. *Gratitude or affection?* She wasn't sure. In the moment, they felt like the same thing.

Startled by her sudden urge, Chelsea removed his coat from her shoulders. "It did work. Thank you. You've been such a help today. Really."

He took the coat and gave a small nod. "Let me know how he does—Socrates."

"I will."

As Chelsea drifted up the path toward the front door, she heard Luka add, "Sweet dreams," and she smiled to herself.

INSIDE, THE COTTAGE was quiet as a tomb, no beating heart inside it except her own. Socrates wasn't a particularly loud or raucous dog—he rarely barked, and when he did, it came out in raspy, punctuated woofs. But knowing he was in another place, frightened and hooked up to IVs while possibly fighting for his life, Chelsea didn't have the energy to do what she needed to do. She couldn't face tidying up after him, making dinner—the takeaway she'd left on the table was surely ruined—grading papers, and heading to bed.

Instead, she walked the few steps to the sofa, lifted a blanket, and folded herself into the cushions with a long sigh.

"THIS IS FANTASTIC NEWS. How did you manage it?" Chelsea asked, pausing in the road, gripping her mobile.

"Adam has a university friend who became a professional archer years ago," Noelle explained. "Or a 'bowman,' I think you Brits call it. And he attends lots of festivals, puts on a display, shows off his technique. Adam phoned him weeks ago, and he was all booked up. But it seems a gap has opened in his schedule, and he can fit us in."

"This will be perfect for the festival." Chelsea picked up her pace again as she approached the church hall. "And the children will love it. I'll contact the manor's owners, see if they'd be willing to provide the venue for the bowman. Their spacious front gardens would be ideal." Chelsea made a strong mental note to ring up the manor after the festival meeting.

"Great idea. And I'll give the bowman your contact info so you can speak to him directly."

"Okay. See you in a bit."

Chelsea clicked off and mused over her week as she continued her walk. Aside from the festival and her teaching—both coming along unusually well—Chelsea had spent the last two days fretting over Socrates's condition and feeling helpless. In the time since she'd taken him to Dr. Renfro's office, she'd only received sporadic updates from Melanie—"Still lethargic, no appetite. We need to run more tests."

Chelsea had even made a visit to see him the day before. She'd been bracing for the sight of her sweet, frightened puffball hooked up to IVs and monitors. But a wag of the tail when he saw her offered her some hope. She whispered soothing words as she stroked his fur, and in that moment, it became crystal clear to Chelsea that this wasn't her mum's dog or even her dad's anymore. This was *her* dog. They were a team, and she wanted him to pull through for her, not for anyone else.

Before leaving, Chelsea had kissed his paw then promised to visit again the next day. Dr. Renfro had said she could swing by after hours for another visit. Fortunately, Mac had been sneaky and replaced her car battery while she was in class, so that Chelsea wouldn't need to lean on anyone for transportation.

Nearing the church hall, Chelsea noticed that nearly every leaf on certain trees along the path had turned either a brilliant crimson or gold. *Beautiful.* She felt her mobile buzz again, and a gust of cold wind whipped her hair near her face, blocking her vision of the screen as she answered. "Hello?"

"Chelsea? It's Dr. Renfro."

Panic shot through her as she halted in the road. She hadn't expected another call from him yet. "How is Socrates?"

"Very well. In fact, that's why I'm ringing you. We took him off the IVs this morning, and he's eaten his first solid food and kept it down this afternoon. And his blood-cell count is back to normal. You can take him home this evening. He's turned a corner, and the crisis, it seems, is over."

Chelsea smiled into the wind. "Such a relief! I've been really worried."

"I must admit, he surprised me today with his rebound. Your visit yesterday must've done him some good."

After she thanked him and clicked off, Chelsea's first thought was how relieved Luka would be too. Since he'd be attending the meeting, she could tell him in person.

She spent a few seconds texting her mother that Socrates was out of the woods then proceeded toward the church hall doors. Inside, Mrs. Pickering had already taken her place near the head of the table, and Rachel was helping Julia arrange the plates and napkins at the refreshments table. Over the next several minutes, the members entered the hall, retrieved their refreshments, and settled in at the table, ready to begin.

But Luka's chair at the opposite end remained empty. They would have to start without him. Chelsea rattled off her announcements then opened up the meeting to the various subcommittees.

Mary reported that her team of seamstress volunteers had already completed the play's costumes and had begun costumes for the madrigal singers, who would make their way around High Street, singing Renaissance-flavored songs during the festival. Holly recounted her decorating efforts—all the orders had been delivered, and everything was on schedule. Mrs. Clementine affirmed that the children's puppet show was coming together, and Fred informed them that the *Romeo and Juliet* sets had been completed and rehearsals were running smoothly. Noelle made her announcement about having confirmed an archery display at the festival.

Even Joe made a rare appearance. He was usually too busy running the pub and taking care of his pregnant wife, Lizzie, to attend. He told the group, "We've decided on turkey legs, if that's okay."

Chelsea peered around the table for consensus. "Fine by me, but why the change?"

Joe shook his head. "Maybe it's her new motherly instinct, but Lizzie says that roasting a whole pig outside the pub will scare the children. Give them nightmares."

Chelsea pictured the grizzly image of an entire deceased pig rotating on a spit over an open flame and was in total agreement. "Good thinking."

The door opened unexpectedly, and Luka stepped inside then moved toward the empty chair. "Sorry. Working on the stalls, lost track of time." He wore Chelsea's most favorite leather coat, and his hair was particularly windblown. He might as well have stepped off the cover of a romance novel. Chelsea hadn't seen him since she'd experienced the unsettling impulse to kiss him.

She flicked away the memory. "No worries. How are they coming along?" Duncan Newbury had insisted on purchasing weatherproof stalls for all future village activities, so rather than having to repair or construct stalls left over from the last village fete, Luka and Mac would simply be learning how to assemble the new ones.

"The delivery arrived today, so Mac and I are inspecting them before we move them to the barn for storage," Luka said. "If anyone wants to keep their old stall, they can. But we're planning on breaking them down. Mac wants to use them for firewood at the festival bonfire."

"Brilliant idea," someone commented.

When it was clear Luka had finished with his update, Chelsea said, "Well, I've been working on a possibility for a few weeks. I didn't want to mention it in case things didn't work out. But this afternoon, I spoke with Mr. Elton, and he confirmed it. His grandson from Kent is available, which means—we *will* have a falcon for the festival."

The members emitted happy gasps.

"I need to confirm it," Chelsea added, "but I'm hoping the owners of Chatsworth Manor will be open to hosting both the falconry and the archery displays on their property."

"Good." Mrs. Pickering nodded firmly. "It wouldn't be a Renaissance fair without a falcon."

Chelsea was unaware of this particular adage. She was glad, at least, that Mrs. Pickering was pleased with the news. Chelsea had finally done something right.

WHEN THE LONGER-THAN-usual meeting ended, the participants gathered up their plates and cups, pushed back chairs, and exited together. But Luka waited behind and appeared at Chelsea's side as she placed her journal and other notes into her tote bag.

"Good meeting." He brushed his arm against hers. "Is that why you're smiling?"

She hadn't realized she was. "Actually, there's another reason. I got a call from Dr. Renfro right before the meeting started."

"Good news?"

"The best possible. Socrates is out of the woods."

"Excellent! I knew he'd make it."

"Did you? I wasn't sure," she admitted. "I've been bracing myself all day for the worst, walking on pins and needles. But I can bring him home. Right now, in fact."

"Need some company? Mac's given me a free evening. And the lorry's parked round the corner."

Half of Chelsea's brain thought an instant *No*. But the other half pushed through with a hesitant *Why not*, and it won out by the slimmest of margins. For whatever reason, Luka's company felt particularly welcome that evening.

THE DRIVE TO THE VET was decidedly different from the one two days before. The solemn, stifling quiet inside the lorry's cab as Chelsea had carried the crate on her knees was replaced by eager conversation, animated and bright. Chelsea chattered on about the falcon and archery additions, Sienna's beautifully heartbreaking version of Juliet—Chelsea had accidentally eavesdropped on her rehearsing behind the school building—and Luka's coffee-table book.

"I might be able to squeeze in a couple of hours this weekend to help with the Joy section," Chelsea told Luka.

"I'll take you up on that. I need a fresh eye. I'm rubbish at the organization side of things."

Chelsea cracked the window to let a hint of crisp air into the cab. It swirled around her face, touched her cheeks, and lifted her hair.

"You look happy," Luka said.

Moving her attention back inside the cab, Chelsea watched through the dashboard lights' reflection as Luka balanced his hand casually on the steering wheel while his eyes darted between her and the road ahead.

"I am. Today feels like a good day."

AT THE VET'S, CHELSEA paid the hefty bill then listened eagerly to Dr. Renfro's instructions as he held a prescription bottle between them then dropped it into a bag. "Finish out these medications and the special food—it's good for his digestion—then gradually reintroduce his normal diet."

When the doctor disappeared, she waited impatiently as the assistant retrieved Socrates. When she saw the wet black nose poking through the crate's wires, a smile stretched across Chelsea's entire face. "There you are! My sweet boy..." She took him from the assistant and heard his tail thump wildly inside the crate.

The drive back to Chilton Crosse seemed only a flash of time as Chelsea talked to Socrates through the crate's air holes, knowing full well she would get little accomplished that night besides coddling him and making sure his every need, great or small, was met. After this week's unexpected trauma, he needed some serious pampering.

Luka pulled up to Nightingale Cottage and parked the lorry then rounded the vehicle to open the door for Chelsea. He unburdened her of the crate, giving her the space she needed to hop down from her seat and snatch her bags. "I'll bring him in," Luka offered, and Chelsea at first wondered if he was angling for an invitation to stay for tea. But the lorry's engine was still running, so likely not.

Inside, when he'd set down the crate on the slate floor, she thanked him. "I seem to be saying that a lot lately. Thanks for pushing down my stubborn kitchen window, thanks for lending me a ride when my battery died... and now this."

"No need," Luka said. "Look at what you've done for me—writing all those photo descriptions, substituting at the poker game, giving me the photographer spot for the festival. People are looking at me differently in the village from how they used to—well, most of them. Because of you."

"I don't think I can take credit for that. But let's say we're even."

"Deal." Luka paused, holding her gaze, then gave a goodbye nod. He backed through the cottage door and closed it behind him with a quiet click.

Socrates whined from inside the crate, and Chelsea's full attention bounced back toward him. As she crouched to click open the gate, he sniffed her fingertips then moved hesitantly forward into her open hands, finally settling there with one last whimper. Chelsea leaned backward to sit then crossed her legs and held Socrates close.

"You're safe now. Welcome home."

Chapter Seventeen

For love, thou know'st, is full
of jealousy. ~William Shakespeare

Luka plodded toward the village center, wishing there was enough time to go back and fetch his coat, but he was already running late. He pulled his sleeves down to his wrists as he pivoted toward the far strip of shops on High Street. He was headed to Mary Cartwright's cottage to take photos of the final fitting of some madrigal costumes.

Six weeks before, on his shoot in Belize for a travel magazine, Luka would never have imagined that he would be living in a quaint but dilapidated old cottage—no airplanes or hotels or exotic locations in sight—with a fairly predictable schedule, his days practically mapped out for him. And even more, he would never have imagined *liking* it.

These days, Luka could easily appreciate the comfort in a routine, the appeal of staying in one place, and the contentment of day-to-day familiarity. Still, he occasionally sensed that familiar pinch of restlessness deep inside. *Wanderlust.* During those brief moments, he contemplated the future and wondered whether he could actually be content staying in a place like Chilton Crosse for the long haul, having predictable days, giving up his traveling lifestyle for good. He knew the answer. With Chelsea, he could. They could be happy here together—if she would only let them.

Halfway down the row of shops, Luka heard a laugh with a familiar lilt around the edges. Slowing, he craned his neck to the other side of the street and saw Chelsea emerging from the gift shop. But she wasn't alone. A lithe man with ginger hair held the door open for her, then they both paused on the pavement.

Luka faced the nearest shop, his back toward Chelsea, still able to see her image across the street inside the shop window's reflection. She looked up at the man as he spoke and leaned into him slightly then touched his sleeve. She laughed again, softer this time.

Their entire exchange lasted less than a minute. Luka wished he could hear every word between them. But he was too far away, frozen in place and hoping she wouldn't spot him.

A tap on the glass drew him out of his thoughts. It came from a little girl inside, trying to get his attention. He didn't realize he'd been gazing steadily at the window of a ladies' boutique shop with two mannequins inside, posed and wearing flowered dresses. Feeling sheepish, he waved at the girl then took a firm step in the direction of Mary's cottage.

Along the way, he slowed his pace, not caring anymore about his tardiness. His thoughts were on this ginger-haired man. Chelsea's ease with him—either friendliness or flirtation—had told Luka that they already knew each other. It wasn't their first meeting. He searched his memory to figure out where in the village he'd already seen the man and remembered one of the early *Romeo and Juliet* rehearsals. He'd been seated in the front row, likely the father of a pupil.

From the looks of him—the short, neat cut of his hair, the necktie, the self-effacing demeanor—Luka determined that he was probably a nice, respectable man, the conservative type who had never cheated on his taxes or strayed in a relationship or cut off another car in traffic. The kind of man who would buy a woman roses for no particular reason or lift an umbrella over her head while his own head got soaked. The type to stay happily in one place and never feel the itch to wander—a man who would provide security and unwavering commitment. He was the type of man Chelsea deserved.

If Luka let his insecurities get the best of him, he might very well take the easy way out and hop on a plane to escape. He knew he was capable of it. And Chelsea knew it too.

THE NEXT MORNING, LUKA awoke in a melancholy mood, uncertain if the overcast skies were the reason or if something bigger might be to blame. Most people probably would have chosen a light, happy task to dissipate the mood, but not Luka. He needed to feed it, to acknowledge it. So he shut the door of his cottage and headed toward the cemetery.

He expected to be alone, but as he threaded his way between the various headstones, he spotted a figure sitting near his father's gravesite. It was Michael.

Luka considered turning back—Michael hadn't seen him yet—but decided to press on. Perhaps his brother needed a bit of company. And perhaps Luka did too.

As he drew nearer, he could see Michael's lips moving, mumbling toward the still-fresh plot where their father lay far beneath. When Luka paused, his brother looked up, squinting. The skies were gray but still held a strong brightness behind the clouds.

"Oh. Hi. I came to see the new headstone." Michael plucked a blade of grass then shook his head. "That's not true. I came for a chat. With Father."

"Should I go?"

"No. Stay."

Luka took the couple of steps to the other side of the grave and sat across from Michael. "It's nice." Luka used his index finger to trace his father's name on the headstone, newly engraved. "The lettering, I mean. And Proverbs 3:5..."

"His favorite scripture. 'Trust in the Lord with all thine heart, and lean not unto thine own understanding.'"

"So, what were you chatting about with Father?"

Michael shrugged and made eye contact across the grave. "Lots of things, I guess. I don't know if *chat* is really the right word. I come out here sometimes for solitude, to clear my head. And then I find myself talking to the air. I'm not sure if I'm talking to Father specifically."

"It's a peaceful place for that sort of thing." Luka heard withering leaves trembling on a tree nearby.

Michael drew his attention back to the blade of grass he'd rolled between his thumb and finger. "I've delivered dozens of eulogies, sat at bedsides of dying parishioners. I've comforted the loved ones as they grieved. But *this* death..." He flicked the gnarled blade of grass onto the grave. "It makes me think about specific things in my own life."

"Such as?" Luka's hesitant voice nearly disappeared into the wind.

"Mortality. And immortality. The importance of family. What it all means." His eyes held palpable pain. "I'm a failure, Luka."

"How can you say that? You have a wife you love, a village full of people who adore you and look up to you, and a career you're obviously meant to be in."

"I'm lucky, I know. And my job is satisfying most days. But as far as my marriage goes, I'm failing Rachel every day."

Luka cocked his head and waited through the uncomfortable seconds of silence, watching Michael ponder the air and search for the words to explain.

"I haven't mentioned this, but... we've been trying to start a family. For years, actually. Rachel's had three miscarriages."

"Blimey. I'm sorry. I had no idea."

"Nobody did. We've kept it private, even from Father. We put on a good show for everyone else—which is frighteningly easy to do. Stay busy, be active, do God's work around the village, pretend you're not in pain."

"But it isn't *your* failure, Michael. Or Rachel's."

"I'm not really speaking biologically. Every single day in this village, I have the precise words to comfort people. It's almost innate. When they've got financial burdens, when they've lost someone, when a couple is headed for divorce, I never struggle to find the words—they flow easily in those situations. But when it's my own wife, when it's her burden and her loss... *our* loss... well, I haven't a single clue what to say. Words fail me around her. And it's affected the marriage over time. I've stopped trying—I've pushed Rachel away, and she knows it. She's pulled away too. I don't even know if she's in love with me anymore. I think she only tolerates me."

"That can't be true."

"It's mostly obvious when we're alone, when there are no distractions—in those quiet dinners we have, just the two of us. Or our bedtime routines when we barely speak anymore except a cursory 'good night' before clicking off the light. We're strangers, Luka. I'm afraid we've lost a closeness that we'll never get back. I can sense this widening gap, with a bridge between us that neither one is willing to cross, to set things right."

Luka shifted, uncomfortable with being suddenly thrust into the role of counselor and comforter. He was ill-equipped to do this, especially since he had no wife and no glimmer of possibility for children in the near future. But he had to try. His brother was in pain.

"At least there *is* a bridge. There's clearly something there, holding you two together, or else you wouldn't be sitting here, beating yourself up about it. Do you love her?"

Michael blinked hard, as though the question were either absurd or unexpected. "Yes. I do. Of course I do."

"Tell me what you love about her."

Michael looked past Luka's shoulder into the field beyond. "Her paradoxes. I love how she's both gentle and stubborn. How she can seem sweet and innocent one minute but turn sarcastic and wickedly funny the next. Not many people see that side of her. And she still has that beautiful laugh that sounds like a song. And more than anything, I love how selfless she is. She's never once complained about being a vicar's wife. The sacrifices and duties, the heavy burdens. I don't think she knew what she was in for, marrying me. But she's borne it with real grace. She teaches *me* every day what a servant's heart looks like. I don't think she understands how much I've learned from her—how much I look to her as an example of how to show compassion."

"Have you told *her* this?"

"Not in those words. And not recently."

"I think you have your answer. Take that first step across the bridge. She'll meet you halfway."

"You make it sound simple."

"Isn't it?" Luka asked.

"I think you missed your calling. That's pretty wise counsel. Where did it come from?"

"Maybe I learned it from watching Father all those years. Picked it up through osmosis."

"You'll hate this question, but... why aren't you taking your own advice? I know you're being cautious with Chelsea, but maybe it's time for you to take a firm step in her direction on that bridge between you."

Luka snickered. "Well, let's just say my bridge is a lot longer and more treacherous-looking than yours. And less stable. It doesn't have the same strong foundation yours and Rachel's does. Plus, I'm not exactly sure Chelsea will be waiting on the other side when I get there."

ON THE TREK BACK TO Mac's property, Luka realized his melancholy mood had been lifted by his talk with his brother. But he wasn't sure why. They hadn't swapped jokes or talked about sports. They'd sat at their father's graveside and bared their souls to each other, talking about serious life problems, something Luka couldn't *ever* remember doing with Michael before—not to that degree. But it was precisely what they'd both needed. Too bad their father couldn't have seen their exchange and watched his boys bonding. But maybe, somehow, he had seen. Or maybe he'd even been responsible for drawing them both to the graveyard at the same time.

The ping of his mobile interrupted Luka's thoughts, and he looked down to see a text from Chelsea: *Work on the Joy chapter tonight? I'll bring takeaway. Indian or fish and chips?*

Grinning, Luka stopped in the middle of the road to type his response: *You choose. Tonight is perfect. 6?*

He waited impatiently then heard the ping again.

I'll be there.

Chapter Eighteen

How far that little candle throws its beams! So shines a good deed
in a naughty world. ~Shakespeare

Chelsea finished her text to Luka then paused, trying to decide which he might prefer—pub food or Indian takeaway. Teenage Luka would have chosen a simple fish-and-chips dinner, but adult Luka had probably developed more sophisticated tastes in his years of exotic travels. *Indian, it is, then.*

She chucked her mobile onto the sofa and unwrapped a mini chocolate bar. "Shh. Don't tell anyone," she told Socrates, who lay half-asleep on the floor beside her foot. She popped the entire bar into her mouth.

Socrates had been growing stronger every day since she'd picked him up from Dr. Renfro's. And when he'd eaten his first full meal a couple of days before, licking the bowl clean, she knew he was fully recuperated.

Chewing the delicious chocolate-and-caramel combination, Chelsea returned to her task of sorting through the chocolate bars and sweets she'd purchased the day before. Bars in one basket, sweets in the other. At university, one of her lecturers had used an unorthodox—and fattening—tactic in one of his classes to entice pupils into learning details of basic economic theory. He would ask a question, call on the first pupil who lifted a hand, then toss a chocolate his or her way. If the pupil answered correctly, he or she got to keep the chocolate. But if not, the student would have to throw it to the next one who answered, and so on until the correct answer was offered. Chelsea had never forgotten that lesson and hoped his technique would help her own pupils during the upcoming review for exams. She could sense their weariness, with research essays due, then exams, and the Renaissance festival after that. She couldn't lessen her pupils' burdens, but she could lighten them with a bit of fun. And chocolate.

As Chelsea continued her sorting, she recalled the previous day's outing to buy these treats at the gift shop. On the way to the till, she'd halted at one of the aisles. Sienna's father, Dan, was staring intently up at one of the shelves, his hand paused in midair. Chelsea took a few steps into the aisle and asked if she could help.

"Oh!" His confusion transformed into a bashful grin as he shook his head. "Sorry. I must look daft, standing here. I can't remember which brand of earbuds Sienna told me to get."

Chelsea stepped closer and stood on tiptoes. "Hmm. Lots to choose from."

"Precisely."

She rocked back onto her heels and peered up at him. "Why don't you text her? See which brand she prefers."

"Of course. Brilliant," he said.

Chelsea left the aisle to make her purchase up front, and during her transaction, Dan came to stand beside her and to thank her for the suggestion.

He held up the earbud package between them. "I was off the mark by a mile. She wanted this brand."

"Earbuds are a very personal choice for some people, especially teenagers."

"Who knew?"

After the clerk handed Chelsea her bags, she stepped aside to reinsert her credit card into her wallet. By the time she was done, Dan's swift purchase was already complete. He reached to open the door for her but awkwardly tangled himself up in her bags as he did so. She detangled herself with a nervous laugh as they stepped out into the chilly afternoon together.

She was about to wish him a good afternoon when he paused outside and ran a hand through his ginger hair. "Listen, you wouldn't want to... get a coffee, maybe? Or even a quick bite tonight?" The wind had snatched away his words—they were soft enough, already—so Chelsea leaned in to hear them better. "I'm on my own since Sienna's studying with her friends. Well, supposedly studying. They're probably talking about boys or social media."

This invitation hadn't caught Chelsea entirely off guard. In her sparse interactions with Dan, she'd recognized his interest in her. Nothing overt—a lingering glance or warm smile that went beyond polite niceties. Because romantic relationships with pupils' parents were strictly forbidden by the headmistress, Chelsea wasn't even allowed to entertain the idea of a date with Dan, at least not until his daughter was well out of her class. But even if the path were free and clear, she wondered if she would have accepted. Dan's clean-cut looks, admirable devotion to his daughter, and good standing in the community were all incredibly appealing on the surface. But not appealing enough for Chelsea. The spark simply wasn't there.

"I'm sorry—I have a *lot* of work to do." She touched his sleeve for emphasis then pulled her hand away, hoping he would understand her sincerity. "But thanks anyway."

"Right. Okay. Well, I certainly understand. And I appreciate the help. You saved me from having Sienna hate me for the rest of her life."

"You're very welcome." She added another laugh for good measure. At least she could give him that.

When they parted, Chelsea's gaze fell on someone across the street, walking in the opposite direction. She recognized Luka and almost called out his name, but he seemed distracted. She decided not to intrude on his mission, whatever it was.

As Chelsea tossed the next chocolate into the correct pile, her mobile pinged with a message from her mum: *My answer is yes! Looking forward to it.*

Earlier that morning, Chelsea had texted her mother an invitation to come stay at the cottage, the week after next, to enjoy the Renaissance festivities.

"She's coming!" Chelsea told Socrates, thrilled to have her first official cottage guest.

CHELSEA THOUGHT SHE'D timed it correctly, arriving early at the Indian restaurant and expecting a lengthy queue on a Saturday night. But she walked in during a rare lull, quickly placed her order, then walked out minutes later, leaving her with another half hour before meeting with Luka. So she took her time on the way to Mac's, gripping her sleeves to shut out the cold while trying to enjoy the tangerine-colored sunset before her and the glorious trill of a robin that seemed to follow her all the way there, from tree to tree.

Approaching Mac's cottage, Chelsea noticed a shaft of light coming from farther off, inside the shed. Walking toward it, she heard Luka and Mac having a conversation. Not wishing to interrupt but also not knowing what to do for the next twentysomething minutes—*Should I just stand at the cottage door until one of them lets me in?*—she continued toward the shed until she could distinguish which voice was which and what they were discussing.

"The foundation will donate the service dog, so that's covered," Luka was saying. "But the expense of feeding the dog, training it..."

"Aye," Mac said. "We could provide a year's supply of both, then?"

"Sure, that would work."

Chelsea paused just beyond the open door. *Service dog?* Ironically, Rachel had mentioned recently that the parents of her pupil, Patrick, were inquiring whether a dog would be allowed in Rachel's classroom next term. Patrick had been recently diagnosed with epilepsy, and his parents told Rachel that a dog could help anticipate the seizures before they began. *But how would Luka or Mac know about that? Through Michael? And why are they discussing it in the first place?*

"The family already has a dog picked out, in Bristol," Mac added. "The boy has to train with it over the coming weeks, but it'll be home in time for Christmas."

"Impressive intel on your part," Luka said. "So I could go for a visit, ask the foundation about handling the training expenses. That would keep your cover intact."

Cover? Chelsea struggled to make sense of it all, not caring that her innocent pause at the door had manifested into full-on eavesdropping. An expensive—and anonymous—gift, ready for Christmastime. It was all adding up to something very specific.

"'Tis always nice to see their faces or hear about the family's reactions, even secondhand. Will ye be here for the holidays to see the results?"

"Not sure yet," Luka said. "Hard to say what Christmas will look like for me this year."

Even more than the mystery of the service dog, Luka's noncommittal answer to Mac's question intrigued Chelsea. Over the weeks, as she'd watched Luka become more comfortable with village life, a sliver of her had wondered if he might actually stay past the festival. But now...

Behind her, Chelsea heard a faint panting that grew stronger. She turned slowly to find a shaggy white sheepdog ambling in her direction. She wasn't aware that Mac had a dog. Skittish, she extended her hand, hoping the dog would keep quiet, but the gesture only made

him lunge toward her and issue a friendly bark. As he dipped his furry head beneath her hand for a scratch then barked once more, all
conversation inside the shed ceased. Chelsea's own cover was blown.

Luka peered around the doorframe and squinted in the dusky
light. "Chelsea?"

"It's me," she admitted.

The dog followed her toward the shed's entrance then stood in
the doorway. Mac sat on a stool, holding a knife and a wooden figurine he was whittling, while Luka stood to her side.

"Sorry." She winced. "I was early with the food, and I'd headed
to the cottage, but then I saw the light on, and—"

"How much did you hear?" Luka asked.

She could have lied and said she'd just walked up, rather than
confess to overhearing every word like the intrusive eavesdropper she
was. But she had to know the truth.

"Enough," she said. "Service dog, a year's worth of food, a Christmas gift you don't want people to know about. Are you... the village's
Mystery Claus?"

Mac nodded. "Tell her, lad."

Luka gestured toward his own stool, so Chelsea sat and placed
the takeaway bag on her lap, feeling the warmth through her jeans.
Mac's sheepdog ambled over to plop down at his feet.

Luka leaned against the doorframe. "Actually, Mac's the Mystery
Claus. He's been doing it for, what, twenty years?"

"Thereabouts," Mac said, still whittling away.

"And he let me know about it one day, back when I was a teenager. He needed my help and said he could trust me. So we played Father Christmas together for those two years I lived here."

"But then you left the village..." Chelsea prompted.

"Right, but I've sent donations to Mac each year since then. He
kept me apprised of the needs in the village, and we brainstormed together. When Michael told me last week about Patrick, the little boy

who needed a service dog for his seizures, I knew we had our gift for this year."

Chelsea struggled to process the details. It didn't surprise her one bit that Mac was the generous Mystery Claus. It made perfect sense. He had a servant's heart, and his humility would keep him from seeking any credit or praise. Plus, he genuinely loved the village and had his ear to the ground, concerning individual needs. *But Luka?*

"They were... horrible to you," Chelsea said. "The villagers, I mean. They gossiped about you and shunned you. Some even accused you of that vandalism incident at the churchyard."

"Yes."

"So then, why? Why would you help them out—and continue to do it years after you left? You certainly didn't owe them anything."

Luka took a long pause as though he'd never been faced with the question before. "At the start, I saw it as helping Mac, not the villagers. But when I was gone and Mac told me who the gifts were helping—a wheelchair for Mrs. Bascom, a bag of toys for the Martins' children when the father lost his job—"

"And my mum when Dad passed." Chelsea felt the hint of unexpected tears at hearing the list of good deeds quietly done behind the scenes, picturing the recipients' delighted faces, and knowing that Mac and Luka had been solely responsible all this time.

"It was the right thing to do. That's the best way I can explain it," Luka said.

Chelsea studied Luka's face—*this* Luka, the adult Luka—and realized she had much more to learn about him. Politely opening a door for Mrs. Pickering and ignoring her in-his-face rudeness was one thing. But it was quite another thing to offer ongoing money and time, for years, to a village he no longer held any loyalty toward... simply because it was the right thing to do. And without receiving a stitch of credit or accolades.

"Does anybody else know?" Chelsea asked. "Besides the three of us?"

"Aye, Dr. Ben," Mac said. "He found out last year. But I trust him to keep the secret." He lifted his brow, likely wondering the same about Chelsea.

"You can trust me too. I'll never tell, Mac. I promise. But... I want to help. I'd like to contribute."

"'Tis not necessary, lass." Mac waved away her offer.

"Please. Let me," Chelsea insisted. "I can't know about this and *not* help out. I want to."

"A female Father Christmas." Luka grinned. "High time, I think."

Mac gave a nod. "All right, then. You're in."

A FURRY SHEEPDOG SNORING at her feet, a fire blazing near-by, a blissfully full stomach, and a half-empty glass of wine. Chelsea should have been made drowsy by any one of these elements, but instead, she was alert and sharp-witted. Perhaps it was because she and Luka had spent the last couple of hours enthusiastically scrolling through photos of Joy's paintings and matching them up with the preliminary descriptions Chelsea had brainstormed over the past week, as well as those old interviews she'd conducted with Joy years before. They all fit like puzzle pieces snapping satisfyingly into place.

Earlier, after they'd all eaten Indian takeaway at the cottage's kitchen table, Mac left for the pub, saying that he wouldn't be back until late. Since then, Luka and Chelsea had been sprawled comfort-ably on the rug near the living room's fireplace, with Chelsea's laptop on the coffee table. They sat nearly knee to knee, backs against the sofa, as they swapped ideas and kicked around potential formatting or new pieces to include.

Chelsea pointed to the screen. "What about this snippet... down here instead, under the gallery's photo?"

Luka considered it then agreed, dragging the text box and settling it where Chelsea's finger was still perched. "That works." He sat back and finished off his wine in one gulp. "We made good progress tonight."

"Agreed. I think Joy would be happy with it. We somehow struck this balance of showing all her accomplishments while still managing to—tastefully—address the low points of her life."

"Yeah, it would've been impossible to leave out her reclusive years. Everyone already knows about them. Plus, she produced her best work when she was holed up in that cottage."

"Just imagine... all those paintings locked away upstairs, and nobody even knew. What an amazing find." Chelsea pictured Noelle twisting the knob to enter the room and find a treasure trove of her great-aunt's paintings in every corner, on every wall. "What do you think made Joy hide away in her cottage? I mean, I know all the rumors—health issues, or that she couldn't take the celebrity status. Or maybe she went mad. What's your theory?"

Luka stretched his arms in front of him then crossed them over his chest. "Not sure. Maybe all of the above."

"We never really know someone, do we?" Feeling pensive and groggy from the previous bursts of energy, Chelsea moved her arm backward to the sofa's cushion and rested her head on her open palm, shifting in Luka's direction. "I mean, people only know what we show them, don't they?"

"I guess that's true..." He tilted his face toward her.

"We *assume* what people think or feel. But we don't really know, for a fact, until they tell us. And even then, everything is subject to interpretation. I might say something, and intend it one way but you could interpret it completely opposite. And vice versa." She suppressed a yawn with her fist.

"That's a depressing thought," Luka mused.

"Why?"

"Well, it would mean that we're all just going around, building relationships with each other using gut instinct, interpreting each other through our own lenses. But what if we're wrong? What if the lens is distorted?"

"Maybe that's the fun of it. Keeps things interesting. Relationships are just one big guessing game."

"You're tipsy, aren't you?" He grinned at her.

"On half a glass and a full stomach? No. But I am relaxed. More relaxed than I've been in a long while, in fact. Did I tell you that I've started writing again? Well, considering it, at least. When there's time for it."

His eyes widened. "Really?"

"I found that old novel, the one I wrote when I was sixteen. And it's awful. But it reminded me how much fun I had, being creative. I suppose you're to blame for all this."

"How do you figure?"

"You got me thinking about it again. First, you pushed me into writing those descriptions—"

"I hardly pushed."

"Strongly encouraged, then. And you mentioned my novel when I'd practically forgotten about it." She explored his face, comfortable with letting her eyes roam a little. "You have this very specific way of challenging me. Without even trying."

"Is that a good thing?"

After a long pause, Chelsea whispered, "I think it could be."

Chapter Nineteen

Knowing is not enough; we must apply.
Being willing is not enough; we must do. ~Leonardo da Vinci

"Frank, take a deep breath. It will all be fine," Chelsea said through the phone.

"But I'm such a bloody idiot!"

"You are not an idiot. And this is not your fault." She peeked at the classroom clock to be sure she had enough time for this conversation. Her lunch break was nearly over. "Besides, you took care of things before they got out of hand. Right?"

A minute earlier, Frank had rung Chelsea to say that the festival tickets were *all* incorrect. The prices for the archery show, falconry display, and *Romeo and Juliet* performance had been mixed up by some incompetent employee at the online site through which he'd acquired the tickets.

"Right." His voice had lost its hard edge, evidence that his anxiety was dissipating. "They're correcting the problem and will rush order them to us this weekend. And they apologized profusely."

"So, then, all is well." Chelsea saw Rachel appear at the classroom's doorway and waved her in.

"Okay," Frank said. "But I still feel a fool. I only had one job..."

"And you did it! This will all work out in the end, Frank."

Rachel sat in the chair beside Chelsea's desk.

"Well, thank you," he said, finally sounding like his usual self. "For not wanting to kill me over this."

221

"The thought would never cross my mind. I'll see you at Thursday's meeting."

They rang off, and Chelsea set the phone down with a roll of her eyes. "One thing after another."

"Festival issues?" Rachel asked.

"We nearly had a blazing fire to put out, but I think Frank has contained it." Chelsea studied her friend and noticed that the weariness she'd grown accustomed to seeing on Rachel's face—the thin creases of worry around her eyes, the pursed lips—had all but disappeared. Her friend looked fresh as a daisy and years younger than her age. "Okay, tell me. What have you done? Something's different. New haircut? Lipstick?"

Rachel touched the tips of her hair. "Well, I did get a trim last weekend." She lowered her hand. "But that's not why I'm here. I have news. Did you hear about Lizzie? She's in labor with the twins!"

"Oh!" Chelsea gave an elated gasp then remembered the timing. "Isn't it too early?"

"Only a few days. She's been miserable, poor thing, on bed rest for weeks. Anyway, Joe whisked Lizzie away to hospital in Bath this morning. I'm sure he'll open up a message chain soon and text us some updates."

Rachel's phone vibrated, and she peered down at the mobile in her lap, read the text, then smiled.

"From Joe?" Chelsea asked.

"Oh. No. It's Michael." She was still smiling as she tapped her reply.

Chelsea crossed her arms. "Okay, what's going on? Something *is* different with you today. You're being so mysterious."

Rachel returned the mobile to her lap then leaned in across the desk, lowering her voice. "I'm almost afraid to say it out loud, but I have to tell someone. Chels, something's changed. I can't explain it.

Last night, Michael and I stayed up until *almost two*, just talking. We haven't done that in years."

"What did you talk about?"

"Everything. About his father, about the church and his ministry, about the future. We even discussed having children. Michael is open to trying again, even finding a way to finance in vitro."

"That's astonishing. What changed?"

"I'm still not sure. I can trace it back to a few days ago. Last week, he came in looking sort of... thoughtful and serious. I was busy, in the middle of dusting, so I expected him to pass me by without a glance then go to his study and shut the door, like always. But he didn't. He looked me in the eye, saying he'd just been to his father's gravesite. And that he got 'clarity' there, whatever that means. Then he leaned in and hugged me—a proper hug, long and tight—and whispered that he appreciates me. And that he's sorry he hasn't told me lately."

"Incredible. What sort of clarity did he get at the gravesite?"

"I'm too afraid to jinx it and ask. But since then, Michael has been sweet and attentive. He even helped me wash a load of dishes over the weekend, unasked. He's back to the old Michael. And... I can feel myself relaxing, letting him back in a little at a time."

"I'm so happy. I knew you would find your way back to each other."

"I wasn't that sure." Rachel lowered her eyes as she smoothed out her skirt. "I've been worried for us, Chels. More than I've let on."

"Worried about splitting up?" Chelsea had a hard time even forming the words. *Rachel and Michael, not together? Impossible.*

Rachel made eye contact again. "No, not splitting up. That never crossed my mind. But something worse did—that we might keep floating along as we had been, going through the motions, putting on a fake face for the villagers for the rest of our lives. That would kill a marriage as sure as a divorce decree could. I didn't realize how stale our marriage was getting until it started to improve. Why couldn't *I* have been the one to humble myself and reach out to Michael first? Was I that stubborn?"

"You just didn't know where to begin," Chelsea offered.

"Maybe. But I feel ridiculous now, not taking the lead, not trying harder with him. At least one of us finally did. We've stopped sniping at each other, but the biggest change is Michael *sees* me again. He doesn't look through me anymore, as though I'm some figurine on a shelf that he has to walk past every day. He pays attention." Rachel recrossed her legs and took in a sharp breath. "Anyway—that's where things stand, at least for now. It's a start."

"It certainly is." Chelsea hoped this afterglow would last, both for them as a couple and, selfishly, for their own friendship. Because just as Rachel recognized the old Michael, Chelsea was seeing hints of the old Rachel too—relaxed and content. Happy.

"Okay. Enough about me!" Rachel said. "This is a huge week for you, prepping for the festival. Besides the Frank situation, how are things coming along? Can I help out?"

Chelsea sucked in a breath as she recalled her long-and-getting-longer list of things to do. She'd been able to cross off a couple of items that morning, but it had barely made a dent.

"Well, aside from Frank, things seem generally under control. I'm meeting with the falconer this afternoon, then it's home to grade and return some calls. I have to tell myself to breathe sometimes. But it's not really the planning I'm worried about. I think it's the actual festival and making sure everything comes together. As we get closer, I feel this strong weight. Like, if something fails or goes wrong, it will all be on my shoulders. My responsibility alone."

"You know that's not true. This is a group effort. We're all responsible. And if anything happens, we'll fix it together."

Rachel was right. Really, the only person who might hold a failure against Chelsea would be Mrs. Pickering.

"All I know is, this half-term holiday is coming at the perfect time. The pupils are restless, and it's hard to keep them on task. But after Friday, I'll be able to put all my focus on the festival. Big relief."

"Amen to that. So, what else has been happening, outside the festival?"

"Nothing much. Oh, well, Luka and I have made some good progress on his coffee-table book. We worked on the Joy chapter over the weekend."

"Did you?" Rachel's tone lilted.

"Stop that." Chelsea smirked. "It was work. I'd promised to help him, and so I met that obligation. Nothing more." But the image of Luka and Mac came to her—the two of them inside that shed, quietly planning out their secret mission for their next Mystery Claus project. *If Rachel only knew.*

The bell rang, indicating that the next class would begin shortly. "Is that the time?" Rachel rose from the chair. "I'd better dart away."

"Thanks for coming in. I'm thrilled for your news."

"Which bit? Lizzie or Michael?"

"Both!"

WHEN SHE'D FIRST RETURNED to Chilton Crosse, Chelsea had made a point, at the height of autumn, to take a leisurely walk to Chatsworth Manor to enjoy the seasonal changes in all their glory. Last year, she had ambled up the extensive tree-lined drive, browsed the public gardens in back, and even had a solitary picnic. She hadn't had time yet, this season, to visit again, but her upcoming meeting with the falconer gave her the perfect opportunity for it, so she arrived a half-hour early, to walk and browse.

When she reached the manor's entrance, she smiled to see the glorious stone facade dripping with Virginia creeper vines, which turned a vibrant red each autumn, drawing visitors and tourists to it in droves. This first day in October, as the sun winked from behind a passing cloud, Chelsea was greeted with the unique image of vivid green leaves dipped in red at their tips, a sort of half-and-half mixture. She snapped a photo of the manor with her mobile just before it buzzed with a text from Luka.

Did you hear about Lizzie? Having twins?

Chelsea texted back: *False alarm. They're headed back home. Rachel just texted me.*

Are you at school? he asked.

The manor. Meeting with falconer.

The long pause that followed led Chelsea to believe that Luka had either gotten distracted or hadn't seen her response. But then his reply came: *Mind if I tag along? Snap a few photos for the website?*

Great idea. Come on, she texted then immediately wondered whether it would be worth his time. She wasn't even sure if the falcon itself would be here.

This was actually an impromptu meeting. Rufus, the falconer, had surprised her with a call before school, saying that he'd be in the vicinity of Chilton Crosse in the afternoon, eager to scope out the property for next week's festival. So she had agreed to meet him at the manor after school.

She ambled toward the front garden—a vast lawn of manicured grass, bordered by shrubs and flowers, the perfect setting for a falconry display. She started to snap another photo, but her mobile vibrated again, interrupting her efforts. It was an unknown number, but Chelsea answered the call anyway in case it was about the festival.

"Miss Barrett?" a woman's voice asked.

"This is she."

"I'm Matthew's mum, Antonia. I have some rather... unfortunate news."

Chelsea could almost literally feel her heart drop down in her chest. Matthew, the play's Romeo. Unfortunate news was *not* what Chelsea needed to hear.

Antonia continued. "You see, Matthew's had a cough—getting worse—and sneezing too. Well, this morning he woke up with a sore throat."

Chelsea recalled marking Matthew as absent in class.

"We hoped it was only a chest cold. But Dr. Granger confirmed it this morning—strep throat."

Chelsea was glad that Antonia couldn't see her horrified expression through the mobile. "I'm so sorry to hear it. What's the prognosis for him?"

Matthew's mother explained that he'd promptly been put on a strong round of antibiotics and might improve in time for next week's play. But "might" wasn't good enough.

"Well, thank you for calling. Please give Matthew my best, and tell him to follow doctor's orders and get plenty of rest."

"What about... the play?" Antonia asked.

"If he's up to it next week, Matthew still has the role, of course. But to be practical, I need to ring his understudy and let him know."

"I understand."

They ended the call, and Chelsea stood in the middle of the manicured gardens and stared up at the sky, watching clusters of lazy clouds drift aimlessly along, and wishing she had nothing else to do *but* watch clouds drift. She thought it through. Matthew's understudy was Andrew, a sweet young man but hardly an acceptable Romeo. His tryout had been shaky at best, and Chelsea wasn't certain he had the courage to step onto a stage and spout Shakespeare convincingly. Especially under these last-minute conditions. But at this point, he was their only option.

She rang Fred. Perhaps he could be the one to inform Andrew that he needed to put extra time into studying those lines. Maybe the two of them could even run through some scenes and get Andrew up to speed.

Fred's phone went to voicemail, so Chelsea explained the situation and asked him to please ring up Andrew ASAP. As she clicked off, a weather alert popped up on her screen, and she glowered at the extended forecast: *Spotty rains next week with a chance for storms.*

One minor disaster after another, rolling in...

"Chels?"

She swiveled to see Luka walking toward her with his backpack slung over his shoulders. He crinkled his brow at her, his eyes darker than usual in the muted hues of the cloudy day. "Something's wrong." He came closer, his look of concern growing stronger, and she realized that panic must be written all over her face.

"Where to begin?" She attempted a half smirk but was on the verge of tears. Instead of letting them have their way, she took in a sharp breath, precisely as she'd advised Frank hours earlier. She refused to let the stress take over. "A lot of unexpected fires to put out today, with the festival. They just keep coming."

Luka placed a gentle hand on her arm as she spoke. His steady gaze was comforting instead of disarming. Someone was listening to her. She wasn't alone.

She explained about Frank and the tickets then the call from Matthew's mother and the strong possibility of a less-than-competent understudy. "And now, there's the weather." She held up her screen, which still contained the festival week's bleak forecast. "Even *that's* refusing to cooperate. I mean, most of the activities planned are outdoors and weather dependent. The stalls, the archery, the falcon show. And the bonfire! We *need* good weather to make this a success, Luka."

"True, but we won't know until we're closer to the festival day." His tone was soothing. "Sometimes those forecasts are spot on, but sometimes, they're dead wrong." Luka rubbed her back reassuringly.

"That's true." She thought about how she'd carried her umbrella around last Tuesday, all day, in anticipation of the expected heavy rains that never arrived.

Luka removed his hand then readjusted his backpack. "Plus, the new stalls are weatherproof. And if worse comes to worst, and it's a downpour, we could even... move to the assembly hall and have the vendors peddle their wares there."

Chelsea was doubtful they could cram all those people comfortably into that building. But still, it was an option—a last resort. Perhaps she could bring it up at the meeting and collect other people's contingency plans and ideas.

"As far as the archery and falconry go," he continued, "well, a bit of English rain won't keep people away. And the rest is under control. I mean, the tickets are being corrected, the understudy situation has been taken care of... in the end, the fires have been quenched. You've done all you can do."

Luka's perspective was refreshing. He was correct—there *had* been a solution to each of these issues. And Chelsea had handled them calmly and rationally, one at a time. Still, a small tornado of worry kept churning inside her.

"You're right. I know you are. I think I needed to hear it said out loud. Because all at once, these problems seemed overwhelming. In fact, they had come to a head just as you walked up." She shook her head. "I knew things wouldn't go perfectly. There were bound to be issues and glitches with this festival. I've been expecting them for weeks. But I was hoping..."

"That you'd be immune? You're a perfectionist, Chels. That's a good trait for a committee chair, but it also means you're hard on yourself. You've got incredibly high standards."

"Unattainable, you mean."

"Maybe. Sometimes."

"In any case..." She clicked off her phone. "It is what it is. That's what my dad used to say. We'll deal with things as they come."

"That's the spirit."

Chelsea heard an engine and turned to watch a rumbling 4x4 drive up the manor's path and park at the first available slot in the car park. It was Rufus, the falconer, right on time.

Realizing she wasn't quite finished with this moment with Luka, she reached out for his hand and gave it a firm squeeze. He looked down at her quizzically.

"Thank you," she said. "For listening."

He squeezed back with a knowing smile. "Anytime."

They released hands and turned their attention back to the ruddy blond man who leapt out of the vehicle then lugged an enormous covered cage out of the back seat.

"He brought the bird," Chelsea mused. "I wasn't sure he would."

"Good. I can get some nice shots today. Need a hand?" Luka shouted toward Rufus.

"I've got it, cheers!"

Rufus approached them on the manicured lawn then set down the cage as introductions were exchanged. Rufus's thick beard and stocky build told Chelsea he was probably an all-round outdoorsman—fishing, camping, hunting, rugby. He seemed the type.

"I brought along Finn," he told them, gesturing toward the cage. "Thought you might want to see him in action. And he can familiarize himself with the area."

"We'd love that," Chelsea said. "Luka is the festival photographer. Can he take some snaps today?"

"Absolutely."

"What can we expect on the day of?" she asked. "Assuming we're not rained out."

Rufus squared his frame and rubbed his palms together then told them the basics. He would arrive early on the day to set up barricades that would guide the crowds where to stand safely and watch from afar. He would be dressed in his hunting garb, a traditional Renaissance costume, and then he would address the crowd with the history of falconry, from the Middle Ages to present day. The demonstration itself would last about twenty minutes, and as they'd agreed on the phone the week before, he had three performances planned, to give the villagers and tourists ample opportunity to catch one.

Rufus shrugged. "So, that's pretty much it. How about a demonstration?"

As Rufus took a moment to strap on his thick glove, Luka removed his backpack and brought out his camera. Rufus coaxed the falcon out of his cage, and Chelsea caught her breath, observing the wide wingspan of the bird as he balanced on Rufus's arm. She took a step backward, bumping straight into Luka, who caught her. She felt his hand inside the crook of her arm.

"Sorry," she whispered.

"You can come closer," Rufus assured her. "He's safe for onlookers."

"Well... okay." Chelsea didn't exactly have a fear of birds, but those sharp talons that gripped Rufus's thick glove made her swallow hard. She pushed down her nerves and took a step forward, then another. Finn had settled comfortably by then and looked like a regal statue rather than a living, breathing falcon.

"He's beautiful." She felt calmer as she studied the multicolored feathers and the curve of his powerful beak. She could hear Luka in the background, snapping photos, but she held most of her concentration on Finn. "What's on his head?"

"It's a hood," Rufus explained. "It removes all distractions until it's time to fly. If you're ready to go, then? We'll need quite a lot of space for this." Chelsea and Luka complied, and Rufus raised his free hand in a *stop* gesture when they'd both backed away far enough.

In the moment before Rufus removed the hood, Chelsea felt the rush of anticipation that she hoped the villagers and tourists would experience next week. "This is exciting," she whispered to Luka, who stood close. She watched Finn blink then shake out his head feathers and strain his neck to assess this new wide-open space.

"When I release him," Rufus explained in a loud voice, "he'll fly off, and then I'll lure him in with a fake bait. Get ready for him to swoop down toward me."

Luka poised his camera, and Chelsea readied herself for the flight. Suddenly, Rufus flicked his arm, and Finn was released. The bird took swift flight, wings flapping, and Chelsea's gaze nearly couldn't follow him fast enough as he flew toward the top of the manor's gables.

Rufus whistled sharply, and the bird reversed course, flying toward his trainer, who was deftly twirling a long lure. The bird dive-bombed toward the lawn, and Chelsea sidestepped closer to Luka with a quiet shriek, clutching at his coat sleeve, probably messing up his photo. "Sorry," she told him, eyes still on the falcon as it swooped down to attack the lure then continued on in the opposite direction. Finn made another U-turn in the sky and dived once again toward Rufus.

Finn made two more passes before Rufus called out, "Ho!" which signaled to the bird to land on the ground near him, where he feasted on his reward, a generous piece of meat.

"Amazing," Chelsea said under her breath while Luka continued to take photos.

Rufus whistled once more, and the bird flew up to his arm and settled his talons onto the thick glove. When the hood was safely replaced on Finn's head, Chelsea came nearer with Luka by her side.

"Absolutely incredible. The attendees will love this," Chelsea told Rufus as he lowered Finn back to his cage. "Especially the children."

Once they'd finalized the details for next week's setup time, Rufus lifted the cage back into his vehicle and went on his way.

"Did you get some good shots?" Chelsea asked Luka.

"I think so." He scrolled through the digital photos then paused on one and leaned in to show her. "The skies were too gray to handle the contrast, but here's a clear one. I'll sift through later and find more for the site. Tristan will be pleased."

"Oh. Speaking of Tristan, he texted this morning—told me to ask you a couple of photography questions. He's putting your profile up on the festival webpage and wanted it to be more than a standard bio. He asked me to write it up. Do you have a minute now?"

"Sure. Ask me anything."

Chelsea opened her journal and clicked her pen. "So, I actually thought of this while Finn was flying. Since I wasn't taking photos myself, I was able to watch everything—the skies, the bird, Rufus's lure. But as a photographer, don't you sometimes... miss things? I mean, you're stuck behind the lens, capturing *one* specific image. Do you ever think that you're missing out on other things? Like, you're not able to be totally in the moment?"

Luka seemed to ponder this as he palmed his camera. "I actually think it's the opposite. Focusing on a specific image forces me to pay closer attention. I'm more in the moment with a camera than without it. Not sure if that makes sense."

"It does." Chelsea jotted down the key words of his answer. "Okay, one more. What's your all-time favorite image to shoot?"

"A sunrise."

"Fast answer." Chelsea scribbled it down. She'd expected something grander—perhaps the majesty of the snowy Alps or the depths of some unknown jungle. Not a common sunrise, a daily event accessible to everyone all over the world.

Luka capped the lens then replaced his camera inside the backpack. "A sunrise is ever changing. I could snap one every day for a year, and I'd never get the same two results. The lighting, the colors, the clouds—they always surprise me. It's fresh every time. I've photographed more sunrises than anything else."

"Maybe that should be your next book—sunrises."

Luka's eyebrows lifted. "Maybe it should."

She closed her journal and hugged it. "This was good. Thanks. I'll get the info to Tristan."

Luka slung his backpack around both shoulders with a quiet grunt. "Fancy a bite of dinner?" He gestured toward the manor.

Chelsea weighed her options, peering ahead in her mind at all the paperwork impatiently waiting for her at the cottage. "I'd better not. Too much to do. I was going to scarf down a sandwich while I got some work done at home. A thousand calls and emails to return too. Another time, maybe?"

"Sure. I might stick around, take some more shots of the manor. For the book."

They exchanged a friendly nod before Chelsea meandered down the long drive back toward the village, part of her wishing she *could* stay behind and fling all responsibility to the wind, as carefree as a falcon in flight.

BY BEDTIME, CHELSEA had ticked through her entire to-do list for the day. Feeling accomplished but knackered, she trudged upstairs to draw a bath. But seconds before she was about to turn the handle and get the water running, she heard her mobile ringing from her bed.

"What now?" she grumbled, abandoning the bath and making her way to the bed, where Socrates snored quietly near her pillow. She saw Rachel's name on the screen and clicked to answer. "Hey."

"You sound a bit ragged. Is it the festival? Everything okay?"

Chelsea sat on the bed and stretched out her hand to pet Socrates. "Not really, but it will be." She relayed quick details about the ticket mishap then the Romeo disaster. She didn't have the heart to vocalize her ongoing worries about the possible weather issues.

"Oh, that's terrible. All at the last minute?"

"Serves me right for assuming things would go smoothly." Chelsea managed a chuckle. "But Frank's on it with the tickets, and we've got an understudy for Romeo. I'm secretly hoping the antibiotics kick in and Matthew will be up to performing. Anyway, thanks for checking on me."

"Well, I *was* checking on you, but also wondered whether you'd... seen the website? Tristan uploaded some new photos tonight."

"Oh. The falconry pics. I was there when Luka took them this afternoon. That falcon was amazing! The kids will love it. Well, if the weather holds."

"It's very obvious you were there, because... you're *in* the photos."

"What do you mean?" Chelsea reached for her laptop, which she'd brought up to bed earlier. "He was taking shots of the falcon and Rufus, not me. Maybe I got in the way for a couple of them. It has to be an accident."

"It's no accident. In fact, it seems quite... deliberate."

Chelsea put the mobile on speaker and set it down while she clicked on Tristan's website. Finding the latest uploads, she scrolled through photo after photo of the falcon in flight, wings spread wide. *Absolutely stunning.* Then she came to closeups of the bird, with every color of the feathers vivid and gorgeous.

"I'm not seeing it," she said, still scrolling.

"Keep going. At the bottom," Rachel instructed.

And there it was. The last photo, in the right-hand bottom corner, was of Chelsea. Only of Chelsea, nothing else. It was a profile, a candid shot, a closeup of her staring at something—probably the falcon, when Rufus had first lifted him out of the cage. She appeared wide-eyed and captivated. Normally, Chelsea hated seeing her own image in photos. She'd never taken a selfie in her life, and there were very few photos of herself she'd ever really liked. She was always overly critical of her too-pert nose, her awkward smile, her imperfect hair. But this photo... it was natural. It was how Chelsea pictured herself. The lighting was delicate, and the angle was perfect. Her lips were parted with the hint of a dimple showing, her eyebrows were lifted, and her hazel eyes were bright with wonder.

"When did he take this? And why?" she asked. "I mean, the shoot was all about the bird. Why would he include this photo with the others? Seriously. It had to be a mistake."

"Even if it were, one thing is obvious. Luka couldn't help himself. He saw a moment and seized it. The photo is beautiful—he really captured you."

"Thanks. But I..."

"This is the way he sees you. It's very telling, I think."

"Telling?"

"Well, if I were looking at this situation blindly, without knowing the players involved, I would imagine that whoever took this photo was *clearly* in great admiration of its subject. But since I actually know the players, this photo leads me to one strong possibility—that the photographer is falling in love with his subject. Or maybe he never stopped."

Chelsea frowned at the screen. "That's ridiculous."

"Is it?"

Chelsea closed the laptop then grasped the mobile, hoping to talk sense into her friend. "It's rubbish. Rachel, it's only a photo. One of millions Luka has taken in his lifetime. It's his job. It isn't love."

Rachel continued, undeterred. "Even Michael came to a similar conclusion when he saw the photo tonight. It's clear to us—and probably to everyone else who sees it. It's just not clear to you yet." After a pause, she added, "It might be time to give some serious thought to where this might be headed. Luka has been staying in the village all along for you. And I think you need to sort out what that means."

"Why are you pushing this?"

"I don't mean to. But I also don't want you to have any regrets, in the end. Maybe you should explore all your options while there's still time. There could be a second chance here. And not many people get that, especially with a first love."

Chelsea flicked a piece of lint from her jeans. "It's not that simple."

"I know it's not. You two have a strong history, and it's unresolved."

Rachel probably didn't realize how true—and timely—that statement was. The past, no matter how strongly Chelsea tried to swat it away, still haunted her at the most unexpected and unwelcome of times. In fact, just that afternoon, on her walk back to the cottage after the falconry display, Chelsea experienced a déjà vu moment as she recalled the last time she and Luka had shared a meal in the manor's ritzy restaurant. She was turning seventeen, and Luka had saved up his wages to take her there. That night, she had seen no shadow of doubt in his eyes, no hesitancy about their relationship—not a single indication that, in two weeks' time, he was about to abandon her and change her life course forever.

"Our history is part of it," Chelsea said. "But honestly, it's about now too. Luka has a wandering spirit. And he's only committed to staying in Chilton Crosse for the festival, which ends next week." Luka had practically verified this when he gave an evasive answer to Mac's question about staying through the holidays. Chelsea had heard it with her own ears. "What if I take the risk, fall for him hard—again—and he ends up disappearing?"

"I get it. I do. This is your life and your decision entirely. The thing is, you deserve to be happy. And quite honestly, right now, Luka is the one making you happy. But you're the only one who can decide if it's worth the risk." After a beat, she added, "Okay, I've said my piece. I didn't mean to add to your burdens today. Forgive me?"

"There's nothing to forgive. I know you're only trying to help."

"I am. Go get some rest, my friend. Tomorrow's a new day. I'll be here to help you put out any more festival fires."

When the call ended, Chelsea set down the phone and resisted the urge to take one final peek at Luka's photo, to see it through Rachel's very opinionated and subjective eyes.

She's only seeing what she wants to see. Chelsea knew that people who were in love—or in Rachel's case, *back* in love—often felt obligated to spread that intoxicating sensation to everyone in sight, sprinkling it around like pixie dust. Because they were paired up, it meant that every other person in the world should be too.

Chelsea pushed aside the laptop then returned calmly to her clawfoot bathtub, more eager than ever to draw a relaxing bath and drain all the day's troubles away. As she watched the water flow from the tap, she pictured the tenderness in Luka's brown eyes that afternoon as he listened to all her woes about the festival. Then she felt his hand on her back, giving her reassurance as he coaxed her down from her panicked ledge.

There might be a second chance here.

But something deep inside Chelsea continued to resist—it couldn't be helped. She poured lavender-scented bubbles into the water's stream and wished that the rest of her life could be as sweet and uncomplicated as a bubble bath.

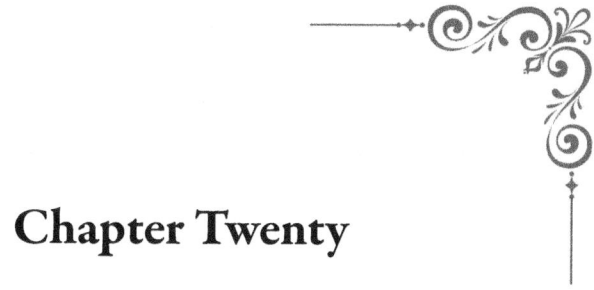

Chapter Twenty

Fill'd with her love, may I be rather grown
mad with much heart, than idiot with none. ~John Donne

Luka sipped his coffee while he listened to Frank recount his ticket-error ordeal to the committee in great and dramatic detail. In this final meeting, Chelsea had asked the committee members to update everyone on their specific area of interest. Luka half listened as he stole occasional glances at Chelsea, while she nodded and scratched down notes. She wore a silky lavender paisley top with jeans, and her chestnut hair was sleek and thick. She'd gotten it trimmed since he last saw her at the falconry display two days before. She looked beautiful.

Luka shifted in his seat as Mary took her turn beside him, telling everyone about the costumes. Although Luka thoroughly enjoyed his role as festival photographer, these weekly gatherings felt static and planned, unlike what he'd been accustomed to in his usual day-to-day life. Still, they held enormous value because they gave him a sure opportunity to be in Chelsea's trajectory—even though he sometimes wondered if she wanted him there.

He hadn't heard from Chelsea since he'd asked her to share a meal at the manor. *Did she interpret it as a date? Did I intend it as one?* He wasn't even sure. All he knew was that even when he'd texted her additional falconry photos for book descriptions, he had waited for replies that never came. He told himself that Chelsea was occupied with the festival and with school. He couldn't expect anything from her these next few days, understandably. She had other priorities.

"Luka?" Chelsea called from the table's other end.

"Oh. Sorry." He snapped out of his musings, realizing it was the second time she'd said his name. "Things are good on my end. Mac and I finished breaking down the old stalls for firewood—with help from Fletcher and Adam—and the outside stage is nearly finished. We'll start setting up the new stalls on High Street early Monday morning. Volunteers are welcome—we've gotten a few offers already. And more photos have been added to the site this week as well."

"Oh! The falcon!" Mary exclaimed beside him. "Wasn't he stunning?" She posed the question to the entire table, eliciting enthusiastic nods. She turned to Luka. "You did excellent work."

"Thanks. And as for the festival next week, the plan is to be everywhere at once. I'll do my best to take photos of all the stalls and cover every event. And then Tristan will upload the proofs to the website, keep the buzz going."

"I think we should give Luka some serious praise," Tristan interjected. "His efforts have been widely unsung, since he *is* behind the scenes. And he's got busy days ahead."

The applause began, and everyone, including a hesitant Mrs. Pickering, joined in. Luka dipped his head and reached for his coffee.

The next person to share was a special guest seated beside Luka—Rosalee Newbury, Holly's younger sister. Chelsea introduced her as "our famous actress" who was taking a quick break from her shoot in Derbyshire, where she was playing one of the Bennet sisters in a new remake of *Pride and Prejudice* for the BBC. Her role in the festival would be to deliver monologues from various works of Renaissance literature.

The meeting soon came to its natural conclusion, and Luka was able to stand and stretch his legs. He wanted to slip quickly out the door, knowing the inevitable small talk would ensue as people cleared their rubbish and gathered their belongings. But he didn't know when he might see Chelsea again and couldn't waste this chance.

Meandering through the sea of people, he finally reached Chelsea's end of the table. She was finishing up a talk with Joe about Lizzie's condition.

"'Any minute now,' says the doc. I'm eager to finally meet them."

Chelsea rested her hand on Joe's arm. "We're all praying for a safe delivery. Please let her know."

"Thanks for that. Cheers," he said then pivoted to leave.

Luka approached her. "Good meeting. Everything's coming along."

"Yes." Chelsea gave a polite smile, nodded, and glanced at her phone. "But I won't be relaxed until this is *all* over."

"Understandable." Luka struggled to fill the window of silence then remembered Chelsea's visitor. "Your mum is coming, too, right?"

"Yes." She tapped on her phone. "Sunday evening, I hope. I need to get the cottage ready. *So* much still to do..." she muttered then puffed out a small sigh.

Luka wanted to hold her attention, look steadily into her eyes, and reassure her that it would all be fine. *Lean on me. Let me help. We can do this together if you'll only open the door. I'm right here.*

Instead, he shifted his weight, kept his distance, and said, "If I can do anything, let me know."

Chelsea made eye contact with him, her gaze softening. "Thank you for that."

Mrs. Clementine, the headmistress, pulled Chelsea's focus away. "Could we talk about the madrigal group? The girls were hoping for a schedule."

"Oh. Of course." She set down her phone and began shuffling through some papers on the table—Luka's cue to exit. At that point, he wasn't doing her any good—he was only one of dozens needing her feedback, standing in her way.

He turned on his heel and headed out the door and into the chilly night air. As he passed by the church, his mobile vibrated, and he paused to read the text from Todd: *Australia is back on the table. Other photographer backed out. Last chance. Take it?*

Luka hovered his thumb over the word *Australia* and imagined the trip—the twentysomething-hour flight, the beaches and rain-forests, the famous landmarks and bustling cities, and the ticking-off of a major bucket-list item. But in the same heartbeat, he pictured abandoning the village in the middle of the festival, when they need-ed him most, leaving them struggling to fill his position and aban-doning their own duties to fulfill his. And then he pictured Chelsea scrambling to deal with the fallout, never trusting him again.

He replied: *Sorry. Committed elsewhere.*

Luka pocketed his phone and continued on toward Mac's. *Com-mitted. To what exactly?* Chelsea had given him recent signals that there might be hope. But sometimes, those signals seemed to evapo-rate, leaving him perplexed about the state of things.

When Luka was a boy, his mum had given him a toy eight-ball. He remembered shaking it fiercely then peering eagerly through a circular window with murky blue liquid to find answers to questions about his future. "Am I going to be six feet tall someday?" "Will I ever win the World Cup?" These were the questions of a small boy hoping for serious answers. Luka would shake and shake until he on-ly got the answers he desired. *It is decidedly so. You may rely on it. Out-look: good.*

Luka wished he still had the eight-ball with him. He would ask it all the questions he wanted to know about Chelsea, hoping for the answers he desired. But Luka wasn't a child anymore. He knew that fate was a complicated beast and that outside forces, decisions peo-ple made, and the ripple effects that came from them all added up to one's "fate." In the end, only *he* was in control of his own actions, his own responses... his fate. But not Chelsea's. She was in control of that. And no toy eight-ball could change it.

AT MAC'S COTTAGE, LUKA gave a cursory knock then walked in as he usually did. He found Mac in the living room, carving a wooden horse. The sheepdog lay at Mac's feet and didn't stir when Luka entered the room.

"Join me, lad." Mac gestured with his knife toward the opposite chair, nearest the fire. "How was the meeting?"

Luka sat and gave Mac the speedy version, telling him the most pertinent parts—the new volunteers for the early Monday-morning setup of stalls, the dodgy weather, the contingency plans.

"We'll work it out." Mac paused his carving and squinted across at Luka. "What else happened at the meeting?"

His friend could still read him with pinpoint accuracy, even after all these years apart. "Or what *didn't* happen, you mean?" Luka shook his head and leaned forward, elbows on knees. "I may have mucked things up with Chelsea."

"How so?" Mac lowered the wooden horse to his lap.

"I'm not exactly sure. Sometimes I feel like the wrong end of a magnet approaching her. Just when we start to get close, when there's a glimpse of hope... I seem to repel her." Luka sat back, remembering the ginger-haired man he'd seen Chelsea with the week before. Maybe her heart was pulling her to a safer port, to a man who *hadn't* hurt her before. "I can't exactly reach backward in time and change things. It's hard to know when to give up and walk away."

"Is that what you want, lad?"

"No. The very opposite." Luka leaned forward again, making strong eye contact, unblinking. "I'm ready for a life with her, Mac.

Here and now—ready to commit, to be the partner she deserves. But only if she wants me. And right now, I'm not certain she does."

Mac scratched at his graying beard. "Tell me, when you're taking photos of nature—in a jungle, sitting amongst the ferns and branches, tasked with the job of getting a perfect shot—how long does that generally take?"

Luka crinkled his brow. "Depends. Sometimes I can get the shot in one day. Sometimes it takes several."

"What are the conditions?"

Uncertain where this was leading, Luka indulged Mac's questions. "Well, the hardest time I had was probably shooting the indri, an endangered lemur in Madagascar. The thick humidity and heat were unbearable, sweltering. And I had to hide away under this camouflaged tarp, camera poised for hours on end. My joints ached, and I had sweat coming out of every pore. It took seven days to get that shot."

"But you got it."

"Yes."

"Was the gamble worth it in the end? The pain, the waiting, the humidity—even knowing you might *never* get that perfect shot?"

Luka saw precisely where Mac was headed with this question. He answered without hesitation. "Absolutely."

"MORNING, MR. BENTLEY," Luka said as he neared the bakery's entrance. Early sunshine slanted onto the cobblestones and onto Mr. Bentley's trousers.

"Good day to you, Luka." Mr. Bentley raised the tray of samples between them. "Care for a bite of lemon cake? Freshly made."

Luka wasn't a fan of lemon anything but couldn't possibly say no to this eager, smiling face. "Cheers." He selected a bite and popped it into his mouth. The lemon was subtle enough that Luka could genuinely say, "Delicious!"

Inside, the bakery bustled with customers, and the aromas of coffee, sugar, and spices blended together and hit his senses. His order was filled swiftly, and as Luka carried away his bag of shortbread and cup of coffee, he spied someone familiar at a corner table. He approached hesitantly, watching the man tap on his tablet, scrolling through a news article.

"Dr. Granger?"

The doctor looked up. "Luka, hello. 'Ben' is fine."

"Didn't mean to disturb." Luka pointed toward the tablet.

"You're not. I'm biding time between patients. Have a seat."

"Only for a minute." Luka slid out the opposite chair and sat. "I need to take advantage of this morning light for some shots of the countryside."

"Mary told me you're compiling photos for a book?" Ben set down his tablet.

"Word gets around fast." Luka hadn't remembered telling very many villagers about the proposed book. But it only took one, he supposed. "Yes. It centers around the village—the people, the landscape, the shops, the festival."

"Nice idea. Good subject material."

Luka saw an opening and took it. "You've been in Chilton Crosse about a year?"

"Just nearly. Since before Christmas."

"And you came from London?" Luka didn't know much about Ben's story except that he was a former Londoner, and Mary's nephew, who'd come to Chilton Crosse for a visit and ended up staying permanently.

"Born and raised."

"So here's my question. Why this village? I mean, you have the obvious connection to Mary. But you've come from this vibrant met ropolitan city full of culture and life. And now you're living here. Do you get bored sometimes or regret leaving London?"

Ben lifted a corner of his mouth in a half smile. "I've never been asked that before." He set down his cup and settled back in his chair to ponder the answer. "I didn't plan on moving here. I was content in London for years, had a busy career, beautiful wife, hectic social calendar. And then, when my wife passed—"

"Blimey, I'm sorry to hear it."

Ben gave a small shrug. "It's getting easier. But that's the main reason I left London. After she was gone, I couldn't stay. The city was suffocating for me, and everything about it held painful reminders. So I quit my job and started wandering. I didn't know at the time, but Chilton Crosse ended up being my saving grace—the people here, Mary and George particularly. And your brother."

Luka hadn't heard Michael mention Ben except in reference to his Sunday organ playing.

Ben smirked. "However, our first conversation didn't go over so well. I was intimidated by the collar. But to be fair, my faith was completely nonexistent in those days. I put a wall up around myself—a high one. Your brother didn't give up, and he became a... quiet presence. I knew that I could speak with him if I ever needed to. And I often did, over time."

"That sounds like him."

"Eventually, my walls came down, spiritually and otherwise, and I embraced this quirky village. I've become quite fond of it, flaws and all. And when I return from Doctors Without Borders—if I go that route—I plan to make Chilton Crosse my permanent home. So to answer your original question, yes, large cities have their appeal, certainly. But they seem rather... soulless, don't they?"

Luka mentally ran through a number of the iconic cities he'd spent significant time in over the years: New York, Milan, Paris, Berlin. Their appeal was deliciously strong—so much to see and do, tantalizing every one of the senses—but he never regretted leaving those cities once his time was up. He had no trouble letting them go without a backward glance. But hearing Ben speak about Chilton Crosse, Luka wasn't sure it would be quite as easy to leave this village behind a second time.

"Thanks for speaking to me about this," he told Ben.

"No problem. There are quite a few transplants in the village. Adam and Tristan came from London too. And Fletcher originates from Texas. Are you considering a long-term stay?"

"I've been mulling it over since I arrived. At first, the visit wasn't meant to be permanent. But I'm slowly coming round to the idea." Luka moved his chair to stand then grasped his coffee, which had cooled to the perfect temperature for drinking without scalding. "Cheers. Have a good one."

He exited the bakery and realized he envied the serenity in Ben's eyes. Up to that point, Luka's stay in the village had only been about Chelsea. But for the first time, he wondered why it couldn't be about him too. Perhaps he needed to see the situation from a more self-focused angle, to view his time here as a chance to settle down, to create a real home and carve out his own unique place in the world.

Chapter Twenty-One

*I freeze and burn, love is bitter and sweet, my sighs are tempests and
my tears are floods,
I am in ecstasy and agony, I am possessed by memories of her
and I am in exile from myself.* ~Petrarch

"Want me to carry it?" Chelsea asked, walking alongside Rachel, who held a potted plant.

"I'm good," Rachel insisted. "We're almost there."

It had been Rachel's idea to purchase the plant for Lizzie and Joe and to visit them directly after that day's church service, before the other well-wishers crowded the cottage. Two days before, in the early hours of Friday morning, Lizzie had experienced intense cramps once again, but this time, it was no false alarm. The twins, Edward and Matilda, were born that afternoon, and the proud new father alerted practically everyone in the village with a joyful text. The next day, receiving a clean bill of health, mother and babies had been sent home from Bath's hospital. Rachel and Chelsea had decided to give them an extra day at home before stopping by for congratulations.

Chelsea gathered her scarf against the chill and kept pace with her friend. A light drizzle began to fall as they made their way to Joe and Lizzie's cottage, located down a narrow path behind the main row of shops.

"Isn't it strange," Chelsea mused, "being off from school? I feel like there are papers waiting for me to mark. But there aren't."

"It's always odd, that first day of holiday. Like a phantom limb—that pull to keep working is still there."

"That's exactly it. But at least we *have* holiday weeks off here and there. Poor Michael. Vicars rarely get time off, especially weekends. Speaking of which, his sermon this morning was particularly inspiring, wasn't it?"

"I thought so too. He practiced it with me last night. He used to do that with all his sermons—ask for my input, run ideas past me."

"Well, it's working. He seemed at ease in the pulpit, more so than usual. It was noticeable."

When they reached the cottage door, Chelsea knocked, glad that she had sent a polite *Okay if we visit?* text to Joe a few minutes before. He'd said yes.

Joe opened the door with a broad grin, ushering Rachel and Chelsea inside. He was a jovial man to begin with, but Chelsea had never seen *this* level of joy in his eyes before. Part of Joe's usual attire at the bar was a dishrag that he habitually slung over his right shoulder so he could keep the bar shiny and tidy at any given moment. But that morning, the rag was replaced with a more delicate cloth for burping his newborn twins.

Rachel handed Joe the plant then followed him into the living room along with Chelsea. They found Lizzie on the sofa, covered in a thin blanket, with her head propped up on pillows. Chelsea could easily imagine Joe doting on her, adding another pillow for comfort, then another, and waiting on her hand and foot. She looked amazingly well rested and content as she waved at them from her makeshift bed.

"Lizzie, you look beautiful," Chelsea said, then caught sight of the two Moses baskets nearby.

Rachel had already made her way over and was peering inside. Chelsea joined her, touching the rim of the first basket. The babies—so tiny—were asleep, breathing in quick spurts, their chests rising and falling, eyes shut tight. Matilda, swaddled in a pink blanket, seemed smaller than her brother, but they both had the same crop of dark hair.

"They're gorgeous," Chelsea whispered to Joe, who had set down the plant and come to stand beside her.

"Thanks. They've just been fed, so they're happy now."

Chelsea and Rachel stared a little longer in silence, appreciating the miracle of new life—the sweep of black eyelashes, the perfect button noses, the tiny fingernails.

"Twice blessed," Rachel said under her breath.

She touched Edward's fingers and gazed at him for a long moment then stood straight and made her way to Lizzie. Chelsea followed her lead, shifting her attention to the new mother.

"How are you feeling?" Rachel asked in that calm, soothing vicar's-wife tone Chelsea recognized so well.

"Better. Last night was rough. I'm quite..." Lizzie bent forward and whispered, "Sore."

"Completely understandable." Rachel offered a warm smile. "Well, your children are beautiful. A gift from God. I'm very happy for you."

"Thank you both for coming to see me."

"We've all been anticipating these babies for a long time," Chelsea said. "It's nice to meet them in person. I'm thrilled for you and Joe. You two will make the most incredible parents."

Lizzie caught her husband's eye. "I hope so. Everything is so new and strange."

"It will get easier," Rachel assured her, as though she knew from experience.

The four of them chatted briefly, touching on other light topics—the weather, the festival, that day's church service. Before they could outstay their welcome, Rachel began the goodbyes then turned to leave. Chelsea thought about all the times Rachel had made similar visits over the years, to parishioners with new infants, and how privately emotional it might have been for her.

Outside, the drizzle had ceased, making the return walk less daunting. They moved in silence for a bit, then Chelsea mused, "Twins. Can you imagine handling two of them at once? Feeding, changing, putting them to bed? Then doing it all over again?"

"At least Joe will be a hands-on father. That will make all the difference for Lizzie."

As they drew near the edge of the high street, Chelsea asked with hesitation, "Rach, was it a hard visit for you, seeing the babies?"

Chelsea never would have dared ask such a potentially insensitive question to anyone else in Rachel's situation—craving a baby of her own, devastated by years of lost efforts and miscarriages. But this was her best friend in the entire world, and they could say anything to each other. The question had hovered in the air this entire visit anyway. Chelsea was merely putting a voice to it.

Rachel slowed her pace almost by half and stared at her shoes as she walked. "Surprisingly, no. I was worried it might be. But the moment I saw those sleeping faces, there was no sadness in me. Only joy." Rachel paused in the road. "It's Lizzie and Joe's time. These babies were meant to be. I believe that Michael and I will have our time, too, someday."

Chelsea clasped her friend's arm. "I know you will."

After they parted at the vicarage and went their separate ways, Chelsea walked the rest of the distance to her cottage and posed that same question to herself. *Was it a hard visit?*

Chelsea was thirty-three, the same age as Rachel. She was certainly not too old to have a child, but time *was* ticking. When Chelsea had been madly in love with Luka, as a teenager, her brain had conjured up a faraway watercolor image of having children with him someday. Then years later, when she got engaged to George, that idea of starting a family became much more tangible.

But when the engagement fell through and then Chelsea's father died, leaving her with a gaping hole in her life and throwing her completely off kilter, her only focus was to trudge through life each day. Time had marched on, and before she knew it, she was back in Chilton Crosse with a new job and a new home but no man in her life or real prospect of one.

No, it wasn't hard to see Lizzie's new babies. But being with them did seem to shine an enormous spotlight on her own life in an area that she'd been dodging for a long, long time. *Will I ever have a family of my own? Can I even envision it anymore?*

Opening her cottage door, Chelsea decided these were questions too heavy to sort out in a few minutes' time. She would save them for another day.

CINNAMON, APPLES, AND ginger—the scents mingled together as they bubbled and baked inside the Aga, a perfect blending of autumn spices that infused the entire cottage. It was a hard-and-fast rule, during Chelsea's childhood, that her mum would always bake *something* on the day company arrived. "I want the cottage to smell welcoming," she would say. That tradition had stayed with Chelsea throughout her adult life.

So, after arriving home from seeing Lizzie's twins then tidying up the cottage—changing sheets, clearing dishes, fluffing cushions, sweeping floors—Chelsea had made a toffee apple cake for her mum's arrival later that evening. She'd stopped by Mrs. Pickering's market the previous day for the ingredients plus some of her mum's favorite breakfast items and snacks.

This was not what Chelsea had pictured doing the day before the festival began—visiting babies, lightly tidying the cottage, baking a cake, waiting for her mum. Or staying calm. For the past several weeks, peering ahead toward this "night before," Chelsea had imagined scurrying, worrying, losing her hair, or getting hives as she put out multiple fires and panicked about the upcoming festival.

But she realized, as the cake baked and she scanned her to-do list, that there were no more items to tick off. At least, not at the moment. She'd returned every call, solved every pressing problem, and thought through every possible scenario. Plus, the unburdening of school had freed up her time inordinately.

This unexpected calm before the storm felt like the eerie few moments before the beginning of a play—the audience gathering in their seats while the actors and stagehands behind the curtain made costume adjustments, rehearsed lines in their heads, and prayed for success. There was an odd serenity inside the nervousness, knowing that time had run out, the event was upon them, like it or not, and there was nothing else to be done but press forward and start the show. All their preparations and anticipation had come down to that moment.

Waiting for the cake to finish baking, Chelsea scrolled through her texts, making sure she didn't have any outstanding ones to answer so that she could enjoy her evening with her mum. Down the list of names, she saw Luka's texts and paused. She tapped to open his messages then scrolled backward to scan them. She remembered receiving occasional texts from him in the last few days, but she hadn't responded to a single one. She was usually in the middle of doing a hundred other things, so she would skim his text, decide that it was a low priority compared to other texts containing time-sensitive questions, and click away. But this time, as she scrolled, she took the time to read them. Luka had sent new photos from around the village then some casual inquiries about how she was doing and whether she needed any help. And she had ignored them all.

Why? He'd done nothing to warrant coldness from Chelsea. Luka had put himself out there, staying in contact with her and offering his aid, this week of all weeks. And she'd responded with silence.

Feeling a small stab of guilt, Chelsea clicked on the text box and typed out a message: *Where are you now? I have something for you.*

A minute later, Luka responded: *Finishing repair job. You're at the cottage? I can be there in half an hour.*

The cake's timer dinged, and just before shutting it off, she managed to type out her response: *I'll be here.*

A mixture of heavenly spices infused the entire space as Chelsea drew the cake out and set it atop the stove. "Perfect," she said, admiring her own efforts, especially since she rarely baked. She hoped, at minimum, it might be the peace offering Luka deserved.

HEARING THE QUIET, muffled woofs of Socrates, Chelsea knew Luka had arrived at the cottage. The forty minutes that had passed since their texting had given her the right amount of time to let the cake cool and to slip a generous slice inside a Tupperware container for him. When she heard Luka's knock, she smoothed out her blouse then lifted Socrates with one hand and opened the door with the other.

"Hey." Luka smiled down at them both.

Chelsea let him inside as he scratched Socrates's head.

"How's he doing these days?" he asked, watching Socrates close his eyes, accepting the attention.

Chelsea closed the door to shut out the cold. "Wonderful. You'd never know he was near death's door a couple of weeks ago." When Luka had finished petting the dog, Chelsea carried Socrates gingerly toward the sofa and placed him onto the cushion, inside his bundle of blankets, then returned to Luka.

He raised his head to inhale deeply. "What's that amazing smell?"

"This." Chelsea fetched the Tupperware from a nearby table then held the container between them. "It's for you, actually."

"What have I done to deserve this?"

Rather than hand him a fake, polite answer, Chelsea chose honesty. "Quite frankly, it's an apology. In cake form." She noticed his confusion. Still clutching the cake, she explained, "This afternoon, I realized I've been completely ignoring you, shutting you out the past few days. Not intentionally—things have just been crazy. And today, I saw all your texts and felt badly about not responding. I was already making a treat for Mum, and I know we can't eat the whole cake between the two of us, so I thought..."

"So it's a guilt gift. An afterthought, then."

Chelsea recognized the spark of teasing in Luka's eyes. "It's neither. It's a gesture of kindness, nothing more or less." She matched his grin as she started to place the cake back onto the table. "But hey, if you don't want it, I can always give it to someone else—"

"I want it." Luka intervened, stepping forward and clasping the cake in his palm. "You know I do."

Chelsea released it to him then crossed her arms.

"Thanks," Luka told her. "I should probably be the guilty one here. All those texts I sent, while you were preoccupied with the festival."

"It's fine—you were trying to help."

"Everything on track? Any catastrophes?"

Chelsea gave him a quick rundown. Romeo's case of strep throat was improving steadily, the corrected tickets had arrived the day before, and even the weather was cooperating—only a ten percent chance of rain forecast for the first day of the festival.

"But the rest of the week still looks dodgy," Chelsea admitted.

"One day at a time, then."

"Right." After an awkward beat, Chelsea asked, "Can you stay for a bit? I'll put the kettle on..."

"I want to, but I've got a conference call with my publisher. I need to get back to the cottage soon to prepare for it."

"Things are good with the book?"

"So far. I've sent them everything I've got, with more to come."

"Well, before you go, I meant to give you something last week but never got around to it." She crooked her finger for him to follow then moved toward the study—a cozy room with tall bookshelves on two walls, a fireplace on the third wall flanked with cushy chairs, and a sturdy oak desk beneath a bank of diamond-paned windows.

"I've never been in here," Luka noted as he ducked his head to avoid hitting the low-arched doorframe.

"It's my favorite room in the cottage, my father's study. Mum kept it the same after he passed—she couldn't bear to do away with his books or this desk." She ran her fingers over the smooth wood grain as she moved to stand behind it. "When I got the cottage, I didn't want to change it either. I've added some of my own books." She nodded toward a section of bookshelves that contained everything from Maeve Binchy and Rosamunde Pilcher to Shakespeare and Frost. "I don't spend much time in here, but sometimes I'll read or do paperwork and pay bills."

Luka set his cake on the corner of the desk and drifted around the room, browsing titles. Chelsea opened the desk drawer and found what she was looking for—her checkbook. In the digital age, she rarely had use for a check, but it seemed the best way to handle this particular task. She flipped to the newest page and began filling it out.

"Your dad had eclectic tastes." Luka paused at one of the bookshelves. "Suspense novels, biographies on Churchill and Einstein. And a book of poetry?"

"Yeah, he was self-taught. He loved to read, but he couldn't afford university. I guess that's why *my* going was always annoyingly important to him."

Luka approached the desk, where Chelsea carefully tore out the check. As she rounded the desk to meet him, Luka perched on its edge, propping his hands beside him on the wood surface. She came closer and realized she and Luka were the same height. She was so used to looking up at him when they stood together that this eye-to-eye perspective was disarming.

"What's this, then?" Luka nodded toward the check Chelsea held between them.

"My portion of the Mystery Claus gift. To put toward Patrick's service dog."

When Luka saw the amount, his eyes widened. "You didn't have to do this."

"But I want to. And count me in for next year's gift too."

Luka folded the check in half and created a firm crease. "Thanks. I'll give this to Mac tonight." He rose from the desk long enough to find his wallet, tuck the check safely inside, then replace the wallet in his back pocket. He sat again on the desk's edge. "I think Patrick and his family will be relieved to have some help. Mac tells me the dad is a bit prideful, so keeping the gift anonymous is crucial."

"I can't wait to hear about the family's reaction," Chelsea said, knowing Rachel would probably be privy to it in the coming weeks.

"It's right around the corner—Christmas."

But will you be here? Chelsea imagined the holidays without Luka, camera in hand, clicking everything in sight. She pictured the hole he would leave behind, once again, when he left the village for a second time.

Breaking her thoughts, Luka asked, "So, your mum's arriving tonight?"

"In a couple of hours."

"I don't think she liked me much. I mean, I barely knew her. But the couple of times we talked, she didn't have much to say."

"Actually, I'm not sure what she knew about you back then. My mum and I didn't have a close relationship. We never talked about boys or the future, and we didn't have much in common. She sort of... lived in my dad's shadow. I used to think she didn't have any opinions of her own. We just never got on well. Not like mothers and daughters should."

"You were a daddy's girl," Luka mused.

"Completely." Chelsea couldn't stop the smile that spread across her face at the mention of her father. "I always wanted to make him proud—never wanted to disappoint him, even as an adult. And when he passed, I had hoped my mother and I would bond over it, finally lean on each other. Become friends even. But it never really happened. I still feel... stilted with her. It's almost like I'm playing the role of her daughter rather than being her actual daughter." Chelsea chuckled. "That sounds really barmy."

"It doesn't. Because that's how it felt with my dad. You just know how to put it into words better than I do."

Chelsea wondered how they'd gotten onto such a deep topic. But with Luka, that was easy to do. It always had been. "Oh, speaking of my mum's visit, I have an odd favor to ask. I need another pair of hands for this. I can't secure the clasp on my own." From inside her jeans pocket, Chelsea removed a charm bracelet her mum had given to her the previous Christmas. Before baking the toffee cake, Chelsea had remembered the bracelet being tucked away inside her upstairs jewelry box and figured her mum would be happy to see her wearing it. But in the rush to put it on, her fingers fumbled, and the bracelet dropped to the floor. Frustrated, she'd picked it up and slipped it into her pocket for a future moment when she might be less rattled.

"This is pretty," Luka noted as Chelsea dropped the bracelet into his open palm then raised her wrist between them.

"A gift from Mum. I wanted her to see me wearing it."

Rather than clasp it swiftly around her wrist and be done with it, Luka paused and examined the delicate bracelet, touching one of the charms with his fingertip. "Is that a Westie?"

"It is." She pointed to the other charm. "And this one's a book."

"Only two charms?"

"I guess I'm supposed to add more on my own. I think Mum was trying to find things she thought were important to me. My interests. But maybe she ran out of ideas."

Luka resumed his task, pinching the ends of the bracelet between his fingers while Chelsea held her wrist steady. She could feel his breath, soft on her skin, as she watched his hands—masculine but graceful, looping the bracelet around her wrist then grazing her skin as he clasped the chain after two attempts. But rather than let go when the job was done, he cupped her hand with his own and traced her skin with a finger, circling the charms. Every touch electrified the nerves under Chelsea's skin. She was helpless to back away.

"Chels," he whispered. He raised his head to peer at her, unblinking.

She could lose herself in those eyes—their tenderness drew her in. Luka's hand moved to her neck, and he cradled it with a hesitant touch. When she saw him leaning in, moving closer and staring at her mouth, she knew what he wanted. And she wanted it, too. In slow motion, her hands moved toward his chest and rested against the smooth leather of his coat as he brushed the hair on her neck with his fingertips. She closed her eyes, craving his kiss.

The moment his mouth grazed hers, a strange sensation hit, from years before—Luka's touch, his smell, his lips. They were starkly familiar, and she was transported in time, a teenager again, heart racing, fire burning in her chest. But something inside Chelsea had to retreat. She let out a small gasp and pulled back from Luka, opening her eyes.

"I can't," she whispered, shaking her head.

Luka still cradled her neck, but his eyes held confusion. "But I thought..."

She lowered her hands and took a step backward, moving out of his embrace.

He dropped his hands to the side of the desk. "I shouldn't have pushed."

"You didn't. This is me. It's all me." She clasped her arms, hugging herself, choosing her words carefully. Her eyes burned with sudden tears. "It's just... I can't let you in again. I thought maybe I could, but... this was a mistake."

Luka threaded both hands through his hair, combing it back, then gripped his neck. He stared at the floor. "A mistake. But I thought we were really building something here. All these weeks. I felt it."

"I did too," she said, wiping a tear. "You've become this big, unexpected part of my life again. But..." She couldn't expect him to understand when she didn't fully understand it herself. But she knew one thing—when her emotions were put to the test in that almost kiss, her body had reacted by physically yanking her away. She just wasn't ready for this. For whatever reason, she couldn't go back down that same road again. It wasn't possible.

She tried to explain again. "We might be confusing new feelings for... old ones. It's easy to get caught up in the past, the way we used to be."

"This isn't nostalgia," Luka retorted. "This is you now. It's me now. Can't we leave the past alone? Start over right here, in this moment, fresh?"

Part of her wanted to say yes—to grasp his face, finish the kiss, get lost in his embrace, and stay there. But the same knot in her stomach that had forced her away from him was still present. And it wouldn't let go. *A protective sixth sense? An intuition?* She wasn't seventeen anymore. She didn't believe in fairy tales and promises the way she used to. This wasn't as simple as dropping the past and starting over. Chelsea had to value her head above her heart this time. Maybe if she'd done that sixteen years before, they wouldn't be in this position in the first place.

"I'm sorry," she whispered. "This is all I can give you."

Luka gave a long, steady look as though trying to read her mind, to make sure her emotions matched up with her words—or maybe to find even a glimmer of discrepancy in her eyes. Then he pushed off from the desk. "If this is what you want..." His voice was flat, neutral. "I won't try to change your mind." He turned to leave the room, almost forgetting to dip his head under the doorframe. Chelsea wanted to follow him to the front door, but his walk was so swift that he'd already reached and opened it before she could. She decided to let him go.

Hearing the door close—not a slam, as she'd half anticipated—Chelsea felt more tears form behind her eyes, and this time, she let them come in quiet sobs. She hated being torn in two—loving him and resenting him at the same time. She wanted to burst open that door, chase after him, and tell him what he wanted to hear. But her old insecurities were too powerful, too entrenched.

Socrates whimpered in the other room, probably still gazing at the front door, wondering why Luka left so abruptly. Her sobs calming, Chelsea saw through her wavy tears the Tupperware teetering on the edge of the desk. In his haste, Luka had forgotten it. Or maybe he'd deliberately abandoned her peace offering, a clear signal that he was leaving her behind too.

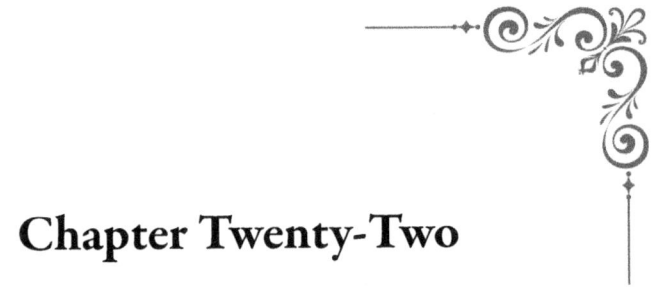

Chapter Twenty-Two

Experience does not err. Only your judgments err
by expecting from her what is not in her power. ~Leonardo da Vinci

Luka shut Chelsea's cottage door, his lips still tingling with the kiss that didn't happen. "So that's it, then," he whispered with a nod.

He took the long way round the village rather than cutting through the village center, heading at a slow pace around the edges of Chilton Crosse. With each step, he surprised himself. He wasn't seething with frustration and regret or concocting some new way to get into Chelsea's good graces or planning an elaborate scheme to win her back and change her mind.

He'd always known this day would come—decision day, when Chelsea made her true feelings known and decided both their fates. But he'd imagined it much differently from this. Luka ran through those last few minutes, from beginning to pitiful end—the casual conversation, the apology cake, the chat about her parents, the bracelet. And then... the kiss. Well, the almost kiss.

Luka hadn't walked into Chelsea's cottage that day with the intention of kissing her. But when he read a longing in her eyes, saw her leaning in, smelled her fragrant scent, then felt her warm lips grazing his, he thought his heart would pound right out of his chest... yet the moment he expected their lips to merge, he received nothing at all. He'd had to open his eyes to realize Chelsea had backed away. Her entire demeanor had changed in the split second it took for him to blink his confusion.

He would hear it in his mind for days, maybe years to come: "This is all I can give you."

And that was his answer. Chelsea had squashed his every hope even before he'd had the chance to declare his love for her or argue his case for why they *could* work out as a couple. Weeks before, or even that morning, Luka might have seen her answer as a sort of challenge. He might have presumed that she meant "It's all I can give you for now."

But something in him changed, too, when she backed away from that kiss. Because it wasn't only a kiss. It was an opportunity, an open door to walk through, a new beginning for them that might last a lifetime. And she had closed that door, albeit gently and courteously, in his face. She'd left him with only a sense of defeat.

He was probably an idiot for not standing his ground and fighting for her. He should have told her that he couldn't live without her—that he wanted to spend all of his future days by her side. But telling that to someone who didn't reciprocate those feelings would have been a fool's errand. He couldn't force someone to love him—couldn't push or cajole or nudge Chelsea to meet him where he was in the relationship. Things didn't work that way.

As he walked toward Mac's, past brilliant-colored countryside and stone-walled properties, Luka came to an important decision. His time in the village was over. He'd been kidding himself all along. It didn't matter if he stayed a few more weeks or months or even if he could give Chelsea more closure and peace about their breakup. None of it mattered if she wasn't in love with him.

Luka had killed their relationship when he'd said goodbye sixteen years before, and that was that. Maybe this was the universe's way of dispensing justice, tit for tat. He deserved this sick feeling in the pit of his stomach. He had earned it.

He paused in the road and pulled his mobile from his pocket to ring up his agent. He was grateful when the call went to voicemail. Luka could forgo all the cursory small talk and get right to the point. "Todd, it's Luka. Plans have changed for me. I can work, starting a week from today. Get me something, anything. Please. I need this."

He rang off, pocketed the phone, and kept moving forward. No other choice.

INSIDE THE BARN, LUKA stood near Mac, arms crossed, staring with him at the folded stalls, ten of them in all. After Luka's conference call with the publisher, which he half-heartedly made his way through, he had asked Mac for an impromptu meeting in the barn to go over their responsibilities for the festival week. Luka needed a distraction.

"We have six men helping, then?" Mac asked.

"Possibly eight. But I'm not sure we can count on Joe... his new twins..."

"Aye."

Before Mac could end the meeting, Luka said, "I spoke with my agent. He's working on some assignments for me."

"Mm." Mac gave him a side-glance. "So, you're leaving the village, then?"

"It's time to get back to my life. My real one. The decision's been made." He didn't add that it was Chelsea who'd made the decision.

"If you're sure about this..."

"I am. I just thought you should know."

Anybody else might have prodded Luka for a reason why his tune had so suddenly changed. Instead, Mac nodded thoughtfully then reached for the barn's door handle.

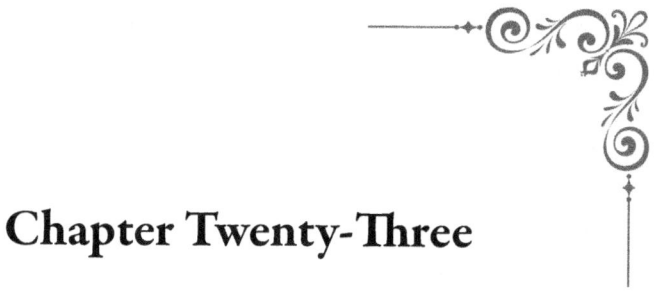

Chapter Twenty-Three

The course of true love never did run smooth. ~Shakespeare

"Here, let me." Chelsea wrapped her fingers around the handle then lifted the luggage from the boot of the car before her mother could do it.

"I also have this other bag, but I can manage," her mother insisted. "It's light."

They walked from her mum's car up the stone path to Nightingale Cottage, where Socrates waited impatiently, whimpering from inside the study.

As soon as Chelsea could securely shut the front door and move the luggage aside, she opened the study door, and out bounded Socrates into the hallway. Chelsea smiled at the reunion. It had been a few months since her mother had been to the cottage, and Socrates whimpered his elation as he leaned upward, trying to plant kisses on her cheek.

"He looks well, doesn't he?" Her mother carried the dog toward the living room.

"He's healed up nicely since his incident. No more rawhides for this little one." She scratched the top of his head. "He gave me such a scare."

"That bracelet. Did I give that to you?"

Chelsea tilted her wrist. "You did. Last Christmas."

"Only two charms? I think you're supposed to add more."

"I will. I've just been busy. This school term was daunting, and then the festival..."

"Of course. And it didn't help, having Mrs. Pickering breathing down your neck, I'm sure."

"That's one way of putting it."

Her mother wandered farther into the cottage, still holding Socrates in the crook of her arm, and peered around the room. "You've made some changes. I like that new chair. A nice place to mark papers?"

"You would think so, but it's too comfy. I'll fall asleep there if I'm not careful."

"And that clock." Her mother pointed to the mantel and frowned. "Is that the time?"

"No, it's broken." She wanted to tell her that she won it in a poker game but wasn't completely sure her mother would approve. "I'll get it repaired... someday." As her mother twirled around, Chelsea asked, "Are you hungry? I've got some soup warming on the Aga, with some cheese and crusty bread. And a toffee cake for later."

"Sounds wonderful." Her mother handed Socrates over to Chelsea. "I need to tidy up first."

"You have the guest bedroom if that's okay..."

"It's more than okay. This is *your* cottage now. In fact, as I drove up and parked, I was thinking—why not change the cottage name, really make it your own? It was named Nightingale when your father and I moved in. But this is a fresh start for you..."

"I'd never considered a name change. It would probably require a mountain of paperwork and research." Chelsea cringed. "I think I'll keep the name. From my Renaissance studies, I know the nightingale has got some dark symbolism attached to it. But I've always loved its song, even as a little girl. It always sounded romantic to me, the bird of love. And a nightingale only makes rare appearances, so it's mysterious, elusive."

"And special. Well suited to this cottage, then."

"I agree."

CHELSEA SLICED TWO pieces of cake then set them on plates and carried them to the kitchen table. Dinner with her mother had been a chatty back-and-forth as they caught up on each other's lives—Chelsea's school, the committee, Lizzie's twins, then her mother's volunteer work, caretaking activities for her sister, and church involvement. All of it was a good diversion for Chelsea. Left alone in the cottage, she would have replayed Luka's visit in her mind a thousand more times, squelching the urge to cry again.

Chelsea lifted her fork to slice into the moist cake.

"This was your father's favorite," her mother said wistfully after taking her first bite. "I probably made it for him a hundred times or more."

Chelsea looked across the table at her mother and *saw* her for the first time since she'd arrived. She appeared the same as always—neatly trimmed ash-blond hair, minimal makeup on her creamy skin, a floral blouse that fit her petite frame perfectly. But there was something new about her this time. A weariness behind the eyes.

"Are you happy in Bristol?" Chelsea asked—a strict departure from their surface-level small talk. She wasn't sure her mother would answer honestly and almost regretted asking.

Her mother pouted her lips as she contemplated her answer. "Most days, yes. Taking care of your aunt can be stressful at times. You know how she can be. But most days, things are good." She turned her attention back toward the cake but then paused, her fork in midair. "I thought moving to Bristol would lessen the pain of losing your father. That removing myself from all the memories of this cottage"—her eyes roamed the kitchen—"would be the salve I needed." Her eyes landed on Chelsea again. "But it's not that way at all.

I carry him with me wherever I go. And the grief as well. Oh, don't get me wrong—I'm not sobbing in a corner every day. I have a life to lead, and I lead it. But you can't escape grief just by moving house, can you? It's a struggle, quite honestly."

"I know, Mum." Chelsea reached her hand across the table and placed it on top of her mother's. "I miss him too. It's never very far away, is it? The sadness."

"No. It isn't. It hovers quite nearby." Her mother abandoned the fork for a sip of tea. "But we carry on, don't we?"

Chelsea squeezed her mum's hand warmly. "We do."

CHELSEA'S EYES FLEW open well before her alarm was set to wake her. She was breathing in quick pants, and her heart was racing. *A bad dream?* She closed her eyes, attempting to remember. She couldn't recall the details, but the dream had everything to do with Luka. No wonder. After saying good night to her mother, Chelsea was left thinking about him while brushing her teeth, changing clothes, settling into her covers—every task was laced with his image. She'd cracked open a book to try to escape, but even that had provided no comfort or relief.

Chelsea shifted onto her side, feeling that same ache in her stomach that had settled there since Luka left her cottage the day before. Maybe that was the nightmare—the confusion in his eyes as Chelsea pushed him away and the disappointment on his face before he walked out and closed the door, literally and figuratively.

Luka tried to kiss me. And I stopped him.

She played out the other scenario in her head. She knew a kiss with Luka would have been amazing. She would've been transported, giddy, intoxicated. But what about the afterward?

Chelsea buried her face in her sheets with a quiet moan. During the almost kiss, she'd let her head rule her heart, which was how she'd spent her entire adult life—following rules, being cautious and careful, and avoiding trouble and heartache whenever she spotted it. And where had it gotten her? To this very moment, feeling sick to her stomach, questioning her instincts, and pondering the excruciating question: *What if?*

CHELSEA QUIETLY CLICKED the cottage door shut, hoping Socrates wouldn't wake up her mother with his barking. The early-morning darkness hovered like a blanket as Chelsea clutched her journal to her chest and ventured out toward the village's high street. She had trusted that Mac and the rest would begin setting up the stalls promptly at five o' clock, as planned.

After her bad dream had awoken her, Chelsea had decided to thrust off her covers, brush her teeth, and start her day, busying herself with preparations—looking over to-do lists, jotting down a reminder to arrive at the archery display an hour early, and deciding what her first-day-of-festival attire should be. Her one and only priority that day was the festival. It had to be.

As she approached the village center, Chelsea could hear the commotion of a busy morning—the clanging and banging of stalls being slid from lorry beds then being assembled in their rightful positions. Chelsea rounded the corner to see more people than expected. Not only were Mac and his staff securing the stalls, but some of the shopkeepers were out, too, beginning to fill their spaces with merchandise. An orange sun made its presence known over the horizon beyond the street, filling a portion of the sky with a comforting glow.

Chelsea immediately recognized Luka across the way, lifting a section of a stall into place while Mac helped secure it. So he hadn't hopped a plane as she'd expected—not yet, at least. There he was, in the thick of things, honoring his commitment to the villagers. And to her.

"Chels?" Rachel walked toward her with a small wave. Chelsea had nearly forgotten that one of Rachel's duties that morning was to provide tea and refreshments for all the early-rising volunteers.

"Oh, hi," Chelsea said. Her brain was still fuzzy and sluggish.

"You need some good strong tea. Come with me." Rachel clutched her friend's hand and led the way before Chelsea could protest.

Inside the vicarage, the warmth of the fireplace was a magnet, and Chelsea moved toward it and sat while Rachel handed her a cup of tea. "Things are going smoothly. Everything is on schedule with the stalls."

"Good," Chelsea said.

"Did your mum get in last night?" Rachel sat down and raised her tea cup.

"She did." Chelsea told her about their pleasant evening, including their unexpected chat regarding grief. She almost wanted to back up and tell her about Luka, too, but it was all too muddled and confusing. She wouldn't even know where to begin or what language to use to describe what had happened.

The front door opened, letting in a blast of cold air as Michael entered. "Hon, did you make more... oh. Hey, Chelsea." He flashed an easy smile.

"Hi, Michael. Thanks for pitching in with the others this morning. I know it's not exactly a vicar's duty, assembling stalls."

"I don't mind. Nothing wrong with a bit of hard labor. We're making good progress—but the shopkeepers are eager to put out their wares. In fact, Mrs. Perkins is standing there, holding an armful of decorations for the stall, waiting for Fletcher to finish!"

"Need more tea?" Rachel asked, already rising to join him.

"You read my mind," Michael said.

She gave her husband's arm a gentle squeeze then headed for the kitchen.

"Well, I'd better get out there," Chelsea said. "I have to lead by example, not sit indoors all morning by a cozy fire, as tempting as that is."

She walked out of the vicarage, filled with new purpose. She'd worked so hard for this festival—for this moment. She couldn't let her troubles with Luka distract her from her duties or weigh her down with guilt that she wasn't even sure she'd earned. Luka was obviously shoving his own troubles aside, assembling stalls, helping Mac—all business. Chelsea should adopt the same attitude. So she would...

ANY PREDICTIONS THAT Chelsea had made regarding the festival's success were surpassed many times over as she observed the bustling, busy street in the midafternoon of its opening day. Giggling children carried treats and balloons, costumed madrigals sang lilting Renaissance tunes, Joe passed out turkey legs to hungry villagers and tourists, miniature Union Jacks waved proudly from above, and festivalgoers snapped photos with their phones. It was all as merry and jubilant as Chelsea had hoped it might be—Noelle's festive painting of Chilton Crosse come to life. She even spied Mrs. Pickering *smiling* as she browsed a nearby stall.

Chelsea was available all morning to the workers and volunteers, answering questions, solving minor crises, and making sure they had a point of contact should they need anything. She came to the end of the street and saw a new crowd forming around Noelle, who'd set up an easel outside the gallery. She was halfway finished with her oil painting as onlookers marveled. Her aunt Joy would have been proud.

Across the street, Mr. Bentley sat in a prime spot near the bakery's stall. He lifted a plate of samples as he chatted gregariously with those stopping by. In all the hustle and bustle, Chelsea had only spotted Luka twice, discreetly taking photos of various festivalgoers and merchants. She wondered if he'd spotted her too.

"Oh, Chelsea, darling, I'm so proud of you!" Chelsea felt a hand at her elbow and saw her mother holding two shopping bags and a half-eaten turkey leg. "You've pulled *all this* together and managed a teaching job as well. I don't know how you've done it!"

"Thanks, Mum. I had a lot of help."

"Have you eaten anything today? You need to take care of yourself. Let me buy you a turkey leg. They are delicious!"

Chelsea realized she hadn't had anything past a slice of buttered toast before leaving the cottage that morning. But there wasn't time to rectify it. "I'll be okay. I need to meet the archer at the manor before his exhibition."

"Well, promise me you'll eat something after that. You need to take care of yourself."

"I promise."

Chelsea took a couple of deliberate seconds to study her mother's smile. It was childlike, carefree. She barely recalled ever seeing her mother that way, without some invisible weight of responsibility always strapped to her shoulders. She was having a good time, casting off her obligations and duties, like a little girl again. Perhaps this festival, at its core, represented the idea of forgetting one's troubles, being thrilled by sights and smells and sounds, and escaping the mundane tasks of everyday life. Every committee meeting, every scowl from Mrs. Pickering, and every spare minute spent on preparation and planning had been worth it.

THE SECOND DAY OF THE festival saw even more participants than the day before. Chelsea had to wade through a sea of people to reach Joe's stall then stand in a lengthy queue to purchase a turkey leg. She'd learned her lesson the day before. Not taking her mother's advice to "eat something!" had resulted in lightheadedness and a piercing headache. Thus, she would not only eat but would also relax into the festival and become a participant. After dealing with one of Frank's anxious questions about running out of tickets and replying to a call from the falconer, Chelsea pocketed her mobile to browse the stalls as a festivalgoer.

Turkey leg in hand, she roamed the cobblestone street, examining the available wares—beaded jewelry and candles from Mrs. Pennington, historical and Renaissance-related books sold by Holly and Fletcher, antique clocks made available by Mr. Rothchild, antique pipes offered by Mr. Belvedere, and wooden zoo animals crafted by Mac and sold near the gift shop. Chelsea decided it was a good idea to purchase a few items for future Christmas gifts. And by the time she reached the end of the street, she'd disposed of her turkey leg and held two bags stuffed full of merchandise. She paused at the small stage and recognized one of her pupils, sitting cross-legged and playing a lute while Rosalee, in costume, issued a monologue. As Chelsea listened more closely, she realized it wasn't a monologue but one of Shakespeare's most famous sonnets. She whispered the familiar words under her breath:

... Love is not love

Which alters when it alteration finds,

Or bends with the remover to remove.

O no! It is an ever-fixed mark

That looks on tempests and is never shaken;

It is the star to every wandering bark—

Chelsea felt someone at her side and turned to see Mary Cartwright, wearing a look of concern. "Chelsea. I'm sorry to bother you with this..." She was tugging gently at Chelsea's sleeve. "Do you know where we're keeping the shopping bags? I can't remember. And we're about to run out!"

During one of the earlier committee meetings, it was decided that the shop owners should be encouraged to place their merchandise into special bags branded with the Chilton Crosse Renaissance Festival logo, which Noelle and Tristan had designed together.

"They're at the pub. Joe's keeping them behind the bar. Take as many as you need—there should be plenty."

"Thank you. That's a relief." Mary released her grasp of Chelsea's sleeve but paused. "This festival. It's a great success, isn't it?"

"It is!"

"And the rain only came for a bit this morning."

"Let's hope that holds! The falconry display is this afternoon."

"I hope I can get away for that. I would love to see it." Mary waved her goodbye then scurried away toward the pub.

A smattering of applause was directed toward Rosalee as she stepped off the stage. She was soon replaced by the madrigal singers. Though she wanted to stay and hear them, Chelsea knew it was a good time to deposit her bags at the cottage, feed Socrates, then make her way to the falconry show at the manor. To that end, she took a step but stopped short, nearly running straight into Luka.

"Sorry. I was moving too fast—"

"I wasn't watching where I was going..." Luka's gaze froze on her, but then his eyes shifted down to the camera in his hand.

He can't even look at me.

She noticed deep circles under his eyes, a sign that he hadn't gotten much sleep either. Before she could conjure up some awkward small talk about the festival or the weather, Luka had looked past her and gestured toward the stage, where the madrigal group was taking a collective breath before singing its first notes.

"I need to take some photos..."

"Oh. I'm in your way."

Chelsea stepped aside as Luka moved past her with a polite nod. She watched him crouch near the stage. Sucking in a long breath, keeping tears at bay, Chelsea turned in the direction of her cottage and clutched the handles of her bags until her fingernails created crescent-shaped dents in her palms.

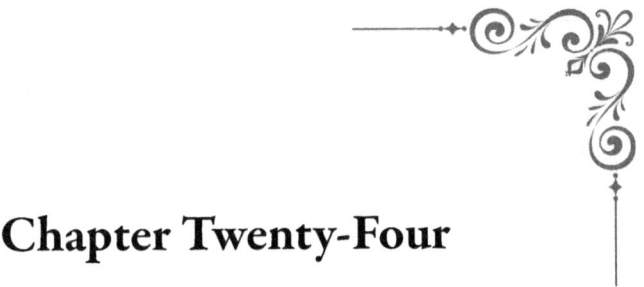

Chapter Twenty-Four

Doubt thou the stars are fire, doubt that the sun doth move,
Doubt truth to be a liar but never doubt I love. ~Shakespeare

Chelsea was chatting with Sienna at the bookshop's stall when the skies burst open and the rain began to pour. It was the festival's third day, midafternoon, and although sinister clouds had been gathering for the past hour, Chelsea had hoped they would keep moving and pass the village by. When the first raindrops fell, a collection of shrieks went up as attendees struggled for umbrellas and tried to protect their purchases, costumes, food, or children. At first, Chelsea thought it was a random burst of rain that would be gone as quickly as it came, but after a few minutes, it fell even steadier and harder, with occasional peals of thunder and whipping winds. The crowds dispersed, forcing an early end to the day's festivities.

After a peek at her mobile's weather app, confirming that a broad cluster of storms would continue to plague the area for at least the next hour or two, Chelsea begrudgingly gave the signal to shut down the stalls. Some vendors had already begun packing up, frantically trying to keep their merchandise from being soaked.

Chelsea's mother shouted over the thunder, "Can I help? What's the plan?"

"Go back to the cottage—get dried off!" Chelsea shouted back. "I'll stay here and help out."

Her mother scurried off toward the cottage while Chelsea pitched in with the nearest stall. Chelsea's umbrella was only a hindrance, so she abandoned it and helped Holly and Fletcher transport their books safely inside the shop. Just as the community had worked together as a cohesive unit to put this festival on, so they worked together now, under dreadful circumstances. Fortunately, this was the final day of vendor stalls, which were scheduled to be disassembled later that evening anyway.

After nearly an hour's work, Chelsea and the others had miraculously managed to stay half-dry in the process of grabbing merchandise and swiftly moving into the shelter of the shops. All the stalls had been emptied, with the merchants restocking their remaining goods inside the shops. There was nothing left for Chelsea to do. From that point, the shop owners could take over—she would only slow them down, not knowing which products went on which shelves.

Mac and his crew had already begun the stall-dismantling process, blinking back raindrops as they each got soaked clean through. She caught Mac's eye from across the street and shouted, "What else can I do?"

"Nothing, lass! We've got it from here. Get yourself dry!"

Officially free of all her duties for the day, Chelsea found her umbrella splayed haphazardly on the pavement where she'd chucked it earlier. She opened it above her head, happy to take Mac's advice.

Inside her cottage was a completely different scene from the one she'd left behind. A cozy fire crackled in the fireplace, her mother sat cross-legged on the sofa with Socrates in her lap, and a soft blanket lay casually across Chelsea's comfy chair, waiting for her to plop down.

"It's positively awful out there," her mother said as Chelsea peeled off her coat and scarf.

"And it's not letting up."

"I'll put the kettle on. I was already planning on it after lighting the fire."

"No, stay put. You two look content. I'll do it in a minute—I need to change clothes and dry off my hair first."

Several minutes later, Chelsea sat across from her mother, feeling restful and serene with a hot cup of tea in her hand and a blanket wrapped around her legs. She hadn't realized the physical toll the entire festival would take on her by midweek. But at least the most taxing part was over. The only events in front of her were the school play and the bonfire, both set for the following night.

"I'm positively knackered," she admitted to her mother then took another sip of tea.

"I should have stayed and helped."

"Nonsense. We did fine, everyone working together. The men are disassembling the stalls. They're probably finished by now, lugging everything up to Mac's."

"Well, even if it had to end earlier than planned, I think the entire festival was a roaring success. The falcon display was probably my favorite. In all my years, I'd never been to one."

"I got a sneak preview last week from the falconer, and Luka got some fantastic shots of the bird. They're on the website if you want to see them."

"Luka?"

"The elder vicar's son. Do you remember him?"

"Yes, of course." Her mother was petting a snoring Socrates in her lap. "I thought I saw him yesterday at the festival. He looks nearly the same as I remember. How long has he been back in the village?"

"Since his father's funeral."

"I regretted missing the funeral. It was a bad day for your aunt—she needed me."

"I understand. Well, Luka's been in town, helping with the festival. He volunteered to be our photographer the past few weeks."

It felt bizarre, saying his name so many times out loud and acting matter-of-fact about him as though he were just some random person she cared little about.

"You and Luka... saw each other." Her mother's gaze was steady, her expression unreadable. "You dated. When you were younger."

Chelsea was surprised her mother had been paying attention back then. "Yes."

"How has it been for you, seeing him again?"

Chelsea moved past her own discomfort, set down her teacup, and contemplated an honest answer. "It's complicated. When I first saw him, it rattled me. My tongue seemed frozen—it was hard to even talk to him. But as the weeks have gone by, and we've been forced to work together for the festival, we've gotten... closer."

"Do you still love him?"

She blinked at her mother, unsure where all this was coming from. Even Rachel hadn't asked her that point-blank question. But Chelsea was tired of hiding the truth and grateful her mother had asked.

"Yes. I still do."

Her mother chewed at her bottom lip. "I feel like there's something you should know. I didn't think it mattered all these years later. But now, I'm not sure..." She stopped petting Socrates, which startled him awake. "Here, little one," she whispered, lifting him to the side, where he snuggled up against her thigh.

Chelsea tilted her head, impatient, wondering what confession she was about to hear.

Her mother rubbed her forehead then gestured to explain. "First, you have to understand—you were my daughter. My *only* child. And we were both worried for you, your father and I. We only ever wanted what was best for you."

"You're talking about Luka. Back then..."

"Yes. He wasn't suited for you. We both firmly believed it. Luka had a poor reputation around the village. He skipped church services, was heard rowing in public with his father, had no intention of going to university. Then there was the graffiti incident."

"Mum... that wasn't Luka."

"Well, most of the villagers assumed it was. Chelsea, try to see this from a parent's point of view. When you were with Luka, *your* grades began to suffer as well. He was having an influence."

Chelsea couldn't deny this. Her grades *were* plummeting in the months before Luka left the village, but she hadn't cared. Her only focus had been on Luka and their future.

"Mum. Tell me." She tried to soften the anxiety in her voice.

Her mother cleared her throat. "Well, one night—this was when you were, oh, maybe seventeen—you were at choir rehearsal, and I was tidying your room, as I usually did. Looking for clothes to be laundered, discarding rubbish from the nightstand, that sort of thing. And as I knelt down to straighten the shoes under your bed, there was something poking out between the mattresses. I'm ashamed to admit this, but curiosity got the better of me, and rather than push the book back where it belonged, I... slipped it out."

"Mum..."

"I'm not proud of it." Her mother's voice was shaky and thin. "When I saw that it was a diary, *even then* I didn't replace it between the mattresses as I should have. 'I'm a concerned parent,' I told myself. The book opened to a specific page near the back, and I skimmed it. You were making plans to leave the village on a backpack trip to Europe. And then I saw the name Luka and gasped. I didn't realize your father had been walking past, on his way downstairs. He must've seen the look of shock on my face. Before I could explain, he took the diary from me and read it for himself. I tried to stop him and tell him we shouldn't interfere, that those were *your* private thoughts. I already felt guilty enough. But he was determined. He took the book and... left the cottage."

Chelsea experienced the story as though she were living it, watching from above as the scene played out. While teenage Chelsea had been singing hymns alongside Rachel in church, she'd been completely oblivious to the drama going on in her very own household.

"What did Daddy do with my diary?"

Her mother leaned back against the cushion, looking as though she'd just run a tiresome marathon and needed to catch her breath. "He never told me. I continued tidying, my heart in my throat, wishing I'd never even seen the diary. About a half hour later, I heard your father return from his errand, climb the stairs for a moment, then move back downstairs. I entered your bedroom and pressed my fingers between the mattresses, and it was there—your diary, replaced."

"He went to see Luka." She imagined her father, intimidating enough in his constable's uniform, going to confront her boyfriend, with *her private diary* in hand.

"He never admitted to it, but yes. I'm sure he did."

Chelsea couldn't suppress her fresh anger toward both her parents for such a clear invasion of her privacy and for the betrayal that she was only just being made aware of. The series of decisions that night, made in haste and anger and without her permission or knowledge, had contained enormous consequences for Chelsea's entire future.

Her mother sniffed back tears. "The next thing I knew, a couple of days later, Luka was gone from the village, and you were inconsolable."

"And Daddy knew exactly why. He watched me being absolutely gutted. I was heartbroken. And he let me suffer."

"Your father thought he was saving you from destruction—from a future with Luka. He wanted the best for you. We both did."

"Tough love." Chelsea stared at the floor, remembering. "That's what he would call it whenever he would punish me for poor grades or bad behavior."

"We hated seeing you hurt. But I suppose we figured... young love, well, it isn't always real love, is it? We hoped you would get over him and move on. I tried to speak with you, but you didn't want to talk. I knew you were brokenhearted and that it was partially my fault. But I couldn't bring myself to tell you the part I'd played. Our relationship was already fragile, and I thought this might be the end of it if I confessed—that you might never forgive me. My sole desire was to protect you. That's all. Please understand. And your father thought he was doing the right thing for your future."

"But it wasn't his decision to make. It was mine." Chelsea struggled to process this incredible news, attempting to connect all the dots, past to present. One thing was crystal clear—everything had changed. She thrust off the blanket and stood. "I need to go."

"Chelsea..." Her mother grasped Chelsea's wrist as she took the first step. "I'm so very sorry. For all of it."

"I know."

Chapter Twenty-Five

*And when love speaks, the voice of all the gods
makes heaven drowsy with the harmony.* ~Shakespeare

Chelsea drove through the open gates of Mac's property and headed straight for the barn. Even during her turmoil after leaving her mother at the cottage, she'd been able to calmly determine that the men had probably set all the stalls inside Mac's barn for storage and that she might still find Luka there. She was right.

As she steered toward the barn and parked haphazardly in the mud, thankful that the fierce rains had been reduced to a light drizzle, she noticed Luka and Mac standing deep inside the barn then taking steps toward the wide-open doors, curious to see who had pulled up. It wasn't until Chelsea opened the car door that she realized the cardigan she'd fetched on her way out wasn't adequate to fight the damp chill.

"Chelsea?" Luka remained frozen in the doorway as she marched swiftly toward the barn.

Mac offered a cordial nod and exited through the doors, probably realizing Chelsea and Luka's need for privacy. The other men had already gone by that point, so Chelsea stood alone with Luka.

"Are you okay?" Luka stepped closer, placing a hand on her shoulder.

She took a step backward, out of his grasp, and crossed her arms after realizing she was shivering. She stared at Luka, unblinking. "Tell me what happened on the night my father came to see you."

"Your father?" Luka's expression was dazed. "I'm not sure what—"

"That night. Sixteen years ago. When he discovered my diary."

Luka looked upward and parted his lips as he sucked in a sharp breath—a clear sign that he knew precisely what she meant.

"My mother just told me everything." Chelsea's voice quivered but somehow grew stronger as she found the words. "How she nicked my diary from my mattress. How she read about my plans with you, running off to Europe. My father took the diary from her and left the cottage. He came to you that night, didn't he?" On the swift journey to the barn, she had promised herself she wouldn't cry. She wanted answers. She had no patience for tears clouding her judgment.

Luka exhaled then shook his head and ran a hand through his hair, still damp from the rain. "I didn't know she knew," he whispered, almost to himself.

Chelsea took a step closer and peered up into Luka's rugged, confused face, desperate to hear his side of the story before she had a chance to make misguided assumptions. "I need to hear it from you. All of it."

He nodded in defeat. "Okay."

He turned away to pace. Chelsea felt her impatience rise but fought it back. Luka had to tell his story his way, in his own time. Chelsea considered this moment from *his* perspective—utterly caught off guard, as she had been earlier with her mother. Luka was probably trying to find his bearings as he rewound his memory back to those details.

Finally, he cleared his throat as he pivoted to face her. "I was actually right here that night." He pointed to the floor. "Inside the barn, finding a tool for Mac, when your father drove up. I watched a police car rush toward me then saw your father—in full uniform—climb out of the car. I was on edge from the start."

He shifted his weight to his other foot and continued. "I greeted him politely, thinking he might be looking for you. But he was looking for me. His face was angry, but his voice was calm, in this... chilling way. He held a pink book in his hand—I'd never seen it before. He said it was your diary and that it talked about our plans to leave together. Then he came a step closer and held the diary between us. He told me to explain myself."

Chelsea could only imagine the fear that had struck young Luka as he was faced with a livid police-constable father.

"I told him the truth—that yes, you and I had planned to explore Europe for a year, and then you would go to university. And that we were planning to tell him about it together. But he didn't like that. His voice grew louder, and he told me it would never happen. That his daughter would be attending Bath University, as scheduled, and nothing would stop it. He would see to it."

Luka's deliberate pause in the story told Chelsea he was holding back. "What else? I need to know everything."

He pushed out a long sigh and tugged at his shirt. "I'm not sure you do. Chels, once I say this stuff, I can't unsay it."

"I can handle it. I deserve the truth."

Luka paced again. "Well, your father used some colorful language to describe 'blokes like me' and said that I wasn't good enough for his little girl. That I was already soiling your reputation around the village, and people were gossiping." Luka gave her a side-glance, perhaps to check and see if she could handle more. "And then he brought up the vandalism as an example of what type of bloke I really was."

"But he knew you were innocent."

Luka winced. "Well, they never caught the person who did it, so technically, it could've been me, from his perspective."

Chelsea's eyes widened. "Did he threaten you?"

"Not overtly. But it was implied that maybe he had the power to..."

"Pin a conviction on you."

Luka hesitated then nodded.

Chelsea filled in the other blanks. "And if that happened, then your own father—a respected vicar—would also be shamed in the village."

"The vandalism charge was only implied, never spoken aloud," Luka clarified again.

"I had no idea he was capable of this." She made eye contact again. "What else?"

"Well, he got this fatherly tone at the end, even placed a hand on my shoulder. He said he only wanted the best for his daughter, and that if I did too—if I *really* loved you—I should prove it and consider leaving for good. He said that your life would be better off without me in it. He told me to do the 'right thing.'"

At that, Chelsea's vision blurred with tears, but ironically, everything came into crystal-clear view. It all made sense. Luka *hadn't* left the village of his own volition. He'd been pressured and intimidated and emotionally blackmailed into it, and by her own father. Had that conversation never occurred, Luka would have stayed in Chilton Crosse. They would have fulfilled their plans and would probably still be together.

Chelsea flicked a tear from her cheek and took a step toward him. She wasn't finished being angry with him. "Why didn't you come to me that night and tell me all this?"

"I considered it. But, Chels, there was no way I could tell you that your dad—the man you adored—had gone behind your back and said those things."

"Okay, but I still don't understand. Why not later on, when I was at university or even after Daddy passed away? For years—and even for these past few weeks—you've still let me believe the worst about you."

"When Michael told me you'd gone to university, I knew you were on a certain path, and I didn't want to mess with that. When I heard you'd gotten engaged, I assumed you were happy. I couldn't ruin that for you. And when your father passed, I still didn't want to taint your impression of him. It would be cruel, and you might blame him. But honestly, those are just excuses. I thought it was too late—that none of this would make a difference even now. I assumed you hated me for how I left."

"I actually did for a bit."

"I hated myself too." Luka turned away from her. "The things your dad said—they echoed inside my head for years afterward. I fought hard not to believe them. It wasn't the first time I'd heard people telling me how bad I was or that I didn't fit in or I wasn't a good influence."

Chelsea could feel her anger dissolve a little. "I'm sorry that my father's words had that effect on you. It wasn't right, what he did." Even with all the new revelations, she was most gobsmacked by the fact that the father she had adored, the person she most trusted in the world, was capable of taking direct action, behind her back, to blow her world—and Luka's—apart. Whether he'd meant to or not, it had been a betrayal of the worst kind, one that held lifelong consequences.

Luka faced her again. "Your father wasn't perfect, but his intentions were pure."

"How can you say that? Why defend him?"

"If I were a father, I might actually do the same in his place. If I saw a potential threat to my daughter and had the power to stop it, I would probably take it. He loved you that much. He thought he was doing the right thing."

It was Chelsea's turn to step away from Luka. As she raised her voice, it echoed into the lofty chambers of the barn. "*Why* does everyone keep doing that—telling me that he meant well, that decisions he made on my behalf were for the best? I should've had a say in all this, Luka. My mum and dad had a choice. You had a choice. But I never had one." Her voice cracked as her heart hammered faster.

"Chels, look at the options I faced that night. What if I'd ignored your dad's advice, told you everything he said, and we went off together to Europe with you hating him and having fractured relationships with both your parents the rest of your life? I didn't want you to choose between me and your family. I couldn't be the reason for that kind of rift."

"So you chose the other path instead," she whispered, remembering the night Luka had said goodbye. She looked up at him, recalling his words. "You told me you had to leave, that I 'deserved better.' And that I would 'find happiness' someday. Empty platitudes with no real explanations. You left me completely confused."

"I didn't know how else to handle it. I was confused too. I actually believed a lot of what your father said. I convinced myself that I would be holding you back—that I wasn't good enough for you. Even so, I'm still responsible for leaving. Your dad was a factor, but he didn't raise a gun to my head. I could have stayed. But I chose to let you go. I'm so sorry." Luka stepped toward her, closing the gap.

He tried to grasp her hands, but Chelsea pulled away. "For sixteen long and agonizing years, I believed that you'd gone away because you stopped loving me. Or maybe because you never loved me in the first place." Tears welled, and she willed them away. "I carried that with me all those years, everywhere I went. I gave you my heart, and I thought you'd given me yours too. But after you left, I told myself it was just a lie. All the moments together, the time we spent, the conversations, the kisses—they started to mean nothing to me because you'd never really loved me. I convinced myself that I wasn't worth your sticking around."

Hearing it stated aloud was both exhausting and liberating. It was out, finally. The lies he'd told himself, the lies she'd told herself, even the lies they'd been telling each other—they were all laid bare, hovering between them inside the damp air of a rustic barn.

After a significant pause, Luka stepped toward her and cradled her face in his hands. Chelsea was too weary to resist. Surrendering, she looked into his eyes, determined to see past her own defenses. It was time to open her heart and really hear him.

"Chelsea Barrett, I loved you then, and I love you now. I should have stayed and fought for you. It's the biggest regret of my life that I didn't." His dark eyes moved even closer in a loving gaze. "Believe this—I will never stop loving you. And I will never leave you again. If you'll have me."

The remaining traces of anger and confusion and pain that had been churning inside Chelsea dissipated. Those were the words she had been craving to hear for over a decade. They became a soothing balm on a wound she had thought would never be healed. And she let herself believe them.

Luka stroked her cheek with his thumb and leaned in. And this time, Chelsea accepted him. His lips pressed against hers with the same urgency that his words had contained, and she reciprocated, tasting his mouth and touching his beard, his shoulders, his waist. She couldn't get close enough.

Luka pulled away, assessing her reaction. She reached up to trace his mouth with her fingertips. "I've never stopped loving you either," Chelsea admitted in a whisper. "I'm tired of fighting it. You're my heart and soul. You always have been."

He looked different to her now, as though a new lens had just been snapped into place. His image was clear—undistorted and unfiltered. She could finally gaze on him with confidence. And she could trust what she was seeing.

Luka smiled that beautiful smile then caught Chelsea up in a tight embrace. It was even more intimate than the kiss they'd just shared. Through his strong grasp, she could feel his heart thumping near her chest as he cradled her neck with his hand. She never wanted to let him go.

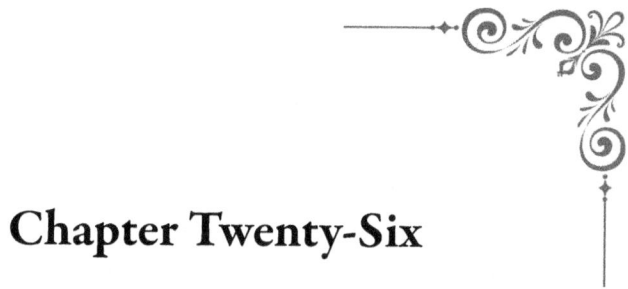

Chapter Twenty-Six

*A person often meets his destiny
on the road he took to avoid it.* ~Jean de La Fontaine

On her drive back to the cottage, Chelsea realized she'd become one of *those* people—the ones who claimed that, because they were deeply in love, the skies looked bluer, the sunsets appeared more vibrant, and the world seemed altogether brighter. As the car bumped along the path toward home, Chelsea realized something else—she couldn't stop smiling. It was a stark contrast from her drive to Mac's barn a half hour earlier. Her world had been dark and confusing then, her faith in other people shaken to its core. But since the moment Luka had kissed her inside the barn, professed his love, and set her doubts to rest, Chelsea's heart had burst wide-open, ready to accept all the love she deserved. It was a delicious euphoria that felt like a page out of a romance novel. But it wasn't. This was her new reality. Luka and Chelsea had made it through to the other side—it was finally their time.

She hadn't wanted to leave the barn so soon, but after more kissing and talking, Luka's mobile had cruelly interrupted their reunion with a reminder of a long-standing appointment for a meeting that night. He and Mac had planned to meet with the foundation, after hours, to discuss paying for the service dog's training.

"I can postpone it or maybe reschedule," Luka offered, stroking Chelsea's cheek.

"No, you need to go," she insisted. "This is important. And Mac's probably waiting."

"You should come with us. You have every right to be there."

For a second, Chelsea considered this, but then she said, "I can't. There's something I need to do."

"Your mum." Luka had read her thoughts.

"We didn't leave things very well when I stormed off to see you. I was emotional and scattered. I can barely remember what I said to her, but I know it was angry. I need to set this right."

WHEN CHELSEA OPENED her cottage's door, she noticed Socrates clicking down the hallway to greet her, but there was no sign of her mum. She shut the door and picked up Socrates, who moistened her cheeks with a series of happy licks.

"Mum?" Chelsea scanned the empty living room and saw the glowing embers of an abandoned fire. Perhaps she'd gone to bed early.

"Are you here? Mum?" Chelsea said again, walking toward the kitchen.

She found her mother at the table, one hand holding a teacup, the other gripping a photo frame. When she glanced up, her expression was dazed. "I wasn't sure you'd come back."

Chelsea gently set the dog down and took a seat. "What have you got there?" She pointed to the frame, wanting to ease into the conversation—to meet her mother where she was.

Her mother tilted the frame then pushed it closer to Chelsea until the photo came into clear view. "After you left the cottage, I didn't know what to do with myself. I roamed around your father's study, looking for a distraction, and discovered this."

Chelsea smiled at the photo—her father propping up eight-year-old Chelsea on his broad shoulders. They were at the seaside, both of them smiling.

"I took that photo," her mother said. "And tonight, I realized it was always that way with us. I was the one on the outside, looking in. You two were a force to be reckoned with—always laughing or chatting intently, heads huddled together. Sometimes I felt... excluded. It's infantile to admit this, but I think I was jealous of you both."

"Oh, Mum." Chelsea abandoned the frame and leaned forward to place a hand on top of hers.

"I'm not playing the victim. I'm not asking for pity." Her eyes searched Chelsea's face. "It's my way of explaining how things went wrong between us—why I was hands-off with you when I should've been more available. If I had been, things would be so different. I should never have invaded your privacy and read the diary. Because you should have been comfortable enough to *tell* me about Luka and about your plans. But we didn't know how to talk, did we? And that's on me. I was the parent."

"Please don't be hard on yourself. I was the one sneaking around, lying to you and Dad, seeing Luka secretly. Those were my choices. I bear responsibility here too."

"Well, at the very least, after finding the diary, I should've insisted that your father sit down with you and hash things out—not bluster off and go repair it on his own. You deserved better than that. And... " Her mother shook her head and lowered her voice. "When you left the cottage earlier, I thought about how far-reaching those consequences were. How *our* choices affected the direction of your whole life. I didn't know it at the time. And I'm sorrier than you'll ever know."

"But, Mum, I came back here to tell you that it *is* repaired. Everything is all hashed out." Chelsea waited until she caught her mother's gaze again. "I went straight to see Luka—well, *stormed in* is more accurate. I was this tempest of emotions, and I spouted off every-thing I'd been holding in for years." She told her mother about Luka's account of that night. "We talked everything out—there was some anger, there were some tears. But it's the most honest conversation I've ever had with anyone. And we said that we loved each other."

"Oh, darling." Her mother squeezed Chelsea's hand as tears glistened in her eyes.

"So you see? Everything is as it's supposed to be. We're together now, and nothing else matters."

GOOD MORNING, BEAUTIFUL.

Chelsea blinked at Luka's text through sleepy eyes, having just been awakened by the ping. So it hadn't been a dream—the barn, the talk, the kisses, the plans for their future. They were every bit as real as the mobile she held in her hand.

Grinning, she rolled over onto her back, adjusted the pillow, and texted: *Hey, my love. Sleep well?*

Blissful. You?

Same.

Chelsea suddenly remembered what day it was—the final day of the festival. She still had a few—thankfully manageable—obligations, such as getting her mother's ticket from Frank and arriving early at the assembly hall to help support and encourage her nervous pupils performing in the play. Their Romeo had made a full recovery and was anxious to step on stage.

When can I see you? she texted.

A couple of jobs for Mac, then I'm free. Meet you at the play?

It's a date. Chelsea set down the mobile on her stomach but heard it ping again.

This time, it was Rachel. *I have news. Can you stop by the vicarage?*

Chelsea tapped out her happy response: *I have news too! Be there soon.*

WHEN RACHEL OPENED the vicarage door, she looked as well rested and fresh-faced as she'd ever been. She offered tea as she shut the door, but Chelsea turned her down. "I had some earlier with a bite of toast."

Rachel led Chelsea to the sofa—remarkably clear of its usual laundry sorting or lesson plans.

As they sat, Chelsea said, "You first. What's this news?" She couldn't read anything significant from her friend's expression.

"No. You go first. I think I know what it is." Rachel raised her brows hopefully. "Luka related?"

Chelsea nodded, and before she could even open her mouth, Rachel squealed. "I knew it! Tell me everything."

Chelsea recounted last evening's drama—her mother's confession, the barn conversation, even Luka's most recent text. With every new detail, Rachel reacted in small gasps, widened eyes, and finally, a broad smile.

"Oh, Chels. I couldn't be any happier for you both. I mean it. You two were made for each other. It only took you sixteen years to figure it out." She chuckled. "So Luka's staying permanently, then? In the village?"

"Yes. His agent gave him one more quick assignment next week. But when Luka returns, he's here to stay. I pressed hard to make sure it's what he really wants, to live in Chilton Crosse. He shouldn't drop everything just for me. I mean, he would essentially be giving up his traveling lifestyle and his career to a great degree. But staying was his idea. He can set up his own studio or have some photography exhibits in London if he wants—possibly even do some mentoring or lecturing. He sounded chuffed about the new possibilities. Plus, he can always create more photography books or take the occasional trip for a travel assignment."

"This is the *best* news. All of it."

"Well, maybe not the best. I haven't heard yours yet!"

Rachel drew in a deep breath then reached for her mobile and began tapping while Chelsea tried to be patient. Finally, Rachel clutched the mobile to her chest and fought tears. "It's happened, Chelsea. I'm going to be a mother." She swiveled the phone so that Chelsea could see the photo—a little girl smiling brightly into the camera, shiny black hair pulled back into two wispy ponytails. Chelsea took the phone slowly as Rachel explained. "Her name is Anna. Well, that's her English name. She's from China, an orphanage there, and she's nearly three years old. The social worker told us about her a few days ago, but we weren't sure we'd be able to get her, so I didn't want to tell anyone. But now we're sure."

"Oh, Rachel. She's beautiful. And she's really yours?" Chelsea's eyes brimmed with tears, matching Rachel's. "I don't even know what to say."

"I'm still having trouble believing it. And Michael is over the moon too."

"I can barely wrap my head around it. This is what you've been wanting for years. Why now, though, after all this time?"

"The social worker said that we'd already been on the waiting list for a long while, and it was just... our turn. She said sometimes these things fall into place when you're not expecting them. A few months ago, we told her we'd love to find an infant but that we were open to older children too. I think that made the difference. And so, a few days ago, she sent us this possibility of Anna. When I saw her face, those sparkling eyes, I knew she was the one for us. I can't explain it, Chelsea, but... she was already ours."

"Incredible, all of it." Chelsea handed the mobile back to Rachel then wiped her cheek. "What happens next?"

"Michael and I will video chat with Anna this weekend so she can see our faces live. And if all goes well, we'll fly to China in the next couple of weeks to meet her in person. There's still loads of paperwork and red tape before she comes home to the village. It's a process, maybe even months long. But at least we're this close."

"I'm ecstatic for both of you. You're going to be a mum, Rachel."

"I am," she whispered through tears.

CHELSEA COULD SEE WHY Fred enjoyed being a drama teacher. There was nothing to match the electric atmosphere and buzz of nervous energy that went on behind the scenes two hours before a play began. Pupils practiced lines with each other, paced while holding a script, or made last-minute adjustments to costumes or sets. A few adults were backstage, as well, helping apply stage makeup, aiding with costume issues, and generally filling in the gaps wherever needed. Chelsea was among them, hovering, trying not to get in anyone's way but helping out as best she could.

"Miss Barrett?" Sienna was calling from a backstage corner, near the exit door. She still wore her civilian clothes—jeans and a jumper—and held a well-worn script tagged with colored tabs.

Chelsea walked toward her with a warm smile. "How are you?"

"Nervous."

"How can I help? Do you want to run some lines?" Chelsea touched the edge of the script.

"No, that's okay. I've memorized them until I can practically speak them in my sleep. But I still feel scared about stepping out on stage for the first time. Rehearsals are easy. But once I'm in front of a real audience, under the lights, knowing people are staring at me... it's that very first step I'm petrified of. I need one of your encouraging talks."

"My what?"

"You know, those enthusiastic speeches you're good at in class."

Chelsea wasn't aware of any such speeches, but if the pupils had interpreted some of her lectures that way, she was flattered. She cleared her throat, knowing how important these next few words might be in helping set Sienna at ease.

"Okay. Well..." Gazing around for inspiration, Chelsea found a thick line of tape on the floor, at the edge of the stage. "The first step of anything is the hardest one. It takes the most courage." She pointed at the tape. "So when you're waiting in the wings for your entrance, and you approach that line, dig deep and find that courage inside then hold it tight in both your fists. Then—cross over with poise and confidence."

Chelsea drew her attention back to her pupil. "You can do this, Sienna. I've watched you all year in my class, in group work, and in rehearsals. You *are* Juliet. You have her quiet strength, her steadfast belief in love, her bravery. Think of what she did—she ignored her parents' command to marry Paris. She fell in love with the enemy. She saw him in secret and *married him* in secret, then she defied her parents to the point of taking a potion to pretend she was dead so she could escape and be with her one true love. That is bravery. Step into her shoes. Be Juliet. And that's where you'll find your confidence."

Sienna took her first significant breath since Chelsea had started speaking. "That was it. That's the speech I needed. Thank you, Miss Barrett." She leaned in for a tight, quick hug then nodded decisively as she rolled up her script and walked away.

Before Chelsea could bask in the glow of relief at somehow finding the right words when she'd needed them, the exit door creaked open behind her, and Luka entered.

"You're here." A smile stretched across her face. "I wasn't expecting you this early."

Luka moved toward her, peeking around at the chaotic scene behind them. "Come over here." He grabbed her hand and led her to a back corner where they were shielded from view—just barely.

He pulled her close, and she felt his body against hers as he kissed her—a luscious, deep, slow kiss. Chelsea nearly drowned inside it, losing all sense of time and place.

When the kiss ended, he told her, "I've wanted to do that all day."

She kept her eyes on his handsome face and found his hands, threading his fingers with her own. She wanted to slow down and take in the sight of him without a single wall between them. After all they'd been through, it was almost too good to be true.

"Did you hear about Rachel and Michael?" she asked. "Their good news?"

"About Anna? Michael showed me the photo. Amazing news."

"You'll be an uncle! An incredible one."

"Looking forward to it." Luka released her hands and slipped his own around her waist. "I have other news. Mac has agreed to let me stay on at his guest cottage. Long as I like."

"That's nice of him."

"Yeah. It's all working out."

Chelsea leaned in. "It is, isn't it?"

As their lips met again, Chelsea heard her name being called. And before she could fully pull away from Luka to answer, Sienna appeared again then stepped back and averted her eyes.

"Oh. Sorry." Sienna stared down at her own shoes. "Mr. Rutherford had a question for you, Miss Barrett."

"Tell him I'll be right there, thanks."

When Sienna disappeared again, Chelsea giggled into Luka's shoulder. "Why do I feel like the teenager here?"

"Aren't we, though?" Luka's face turned unexpectedly serious as Chelsea backed away to see him. "It feels like it used to. You and me."

"The way it was supposed to be."

They met together in a kiss—mutual, equal, fully invested. All in.

MINUTES BEFORE THE curtain rose on the afternoon performance, Chelsea asked her mother, "Are you sure these seats are okay?"

"Perfectly fine."

They sat on the first row of the assembly hall, with one seat saved for Luka. Earlier, he'd told Chelsea he couldn't view the play as a casual observer—he had a role of his own to play. When the curtain rose, he would become a phantom—crouching in the dark corners of the assembly hall, both behind stage and off, snapping photos of the play without obstructing anyone's vision or distracting them from the performances. Occasionally, he might be able to sit beside Chelsea, hold her hand, and watch the play with her. But as the scene changed, he would have to slip away again to continue snapping photos.

Chelsea opened the paper program handed to her at the entrance.

"Hey." Luka appeared at Chelsea's side and crouched near her seat with a wince. "I hate that we're so close to the stage. You're sure these are okay?"

"I just asked Mum the same thing. They're fine." She watched Luka's gaze drift in her mother's direction.

"Mrs. Barrett." Luka nodded hesitantly. "It's nice to see you."

"You as well."

Her mum studied Luka's face, probably comparing it with the one she'd remembered from all those years before. Then she rose from her seat and approached Luka. He stood, too, and faced her as she leaned into him for an embrace.

Chelsea watched it play out in front of her, unsure of what to do, expecting some verbal exchange between them as they drew apart again. But they said it all with their eyes. Her mum beamed up toward Luka and gave his arms one last squeeze before taking her seat again. Luka let out a measured breath as he reached for Chelsea's hand.

MINUTES LATER, AS THE thick curtain rose, Chelsea realized that being this close to the stage had its advantages. She could view the finer points that other audience members couldn't—the beading of the stunning costumes, the nuances on the faces of the actors as they slipped into their roles, the details of the balcony set, and the vivid colors of the video-screen backdrops.

Shortly after the prologue, Chelsea was thrilled to see Matthew enter as Romeo, healthy and strong and delivering his lines with ease. A couple of scenes later, Sienna stepped onto the stage, graceful and confident. When she spoke her first lines to the nurse, it was clear that Sienna had overcome her jitters. She had become Juliet.

When Romeo and Juliet finally met at the Capulets' ball, Chelsea noticed something else that was subtle but significant. As they delivered their lines, Sienna and Matthew stood a bit closer than they'd done in rehearsal. Their nonverbal communication was strong, their connection electric. And when they kissed, it was more intimate and knowing than any of their stage kisses from before.

They're back together. Why didn't Sienna mention it? Maybe she had taken him soup when he was ill, and Matthew had finally appreciated her for the amazing girl she was. Perhaps he'd come to his senses. Chelsea was glad that they hadn't followed in her and Luka's teenage footsteps—that they'd been brave enough to overcome their insecurities before adulthood could separate them.

The play's end was met with thunderous applause, and Chelsea stood to show her support. Her heart was bursting with pride. These pupils—*her* pupils—had exceeded her every expectation.

Afterward, as the crowd began to disperse, Luka told Chelsea, "I have to stay. For the cast photos."

"It's fine. I have a couple of things to do before the bonfire anyway."

"Speaking of which, I need to help Mac and Tristan prep for it. Busy days."

But good days, Chelsea thought as he kissed her cheek.

She walked her mother back to the cottage, where they shared a quick sandwich. Afterward, her mother decided on an impromptu outing to see a couple of her friends in the village. When she left the cottage, Chelsea knew this was her opportunity to slip away.

She patted Socrates on the head, told him, "I'll be back soon," then headed out the front door and walked to the cemetery, in search of her father's headstone. She hadn't visited it since the funeral years before.

When she found the headstone, Chelsea scanned the engraving: *Loving Husband and Father, Honorable Police Constable, and Loyal Mate.*

Someone had already been here with fresh flowers—her mother, Chelsea assumed—a cheerful mixture of colored roses. Chelsea had brought a blanket with her and spread it out beside the grave, feeling awkward as she sat down cross-legged. She knew that other people visited their loved ones' graves, sometimes on a weekly basis. It was quite normal for them. They would sit and have a casual chat with the deceased. But for Chelsea, this was a new experience.

"Dad," she said, her voice timid and thin.

This was harder than she'd thought. When the idea had struck her that morning sometime between her visit with Rachel and the play, Chelsea had swatted it aside. But the idea wouldn't leave her mind, so after the play had ended, she'd succumbed.

"Daddy," she repeated, this time louder.

It was difficult looking at the headstone, so she chose a different focal point—the beautiful flowers. On the walk over, Chelsea had thought she'd known what she wanted to say. She'd imagined herself going over the past twenty-four hours in detail, talking out the wide range of blistering emotions she'd experienced.

But when faced with her father's grave, all she could say was "I forgive you, Daddy. I know why you did it. You thought you were doing me a favor—helping me. But it was really the opposite. You didn't know that, of course. Daddy, Luka's a good man. He always was, but you couldn't see that. And I love him. I wish you were here now to talk with him and see for yourself. He's good for *me*."

She pressed her fingers to her lips then placed her hand against the cold, smooth marble.

"I miss you," she whispered. "So very much."

She remained on the blanket for a few minutes, listening to the wind rattle the brittle autumn leaves overhead, hearing birds talk to each other, limb to limb. She distinguished one song in particular, and it sounded almost like a nightingale's call, though it would have been nearly impossible at that time of year and at that time of day. *A robin?* For a moment, she pretended it *was* a nightingale, bringing her a peaceful tune in a morbid, bittersweet setting precisely when she needed it. Pushing to her feet then folding the blanket, she finally understood the strange appeal of visiting loved ones inside a graveyard—life and death meeting together in nature's backyard.

"I'll visit again sometime," she told the air, believing that somewhere, somehow, her father could hear.

DURING THE EARLIEST planning stages of the Renaissance festival, Chelsea had almost cancelled Frank's bonfire idea, thinking it was too much trouble after an exhausting week of activities, and believing that no one would be interested in attending. But how wrong she'd been. A few minutes after Mac had lit the bonfire, which was located on an open, spacious clearing on Mr. Elton's land, Chelsea focused on the crowd—close to a *hundred* people—and shook her head in amazement. It was the perfect ending to an incredible week. The blaze climbed higher and higher toward a clear night's sky, and Chelsea felt the warmth of it touch her cheeks as embers popped and smoke billowed. The crowd seemed to love it too. The children, held back at a safe distance by anxious mothers, squealed their glee, pointing to the blaze with wide eyes. Families stood together, and couples in love—including Sienna and Matthew—grasped each other and swayed or held hands as they watched the sights. Chelsea wished her mother had attended—she'd turned in early, tired from the week. She planned to go back to Bristol and her sister in the early morning.

After Luka had finished taking his photos of the unlit bonfire, then the lighting of it, then all the people around it, he took a final photo of Chelsea.

"Stop!" She grinned and waved him away.

"But you're my favorite subject," he teased, tucking his camera away for the night.

"Even above sunrises?"

"*Far* above sunrises." As Luka came to stand at Chelsea's side, she leaned against him. "This is grand," he mused as they gazed together at the fire, its flames licking the air.

"It's perfect. All of it."

"There's no place I'd rather be." Luka moved behind Chelsea then wrapped both his arms securely around her. Snuggling into him, Chelsea watched the hypnotic flames rise higher, knowing she had never felt so warm and safe in all her life. Or so loved.

Acknowledgements

To my mom, who's always been my biggest fan and supporter. I'm grateful to have her as my sounding board and best friend.

To my entire extended family, whose support and encouragement mean everything.

To beloved family members who are no longer with me and have made their exit to heaven: Daddy, Maw, Pa-Paw, Grammy, Pappy, and Mark. They would have been so supportive of this new book and series. I miss them every day.

To my dearest friends, and to those who continue to be supportive of my writer's journey: Karen Ingram, Augusta Malvagno, Linda Bratcher, Sandy Graham, Becky Bray, Karen Peterson, Michelle Cotter, Doris Lininger, Sue Willis, Sheree Webb, Stephen and Laurie Stine, Carla Krae, Rae Champagne, Rebecca Sanders, Corina and Ellie Fauley, Deanna Markham, Brittni Tracy, Leigh Ann Olejnik, Silvana Vierkant-Waller, Kerry Coleman, Penny Gamache, my TJC friends and colleagues, and my beloved Commando sisters.

To Melanie Bankston, who read through the book to double-check the Britishisms. Also special thanks to Rich and Jaimee Sawrey, and Barbara Peachey for their extremely helpful input on all my British questions.

To Rex Enochs, Heidi Borum, Kristi Kuczkowski, and Rebecca Sanders, for their input on the photography sections of the novel. Your details and advice were so helpful and interesting. I learned a lot!

To Joy Neely for her advice on the falconry scenes.

Special thanks to my publisher, Lynn McNamee, whose professionalism, knowledge, and ambition have helped to create an amazing publishing company that produces high-quality books. I'm honored to be on board with Red Adept. Also special thanks to my editor, Sarah Carleton. Her careful input and guidance has heightened the quality of the book in every way.

To the entire Red Adept team, but especially Erica Lucke Dean, Streetlight Graphics (particularly Glendon Haddix), and all the proofreaders and formatters. This novel is what it is because of your diligence and dedication and talents. I'm so grateful to you.

To Clint Jones at Motophoto for my author photo.

Finally, all thanks to God, who makes everything in this life worthwhile. He is the Source.

About the Author

Traci Borum is an insatiable bookworm whose first love is fiction. As a little girl, she became mesmerized with books—with the textures, the smells, and most especially, the worlds created between the pages. Years later, she discovered she could create her *own* worlds by writing. She's been scribbling away ever since, writing bits of poetry, articles, and especially fiction.

Traci has been a Creative Writing teacher at a community college for the past ten years. She's a native Texan and an Anglophile at heart. She owns two "British" dogs—a Corgi and a Sheltie—and she's completely addicted to Masterpiece Theater (must be those dreamy British accents!). More than anything, she treasures the friendships in her life and adores her supportive family.

Read more at writerscorner-traci.blogspot.com.

About the Publisher

Dear Reader,

We hope you enjoyed this book. Please consider leaving a review on your favorite book site.

Visit https://RedAdeptPublishing.com to see our entire catalogue.

Don't forget to subscribe to our monthly newsletter to be notified of future releases and special sales.

www.ingramcontent.com/pod-product-compliance
Lightning Source LLC
Chambersburg PA
CBHW071127200626
46817CB00018B/2325

* 9 7 8 1 9 4 8 0 5 1 7 6 7 *